THE CONVERT

ALSO BY ISRAEL JACOBS

Fiction

TEN FOR KADDISH

Non-fiction

DID GOD CHOOSE THE JEWS?

THE CONVERT

by

Israel Jacobs

With deep appreciation
to my friend and colleague
Rabbi Paul Teicher
For his editing and advice.

Copyright © 1994, 2001
Israel Jacobs

Cover by Ricia Docobo and Tim Andexler

All rights reserved. Except for brief excerpts by reviewers, no part
of this book may be reproduced or used in any form, mechanical or
electronic, including recording or photocopying, or by computer-
ized storage/retrieval system, unless permission is obtained in
writing from the Publisher.

All names and characters in this novel are fictitious;
resemblance to any person or persons is entirely coincidental.

Printed in the United States of America. *First Edition*

Library of Congress Catalogue Number: 2001098531
ISBN: 0-940121-73-5

Published by Cross Cultural Publications, Inc., Cross Roads Books

To Selma
for her encouragement and support
when I needed it the most.

I am dark, but comely,
O daughters of Jerusalem—
Like the tents of Kedar,
Like the pavilions of Solomon.
Don't stare at me because I am swarthy,
because the sun has gazed upon me.
My mother's sons quarreled with me,
They made me guard the vineyards;
My own vineyard I did not guard.
(Song of Songs, 1:5–6)

Chapter One

Even as an adolescent Tali dared challenge God. Why did his best friend die? Why are there earthquakes and floods that kill innocent people? Why did God allow the Nazis to murder six million Jews? Whether God existed was not the issue. It couldn't be otherwise. Can there be a creation without a creator? But his questioning mind pushed him to the conclusion that there had to be a better way for an omnipotent God to pilot the world.

The diploma, hanging proudly in his study, announced that A. Naphtali Zeig had passed the requisite examinations to be *Rabbi, Teacher and Preacher in Israel.* Examinations, however, test book learning, not faith. That is an ongoing test, day after day, year after year.

Jeremy Klein's funeral had stretched Tali's faith to the limit. On the way to Hebrew school the youngster suddenly darted into the street. An oncoming van screeched to a stop. Too late. Jeremy lay in a coma for a week. At the chapel service Jeremy's parents kept staring at Tali as if they expected him to come up with answers.

He had no answers. Millennia ago the author of Proverbs wrote, *Many plans rise in human hearts, however, the designs of God prevail.* But God's designs, Tali silently fretted, too often don't make sense.

He still felt a safe distance from agnosticism. But who knows? If a sage such as Elisha ben Abuyah could become an apostate...

No use whining. He knew what he was getting into when he decided to become a rabbi. He knew it wouldn't all be happy occasions. He knew tragedy would be part of the job. But in this profession you don't really know what you're getting into. You learn on the job.

Tali swivelled his chair a half turn toward the window, trying to chase the depression. He contemplated the scene outside his study. A huge oak tree bordered the far end of the macadam driveway. Branches, bare of leaves just a short month ago, were already thick with foliage, partially blocking his view of the pond across Manor Drive. A white duck, followed by a brown-feathered companion, waddled confidently past the oak. They crossed Manor Drive in tandem and hopped into the pond. Fortunate are ducks, he brooded. They looked contented, without a care. On second thought he reconsidered, "Who knows? Ducks probably have their problems." He rotated his chair back to the desk and checked his appointment book:

<u>10:30 a.m.</u>	Dr. Jeremiah Yarden
<u>2:00 p.m.</u>	Premarital meeting with Harvey Epstein and Joan Becker
<u>4:00 p.m.</u>	Confirmation Class
<u>8:00 p.m.</u>	Ritual Committee meeting

Today promised to be a busy one. Good! He did poorly with large open blocks of time. Too much time to think invited depression. Better for his disposition to be on the run.

His attention wandered to the bookcase. It was custom-built of blonde-mahogany and spanned one entire wall from ceiling to floor. He admired the twenty handsomely bound volumes of the Talmud his uncle had given him as a gift on the occasion of his ordination from the Seminary five years ago. They never failed to impress him. Five-thousand-eight-hundred-four folio pages, divided into sixty-three tractates. It was an intimidating work. He had completed five of the tractates while studying at the Sumtara Yeshiva. To master the entire Talmud seemed to him an impossible project for any mortal. His uncle had gone through it all ten times, at least, and could recite entire chapters from memory.

Tali had been astonished that the Sumtara Rebbe, would acknowledge an ordination from anything but a strictly Orthodox seminary. He read a message into the gift: "Now that you have the title *Rabbi* you are obligated, even more so, to increase your knowledge of Torah." To his uncle that meant a lifetime commitment to studying Talmud.

Easier said than done. The incessant demands on the rabbi's time and energy of a six-hundred-family modern congregation left him little opportunity for serious study. Or perhaps he was rationalizing. "It is a matter of priorities," his uncle would have sternly reminded him. Where there is a will, there is a way; when there is no will, a molehill becomes a mountain.

Tali pondered the ten-thirty appointment with Dr. Jeremiah Yarden. Interesting name, Yarden. He had never come across a Yarden before. Jordan, yes. But few, if any, Jews were named Jordan. Actually, Jordan was a transliteration of the Hebrew, Yarden, the chief river in Palestine, flowing a hundred miles south into the Dead Sea. Some four millennia ago the people of Canaan referred to Abraham as Abraham the Hebrew. Abraham earned the addition to his name, which means to cross over, because he crossed over the Jordan river when he migrated to Canaan.

The intercom buzzed, interrupting his reverie.

"Yes, Stella."

"Rabbi, your ten-thirty appointment is waiting. Shall I send them in?"

"Them? I have an appointment with a Dr. Jeremiah Yarden."

"Well, Rabbi, Dr. Yarden has several gentlemen with him."

"Oh!" Tali had allowed himself half an hour for the appointment. He hoped it would not drag on much beyond. He wanted to take time out for lunch before the premarital session with Harvey and Joan.

"Okay, send the gentlemen into my office."

Stella stayed on the intercom. Apparently she had another message for him. She usually did.

"Rabbi, Mrs. Shapiro mentioned that her daughter, Dr. Allison Shapiro, will be in Pineville this weekend."

"So?" Tali knew what was coming next.

"Well, it would be nice if you would give her a call."

Stella Heyman not only served as Tali's loyal secretary, but also as his surrogate mother, as did a dozen mothers with eligible daughters in his congregation. Stella believed it her special obligation to act as intermediary. To her way of thinking, bachelorhood was unnatural in general, and in particular for rabbis.

"Okay, Stella, I'll keep it in mind. Please send the gentlemen in."

Tali could barely contain his surprise. He hoped it didn't register on his face. The gentlemen were black.

"Dr. Yarden?"

The man in the lead touched his snap-brim hat. He hesitated at the door, apparently waiting to be invited in. He was dressed in a grey vested suit. A mustache looped around the corners of his mouth and penciled down to meet with a meticulously groomed beard. Silver-framed glasses gave his face a professorial appearance. Two companions, partly in the shadow of the hallway, stood behind him.

"Come in, gentlemen," Tali walked around his desk. Dr. Yarden was small in height, but his authoritative bearing seemed to cancel the difference.

"Mr. Gever Silvano," Yarden presented a chunky ebony-skinned man. He had a broad friendly face, with a bald spot the size of a silver dollar in the center of his pate.

"And Tom Carter." The handsome young black man nodded. Tali guessed him to be in his late twenties. He wore a light-green turtleneck shirt, tucked neatly into dark green slacks.

"Tom is Mr. Silvano's son-in-law," Yarden explained.

Tali said, "Please make yourselves comfortable."

Yarden and Silvano settled into chairs adjacent to Tali's desk. Tom Carter selected a chair further back, near the rear window.

"We appreciate your granting us this interview," Yarden spoke with a faint accent that hinted at West Indies origins.

"You are wondering, I'm certain, Rabbi Zeig, why I called to arrange this meeting."

"Whatever it is, Dr. Yarden, I'm delighted to meet you."

"I hope you will be as pleased after I explain the reason for our visit."

"That sounds ominous. I'm confident that whatever the problem is that brings you here, we shall overcome."

Israel Jacobs 5

"In that case I will come right to the point. Twelve families from Northville would like to join your congregation. And I suspect that in the not too distant future more will be moving in from the city, who also will want to join."

Tali gave himself a long moment for the request to sink in.

"Did I read you right? Twelve black families want to join this congregation?"

"That is correct."

Tali adjusted his skullcap. "Don't you have enough problems? What do you want ours for?"

Yarden sat like a block of ice. "Will you or will you not consider our application?"

"Dr. Yarden, I'm sorry for seeming a bit startled, but I don't get this kind of a request every day. Twelve black families want to join the Pineville Jewish Center?"

"Why should an application to join your synagogue astound you, Rabbi Zeig? Are you oversubscribed? Are you a closed corporation?"

"Uh... well... no..." Tali stammered. "We're not a closed corporation. Certainly not. But to be a member of a synagogue you do have to be Jewish."

Dr. Yarden studied Tali as if examining a patient.

"Rabbi Zeig, we *are* Jewish."

The room plunged into silence.

Gever Silvano leaned forward. He said softly, "Dr. Yarden's father was Rabbi Matityahu Yarden."

"You are Rabbi Matityahu's son? Oh, my God!" Tali slapped his cheek, leaving a finger-length welt. "Yes, I should have made the connection when you walked into the study. I apologize. I've read your father's autobiography." Tali reached behind him and extracted a book prominently displayed on the book shelf next to his desk. "Here it is, *Black Israelite*. I intend to review it for my adult study class. An extraordinary story." Tali flipped open the cover:

My odyssey begins on a Friday morning in March nineteen hundred and forty-four. I had been tossing and turning, sleepless most of the night. Thinking that I may as well start on my Sunday sermon, I sat at my desk searching for a theme.

Not a usable thought came to mind. Preaching, which had always come easily, was becoming a burden. I seemed to have little to say to my congregation that was meaningful. Something was troubling me. Precisely what, I couldn't put my finger on. Faith? God? Jesus? Although it was a cool morning, I felt myself perspiring. The walls seemed to be pressing in on me. Fresh air might get my mind working. I stepped into the brisk March air and nearly collided with a group of dark suited bearded elderly men. I had seen them pass my house numerous times, but paid them no attention. For reasons I can't explain I trailed them to their synagogue. An overwhelming urge to see the "Church" in which Jews worshiped propelled me down the steps to their basement synagogue. I sat through the service, watching the men drape themselves in woolen prayer shawls and strap black cubes to their arms and foreheads. At the conclusion of the service one of the men who seemed to be in charge asked whether I would return that evening. I said I would, and I did, and returned again the following morning.

That Sabbath started me on the road to conversion. Ten years of soul-searching, of studying Judaism on my own, hardly knowing where to begin. Ten years later, I George Cariota, became Matityahu Yarden.

"Rabbi Zeig," Dr. Yarden brought Tali back to the present. "I am pleased that you find my father's autobiography interesting. But I'm quite familiar with his book."

"Of course, Dr. Yarden. Forgive me for being carried away.' But, the book is absolutely fascinating. Not only did your father convert, but he influenced his congregation to convert with him. By the sixties, according to the Jewish Encyclopedia, black Jewish congregations had sprouted in New York, Chicago, and Boston with an estimated six thousand members. And I believe your father was the inspiration."

Dr. Yarden smiled for the first time since he had entered the study. "I see you've done your homework. I'm impressed. But now, to the matter at hand. About our joining your synagogue, Rabbi."

"That will present no problem. But first, I'm curious. How long have you all been living in Northville?"

"Most of us have moved out from the city in the last three to five years," Yarden said. "I've been practicing in Northville four years. Gever is the trailblazer. He was the first to settle here." Yarden favored the older man with one of his rare smiles. "How long has it been, Gever?"

Gever Silvano knitted his brow. "Fifteen years, as of next month."

"Gever owns Northville Pharmacy," Yarden added.

Silvano grinned. "Our pharmacy has been on the same corner since I started the business. We've expanded several times, but I'm still located on Sixth and Main."

"Right in my own back yard. Twelve black Jewish families, and I never knew." Tali shook his head. "What took you so long to surface?"

Yarden shrugged. "To everything there is a season. Until now we have been managing nicely by meeting in homes. But we are on the increase. Mira Carter, Tom's wife, made Gever a grandfather three weeks ago. At least six other Jewish families we know of have put deposits down on homes in Northville. We are rapidly outgrowing basements. We have toyed with the idea of building our own synagogue, but there aren't enough of us yet to support such an ambitious project. Besides, we need a rabbi. I've been drafted to serve as interim rabbi, but I don't have the time nor, truth to tell, am I qualified. We have been debating what to do for several months. Last week we came to a decision. If you will have us, we would like to join your synagogue."

"I would consider it an honor to have you as members of the Pineville Jewish Center."

Tom Carter had been sitting glumly silent. He scraped his chair closer to Tali's desk. "Rabbi Zeig, can I ask you a question?"

"Sure."

"When we walked into your office, you didn't think we were Jewish, did you?"

"That's right."

"Would we have been the first non-Jews to have asked you about converting to Judaism?"

"No, you wouldn't have been the first. As a matter of fact we have about twenty converts in our congregation. I converted four of them myself."

"Then why were you so rattled when Dr. Yarden told you we wanted to join your synagogue? Was it, maybe, because we're black?"

Silvano glared at his son-in-law. Tali drummed his fingers on the desk top. He meditated at a Bible stacked on the desk between two bookends. After a moment, he flicked the Bible open and riffled through the pages. "Here it is." Tali shoved the Bible toward Carter. *To Me, O Israel, you are just like the Ethiopians. I brought up Israel from Egypt, but also the Philistines from Caphtor and the Arameans from Kir.* "Amos, chapter nine, verse seven."

Carter retorted, "I know that passage. My father-in-law's been quoting it over and over, as if it's the whole Jewish Bible."

"Well, it isn't the whole of our Bible," Tali snapped. "There's a lot more to it. But before we go further, friend, let's get one thing straight. I interpret that verse to mean that as far as God is concerned a man is judged by his actions, not the color of his skin."

"What about as far as white Jews are concerned? How do they judge?"

Gever Silvano flashed a warning look. Yarden interjected.

"What is the procedure for joining your synagogue?"

"Fill out the membership forms as you leave. Your names will be presented at the next membership meeting."

"How long before we are officially members?"

"About a month."

Tom Carter said, "Why so long?"

"That's the routine."

"The same routine for everybody?"

"For everybody."

Tali had sensed hostility pouring out of Tom Carter from the moment the junior of the three men walked through the door. He asked, "Are you a convert, Mr. Carter?"

"Yeah, I am."

"Who converted you?"

"Does it make any difference?"

"It might."

Gever Silvano intervened. "Rabbi Matityahu Yarden converted Tom."

Tali pressed on. "Tell me, Mr. Carter, why did you convert?"

Israel Jacobs 9

Carter hesitated, as if debating whether to answer. After a tension-filled moment he said, "My father-in-law put the pressure on Mira, and she high-pressured me."

"What about you? Do you see Judaism as having merit?"

Again Carter hesitated. "Maybe."

"What do you mean, 'maybe?' Don't you have an opinion?"

"Yeah, I have, but I haven't been Jewish long enough to be sure."

"I can't fault you on that score. Do you have thoughts on the subject?"

"Yeah, I have lots of thoughts."

"Would you share some of them with me?"

"Okay, I'll tell you what I think. You may not like it."

"Try me."

"Well for one, Jews are cliquish. They give me the feeling they think they're better than anyone else." Carter brushed his brow, "I do respect the Jewish family. They hang together no matter what."

"Mr. Carter you're correct on one count. There are Jews who think they're something special, though only God knows why. But there is more to Jews sticking together than snobbishness, much more. On the second count, I hate to disillusion you. The Jewish divorce rate is fast catching up to the general population. Is there anything else you believe may be a possible plus to Jews or Judaism worth pursuing?"

Carter's belligerence seemed to have cooled. He said, "Yeah. I was raised Baptist, and just about every minister I heard was sure he had the key to paradise, And only his key fit. That's okay if you can buy it. My momma did. She was a Baptist till the day she died. Nothing could have made her change faith. My daddy didn't buy it. My momma couldn't get him to church nohow. One day he took off and left us. I'm not saying that's the main reason my folks split, but my mamma's nagging Sunday after Sunday didn't help the marriage. Me, I've got some of daddy in me. I need thinking space. Dr. Yarden, the rest of the brothers and sisters who converted don't act like only they got the answers. They don't make a man feel that doubting means you're gonna burn."

Tali said, "Mr. Carter you've got a feel for Judaism, but, you're not eager to join our synagogue, why?"

"I don't think the mix can work. I see it leading to grief."

"Mr. Carter, I can't guarantee it'll work. But if you meet me part way, I promise I'll do whatever it takes to make it work. Will you give it a try?"

"I'll go along."

"Good enough."

Tali held out his hand. Tentatively, Carter accepted the handclasp. Tali said, "Tom, we both have a distance to go."

Yarden asked, "While we are waiting for your Board of Trustees to act on our application, may we attend services at your synagogue?"

Tali smiled. "Dr. Yarden, it isn't often anyone asks permission to attend services. This time of year it's a buyer's market. We've got seats to spare."

Gever Silvano said, "We wouldn't have to wait until we're voted in as members?"

"Not at all, Mr. Silvano. Anybody is welcome to attend services at the Pineville Jewish Center. For that matter, at any synagogue. To paraphrase a popular commercial, you don't have to be Jewish to worship in a synagogue."

Silvano laughed. "Rabbi, I'll spread the word to the others. I believe you will see most of our group at services this coming Sabbath eve."

Yarden signaled it was time to leave. The three men stood up.

Tali shook hands with each of the men as they filed out of his office. "Looking forward to seeing you this Friday night. We start promptly at eight."

He may be looking forward, Tali speculated over the impact this would have on the congregation. Perhaps he should prepare the membership committee. This was not a run-of-the-mill application. He considered the possibility that undue attention to this application would invite prolonged debate, which he didn't want. Tali came to a decision, no preparation warranted. When he urged a go-slow-policy in matters pertaining to Jewish law and tradition, his upper-middle-income liberal intellectuals were quick enough to challenge him:

"Rabbi, we must be open to change. We need to encourage new ideas. We live in fast-moving times. We can't afford to stand still. If we don't keep up, we'll be left so far behind no one will take us seriously."

Well, their much touted liberalism would soon be put to the test. We'll soon see how fast they're willing and able to move on this one.

Chapter Two

Excluding the High Holy Days and special occasions, Tali normally preached to about fifty congregants, and eight hundred fifty empty pews. Tonight should be different, he predicted to himself.

Eric Epstein was scheduled to be bar mitzvah the following morning. Tali required the celebrant and family to attend Friday evening services. This served a dual purpose—an opportunity for the family to experience a Friday night service, and it filled some empty pews.

And, expectantly, Dr. Jeremiah Yarden and his contingent.

Everett Russel, president of the congregation, and his wife Sandra, stopped off in the lobby to chat with the Epsteins. They were joined by Maurice Cline, a vice president of the congregation. Cline, a prominent local attorney, rarely attended services. This Sabbath eve was the *Yahrzeit*—the anniversary of his father's death. He had come to pay his respects by reciting the traditional mourner's *Kaddish*.

The three couples ambled down the aisle, selecting seats a comfortable distance from the pulpit. Ten other couples, several with children, drifted into the sanctuary. At seven-fifty Tali mounted the pulpit dressed in his formal black robe and prayer shawl. Cantor Bindel followed, escorting a nervous Eric Epstein. Tali motioned for Eric to sit next to him. Bindel checked to see that the silver wine goblet was full.

At exactly seven fifty-five the blacks marched in.

Israel Jacobs   **13**

From the moment Tali had met Jeremiah, the physician had struck him as a precise man. Yarden had said twelve families. That apparently was exactly what he meant. Not twelve blacks. Not twelve couples, but twelve families. Forty-five in all, by a fast count Tali made from the pulpit. They filed down the aisle: men, women and children, Jeremiah Yarden at the head of the line like a black Moses. They sidled quietly into the first six rows to the right, sat down and waited for the service to begin. A buzzing started up in the back pews. Maurice and Everett shushed their wives.

Tali glanced at his watch. He rose, and taking no special note of the blacks, as if their attendance was an everyday occurrence, he announced, "Please turn to page two."

Albert Shakter, a trustee, strolled in with his wife, Muriel. The Shakters had come because they were friends of the Epsteins. Also, Albert, a clinical psychologist, was treating Eric. Tali observed the Shakters halt midway down the aisle, stare wide-eyed and squeeze hurriedly into the nearest pew. Seymour Kraft, another trustee and friend of the Epsteins, charged into the sanctuary. Lucy, his wife, walked daintily behind him. Kraft was short, extremely stout with pendulous jowls, aggressive, and a millionaire several times over. He flounced heavily toward his regular pew in the front row, wearing a navy blue double-breasted jacket, which accentuated his bulk. He stopped suddenly and gaped at the newcomers who had preempted his seat. He retreated hastily, crashing backwards into Lucy. Tali crouched closer to the microphone.

"Please rise and turn to page two for the opening prayer."

Forty-five blacks bolted upright.

"Let us pray in unison. The last paragraph on page two."

The blacks answered like a trumpet call.

Tali announced, "Let us now chant the Shema in the Hebrew and in the English: *Shema Yisrael Adonoy Eloheynu Adonoy Ehad*, Hear O Israel, the Lord is our God, the Lord is One." The stalwart response from the front rows all but drowned out the rabbi. In the back, silence. Choral refrains led by Cantor Bindel elicited a continued blank from the white section. Tali prodded Eric Epstein to the lectern. Cantor

Bindel handed the goblet to Eric.

"We will now sanctify the Sabbath by chanting the *Kiddush*—the prayer over the cup of wine, page twenty-eight, please rise. Eric, who will be bar mitzvah tomorrow at our Sabbath morning services, will chant the Kiddush."

The blacks rose as instructed; the whites seemed glued to their seats.

"Please rise for the Kiddush," Tali repeated.

Eric stumbled through the prayer, in a jittery soprano. At the conclusion Tali reminded Eric to sip from the goblet. Eric sipped into the goblet, grimaced and sat down. Tali announced, "Tonight my subject is *Judaism is a Do-it-Yourself Religion.*"

"Prayer, study, Sabbath and festival observances, all the ritual and ethical precepts of the Torah," Tali struck the lectern to emphasize his point, "are do-it-yourself projects..."

"AMEN!"

Tali lost his train of thought. He searched for the voice. Gever Silvano, seated next to Yarden, beamed approval. Tali looked at the white section; they seemed disjointed. Tali returned to his theme:

"No rabbi or cantor, no Jew can observe Judaism for you. We have no intermediaries between man and God."

"AMEN!"

Apparently, taking their cue from Silvano, the entire black section barreled up approval. This time Tali was prepared. He smiled, thinking to himself, what an effective way to let a preacher know that he is hitting the mark, or conversely, by silence, telling him that he is rambling.

Tali continued, "The Torah teaches that every man is created in God's image, that means, every one of us is equally privileged, and equally responsible for his or her actions."

The black section exploded: "AY-MEN!"

A quick glance to the back showed Seymour Kraft cringing in his pew. Tali asked the congregation to rise for the *Alenu*— the Adoration. Blacks and whites were about evenly divided, with the whites enjoying a slight edge. Though not up to their usual exuberance, the white

Israel Jacobs 15

section picked up volume. They were still in shock, but alive, Tali wryly observed to himself. Congregants in mourning or commemorating the *yahrzeit* of a relative remained standing to recite the Kaddish. The mourner's prayer concluded, Tali leaned into the lectern:

"On behalf of the congregation, and on my own behalf, I extend sincerest condolences to Mrs. Herzog on the loss of her dear mother, Sadie Schwartz. May the family be consoled by the memory of the many years she was granted, and loved. Tomorrow morning services begin promptly at nine, at which time we will celebrate the bar mitzvah of Eric Epstein. A reminder, our adult study classes will recess for Passover. Both Hebrew and Bible classes will resume the first Tuesday following Passover. New registration for these classes will be accepted. Please call the office for further information.

"I also want to say Shalom to those families who are worshiping with us for the first time this Sabbath eve."

Tali continued, exhibiting no change in expression. He read the list, starting with Dr. Jeremiah Yarden, as if having blacks at Sabbath eve services was commonplace. "I hope you have found our services meaningful, and will want to join us every Sabbath."

"AMEN." The response thundered from the black section like a cloudburst.

"Mr. And Mrs. Epstein are sponsoring the Oneg Shabbat tonight, in honor of Eric's bar mitzvah tomorrow morning. The *entire* congregation is invited." Tali announced the invitation with heavy emphasis on *entire*. He hurried to the clergy dressing room behind the pulpit, disrobed and raced to the ballroom.

For a moment he thought he was alone, so unnatural was the quiet.

An invisible wall separated whites from blacks. Each camp had marked off a section of the spacious ballroom. In one corner the blacks poured tea for themselves. The whites clustered in tight circles at the opposite end. Punch and a colorful spread of finger cakes and cookies decorated the tables. Twenty or so black children milled close to their elders, so well behaved it was eerie. Down to the youngest, who could not have been more than four years old, the children's conduct was punctilious. Not a child approached the tables without an adult signaling permission. Never had Tali seen children mind their manners so, certainly not Jewish children in a synagogue. The quiet pressed down awkwardly even more so on the white side. Conversation was held in self-conscious whispers. Tali searched for Yarden, locating him at the far end of the reception hall talking in sotto voce with Gever Silvano.

"Shabbat Shalom, Dr. Yarden. Mr. Silvano." Tali assumed a happy grin. "Tell me, do these youngsters always act like angels?"

Yarden said, "Not quite."

"They sure are tonight," Tali said.

"Your synagogue is strange to them," Yarden said. "They don't feel at home yet."

"Somebody must have drilled them."

"I suppose some of the parents did suggest to the youngsters to especially mind their manners tonight."

"I suppose some of the parents did," Tali chuckled. "Would you excuse me a moment? I want to find our president and introduce you."

Tali strode tight-lipped to the white enclave. Everett Russel, Kraft and Cline were in a huddle off to one side. Tali broke in.

"Everett, as president of the congregation, I think you should welcome our guests."

"Sure, Rabbi." Everett, as if in a partial daze, let Tali lead him to the other side. Kraft and Cline remained cloistered in their corner, following the two men with hard stares. Yarden and Silvano were positioned in the same area where Tali had left them. He made the introductions:

Dr. Yarden, I'd like you to meet Mr. Everett Russel, president of our congregation. Everett, Dr. Jeremiah Yarden."

"I'm pleased to meet you," Everett said in a stilted voice.

"My pleasure, Mr. Russel," Yarden said equally stilted.

Yarden introduced Everett to Gever Silvano. Everett stayed to shake hands with several other blacks then retreated to the white section. Yarden made ready to leave.

"Rabbi Zeig, you will see to our membership application?"

Israel Jacobs 17

"Yes, I'll handle it personally." Tali halted Yarden's departure. "Before you leave, Dr. Yarden. I'd like to stop in for a visit with you at your home. About two o'clock this Sunday. Would that be convenient for you and Mrs. Yarden?"

Rebecca Yarden, a plump pleasant-faced woman with caramel-colored skin, smiled broadly. "Rabbi Zeig, you're welcome to our home any time. Just give us a call to make sure we are in."

Yarden touched his wife's elbow. "Angela and Gabriel are coming this Sunday."

"You're right, I forgot." Rebecca Yarden mulled over the problem. She brightened again. "That makes no difference. In fact, it might do Angela some good to meet a rabbi."

Yarden gave his wife a skeptical look. "I suppose anything is possible." He said to Tali. "Please do come. We would be honored."

The blacks marched out in step, as they had arrived.

Seymour Kraft rushed Tali. "Rabbi, what was that all about?"

"What was what all about?"

Kraft waved a finger at the door. "You knew they were coming?"

Tali chewed on a biscuit very deliberately. He took a long sip of tea. "Knew who was coming?"

"Let's not play games, Rabbi," Kraft's jowls shuddered. "Them."

"Oh, you mean Jeremiah Yarden and his gang?"

"Yeah, I mean those blacks."

"That's right, Seymour. I knew they were coming. So, what's the problem?"

"Why didn't you warn us you were expecting a heap of blacks at services tonight?"

Tali set the tea down hard on the table. The cup rattled dangerously around the saucer. "Since when do I have to announce who is coming to services?"

A circle formed around Tali and Kraft. The ballroom took on the atmosphere of a boxing ring. Maurice Cline placed himself between the men.

"No need to get excited, Rabbi. I'm sure Seymour has no

18   *The Convert*

objections to you inviting anyone you please to services. But if you had given us some advance notice, we would have been better prepared to show them good Jewish hospitality."

"They didn't expect special treatment. All they wanted was to attend services." Tali scowled at Kraft.

"Okay, Rabbi. You were perfectly in the right to invite them. What I'm saying is since it's not the usual thing to have blacks at our services, we would have appreciated being notified. I don't think that's being unreasonable, is it?" The attorney checked to see if Kraft approved of his efforts at mediation. Kraft was still puffing hot. Cline returned to Tali. "Will they really be coming regularly?"

"They seemed to have enjoyed the service. They'll be back."

"Every Friday night?"

"Maybe Saturday mornings, too. There's no crush on seats."

Cline said, "Why would blacks want to come to synagogue?"

"Because they're Jews."

Lucy Kraft's teacup crashed to the table. The white tablecloth soaked up the spill; a brown stain zigzagged across the width of the table. No one moved. Tali's eyes narrowed.

"Anything wrong with Jews coming to synagogue?"

Chapter Three

Tali edged his Mustang to the curb. He read the street sign, PETULIA LANE. The homes, on half-acre plots, were set well back along the tree-shaded street. A Cadillac backed out of the circular driveway up ahead. He hailed the driver. The man, very dark-skinned with a short beard and closely cropped hair, braked to a full stop. Beside him sat an attractive middle-aged woman. A girl about ten, with a long ponytail held in place by a pink ribbon, and a younger boy, poked their heads through the rear window.

The driver rolled down his window, "Can I help you?"

"I'm looking for Jericho Lane," Tali said.

"Jericho is one block north. Make a right turn at the corner. What number do you want?"

"Twenty-four."

"That would be Dr. Jeremiah Yarden's house. The first house on the street. You can't miss it."

"Thank you." Tali eased away from the curb. He turned the corner and braked in front of a Dutch colonial-style house. Number twenty-four was posted in large italic letters on the gabled entrance. He cut the ignition and walked up the cobblestone path, catching spray from a sprinkler rotating a jet-stream over the lawn. A slender black teenager, wearing white shorts and swinging a tennis racquet, sprinted from the house next door. She stumbled over a tricycle, kicked at it angrily, then limped down the street. Tali pressed the doorbell. He waited a moment and pressed once more. Rebecca Yarden opened the

20   *The Convert*

door wide.

"Rabbi Zeig! I just about gave up on you."

"I'm terribly sorry, Mrs. Yarden, but I stopped off to pay a condolence call. I couldn't break away any sooner. I hope I'm not inconveniencing you."

"Not at all, Rabbi. I'm so glad you could come."

Rebecca Yarden invited him into the foyer. The room enjoyed a vaulted ceiling, and a highly polished parquet floor partially covered by an intricately designed oriental rug. Sunlight poured through two windows spaced several feet apart over a circular staircase.

"Jeremiah left for Northville Hospital about an hour ago," Rebecca Yarden said apologetically. "He's on call this weekend. His partner took sick suddenly; he had to cover for him." An antique grandfather clock, standing elegantly against the wall, pealed the half-hour. "Two-thirty already. Jeremiah should be back any minute." She marched Tali past the living room. "I suppose you've already eaten lunch, Rabbi."

"Twice," Tali chuckled, "at home, and at the condolence call. They wouldn't let me leave until I surrendered and had a second lunch."

Rebecca Yarden gave a short laugh. "I won't force another one on you. But before you leave you must have a slice of my cherry cheese cake."

Tali patted his stomach. "I don't think there's room left."

"I'm sure, in a half hour or so, you'll find room for a tiny piece." Rebecca Yarden led him by the arm. "Come into the den; there's someone I'd like you to meet."

The living room ended in a wide archway through which Tali saw directly into the den. It was a long rectangular room comfortably furnished and paneled in light mahogany. An electric typewriter perched on a modern L-shaped desk. Several scatter rugs decorated the polished parquet floor. A young woman, leaning on an elbow, reclined on one of the scatter rugs, her back to the living room. She tilted her head slightly. Sunlight percolating through the curtains sprayed her hair creating, in silhouette, the illusion of a dark cupola-shaped crown. She was building a domino tower assisted by Jonathan, the Yarden's four-year-old son. Carefully, she fit a domino to the top layer. The tower

Israel Jacobs   21

swayed precariously. Jonathan looked at the woman with adoring eyes.

"That's the biggest castle I ever built."

"Want to try for higher?"

Jonathan suddenly said, "Angela, I want to marry you."

Angela laughed. "Let's finish the castle first."

Jonathan persisted. "I want to marry you."

"Well, Jonathan, I don't think I can right now. It's not that I don't love you," Angela kissed Jonathan on the forehead. "But I don't earn enough money to support us both." Angela retrieved a domino from the floor.

"I'll take care of you, Angela. I have lots of pennies in my piggy-bank."

"Well, I'll have to think about it. You know, a girl's got to be given time to—"

The castle crashed to the floor, scattering dominoes on the carpet helter-skelter. She turned toward the archway full face.

She was stunning—the large questioning eyes, her high sculptured cheeks, the full sensuous mouth, suggested an exotic princess. He realized he was staring like a moonstruck idiot, but he couldn't tear his eyes away. Angela bounced to her feet. She was quite tall, reaching his cheekbones, and he was six-two. She wore a body-hugging jump-suit, which emphasized the curvature of her breasts and narrow waist, exciting erogenous impulses he was hard-pressed to keep from showing. For a moment she appeared startled. The astonishment quickly faded. She clamped her lips shut tightly. Her eyes flashed belligerently. Rebecca Yarden prodded him into the den.

"Angela, I would like you to meet Rabbi Zeig."

She ignored him. "Aunt Rebecca, Gunner and I have to be going."

"There's no hurry, Angela. It's only a ten minute drive to the station."

"I'd rather wait there. I don't want to miss the train."

"Nonsense, You have plenty of time. I don't want you and Gabriel waiting hours at the station."

Angela started for the living room, stepping cautiously around Tali. "I'm going upstairs to check on Gunner. He's been too quiet."

22   *The Convert*

Rebecca Yarden blocked Angela's exit. She said in an irritated tone, "Gabriel doesn't need checking. He's just fine. He's watching television."

Slowly, tentatively, like a child after a scolding, Angela retreated back into the den. The doorbell chimed.

"That must be Jeremiah," Rebecca Yarden said.

Jonathan scrambled to his feet. "I'll open the door for daddy." He hop-skipped past Rebecca, "I'm coming, Daddy." The doorknob rattled several times, followed by Jonathan's excited report, "Daddy, there's a man with Mommy and Angela, Rabbi Tiger."

Jeremiah plodded through the living room, tilting to his right side trying to balance Jonathan, who was cavorting around his neck. He peered around the boy's head to see Tali floundering between his wife and Angela.

"Thank you for coming, Rabbi," Jeremiah said. "I'm sorry I wasn't here to greet you."

"Not your fault," Tali said. "I was delayed getting here."

"Has Rebecca introduced you to Angela?"

Rebecca said, "Not yet, Rabbi Zeig arrived just a few moments ago."

"Good. I'll do the honors." Jeremiah secured Angela's hand in his, angled it toward Tali then let it hang in midair. "Rabbi Zeig. Angela Adams."

Angela allowed her hand to languish limply in his for a moment. The contact of skin to skin discharged tingles up to his elbow.

"Now that the formalities are done with, let's chat." Jeremiah beckoned Tali to a comfortable wicker chair. "Angela, come sit beside me."

Angela arranged herself rigidly on the sofa. Rebecca appeared relieved to have her husband take over. "I'll perk up a fresh pot of coffee."

"And some of that cherry cheese cake I never got a chance to finish," Jeremiah called to his wife's back. He settled into the sofa. "What train are you catching, Angela?"

"Four-fifteen."

Jeremiah consulted his watch. "That gives you an hour." He shifted to Tali. "Angela lives in Upper Chelsea. We've been trying to convince her to move out to Northville."

The freeze in Angela's stance thawed a bit. "What would I do in Northville, Uncle Jeremiah?"

"For one, you could stay with us. We have plenty of room."

"I can't make a career of sponging on you and Aunt Rebecca."

"I don't mean for you to live with us forever. Just till you get a place of your own."

"Gunner and I have a place of our own."

"That apartment?" Jeremiah sniffed. "I won't dignify it by calling it an apartment. It isn't fit to live in."

"At the moment that's what I can afford."

"If you would give it a try, you might find a position here."

"You know I don't stand a chance of finding a teaching job anywhere out this way."

Tali followed the dialogue with interest, anxious to know more about this young woman. He was tempted to put a few questions to her on his own. Perhaps offer suggestions as to where she might apply for a teaching appointment. As Rabbi of the Pineville Jewish Center he was in a position to help her make connections. At the least, a reference from him would carry weight. He held back for fear that intruding himself might ignite her. Jeremiah veered the conversation in Tali's direction.

"How did the congregation take to our presence?"

"You added flavor to the service. It was a pleasure having you."

The answer did not satisfy Jeremiah Yarden. The rabbi was being evasive. He decided on another tack, "How is our membership application faring?"

"It's being processed. As I mentioned to you at our first meeting, the application is merely a formality."

"And may we continue to attend services pending our acceptance?"

"By all means, Dr. Yarden. The synagogue facilities, my services are at your disposal. Please feel free to make full use of them. In fact,

I'm here on what you might call synagogue business. "Tali rotated a finger-length rectangular box from his pocket. "On behalf of the synagogue it's my pleasure to present you with this *mezuzah*." Tali handed the box to Yarden.

"Why thank you, Rabbi." Yarden snapped open the cellophane lid. The mezuzah was sculpted in patina in the shape of an oil lamp. The Hebrew letter Shin, the first letter of *Shaddai*, one of God's many names, was embossed in bright yellow.

"It is quite beautiful. I feel guilty at not having put one up before. I suppose you noticed when you entered."

"We could put it up now."

"Yes, I would appreciate that, Rabbi."

Rebecca Yarden made a cheerful entrance. "I hope you all are ready for my cheese cake." She piloted a tray laden with finely textured small cheese cakes toward Tali and set it down on the coffee table. "The coffee should be about ready. Help yourselves while I dash back to the kitchen."

"Wait a minute, Rebecca." Jeremiah displayed the mezuzah. "Look at what Rabbi brought us."

Rebecca examined the mezuzah, turning it wrong side up. By the manner in which she handled it, Tali surmised she had no idea what it was for. "It's lovely," she said and returned it to Jeremiah. He pushed himself upright. "I'll get a hammer and we'll nail it to the doorpost. Rabbi Zeig will help us consecrate our home."

"How very nice," Rebecca said. "Will we have a ceremony?"

"Yes, a brief one," Tali said.

"Rebecca, would you get Jonathan while I look for a hammer? And Gabriel, I'd like him to see the ceremony as well."

Angela said. "They're both still upstairs glued to the TV. I'll bring them down." Angela retreated to the stairs, giving Tali a wide berth.

"I've never seen a Jewish home being consecrated," Rebecca said. "Shouldn't it be done when a family first moves in?"

"Yes, but it's never too late."

"I wonder why Jeremiah didn't take care of it before?"

"Probably slipped his mind."

Israel Jacobs 25

"I suppose that's it. He is such a busy man. Sometimes he takes on too much for his own good."

Jeremiah trudged into the den, clutching a tool chest in his right hand. "Where are Gabriel and Jonathan?"

"Angela is getting them," Rebecca said. "There they are."

Jonathan hop-skipped into the den, trailed by a slender black pre-adolescent. The boy had an impish grin and clever eyes, as if the world was his plaything. He wore tan Levis and an oversized striped short-sleeved shirt. At the sight of Tali, he stopped short. Rebecca nudged him forward.

"Gabriel, say hello to Rabbi Zeig."

Rebecca thrust the boy's hand into Tali's palm. The boy smiled mechanically, shook hands briefly then wiggled free. He wiped the hand on the back of his pants and retreated expressionlessly to Angela.

"Everyone to the front door," Jeremiah ordered. The company filed after him. He set the tool chest down in the alcove and fished inside for a hammer. "Which post do I nail it to, Rabbi?"

"The right, as you enter."

Jeremiah threaded two nails through tiny eyelets at each end of the mezuzah.

Tali said, "Before you hammer the mezuzah into the doorpost please recite the prescribed blessings after me: Praised are You O Lord our God King of the Universe, who has sanctified us with Your commandments and instructed us to affix a mezuzah to the doorposts of our homes." Tali waited a moment then recited the second blessing. "Praised are You O Lord our God who has kept us in life, sustained us and enabled us to reach this happy moment."

Jeremiah hammered the mezuzah into the doorpost. Tali concluded the ceremony with a prayer, "May this home be blessed with harmony, health and happiness."

Rebecca dabbed a handkerchief to her eyes. "That was a lovely ceremony, Rabbi, thank you. Now for my cheese cake. Back into the den, everybody, while I get the coffee."

Rebecca mustered them out of the foyer. She returned with a steaming coffee urn, placed it on the table and doled out generous slices of cheese cake.

"Help yourselves. And there's plenty more on the way."

Angela sliced a piece of cake with her fork, nibbled, then set the plate on her lap. She stared at Tali quizzically.

"What's the purpose of a mezuzah? Is it like an amulet, a magic charm?"

Tali tried to gauge what prompted Angela to ask the question. Honest curiosity? Or was she baiting him? At least she was talking to him. "No, a mezuzah is not meant to be an amulet, although some Jews mistake it for one. It's to remind us that God is present in a Jewish home."

"You mean God limits his presence to Jewish homes only?"

This black girl carried a chip on her shoulders, Tali thought. He decided to play the teacher, and see where she was heading.

"Jews do not believe they have a monopoly on God. We believe God is infinite. As Isaiah said, *All the world is filled with His glory.* God can be found everywhere."

Angela wasn't finished. "Well, if God is in our neighborhood, He sure isn't paying any attention to all the misery in plain sight. Like He doesn't give a damn. So what difference does it make whether He's there or not?"

"God cares…He cares… He makes a difference…"

Angela failed to catch the lack of conviction in Tali's tone. "Easy for you to say, Rabbi. Try spending some real time in my part of town, then tell me God cares, that He makes a difference."

Angela swerved to Rebecca. "Aunt Rebecca, please take us to the station. I don't want to miss the train."

Rebecca hooked arms with Angela. "Excuse us, gentlemen. Angela and I need to have a woman-to-woman talk." She marched Angela forcefully into the foyer out of earshot. She whispered sternly, "That was rude. What do you have against the man? Rabbi never did you harm."

Angela said, "I've no right to tell you who you can or can't invite to your house, but you should have let me know he was coming."

"It's hard to get in touch with you, Angela. You don't even have

Israel Jacobs   27

a phone."

"Even if I did, you wouldn't have called, would you have?"

"I won't lie to you child, probably not."

"Why do you insist on trying to make me over, Aunt Rebecca?

"You can't go on like that."

"I can't help it, Aunt Rebecca, white people make me nervous."

Rebecca sighed, "Angela, there's good and bad in white people just like in us."

"Maybe so, but I don't have a mind to weed out the bad ones."

"You can't go on living with all that bitterness in your heart. You've got to change your attitude, Angela."

Angela shook her head. "White people didn't do to you what they did to Gunner and me."

Rebecca spread her hands helplessly "I give up. Say goodbye to Uncle Jeremiah, and I'll drive you and Gabriel to the station."

Rebecca made the round trip in twelve minutes. She huffed back into the den. "I love that girl, but she is stubborn as a mule."

"Yes, she is," Yarden agreed. "If you recall, Rebecca, I did not think it a good idea for the rabbi and Angela to meet. It was premature."

As far as you're concerned, Jeremiah, it will always be premature."

"Well, Rebecca, You saw for yourself how she behaved."

"I did. But I'm sure Rabbi Zeig understands."

Tali shrugged. "Not to worry about me. Rabbis are battle-hardened to criticism. We're subjected to worse rebuffs from congregants."

Yarden said solemnly, "It isn't you, Rabbi, that concerns me. I'm aware that you must deal with angry congregants, as I often must with angry patients. It is Angela that concerns me."

Rebecca interjected. "It's healthier to vent anger than to bottle it up inside, which you well know, Dr. Yarden."

Yarden hesitated, as if considering whether to pursue the subject. "Rebecca, I appreciate your good intentions, but sometimes your feminine instincts cloud your better judgment."

Rebecca glowered, "My feminine instincts! Listen to that male chauvinist. Let me tell you— "

Tali half rose from his chair. "I think it's time for me to leave."

Yarden tapped his shoulder lightly. "Please stay, Rabbi. This is as good a time as any to discuss Angela. And related matters."

Tali fell back into his chair.

"Angela, like many of us, lives with false equations: Judaism equals Jew. Jew equals white man. Hence Judaism equals white man. I want Angela to understand that Judaism does not necessarily mean white."

Tali said, "Suppose she does drop her equation, what then? Would you like her to convert?"

"What I'd like is for Angela to realize that like black people, not every Jew is cut of the same cloth. If she wants to convert, so be it."

"But you wouldn't mind if she converted. Is that why you want to join our congregation? To give her a bit of a push?"

"No, Angela can't be pushed. She is very strong-willed, as you saw for yourself. As far as joining the congregation, I must say I have reservations, but one must take risks."

"What risks?" Tali said sourly, as if the integrity his synagogue was being questioned.

"Rabbi, I'll be candid. As you probably inferred, not all my people think this will work."

Why shouldn't it?"

"Rabbi, you read my father's autobiography. He was a wise man. But, like most teenagers, I was not attuned to listen to sermons. However, one sermon he preached I will not forget. Probably, because it is constantly being reinforced.

"You remember the biblical narrative of the twelve scouts sent to reconnoiter Canaan. Ten returned dejected, dashing hopes that the Israelites would ever enter the Promised Land. 'The Canaanites are too powerful,' the scouts wailed. 'We encountered warriors so tall we felt like insects, and so we must have seemed to them.'

"God had performed miracle after miracle on behalf of the Israelites. Why, my father wondered, did they lose confidence in God? He answered, 'Not even God can help people who feel like insects.

That generation was condemned to die in the wilderness. The Promised Land would have to wait until a new generation matured, one that would feel like men, not insects.'

"An invitation my father declined prompted that sermon. A white congregation had invited my father to join them. Had he accepted it would have considerably lightened my father's burden. The host congregation boasted a lovely building, and was financially viable."

Tali shook his head. "Your father is invited to join a white congregation. He declines. His son initiates the idea. What's changed?"

"Success."

"I don't understand."

Roles seemed to have been reversed. Rabbi had become student, and layman teacher. Yarden continued patiently.

"The black man's fury at the white race is born of two causes. Fear, which is grounded on the oppression and prejudice we have experienced at the hands of the white race. The second cause is a sense of inferiority. Success mitigates the first cause. An inferiority complex is more difficult to cure."

Tali interjected. "I know. Some of my congregants have achieved phenomenal success in business, in professions, and still carry an inferiority complex about being Jewish."

"Then you grasp the problem. Much of the fury directed at the white race is a cover for a sense of inferiority. My father felt that his flock was not prepared to join a white congregation as equals. Success has made it possible for my people to hold their heads high. They are ready to join you as equals."

Rebecca had been listening intently. She said gravely, "This is all very interesting, but what has it to do with Angela?"

Yarden turned his attention to Rebecca. "The one thing we know about Angela, she definitely does not have an inferiority complex. There is good reason. She was raised in a loving home. Her parents were educated, proud people, and they transmitted that pride to their daughter. Angela is an angry young woman. There is reason for that. But the cause is not an inferiority complex. I firmly believe that she would respond positively to success and forget her anger."

Again Rebecca gave expression to her doubts. "So, why do you want to keep her from the white world? She's come a long way."

"That is true," Yarden agreed, "but not far enough."

"How far does she have to go?"

"To the point where if she did begin to trust white people and one white person betrayed her, she would not tar the entire white race with the same brush."

Tali interjected, "Jews are not racists, but most every synagogue has its share of misfits. Doesn't that worry you?"

"No, if it doesn't work out between us we can move ahead on our own. It would be difficult at first, but we have the talent and resources. If Angela begins to trust and her trust is betrayed, God knows if she would ever give the white world another chance."

Tali stroked his chin meditatively. "This has been quite a learning experience. *Mikal milamdai hiskalti*—I have learned from all my teachers."

"Aha yes," Yarden nodded recognition of the maxim. "From *Ethics of the Fathers*. My father prescribed that principle to his congregants many times. It is kind of you, Rabbi, to think I have something to teach you."

Tali said, "If you think I'm being too inquisitive don't hesitate to tell me. I'm curious about Angela's brother. He seems unusually attached to his sister, yet he gives the impression of being very independent. I can't put my finger on it, but it seems there's more to him than meets the eye."

Rebecca said. "Yes, Angela and Gabriel are very close. After their parents died all they had was each other. Now they have Jeremiah and me, but that's not the same thing. And he is a bundle of contradictions, also very bright. To us he is polite, but it is hard to know what goes on in his mind."

Yarden said, "I think that trait goes with being street-smart, which he has to be in order to survive in his neighborhood."

Rebecca said, "We worry about Gabriel even more than Angela. Her character is fixed. She will be what she already is. Gabriel is still

Israel Jacobs   **31**

malleable. Youngsters that age are easily influenced. And his environment brutalizes young people. I wish we could remove him from that neighborhood, the sooner the better. Otherwise, God knows what will become of him."

"I notice that Angela calls her brother Gunner, not Gabriel." Tali directed the observation to both Jeremiah and Rebecca Yarden.

Jeremiah said, "You are perceptive, Rabbi. Gabriel is his Christian name, Gunner his street name. He throws a fit when called Gabriel, except for Rebecca. He has learned that my wife is not impressed by his tantrums."

The chug of a balking engine squealed into the den from the street. The ignition wailed several times, caught, then the sound of a car fading off into the distance. Tali asked, "Is Angela your niece?"

"No. She's the daughter of a distant cousin on Rebecca's side. We are the only relatives Gunner and Angela have."

"You mentioned that you'd like Angela to teach out here. Is she teaching now?"

"Not full time. She has earned her degree. Now and then she gets a call to substitute. She also teaches part-time at the Office of Economic Opportunity in Upper Chelsea as assistant to a Reverend Malcolm Wood who is in charge of the Head Start program."

"That name sounds familiar. I remember hearing it recently." Tali tugged a pocket calendar from inside his jacket and shuffled through May and June. "I remember. The Christian-Jewish Conference. They meet bimonthly at the Seminary. Reverend Malcolm Wood. Yes, he's scheduled to be the speaker on June twenty-eight."

"That is quite a coincidence."

"Coincidence? Life is full of coincidences, Dr. Yarden. Your father can't sleep, has writer's block, can't find an idea for a sermon, he goes for a walk, chances on a group of elderly Orthodox Jews on their way to synagogue, and he and his congregation embark on a remarkable journey to Judaism. I remember my history professor telling the class that if you turn back the pages of life, you'll discover that what follows is mostly based on coincidence. The older I get the more it rings true."

"You are still young, Rabbi. Perhaps in time you will see things differently."

"Maybe. In any event I'll make it a point to meet Reverend Wood."

"Do that, Rabbi. Angela thinks highly of him. I would like to hear your opinion."

Chapter Four

On his instruction, Stella had mailed reminders that classes would resume the first Tuesday evening following Passover. Based on past experience, Tali doubted half of the twenty students he started with would be back. Once spring set in, the outdoors beckoned and adult-study programs fell on hard times. The muted voices drifting through the school corridor confirmed his prediction. He tugged the door open slowly, expecting to be greeted by an empty classroom.

Every chair was taken. Twelve of his regulars had returned. The other eighteen chairs were occupied by blacks.

In the ensuing weeks Tali discovered ramifications that had not occurred to him.

It had taken Tali awhile, but finally he had capitulated to reality. To the average synagogue member, lectures and seminars were a pleasant diversion. Undemanding, no reading assignments, no preparation required. You sat, you listened, asked questions. Occasionally, you dozed.

The blacks had come to learn. They were in dead earnest. They marched in week after week mentally armed to put in the time and effort. Within a few weeks they caught up with the whites, then moved ahead. Normally, the number of students tapered off after a few sessions. Not the blacks, their numbers increased. They started out with eighteen; by mid-May they were twenty-five strong. While the whites squirmed in their seats, the blacks came up with the answers, and exciting questions. Tali found himself enjoying the discomfiture of his white students, then began to worry that the competition might prove too stiff for the whites. He cut back on the assignments. But the blacks were eager. Whatever he taught they soaked up like sponges. They pushed for more. He got caught up in their excitement. They wanted to learn. Well, he was there to teach. He poured on the work. Marvels began to happen.

The whites stayed. They discovered their minds. They were reminded that rumps were to sit on, heads to think with. They began to take classes seriously. Word spread. Curiosity attracted synagogue members who hadn't opened a Jewish book since their bar mitzvah. They came to find out what was going on. Dozens stayed to learn. Classes were transferred to the library, which could accommodate a hundred chairs.

An equally phenomenal change occurred at Sabbath eve services. Fair weather or foul, the blacks attended services. Their presence doubled the number of worshipers. Attendance increased to a hundred, two hundred. Additional prayer books had to be ordered. With a congregation that size attending weekly, Cantor Bindel performed as if he were First Tenor at the Met. Tali, also, became more serious about preparing sermons.

Sabbath followed Sabbath. Every Friday night, without fail, five minutes before services began, the blacks marched down the aisle, the same forty-five, give or take a few, and to the same pews. The burgeoning white attendance made the blacks less conspicuous; they were now a minority, though their presence was never in question. Tali easily picked out their enthusiastic responses. He noted with satisfaction that they were becoming fluent in the Hebrew chants. Sabbath eve succeeded Sabbath eve. Gradually, the blacks began to feel and act more at home. They ceased parading in as a group. Some black families, taking their cue from the whites, would straggle in late, slipping quietly into rear pews. From Tali's vantage point on the pulpit the blacks no longer appeared as a sharply demarcated island in a sea of whites. Integration still had a long way to go. But a mix was blossoming in the Pineville Jewish Center. It disturbed Tali that the blacks insisted on departing for home immediately after services. Remembering the initial reception they were tendered, he appreciated why they were reluctant to remain for the *Oneg Shabbat*—the fellowship hour. He thought it wiser not to press. Hopefully, given time, both sides would warm to one another. In the meanwhile, Jews, whites and blacks, were worshiping in the same sanctuary.

At the May meeting of the Board of Trustees, the blacks were voted in as members of the Pineville Jewish Center.

Chapter Five

Tali lingered in the air-conditioned foyer. He shrugged to the silence, stepped outside and closed the door, squinting away from the sun. It hovered low over Albert Shakter's sprawling ranch house, a bright orange disc, promising another scorcher. A soft breeze ruffled the topmost branches of the elm trees lining the street, but provoked little motion below. Tali slipped on wraparound sunglasses. He disliked wearing them; on hot muggy days the glasses made the bridge of his nose perspire. But he preferred a damp nose to another migraine. Since his teens he suffered from migraines. Tiny bubbles would explode around one eye, usually the left. Within the hour, pain would split the back of his head, putting him out of commission for the rest of the day. He still remembered his first attack: the *yahrzeit*—the anniversary of his father's death. He was reciting the Mourner's Kaddish, his uncle looking on with sad eyes, when the bubbles suddenly danced on the pages of his prayer book. Then the sharp pain and the nausea.

Since his election to the Pineville Jewish Center, the attacks struck almost monthly. He was examined by an ophthalmologist, who referred him to a neurologist. All tests came back negative. He enjoyed twenty-twenty vision; other than the headaches he was a perfect specimen of young manhood, according to the specialists. Albert Shakter, psychologist and trustee of the Pineville Jewish Center, offered Tali a different prescription, "You don't need glasses, Rabbi. What you need is to get married. A wife, regular sex. That'll cure your migraines in no time."

Tali wondered how much of this free advice originated with

Israel Jacobs 37

Muriel, Al's wife. Muriel worried about Alice, her daughter. Twenty-five, unattached and no prospects in sight, drove Muriel to do the Jewish-mother routine. Tali laughed to himself whenever Al insisted that sex was the rabbi's problem. Al, philanderer that he was, should know first hand there was no lack of women willing and able to satisfy a bachelor. Like most laymen, Al had been programmed to stereotype rabbis as virgin-monks, until married.

Tali expected to marry, eventually. In principle he agreed that eventually should be soon, should have been already. Many of his Seminary classmates had walked down the aisle while still students. The few holdouts didn't hold out for more than a year after ordination. By now most of them were fathers. Yes, he should have started a family of his own. He had a well-paying position, and a large house that came with the job. But, to date, the woman with whom he'd like to share the rest of his life hadn't materialized.

Tali lifted the garage door and slid into the Mustang. The engine started up with a roar. He rolled up the window on the driver's side, jiggling the air-conditioning knob as he eased out of the garage. The knob jammed.

"Damn it, they were supposed to have fixed it."

Tali rolled down the window, shifted to park and drew a set of pliers from the glove compartment. He twisted the knob. It came loose and tripped to the floor. "Damn it again," he swore at the dashboard. He squirmed down, groping blindly into the grooved rubber mat. His elbow smashed against the steering wheel. A shock wave raced from his elbow to the tip of his fingers.

"Damn it! God damn it!"

"Gosh, Rabbi, you sure can swear." Vanessa, the Shakter's eleven-year-old daughter peeped through the car-window. An oversized collie strained at the end of a leash, which she gripped hard with both hands. She wore tight yellow shorts and halter to match. "You having car trouble?"

The tingling in his elbow simmered to a dull throb. He forced a smile. "It's the air-conditioner."

"Hey, you really banged your arm, Rabbi." Vanessa emitted a low whistle. "It's all black and blue."

Tali raised the bruised arm to window level. "That's not from now. I hurt it Monday night at karate. Made a lousy shuto-uke."

"What's a shuto-uke?"

"A knife-hand block," Tali explained, wincing. "And this bang didn't help any."

Vanessa stared at the arm. "Gee, it really looks swollen."

Tali massaged the arm, tenderly. "Not the first black and blue mark I picked up at karate. Probably not the last."

"Whatever for are you taking karate? You afraid the girls are gonna attack you?"

Tali grinned. "Could happen."

"Nah, not to a rabbi."

"You think rabbis can't have sex appeal?"

"Well, I never really thought about rabbis having sex... but I guess they do." The collie tugged impatiently. Vanessa choked down on the leash. "Anyway, rabbis are supposed to be peaceable. Like you're always praying for shalom. So, who do you expect to chop with all that karate stuff?"

"Oh, I don't expect to chop anybody. It keeps me in shape."

The collie yelped at Vanessa's ankles.

"Be quiet, Putzy." Vanessa poked closer to the car. "You going to the city today?"

"Generally do on Wednesdays."

"I can tell it's your day off."

"Now how can you tell that, Vanessa?"

"By the way you're dressed. A sport shirt, no tie." Vanessa tucked her head into the car. "And those... ugh..." she crinkled her nose... "green pants."

Tali chuckled. "The fella that gets you, Vanessa, is gonna get himself one smart gal."

"Not available yet," Vanessa giggled prettily. She pointed to her house. "Alice is." The collie pitched violently against the leash.

"Putzy wants to go. Hope you get your air-conditioner fixed. The weatherman said today's gonna be a scorcher."

Tali waved Vanessa off. He stooped to the floor, this time carefully avoiding the steering wheel, and retrieved the knob. It showed a crack running lengthwise. He shoved the knob into the glove compartment, rolled down the rear windows and backed out of the driveway into Flower Lane. He glanced at his wristwatch. Expressway traffic was peaking by now. He cruised lazily through town, taking in the kaleidoscope of color sprinkling Pineville.

It would be hard to find a prettier place to live, Tali mused to himself. Having been reared in Downtown Chelsea where a blade of grass was a rarity, he appreciated the flora exploding into life all around him. Peculiarly, the plush loveliness cast a pall over him. He felt depressed by the scenery. It fed his sense of isolation. He couldn't pin down the cause. Maybe the anomaly of being a bachelor in suburbia, where just about everyone else was married and had families. Or was it the rabbinate? So long as he was busy and working he didn't fret over it, but of late, the nights at home were unbearably long. More and more he found the rabbinate a lonely profession. It quarantined a man, set him apart. Merely, the title Rabbi put psychological distance between him and the rest of humanity. A congregation might have dozens of doctors, lawyers, accountants, teachers, business men. But per congregation there was only one working rabbi; in large congregations, sometimes an associate.

Five years a rabbi, and he found himself living in an eight-room colonial house, spiritual leader of a six-hundred-family upper-middle income suburban congregation, in the 20 percent tax bracket. And no deductions.

As luck would have it, the congregation had been on a youth kick at the time of his interview. His predecessor Rabbi Simon Klarsfeld, a Hungarian-trained rabbi with a heavy accent, had served the congregation for ten years. At the age of seventy the Board retired him with a comfortable pension. The younger set now demanded a voice in the selection of the next rabbi. They insisted that he be a graduate of an American university and ordained by the Seminary. Tali arrived with the right credentials. Shortly after being elected he wondered whether he was right for the job. Lately, he had become uncertain whether he was right for the rabbinate.

The synagogue's annual dinner-dance came to mind. Muriel Shakter had made a remark that had pushed him to the bottom. She hadn't been aware that he was within earshot.

"Where are you sitting?" Muriel asked Rochelle Feld, while waiting for the bartender to pour a Chablis.

"Table one," Rochelle said.

"With Rabbi?"

"I guess so. As Sisterhood president I suppose I have to."

"Too bad," Muriel offered condolences. "There goes your evening."

Most insults rolled of his back. This one had cut him to the quick.

Still, he had no cause to complain. Tali argued himself into taking a happier perspective of life. Lately, he had gotten into the habit of carrying on long solo conversations. He worried whether all this talking to himself signaled a breakdown. He considered asking Al, but decided against seeking the psychoanalyst's advice. Al would tell him the cure is marriage. To Alice.

Tali stopped for a long light on Cortez Drive. He observed the cars turning off at the mall. Not quite nine a.m., and the women were already cramming the parking fields. He drove by the one-story brick post office. Dan Myles, village postmaster, was pulling packages from his Thunderbird. He hailed Tali cheerfully. Tali waved back. Yes, it was a nice town, with all the amenities that made for good living. Friendly. You weren't a cipher. So Muriel Shakter didn't think he made a good table companion. That's her loss. Her logic was a conundrum anyway: He was a dinner-dance spoiler, but okay to have as a son-in-law. Must be the lady is desperate to marry off her daughter.

Chapter Six

Tali scanned the Seminary bulletin board: "Christian-Jewish Conference" headed the roster of meetings for the day. The Conference was scheduled to begin at 9:45 a.m. in the Winestock Auditorium. Reverend Malcolm Wood was listed as the speaker.

Memories of student days and of his brief post-student involvement in the black man's struggle still smoldered. Though the passion had cooled, Tali on occasion felt the old commitments flare up. Not sufficiently to impel him to action as it once did, but empathy for the black man's cause still lived. Enough to make him give up one morning to hear this black clergyman.

And, there was Angela Adams. Forgetful as he was about names, he was not likely to forget her name, or face.

Reverend Malcolm Wood spoke—without notes—for about thirty-five minutes. He delivered his message calmly, in a matter-of-fact style. But the bitterness brewing beneath the surface stirred Tali's memory. About eighty people sat in the audience, including three youthful looking nuns wearing short-skirted habits. Less than half the folding chairs lined up between the thick Gothic pillars were occupied. A popular God-is-Dead theologian had lectured at the Conference several months ago. That lecture had drawn a full house, with rabbis well represented. No other rabbis were in the audience today.

Reverend Wood described the poverty and frustration building to a head in Upper Chelsea's black ghetto. He laced his lecture with horror stories of ghetto life that Tali found hard to digest. The audience listened politely. At Tali's side a corpulent grey-haired minister wearing a heavy gold crucifix had dozed off. The speaker accused white Christian America—and the Jewish community—of passivity in the face of black misery. He warned that the black man's despair was turning into a murderous militancy that could explode any day, in Upper Chelsea as it had in other cities.

"The black man's tragedy will not be confined to the inner cities," Reverend Wood predicted. "It will surely spill over to the suburbs, to every neighborhood. America has been fouled by the black man's suffering, for more than two hundred years. There will be a payback."

Tali had heard these threats time and again. In fact, he heard them repeated so often they grated. Particularly disturbing was the anti-Semitism spewed by some black militants who seemed determined to climb out of the ghetto over Jewish bodies. Norville Wright, director of Triton University's Black Studies program was quoted as saying that white Jewish teachers are "committing cultural genocide and mentally poisoning black children." Barakav X Amitoo, heralded as the black Shakespeare by his small but vocal following, catalogued Jews as, "arty bastards whose time is coming and who deserve to be beaten, killed and tied up in a box marked, *contagious germs*." Tali believed this hate reflected no more than a fraction of black sentiment. He understood the provocation that produced such hostility. Were he black, were he forced to endure the poverty and oppression blacks did, every white face could very well be as hateful to him as every Nazi and neo-Nazi are to Jews. But to mobilize blacks by demonizing Jews is unforgivable. That was *Hitler's* game-plan.

It seemed only yesterday that he ran the gauntlet for the black cause. His first pulpit, Temple Shalom, a seventy-five-family southern congregation, allowed time for extra curricular activities, which he exploited to volunteer three hours a week at the Montgomery Freedom School, some twenty miles west of Temple Shalom. One night a gang of town bigots sprayed a swastika on the Temple's front entrance. The Board connected the swastika incident to his activities at the Freedom School. They gave him a choice: "Confine your activities to the Jewish community, or you're out." Tali chose out. He had counseled blacks how to avoid the draft. He believed the Vietnam war was evil. More evil was the fact that blacks were drafted while white affluent boys were safely tucked away in college dorms. While a student at the Seminary, he had helped register black voters. He had marched with civil rights leaders, black and white. He had "sat in" with blacks, spent a night in a southern jail with them. However, as incidents of covert and overt anti-Semitism multiplied in the black community, he had become disillusioned. Perhaps it was time for Jews to step to the rear. Let the white Christian community sound the trumpets for the black cause.

The speaker made him feel like a turncoat.

Malcolm Wood's militancy was of a different order. The anger was apparent, but it was not indiscriminate. He accused the white man of being indifferent to the degradation of his black brother, and in the process degrading himself. "The white man has a debt to pay, and he will have to make good, if he hopes to retrieve his humanity." The reverend did not simply denounce white passivity. He added, "the black man will have to lift himself up from his misery. And, we need all the help we can get. I for one will gratefully accept it, black militants and reverse segregationists notwithstanding. In the final crunch, however, we blacks have to help ourselves. We cannot depend on benefactors to do our work for us."

The reverend triggered feelings that went beyond guilt. Tali felt an atavistic kinship with the speaker. Malcolm Wood raised memories of events Jews had experienced, similar to the hells the black race was experiencing. If you ever hope to retrieve your humanity... that challenge kept reverberating in Tali's head.

During the half hour question and answer period, Tali sat deep in thought. Finally, it was over. Malcolm Wood walked off the stage and down the center aisle in Tali's direction. Up close, the reverend proved to be a man of wider girth than he appeared on stage, and shorter. He wore a lightweight tan suit. Horn-rimmed glasses squatted on the bridge of his nose. His hair was cropped close to the skull; a thick black mustache, spotted with grey, hid his upper lip. Tali stepped into the aisle and introduced himself.

Malcolm Wood studied Tali. "You sure don't look like any rabbi I ever met."

Tali made a lame effort to smooth his wrinkled sport shirt. "My day-off outfit. Actually, I dress very clerically when on duty."

Reverend Wood continued to examine Tali. He shrugged. "Okay, I'll take your word for it. You're a rabbi. What can I do for you?"

"I'd like to talk to you."

"Short or long?"

"I don't know; it depends. But I'd like to talk to you. About what you said... needing all the help you can get."

Reverend Wood glanced at his watch. "Look, I haven't eaten since early this morning. I'm famished. You know a good restaurant hereabouts? Not too expensive. We can talk and chat."

Tali introduced Reverend Malcolm Wood to "Yoinee's Kosher Delicatessen."

Tali ordered a triple-decker pastrami and corned beef sandwich, cola, and a family size plate of French-fries. Reverend Wood put his stomach in Tali's hands and ordered the same, with iced tea. Tali stared soberly across the table.

"I want to help. Tell me how."

The waiter, an agile pencil-thin Jew, wearing a black skull cap asked, "Anything else you want I should bring you gentlemen?"

Tali said, "That's it for me. How about you, Reverend?"

"Enough for me, too."

The waiter tucked the bill face up under a glass, and scurried to take the order of a noisy trio at the next table. Malcolm Wood studied Tali. "Before you leap, I suggest you visit our office and see what it's all about."

"I think I'll take you up on that invitation." Tali picked up the bill. "By the way, there's a girl I met not long ago. I believe she worked at your office. Name is Angela. Angela Adams, If I remember correctly." Tali pretended nonchalance. "She still work there?"

Malcolm Wood reached for his wallet. "Yes, she's still working at our office. How did you ever get to meet Angela?"

"Oh, she's distantly related to a family that recently joined my congregation."

"That's very interesting."

Reverend Malcolm Wood insisted on paying his share of the bill. He bid Tali good afternoon and strode out of Yoinee's Delicatessen, wondering how a relative of Angela came to be a member of a Jewish Temple.

Chapter Seven

Entrance to the O.E.O. office was via a rust-encrusted iron gate, which squeaked torturously when opened or closed. A corroded metal sign announced that this was the headquarters of the Office of Economic Opportunity.

Reverend Malcolm Wood stopped to inspect the cracked window fronting Lincoln Street. The jagged edges, sutured with Mystic tape, had begun to spread apart. A little pressure and the glass would crumble into the street, maybe on someone's head. A year had come and gone since he had been installed as Director of Upper Chelsea's O.E.O. by Mayor Goodrich. The mayor had cut the ribbon, smiled for the photographers while shaking the good Reverend Wood's hand, then hastened to his limousine. That was the last Malcolm Wood heard from City Hall. They allotted him a title, funds for a part-time assistant, a second hand desk, one filing cabinet, chairs and tables. That one-time allocation was it; for the rest, he had to forage, or do without. Not even funds to repair a cracked window. Whoever had tossed that garbage can lid should have finished the job. He had called maintenance to have the window replaced. The Task Force office sent the forms, in triplicate, which he had promptly filled in. A month had gone by, and still no word. Malcolm Wood was tempted to help the window die. That just might move the paper-shufflers downtown to send a man over.

Animal-like shrieks crackled into the room. It took a moment to realize these were coming from humans.

"Come on, man. Get that fuckin' hydrant goin'."

Israel Jacobs 47

The midmorning sun had turned the pavement pasty. Gooey tar-chunks adhered to the soles at every step. Auto hoods sizzled hot enough to fry bacon. An emaciated coal-skinned thirteen-year-old, whom Malcolm Wood knew only by his street name, Geronimo, was unscrewing the fireplug with a plumber's wrench, heaving with all the strength his thin arms could muster.

Malcolm had argued with the powers that be to permit the kids to open the fire-plugs a few hours a day, though he realized it made for a dangerous situation. With the fire-plugs on full blast, water pressure dropped. Should there be a fire, which in this neighborhood was as common as uncollected garbage, there would be a major tragedy. But you couldn't explain that to kids. The sanitation department used to send men to shut the fire-plugs. To little avail. The kids merely waited for them to leave then turned the fire-plugs on again. And there wasn't a lock these kids couldn't break. Apparently, the department had given up, probably calculating that another tenement burned to the ground didn't matter much.

Malcolm Wood agreed. Except for the fact that people lived in those tenements.

The first outpouring smacked onto the heat-blistered pavement and whipped up a storm cloud that reached to the sidewalk, fogging the lower half of the O.E.O. window.

Malcolm Wood observed with amusement as Gunner Adams shoved Geronimo aside. Gunner, though a couple of years younger, was half a head taller. Malcolm chuckled as he watched Gunner train the jet stream on another boy they called Fish-ears. The powerful stream pushed Fish-ears off balance and flipped him over on his rump. The youngster scampered out of range as fast as his short legs could move. Geronimo, standing barefoot in soaked tattered denims, waving his hands wildly and making ugly faces, challenged Gunner to hit him. Three older youths, in their early twenties with little but time on their hands, were leaning against a junked car tilted sideways on rims bereft of tires, the guts underneath long since cannibalized. They watched patronizingly as their juniors frolicked under the stream. Across the street, on the shady side, two winos and an extremely corpulent woman with rolled up stockings and bloated face were sitting on a stoop swilling from a bottle they were passing from hand to mouth.

Suddenly, Geronimo froze. Gunner prepared to fire. Geronimo's arm jerked up, his fingers pointing down-street. Gunner held back. Water swirled around Geronimo's feet. A Machiavellian grin spread from earlobe to earlobe. Curious as to what it was that stopped Gunner from firing his water-cannon, Reverend Wood followed Geronimo's fingers.

A red Mustang inched a bit forward. About twenty yards from the fire-plug, just out of range, it came to a halt. Sitting behind the wheel, one hand dangling out the window, was a white man who looked vaguely familiar. He wore a yellow sport shirt, wraparound sunglasses and a straw hat decorated with a yellow feather. He tipped his hat back and scratched his forehead several times, as if undecided how to proceed.

Gunner assumed an innocent pose. He waved the stranger on, laboring to give the impression that he merely wanted the car out of the way so that he and his friends might resume their splash-party. Malcolm Wood knew better. He considered intervening, then decided against it. Worst that could happen was that the car got a free wash. The driver, who looked more familiar to the O.E.O. director with every passing moment, put both hands to the wheel.

Gunner made a megaphone of his hands. "Come on, man, we ain't gonna wait all day. Move the fuckin' car." He positioned himself securely behind the fire-plug.

The Mustang raced its engines in neutral. Fumes spurted from twin exhausts.

An audience began to congregate. The three older youths, who had been leaning against the junked auto, stepped in for a closer view. Across the street, the winos perked up. The corpulent lady made an effort to join them, then plopped back. More Lincoln Street residents emerged from doorways and alleys. Gunner had drawn a sizeable audience. They trumpeted directives his way.

"Drown fuckin' whitey! Shoot it up his asshole."

A torrent continued to spurt from the fireplug, building to curb-

Israel Jacobs 49

high streams on both sides of the street.

Gunner readied himself for the attack. The Mustang clicked into gear. Gunner interlocked both hands under the mouth of the fire-plug. Excitement mounted among the bystanders. Malcolm Wood felt the battle thrill charging Lincoln Street. Whitey was about to take a bath, and from an eleven-year-old black boy. Gunner looked as if he already heard the applause. The reverend regretted not stepping in before. At this stage it was not advisable to interfere. Emotions were running too high. Whatever happens, happens.

Gunner arched over the fire-plug, digging his toes into the wet pavement. The crowd tensed.

The Mustang began to move.

In reverse.

Gunner appeared confused. Geronimo urged the driver to change direction. "Come on, man, we ain't gonna do nothin'." Shrill catcalls welled up from the spectators. Geronimo coaxed, cajoled, teased.

The Mustang continued to retreat. Gunner's hands dropped away from the fire-plug.

An earsplitting roar suddenly wrenched from the Mustang. The rear tires squealed insanely. Geronimo screamed over the din, his arms flailing wildly. Gunner leaped back into firing position. He slipped. One foot whipped air. He grabbed for a hold, missed the fire-plug and fell. The wet pavement crunched into his buttocks. The audience's attention switched from the Mustang to Gunner.

"Git you fuckin' ass up, Gunner. Hit him! Drown the mother fuckin' sonnabitch!"

Gunner sat on his hands, bewildered and in pain.

The Mustang roared past the fireplug. Twenty yards on the other side it screeched to a halt. Out of range again.

The door opened. One long leg protruded. The other followed. Slowly, the rest of the white man emerged from the car. He stood up to his full height, taking stock of the crowd. Malcolm Wood strained to recall when he had seen this young man before. The white stranger's gaze settled on Gunner. He sat drenched, half on the curb, half under the fire-plug, his legs spread-eagled. A shout went up from the crowd,

"He got a fuckin' asshole where his head ought to be."

Gunner hugged his waist, staying close to the fire-plug, as if it were his last refuge. Water sluiced down his ears and nose. The heavy stream continued to gurgle out of the fire-plug. Fish-ears, whom Gunner had sent tumbling before the stranger's arrival, gave him the finger. A woman pushed through the crowd, heading stridently toward Gunner.

"What in hell is going on here?"

Malcolm Wood turned to see Angela sweep into view. Her demand, directed at Gunner, carried part of the crowd back.

"How are you, Miss Adams?" The white stranger smiled at Angela. She stared at Tali. "And who are you?"

For a long moment the only sound to be heard on Lincoln Street was water coughing out of the fire-plug. The crowd tightened the circle around Tali and Angela.

Fish-ears, on the outer edge of the circle shrieked, "Yeah, who the fuck is you? Get yo' fuckin' asshole outta here fo' we slit yo' balls."

Malcolm Wood became concerned. The crowd was, as of the moment, merely curious. But the mood could grow ugly in an instant. Fish-ears' warning was no idle threat. Anyone in that throng was capable of pulling a knife. Malcolm Wood tried to push through, thinking to head off trouble. The stranger stepped closer to Angela.

"Don't you remember me, Miss Adams?"

Angela appeared baffled. "How do you know my name, Mister?"

"We met at Dr. Yarden's house. Remember?"

It's him! Malcolm Wood suddenly remembered. A rotund woman with enormous thighs blocked his path to Angela and Tali. Recognition flashed across Angela's face.

"You're way out of your territory, Rabbi. What're you doing here?"

"I was invited."

"Invited? By whom?"

"Your boss, Reverend Wood."

"Malcolm asked you here! What for?"

Tali pointed to the O.E.O. sign. "Your program is short-handed. I volunteered to help."

"To help? How?"

"Teach. I'm a very good teacher."

"Malcolm Wood asked you to teach? Teach whom? When?"

"The reverend didn't fill me in on the details. But I'm willing and able. I hope that's okay with you."

Chapter Eight

The O.E.O. "suite" consisted of a three-room railroad flat. Malcolm Wood's office looked out on Lincoln Street. It was sufficiently spacious to accommodate his desk, a book case and three chairs. The walls were whitewashed plaster. The floor, of slatted wood, though rutted in spots, had a sheen to it. A photograph of a clean-shaven black man in a pin-striped suit hung on one wall. Educated eyes peered through old fashioned rimless spectacles. Affixed to the wall a placard, in cursive writing, read:

Judge Lawrence Frost
Black is what you make it

Lace curtains—Angela's contribution to the decor—dressed a narrow window opposite the wall bearing the judge's photograph. Patches of sunlight strained through the window, which also acted as a conduit for the outside din and odors. The two rear rooms, crammed with folding chairs and bridge tables, were visible from the entrance. Malcolm Wood sat behind his desk, squeezed in a space too narrow for his ample bulk.

"Slow down, Angela. Have a seat, let's discuss this rationally."

Angela declined a seat. Her eyes pounced from Tali to the desk, drilling into Malcolm Wood. "There is nothing to discuss."

"Please, Angela, let's be reasonable about this. Threats don't become you. Give the rabbi a chance. What have we got to lose?"

Reverend Wood contemplated Tali. He still felt hard-pressed to reconcile his image of rabbis with this young man.

Israel Jacobs 53

The rabbi was tall, six feet two, Malcolm estimated. He wore a yellow short-sleeved shirt open at the collar and flared green trousers. A wide belt with an ornate silver buckle circled his waist. His legs, disproportionately long, terminated in scuffed Hush-Puppies, which fitted snugly to the rabbi's oversized feet. The rabbi—Malcolm would have to revise his image of rabbis—needed a haircut. Thick brown strands curled around both ears. The nose was a trifle long and hooked slightly at the bottom. The mouth, wide and poised over a firm chin, gave the impression that this young man spoke what was on his mind. The reverend found the eyes a contradiction to the rest of what he perceived in the rabbi. You could judge a man by his eyes, the reverend believed. The rabbi's liquid brown eyes belied the surface bravado; they reflected loneliness, uncertainty.

"Have a seat, Rabbi Zeig," Malcolm Wood abandoned further analysis of the rabbi's personality.

"Thank you." Tali pulled a folding chair close to the desk.

"First off, Rabbi, I want you to know that I appreciate your offer. It's kind of you to want to help us."

Tali crossed one leg over the other. "You're welcome, I'm sure. Now let's get down to *tachlis*."

"To what?"

"*Tachlis*. Jewish for brass tacks."

"Oh, well, yes. As I said the first time we spoke, you should look carefully before you leap. It's important that you know what you're getting into. Better not to start than quit on us next week."

"You don't know me yet, Reverend, so I'll let that comment pass. And I'm well aware of what I'm getting into. I've looked." Tali stole a glance at Angela. She stared back, her eyes angry slits.

"Do you have teaching experience?"

"Education is my business. That's the meaning of rabbi, a teacher. And believe me, I'm good at my trade."

"Angela huffed to Malcolm's side of the desk. "Malcolm, there's no way a white rabbi is gonna be accepted here."

Tali nodded in Malcolm Wood's direction. "He thinks I might be."

Angela glared at the reverend. He shifted in his chair. "I invited him because we need help."

"You invited him to teach black kids?"

"Well, we didn't sign a contract. But the rabbi's price is about what we can afford. He's offering his services gratis."

Tali grinned. "There it is. Straight from the reverend himself."

Malcolm toyed with a paper clip. "Teaching our kids won't be like teaching Sunday School in—where's your congregation?"

"Pineville."

"That in Debb's County?"

"No, further out. Melrose County."

"Well, wherever. There is a huge difference."

"On the surface, maybe. Inside, kids are kids. Anyway, I've taught black kids."

"You have? Where?"

"My first pulpit was down south. I volunteered a few hours a week at the Montgomery Freedom School."

"How long were you with the school?'

"Six, seven months."

"How did it go?"

"Good. We made real progress. I enjoyed working with those kids."

"And your congregation didn't object?"

"Not until they found out about it." Tali omitted the swastika incident.

"You taught black kids on congregation time without telling them about your project?"

"I don't know how it works in your church, Reverend. In ours they only *think* they own their rabbi. Rabbis owe allegiance to the larger community, too. Some of us occasionally put the theory into practice."

"What happened when your congregation found out?"

They offered me a choice. Confine my activities to the Jewish community or resign. I resigned."

"You left a congregation because you wanted to teach black children?"

"I'd be painting myself a saint if I said yes. Truth is, if all else had

Israel Jacobs   55

been good I might have stayed. It was just another negative in the hopper."

"Been doing any teaching since?"

"Not black kids."

"Angela made a wry face. "Malcolm, Are you serious about this?"

"I am. The facts are we need help desperately."

"Malcolm, you are looking for heavy trouble, a white rabbi from all-white suburbia." Angela swerved back to Tali, "No offense, Rabbi, but these kids will cut you to pieces."

Tali made a mock bow, "No offense taken, Miss Adams."

Malcolm looked sternly at Angela. "I think our problem may not be so much with the children as with your attitude."

Before Angela had time to react, Tali intervened. "I'd like to remind you, Miss Adams, that you invited me, as well as Reverend Wood."

" Rabbi, you are hallucinating. When did I invite you?"

"First time we met. At the Yarden's you said, 'spend real time in my part of town and see if God cares, if God makes a difference.' Remember?"

"I... I...didn't think—"

"You didn't think I'd take you up on it. Well, Miss Adams, no offense meant, it isn't nice to extend an invitation if you don't mean it."

Angela's mouth clamped shut. She turned sharply on her heels toward the exit and slammed the door behind her.

Gunner's audience had deserted him. Lincoln Street returned to hot decaying monotony. The winos tottered back to their fat lady companion, who had not budged from the shaded stoop. The three older youths resumed their previous stance, indolently squatting against the junked automobile. Gunner clung to the curb, cut to a bug's size. Geronimo had called him a fuckin' asshole. Geronimo, His friend! No better than the other farts. But, Gunner was forced to admit, they had reason to. He had been given a chance to drown whitey. Instead, in front of the whole neighborhood he fell on his ass. He felt like shit. A wet hand pressed gently against his shoulder. He looked up to see

56 *The Convert*

Geronimo hunched over him.

"Yo can't win 'em all, Gunner."

Disgrace pasted Gunner to the curb.

"Jive your ass off this fuckin' sidewalk," Geronimo urged. "Don' let no sonnabitch honkey fuck you up. They all ain't nothin' but shit."

That sonnabitch honkey was smart enough to stomp him, Gunner thought. He stayed glued to the curb.

"Come on, man. There gonna be other cars."

Gunner was in no mood to contemplate possible future victories. Geronimo gave up in disgust and rambled off to join Fish-ears.

Half an hour went by. To Gunner it seemed an eternity.

So, he missed this one. Nobody scores every time he's up at bat. Geronimo was right. The world began to feel liveable again, and the wet curb uncomfortable. Gunner rubbed his buttocks; he shifted position, away from the water still cascading from the fireplug. The depression began to lift. He crumpled handfuls of his shirt and pants, wringing out pints of water.

Gunner heard heels clicking sharply behind him. Without turning he recognized Angela's walk, and knew she was mad. He looked up. She loomed over him, her nails digging into his shoulder blade.

"You get your dumb ass home now and out of those clothes or else you'll be fasting the rest of the day, maybe tonight also."

Gunner nodded meekly. He wondered what had happened inside the O.E.O. office. His sister was in an uglier mood than when she had stormed in.

Five minutes later the mystery deepened. The honkey emerged from the basement, grinning. He reached out a long arm and patted Gunner on the head.

"Thank you, Gunner, my boy," the honkey crooned.

Gunner slapped the hand away. Curiosity prevailed over the enmity the defeated feel for the victors. He asked, "What for?"

"For having such a beautiful sister."

The white stranger's reply cleared up nothing. Gunner found his rage. "Shit on you, honkey."

The man continued to smile. "Don't fret, son, you may have lost a battle, but you will surely win the war."

The white stranger made a quick about face, hopped into his car and roared through the humidity of Lincoln Street.

Suddenly, Gunner remembered where he had met this honkey before.

Chapter Nine

Angela tapped the soft-boiled egg with the spoon-edge; the eggshell split into two neat halves. She tumbled the egg into a glass cup.

"Gunner, you want me to scramble a couple of eggs?"

"Don't want eggs," Gunner shoved his folding cot into a corner. "I'll take some Krispies."

Angela salted her eggs lightly. She spooned it in silence. Wednesday had arrived. A week since her collision with Zeig. The episode had unsettled her all week. Inviting a white man to teach black kids? Malcolm was a good man, she appreciated his problem, but things weren't that desperate. Well, she had given him her ultimatum. Zeig in, Angela out. Did Malcolm think she was bluffing? Would he actually let her quit, for a white man? Oh, she was getting up steam for no reason. Zeig wouldn't show. He was slumming, thinking maybe, a black girl an easy score. After that scene at the O.E.O. it should be plain he was fishing in hazardous territory.

Still, there was the possibility he would show. Something about this white man spelled caution in her mind.

Gunner watched his sister brood over her coffee. "You goin' down to the O.E.O. today?"

"Yes, I have an eight-thirty class."

Angela dampened the table with a moist cloth. She rinsed the dishes under the cold-water tap; the hot water tap worked on and off. Most of the time, even when it worked, it poured rust. Gunner stashed the dishes into a varnished crate under the sink, which served as a

Israel Jacobs 59

cabinet.

"You want me to walk you down to the O.E.O.?"

Angela smiled. "You that desperate for company?"

Gunner made a pugnacious face. "Ain't never needed no sister for company. I got business with Geronimo there."

"No insult intended," Angela tousled her brother's hair. "I really would like you to walk me down."

Gunner stomped to the sink. He jiggled a fork from the crate and scratched his back, using the fork as a backscratcher.

"What are you doing with that fork?"

"Scratching my back."

"With a fork? That is disgusting."

"My back ain't no more disgusting than my mouth."

Angela snatched the fork from Gunner's hand, rinsed it under the tap, dried it and slammed it back into the crate. Gunner skated to the bathroom door and scraped against the knob, wiggling his back up and down. The knob didn't quite reach the itch. He pushed the door open and scraped sideways against the edge. The toilet-bowl-lid stood at attention, Gunner having urinated a few moments before.

"Will you please shut that bathroom door!"

"Soon's I scratch my itch away."

Angela shoved him aside. She yanked the door shut; it whipped by Gunner's head, raising wind in his ear.

"Did you set the traps like I asked you?"

"What for? Ain't all the traps in the world gonna catch up with the rats runnin' around this building."

"Don't argue. Just set the traps like I say. Maybe if we kill a few more, the others will be scared off."

"Scared off! You kiddin? The way they was scratchin' in the walls last night, it sounded like they were all comin' to the funeral."

Angela submitted. "Okay, you'll set the traps tonight. You ready?"

Gunner saluted smartly. "Yeah, Sarge."

Angela laughed. They stepped into the hallway. The acidic stench of urine wafted up the staircase. Gunner closed the door, rattled the lock twice then followed his sister down the stairs.

After rush hour peaked, barring an accident, expressway traffic usually moved briskly. Tedious housing projects stretched mile after mile along the service roads. The tires clipped monotonously over the blacktopped asphalt. Tali's thoughts turned to his Ph.D. thesis. Now that he had committed Wednesday mornings to the children in the O.E.O program, he would have to cram all the research into the afternoon. Fortunately, for the most part it was finished. He needed time to organize the material. Then the big hurdle—defending it before Professor Teitlebaum. Tali speculated as to what use he might put the Ph.D., if and when he earned it. The rabbinate offered a challenge, satisfying in ways, frustrating in others. Were the doubts he felt about the profession peculiar to the rabbinate, or were they the result of the doubts plaguing him of late? Perhaps marriage would make the difference. Then again, maybe he didn't have the right temperament for the profession. In any case, with a Ph.D. under his belt he would have options. He could continue rabbinating, or look for an appointment at a university.

Wednesdays, Tali divided his time between the Seminary library and Triton University. Both were conveniently located on the edge of Upper Chelsea. At the Seminary, Tali researched sources on the Wisdom Teachers of ancient Israel, concentrating on the period between the destruction of the Temple in 586 B.C.E. and the sacking of the second Temple about 70 C.E. At Triton, Tali investigated sources on early Chinese philosophy.

Sam Yin! Tali recalled his former college roommate with nostalgia. Sam, a pre-med student, was an agnostic and a passionate believer in acupuncture. Tali didn't know what he himself believed in anymore. The philosophy and science courses were eating away at his fundamental orthodox beliefs and practices. First to go was his *yarmulke*—his skullcap. Next, the *tzitzit*—the four-cornered fringed undergarment. Orthodox Jews might go bareheaded when circumstances warranted it. But discarding the *tzitzit* was a major infraction. A covered head was rabbinic in origin, the *tzitzit* biblical.

Haverhill's coeds had taken up much of his time and conversation. And, under Sam Yin's tutelage Tali finally lost his virginity. But his

Israel Jacobs

extracurricular activity was not limited to sex.

Sam Yin had also introduced Tali to Confucius.

Tali had argued that humanism, not founded on a supernatural God, would sooner or later run aground. "This proves," he had insisted dogmatically, "that humanism is the child of the Bible."

Sam Yin waited patiently for him to finish.

"Can I talk now?"

"Yes."

"Okay. 'Do not do unto others what you do not want them to do to you', that sound like humanism to you, Sir?"

"It does."

"Know where it comes from?"

"Plagiarized from the Talmud."

"Jewish chauvinist! I never studied your Talmud. That's Confucius: Analects 17:22."

Tali chewed on the quotation. It paraphrased Hillel's dictum, "What is hateful to you, do not do to others."

"Could be Confucius got it from Hillel," Tali said without conviction.

"When did Hillel live?"

"Beginning of the Common Era, about the time of Jesus."

"Confucius lived five hundred years before, so how the hell could he have picked it up from your Hillel?"

Tali conceded. And Sam Yin had planted a seed in Tali's mind that took root, blossomed, became an obsession, and the basis for his thesis.

Leviticus 19:18 dictates, *Love your neighbor as yourself.* Confucius and Hillel, separated by continents and five centuries had both paraphrased this aphorism in the negative. Tali pondered the coincidence. It was too much to attribute to chance. He concluded that the two sages were influenced by Leviticus, which is older than the Analects. He stewed over the theory, finally becoming convinced that Chinese humanism, its reverence for the scholar and passion for scholarship paralleled Judaism because, in the distant past these two civilizations had communicated with one another.

When Tali first broached the idea at the Seminary he was advised to forget it. Somehow Tali's theory caught the attention of Professor Arthur Teitlebaum, chairman of the Bible Department. The professor invited Tali to lunch in the faculty dining room. Tali described how he got started on the idea. Arthur Teitlebaum asked to hear more. Three assistant professors were at the table. Teitlebaum was actually considering the theory. The assistant professors buzzed it around the hallowed Seminary halls. "Maybe Zeig has latched on to something."

From that watershed moment Tali's theory coasted uphill.

On foot it was a depressing twenty-five minute walk from their apartment to Lincoln Street. This morning the sights and sounds aroused Angela to more than the usual ill-will she bore white politicians, white corporate America, the white world in general—the garbage, in cans and out. Human discards, more dead than alive, shuffling like zombies through the debris. Winos passing rubbing alcohol, urinating and vomiting in hallways. Junkies nodding in those same hallways. Teenagers selling their bodies. Brothers leading johns to sisters; brothers selling their own ass. Dank rat-infested tenements spitting out dank rat-bitten tenants.

The white world had locked her race into this hell; they were responsible, from the president down to the last white bureaucrat. And their sanctimonious commissions with their charts and graphs. That was what black meant to them. A statistic. A line on a graph. Let them haul their asses down to Upper Chelsea and live here like her people were living. Then, maybe, they might understand what those lines were about. People, human beings. Her race pushed down to subhuman level. Angela glanced at Gunner. He paid scant attention to the grime they were wading through, hardly remembering anything else. These streets were home to him.

Boro Bridge loomed ahead. Tali eased on the accelerator, made a full stop to pay the toll and crossed Boro Bridge into the city.

It was as if he had left sanity and sanitation behind. The deafening racket, the melange of odors, the rush of bodies. Bedlam! Humanity

Israel Jacobs 63

run amok. Masses crowding the sidewalks, morose faces, people angrily pushing, shoving, sidestepping garbage, garbage spilling into the streets. Pedestrians recklessly darting into onrushing traffic. Bus drivers grinding their soot-covered vehicles to the curb, shouting curses at cabdrivers making insane U-turns. Mammoth trailer-trucks indifferently blocking traffic. Cars, double and tripled-parked. Music shops screaming ear-splitting atonal rhythms. Theater marquees displaying X-rated movies in grotesque word-pictures. Blacks in multicolored frocks hawking merchandise on the sidewalks. Store fronts plastered with signs advertising Afro-dance lessons and Afro religions. Ten minutes after crossing Boro Bridge, the city felt like home. But those first few moments, until he accommodated, it felt as if he had stumbled into a foul-smelling mind-shattering asylum.

Gunner scuttled around the corner into Lincoln Street. Angela trailed slightly behind. Gunner saw it first.

"Look Angela, the white shit's come back."

The red Mustang did not register on sight. Angela continued on a few paces. She stopped short.

"I don't believe it. God damn it!" Gunner was shocked. His sister sputtered curses he didn't think she knew. She poured it on. She swore at the car, shifted to the O.E.O. sign, back to the car. She bolted for the gate. Gunner pursued her into the basement.

Angela crashed into Malcolm Wood's office. The reverend sat at his desk tucking loose-leaf papers into a binder. A four-drawer filing cabinet, its bottom drawer rolled out to full length, stood to the left of the desk. To the right, one leg crossed over the other, sat Rabbi A. Naphtali Zeig.

Malcolm Wood laid the binder down. Calmly, he looked up. Tali's gaze strayed from Angela to Malcolm and back to Angela. She stormed to Malcolm's desk. Gunner positioned himself well behind his sister. She glared at the reverend, jabbing a finger in Tali's direction.

"Him or me. Which?"

Malcolm Wood pushed his glasses half a length down his nose; he peered over the rims. "Good morning, Angela."

Angela continued to brandish her finger at Tali. "Which one?"

Malcolm Wood tapped one nostril then the other. He slid off his glasses. "First, young lady, it is rude to point. Second, for an intelligent young woman you are acting infantile."

"I want an answer. Who will it be?"

Malcolm Wood fingered his glasses. "Both. I want you both."

"Well, you can't have us both. It's either him or me. Choose!"

Malcolm fitted his glasses back on. He ran his fingers along a paperweight resting next to the binder, quietly studying Angela for a long moment.

"As you say, Angela. I will choose. Before I do, however, let me read this to you." The reverend snapped a sheet from the binder and waved it at Angela like a weapon:

"James Walters, age nine. Lives with aunt. Whereabouts of father not known. Mother is an addict, unable to care for James. School verdict: James incorrigible truant. Missed school 55 days this year."

Malcolm pulled a second sheet from the binder:

"Francis Shaw, age ten. Lives with mother, three brothers, two sisters and grandmother. Father deserted family two years ago. Mother works. Francis stays home to care for younger siblings when grandmother is unavailable. Francis absent forty-nine times this year."

"Now I'm ready to make my choice. But first, you choose. Which child should I accept into our program? Which should I reject? I can't accept both if I don't get another teacher. In fact, I may not be able to accept either one.

"And let me remind you, adding these remedial classes to our Head Start program was your idea. You were the one that said these kids deserved a second chance. Because of you I squeezed an extra grant from City Hall to cover the program."

"Okay! Okay! Accept Walters. Accept Shaw. Accept them all." Angela bit her lip. She seemed on the verge of tears. Quickly, she covered the lapse with rage. "But change my day so I don't have to bump into him."

"I'll do whatever I can to arrange classes so that you two will cross paths as little as possible."

Angela turned to leave. The reverend snagged her wrist.

"Where are you going, Angela? You have an eight-thirty class."

Chapter Ten

Angela tapped her foot impatiently as Malcolm pulled folders from his filing cabinet.

"Here you are, Angela. The new students. Pick fifteen."

"I can handle twenty."

"Too many. It's no good for you or the children."

"And the rest, he gets?"

"Let's not start up that road again."

"Okay, but I'm still waiting for you to change my day."

"I will, soon as it can be arranged."Malcolm handed her the folder.

Tali thrust through the door swinging a bulging briefcase in one hand. Angela affected an indifferent posture.

"Good morning to you, Rabbi, you're early. The children aren't due for another twenty minutes."

Tali slapped his briefcase to the desk. "Good morning, Reverend. Good morning, Miss Adams. And how is every one today?"

Malcolm said, "What have you got there?"

Tali unzipped the briefcase.

"Comic books?"

"Contribution from my confirmation class." Tali capsized the briefcase. Reverend Wood picked through Vulture Man, Zombie Lady, Space Patrol.

"You don't intend to use this stuff for reading material?"

"Why not? It's more exciting than, Run, Jane, run. Run, Dick, run."

The reverend pointed to a cover displaying a fanged monster greedily ogling a scantily clad young woman with amply endowed breasts chained to a wall, all in sparkling technicolor.

"This is trash."

"When the kids master this literature we'll promote them to the assassination of Macbeth."

Angela made a retching sound. "I'll return the files soon as I copy the names." She stalked past Tali to the back room. Malcolm followed her departure with an annoyed look. He turned to Tali. "I'm sorry about Angela. She can be offensive when she has a mind to."

"Don't let it trouble you, Reverend, I've been insulted by experts."

"If Angela is too much for you, I can try getting her students switched to another day."

"Believe me, Reverend, I can handle it."

Malcolm Wood shook his head. "I don't know how you can take that girl's attitude. There are times I'd like to put her over my knee."

Tali chuckled. "Me, too."

"If you can take it, I'll manage to live with it. But it's like living in the middle of a battlefield."

Tali smiled. "Well, Reverend, we are men of the cloth. It's our sacred duty to beat her sword into a plowshare."

"Right... yes... Now about the comic books."

"Any problems?"

"I... I guess not. We'll try it for a while. See what happens."

Tali collected his comic books into a neat pile. "One favor, Reverend."

"Sure. What is it?"

"Wednesday is my day off. I'd be more comfortable if you dropped Rabbi. Tali will do fine."

The reverend held out his hand. "I go by Malcolm, or Cal. Whichever suits you."

Tali rolled both names on his tongue. "Malcolm. I visualize you better as Malcolm, it's got more body to it."

Malcolm Wood poked Tali's shoulder playfully. "I'm not sure what you mean by that. Would you care to explain?"

68   *The Convert*

Tali shrugged, "Just a passing thought." He stuffed the comic books into his briefcase, marched to his room and settled down to wait for the class. Malcolm Wood heard him whistling snatches from "Fiddler on the Roof."

Angela's students quickly learned about the comic books. They raised a howl.

"We want in on Tali's class."

Malcolm Wood tried reason, "You can't all be in the same class. That's why we added a teacher, so we can have smaller classes."

Class-size did not concern the rebels. The protests grew louder, more strident. Malcolm refused to yield. The following Wednesday, Angela's group paraded into Tali's room en-masse. Malcolm faced a sit-in. Tali grinned. Angela looked on bewildered. Malcolm threatened. Not a rebel budged. Tali stepped in to arbitrate.

"Why don't we alternate classes so everybody gets equal time?"

"Great idea," Malcolm agreed. "How about it, kids?"

Horace Clay, one of Angela's students, crossed his arms. "We all gets a chance with Tali?"

Malcolm said, "Yes, all get equal time."

"When we goin' into Tali's class?"

"Soon as I can arrange it?"

"When that gonna be?"

"Next week. By next Wednesday I'll have it all worked out." The reverend raised his palm as in prayer. "I promise."

Janie stuttered over a suffix.

"Shun," Angela checked the urge to call the girl stupid. "How many times do I have to tell you? T-I-O-N is pronounced 'shun.'"

Janie grinned, showing a gap between her front teeth. If not for the hollow cheeks, the eleven-year-old's brown face could be called pretty. She had large eyes and a wide sensuous mouth. At the moment, to Angela, the face looked incredibly, unbearably stupid. Janie did a two-step in front of Angela's table, snapping her fingers to a rhythm inside her head.

"Will you stand still and concentrate?"

"Ah am concentratin'."

Angela slammed the book shut. "Oh go on home. We'll work on it next week."

Janie skipped to the door. "Next week I'll be goin' to Tali's class."

Shit on you, girl; double shit on Tali's class, Angela muttered under her breath.

Before Zeig had dropped into her life, Angela monopolized her students' affections. Not anymore. She used to look forward to Wednesdays. Not anymore. Wednesdays had become hateful. Every Wednesday, between eight-fifteen and eight-thirty a.m., he charged into Lincoln Street with his red Mustang. And for the next hour and a half she had to listen to his cackle through the paper-thin walls. She steamed. Little things set her off. Prior to Zeig she took the horseplay in stride. Now the jiving drove her to distraction. She had become short-tempered, backbiting. She saw herself in the children's eyes turning from a loving surrogate parent into a witch. She couldn't control herself. She blew up at the least provocation. Worst of all, the kids were closing their minds to her. What had gone wrong? Him! That's what had gone wrong. Four weeks she had endured his cackling in the next room. And every week Malcolm had put her off. "Next week, Angela. By next week I'll have it all worked out. Have patience." The middle of July, and Malcolm was still putting her off.

"Have patience—shit!"

Angela thrust the key into the cabinet as if the key was a rapier and the cabinet door Zeig's chest. The lock jammed. Angela shoved the key in further, twisted with a vengeance and yanked. The door gave, swinging open all the way. Angela grabbed to stop the spill. Too late.

"Damn him!" Angela swore at the pencils, notebooks, textbooks pouring out and falling into a jumble at her feet. She squatted to her knees, sweeping her arms in a wide arc to gather in the mess. Her calf snagged on the cabinet edge. She half-turned, still kneeling. A full line in her double knit slacks had unraveled.

"That's it; I've had it!"

70 *The Convert*

She bolted upright, leaving the mess on the floor. She chased through Tali's room. The empty class mocked her. She felt his idiot grin bouncing off the walls. She pictured him standing in front of the blackboard juggling pencils and chalk in his ever busy white hands and cackling with his ever busy white mouth. And the kids, lapping up his every wisecrack. She slammed into Malcolm Wood's office.

The reverend was studying the contents of a folder. Angela rattled the paper weight sitting on his desk.

"You hear me, Malcolm? Enough! I can't take it any more. Either you change my day, or I quit."

Malcolm laid the folder aside. He gave Angela his full attention.

"It's not that simple to get a bunch of mothers and aunts and grandmothers to agree on a switch in schedule."

"Seems to me you haven't been trying too hard to make the switch. I'm telling you for the last time. Either you change my day, or get someone else. I refuse to take another day of him."

"What's the point of switching you to another day if the kids won't show up? My first consideration has got to be for these children."

"What about me? Don't I count for anything?"

"Has it really been that terrible working with the rabbi?"

"It's making me sick to my stomach."

"Alright, Angela. Give me a couple of weeks. I'll really work on it. I'll reschedule half the kids for another day. If they don't come, I'll just have to thank the rabbi and tell him his services are no longer needed."

"What if you can't find anyone to replace him?"

"Well," Malcolm purred, "between the two of you there are twenty-eight students. You can't handle all of them by yourself. I'll have to find someone else. If I can't, we'll just have to cut eight or ten out of the program."

Angela gulped down on air. Malcolm understood the effort it took to cover her hurt pride. He considered calling her back, consoling her, changed his mind, thinking it best to let it drop for the time being, then changed his mind again. He couldn't let her walk out feeling so defeated. He felt her pain.

"Angela, you are one of the best teachers I've had. I can't afford

Israel Jacobs   71

to lose you. I understand why you feel as you do; I don't agree but I understand. Sometimes we have to put our feelings aside. Your anger is not fair to the school, it's not fair to Rabbi Zeig. Most of all it's hurting you. You have to put that anger down. It's too heavy a burden to carry."

"Malcolm," Angela spoke the reverend's name softly. "In this lifetime Gunner and I will never be able to repay you and Clara. Without your help we couldn't have made it. But, Malcolm, It's *my* anger. And much as I'm grateful and love you, you are not my psychiatrist."

"I can't just sit by and watch you fry your insides with so much anger."

"Let it rest, Malcolm. I don't want to talk about it."

"You've got to talk about it. You're feeding on poison. It's destroying you body and soul."

"Malcolm, I don't want to talk about it."

"You have to, Angela. All these years... you've been directing that hate at the wrong target. The accident, it could have been—"   ·

"I DON'T WANT TO HEAR ABOUT IT! I DON'T WANT TO HEAR ABOUT IT!" Angela pressed hard against her ears. Gently, but firmly Malcolm tugged her hands away. "Angela, it could have been a black boy behind that wheel."

"IT WASN'T! IT WASN'T!" Angela broke away. She pounded at her ears. "IT WAS A WHITE BOY! IT WAS A WHITE BOY!"

Malcolm pressed her face into his chest. Tenderly he stroked her hair. "Hate every drunk who drives a car. The fact that it happened to be a white boy doesn't make every white man guilty."

Angela pulled away from Malcolm's embrace. "Every time my life's gone to pieces it's been white people smashing into me. Why don't they just stay on their side of the line? That's all I ask. Just let us be."

Malcolm felt her fighting back tears. If she would only let it pour out, maybe it would wash away the hate. Not Angela. She wouldn't cry. He hadn't seen Angela cry since the accident. Rage. Hysteria. Not tears.

"Angela, talk to the rabbi. He really is a good man."

"I don't want to. I can't."

"You say you owe me. So do it for me."

"That's not fair, Malcolm."

"Okay, it's not fair. I'm asking anyway."

"I can't. I don't have anything to say to him."

"Say, 'good morning,' 'good afternoon.' Talk about the weather, about the kids. Say 'good night.' But talk to the man."

"Alright, alright. I'll talk to him next week."

"Not next week. Now."

"He's left. His room is empty."

"He didn't leave yet. He's outside rapping with the kids. He'll be back to say goodbye. He always does... Here he comes now."

Tali stepped into the office. He loped toward the desk in his usual cavalier way that so irritated Angela. He saw her staring his way and stopped abruptly, as if aware that he was breaking into an intimate conversation between the reverend and Angela. Malcolm prodded her forward. She brushed his hand away. She stared at Tali a long moment.

"Zeig, would you answer a question that's been bothering me?"

Tali rolled a chalk-stick between his fingers. "If I can, sure."

"I need an explanation. Why are you giving up a morning every week coming here to teach black kids to read? What's in it for you?"

"It's hard to explain."

"Give it a try."

"I'm not sure I can. Not right off the cuff."

"Maybe I can help."

"I'd appreciate it. Go on."

"It's to ease a guilty conscience. Coming down here to the black ghetto a couple of hours a week makes it easier for you to sleep the rest of the week. Kind of a token weekly payoff. Have I got it right?"

The chalk snapped in Tali's hand.

"Angela, the truth is I don't know exactly why I keep coming. Maybe you've screened out part of the reason. But let me tell you something you've made me dredge up from my past. I think about it often."

"My father would tell this story over and over. I must have heard it a hundred times. To him every Christian was an anti-Semite. The wisest thing for a Jew to do was avoid contact with Christians. In his world he had good reason for that opinion of Christians. He grew up in a village somewhere in Romania. To him Christians equaled Jew-baiting, drunken peasants raping, burning, beating up on Jews—local priests egging them on, especially at Christmas and Easter time. An occasional murder of a Jew, a pogrom was expected. Then came Hitler, the natural end-product, to my father's mind, of Christian anti-Semitism. And Christian countries, including our own, that turned away the few pitiful refugees that escaped the ovens, because they couldn't care less, confirming my father's opinion of the Christian world.

"The Nazis got my grandparents and most of the family on the first roundup. My parents won a reprieve, ironically, because a Christian couple hid them. They hid my parents five months. Until someone denounced them to the Gestapo. My parents managed to escape in time. The Nazis shot that Christian couple."

Angela said, "Your father change his mind about Christians?"

"It's hard to know. The lifestyle of my parents after they came to the States didn't allow for much contact with Christians. But that Christian couple shattered my father's certainty that every Christian had to be a Jew-hater."

Angela's belligerence still showed. But she was clearly forcing it now. "I expect you think you can be that Christian couple to blacks."

"Maybe, Angela, maybe. It's very possible, unconsciously, that's what's pushing me. Yes, maybe it's my way of repaying a debt. If not for that Christian couple, I would never have known my father. I wouldn't be."

"We're all messed up," Angela said. She stroked her temples, as if trying to contain a throbbing headache.

"I'm drained, Malcolm. Right down to empty. It's been a long morning. I'm going home. Zeig... "

"Yes, Angela."

"I... I... I'll see you next week."

Chapter Eleven

In the presence of white folks keep a low profile. Little colored girls growing up in Redford learned that lesson at a tender age. Angela had digested it before she could read.

Redford's Main Street featured a red-brick courthouse with stately columns and a clock-tower. Courthouse Street was shaded by huge oak trees that branched out over most of the square. A bronze statue of a Confederate soldier with a blanket roll on his back and a long rifle in his hand at the ready guarded the courthouse. No matter from which angle Angela entered the square, the rifle seemed to be pointing at her. Benches lined the square, on which old men sat, whittling and telling each other endless stories. One entrance to the courthouse was reserved for whites, the side entrance for Negroes. Courthouse Street included an ice-cream parlor patronized by Redford's citizens of all ages. The ice-cream parlor had a window looking out on the street where Negroes could stand in line. No Negro dared venture inside to sit at one of the tables. Redford's one movie theater also had two entrances, the main entrance and a side entrance, for Negroes.

But the memories were not all bad. Angela remembered the pasture behind her house, the field and woods. Running barefoot, through the cane thickets and muddy ravines peppered with tracks of mink and coon. Skipping across creeks, scampering over hills, rolling in freshly cut hay.

Her father taught history in Redford's Negro high school. They lived in an old solidly built five-room house. Her mother, Vera, gave

Israel Jacobs   75

birth to Gabriel a month before Angela's eleventh birthday. The following year her father announced they were heading North; he had been promised a job in a city called Chelsea. Angela remembered her mother protesting. She didn't want to uproot the family. Things were changing, her mother argued, and the change would soon reach Redford. Her father was adamant. He had waited for change all his life, as his father had before him. Enough waiting. He wanted his children to breathe free, to go as far as their talents would take them. Angela remembered the excitement of moving. It was like movies she had seen of wagon trains heading West. Except, they rode by U-Haul.

They rented a three-room apartment. Angela no longer had a room of her own. But the apartment was clean and had a bathroom with a needle shower, which made her skin tingle and feel clean all over.

Her father did not get the promised appointment. His teaching license, it turned out, was not valid in this state. He supported the family by working odd jobs, and enrolled in night school in order to qualify for a teaching position. They never went hungry, though tension was building up between her parents. Eleven months after moving North, Clive Adams proudly announced he would again be teaching history. He had secured a position to teach in Upper Chelsea High School. They moved to a larger apartment. Angela adjusted. Redford receded from her mind. The city pulsed to an exciting rhythm. There were no statues of Confederate soldiers. No "For Negro" signs. She could choose any of a dozen movies, pay for a ticket and sit wherever she fancied. She explored Upper Chelsea, as she had run through the woods outside Redford. Ever since she could walk, Angela had exhibited a fierce independence. Clive Adams labeled his daughter spirited. Her mother said the devil wouldn't let her sit for a minute. Angela loved them both. Gabriel grew up fast, faster than kids grew up in Redford, and he learned too much too soon. He began to spend more time in the streets than at home. He demanded a name-change; from Gabriel to Gunner. When asked why, he said all his friends had nicknames. And Gabriel sounded faggish. Her mother would not hear of it. Angela and her father capitulated. The Adams family joined the Second Baptist Church. Reverend Malcolm Wood presided as minister.

Vera saw to it that her brood made it to church every Sunday. When Angela turned fourteen, she acquired a Social Security card and found a part-time job as a salesgirl in Norton's Department Store. Vera protested, the job would interfere with school. Clive Adams thought it a good idea. To her father, Angela could do no wrong. Lucky for Angela, he never found out she had lied about her age. Lying was one thing Clive Adams would not countenance, even in Angela. The Adams, a middle-income family, upper middle by Negro standards, were content with what the good Lord had provided.

One Sunday night, while homeward bound from a church supper, Clive and Vera Adams were killed in an automobile accident. A drunken white boy had smashed his Cadillac into their Datsun.

Angela had been at home with Gunner. Toward midnight she got the news. Two white cops knocked at her door. Frightened, shivering in the bitter February night, she was driven downtown. To the morgue. A somber looking man with a rooster-like face and dressed in a white frock rolled out one drawer from the refrigerator. Then a second. Angela remembered screaming, and little else, until the funeral.

The next six months she recalled as through a fog. She had turned numb. She heard, saw, she felt, but it was as if she were witnessing it all from outside her body. It was like sitting through a movie, a horror movie, not something actually happening to her.

The white boy's lawyer persuaded an all-white jury that the teenager was not drunk. The accident was Clive Adams' fault. He had driven through a stop sign. Being dead, Clive and Vera Adams could not testify to the contrary. The white boy's license was suspended for a year. The deceased's heirs were awarded ten thousand dollars. Five thousand each, her parents had been worth to that all-white jury.

Angela and Gunner became wards of the state. The court-appointed a guardian to manage the estate. Clive Adams had left some insurance. Not much. And after probate by the white court it was much less. By the time the court-appointed guardian was through, their share of the damage-award was near zero.

The white social workers took charge. She and Gunner were farmed out to foster homes. Different foster homes. Angela's foster

Israel Jacobs 77

mother, a prematurely aged mother of six grubby brats, tried to turn Angela into her maid. The woman's husband tried to turn her into his mistress. He would waddle home, fat and filthy, smelling of whiskey, throwing lewd gestures her way. Once he caught Angela alone at home and nearly raped her. Angela threatened to tell his wife, whom he feared like the plague, and he backed off. Gradually, Angela came back to life. The numbness wore off. She began to feel again. New feelings sprouted. Hate, fury. Her foster parents were black, and she despised them and their filthy screeching children, but the hate that raged inside was directed at the white world that had convulsed her life.

One July afternoon she found her foster mother's purse lying on the kitchen table. She reached in and snatched a handful of bills. Quickly she stuffed some clothes into a shopping bag and walked out of the apartment. She rode the subway that night. When she got to count what she had pilfered, it added up to more than a hundred dollars, to her a small fortune. She rented a room, with bathroom facilities in the hallway, for twenty dollars a week. The next morning she went job hunting.

In the following months Angela went from job to menial job. She cleaned floors, did laundry, ushered in a dinky double-feature movie theater, waited tables in a ragtag diner. She found another room in another grisly tenement, but this room boasted its own toilet. Eating and shelter were less of a problem than fending off the parasites— the derelicts and junkies of Upper Chelsea. Angela learned to carry a knife. She began to miss Gunner terribly. One day she waited outside his school. He spotted her and burst into tears. He clutched at her coat, threatened to run off if she didn't take him with her, she would never see him again. Angela brought her brother home. For six months he wasn't missed. His foster parents collected the monthly allotment, not bothering to report that he had run off. To avoid alerting the social workers, Gunner continued in the same school. For a time it appeared they were in the clear. But the white social workers could not be fooled forever. Gunner was placed with another set of foster parents. In three weeks he was back. Angela called on Malcolm Wood, her last resort. Tears welled up in his eyes when he saw Angela. She told him what had transpired since she and Gunner had been farmed out to foster homes. They didn't need foster parents. What they needed was each other. Could he help? Malcolm Wood asked if they had relatives he might contact. None, Angela said. The only relative ever mentioned by her parents was a distant cousin to her mother, a Dr. Yarden, who lived in the suburbs. Angela recalled hearing the name, Northville. Malcolm searched, canvassed phone books, called the Medical Society, to no avail. Meanwhile, Malcolm accepted custody of Gunner. His wife, Clara, invited both Angela and Gunner to live with them. Angela declined. Gunner was free to live with the Woods if he wanted. She was determined to go her own way. Gunner refused to leave Angela. Clara argued, pleaded. Angela would not budge. Clara went apartment hunting. She found a tiny one-room apartment in an antiquated tenement, but an improvement over what Angela and Gunner had been living in, and closer to their own apartment. Out of his own pocket Malcolm paid the first month's rent. Out of a fund the church sisters raised, Clara Wood furnished the apartment with folding cots, dishes, silverware, a table, chairs, linen.

At the time, Angela waited on tables at Chuck's, a local diner. Malcolm Wood took a dim view of the place. The food wasn't bad; occasionally Malcolm stopped in for a sandwich. What troubled the reverend was the clientele, a gruff, uncouth bunch, who felt that the right to pinch the waitress' buttocks came with the service. It was no place for a young woman to work, but Angela had little choice. Meager as the wages were, with tips, the job enabled her and Gunner to eat decently and keep a roof over their heads.

Malcolm renewed his search for Angela's relative. Finally, the Medical Society located a Jeremiah Yarden M.D., who had opened a practice in Northville. Malcolm Wood called immediately. The Yardens lost no time in running out to Upper Chelsea. They pleaded with Angela to move in with them, and came up against the same stubborn streak that had defeated the Woods. Jeremiah Yarden recommended Angela to a Dr. Porter, a colleague practicing in Midtown Chelsea. In later years Angela was to learn that half the salary she was paid that first year as Saturday receptionist in Dr. Porter's office was subsidized by

Israel Jacobs 79

Jeremiah Yarden. She had finished high school, and upon graduation, encouraged by Yarden and Malcolm Wood, Angela had enrolled in Chelsea University. Jeremiah Yarden underwrote the tuition. Angela took summer sessions and had graduated with a degree in Education.

During those early years she and Gunner had missed many a meal, and more. Angela remembered bad nights, Gunner crying in his sleep for Mamma, she fighting back tears, trying to comfort him. At present, life seemed to have taken a half turn for the better. Between her part-time jobs and the money she earned at the O.E.O., she averaged a hundred twenty-five dollars a week. She was a certified teacher in line for an opening at P.S. 413, starting salary ninety-five hundred. If it came through, she and Gunner would have breathing room.

Angela beat a hollow into the pillow with her fist. It had been an emotionally grinding day. Her body ached to sleep, but her mind circled round and around. She reached into the past, skipped forward to the present. Her brain insisted on rehearsing the morning's scenario with Zeig. The murder of his grandparents because they were Jews. Zeig's face kept intruding: his gait, smile, surface bravado, underneath which she now recognized a soul as troubled as she. She felt restive, fidgety. Novel sensations gripped her body. He had plummeted into her life, pummeled her stereotype of the white world. She had grown comfortable with her rage. It filled her, sustained her, a trusted companion from whom she was reluctant to part. Now when her life seemed to be turning the right corner, he jostled in uninvited.

But it wasn't all Zeig's doing. Before Zeig, crevices had opened in her life, an emptiness that rage could not fill. Angela's fingers caressed her belly, stroking between her thighs. A. Naphtali Zeig. She lingered on the name, mentally articulating it. Insane! She was going out of her mind. Maybe Malcolm was right. Maybe she was ripe for the couch.

Friend rage, of late, failed to fill the expanding emptiness. Not her work at the O.E.O, nor the hope of an appointment at P.S. 413, nor Gunner, or the Woods, or the Yardens. God, she felt so alone.

Gunner's rhythmic breathing lulled her. She fell asleep crouched in the fetal position, hands tightly pressed between her legs.

Chapter Twelve

Everett Russel chaired the Board meeting, hoping for a fast adjournment. No problems thus far. Nine-thirty, and the president had managed to plow through old and new business without any wrangling. Remarkable, Tali thought, for a Pineville Jewish Center Board meeting.

"Good and welfare," Everett moved to the next item on the agenda. Out of the corner of his eye, Tali caught Rochelle Feld's hand spring up.

"Yes, Rochelle, the floor is yours," Everett recognized the Sisterhood president. Tali had a sudden premonition of gathering storm clouds.

"Thank you, Everett," Rochelle smiled sweetly. "I've been delegated by Sisterhood to insist that the Board discuss the question of giving women the right, and may I add a right long overdue, to participate equally with the men in all the honors and privileges of synagogue worship. We refuse to tolerate any longer being second class citizens in our Temple. We contribute and work at least as hard as the men to maintain the Pineville Jewish Center. It's time we joined the mainstream of the Conservative movement."

Tali sighed. "That shoots down prospects for an early adjournment."

"To be specific," Rochelle continued, her tone now turning militant. "We woman want *aylos*."

Old man Lutvak snorted. "*Aliyos!* You want to be called to the Torah at least you should know how to pronounce the word correctly."

Israel Jacobs 81

Lutvak's distemper failed to ruffle Rochelle Feld. "Yes, Mr. Lutvak. Thank you for the correction. We want *aliyos*. We women refuse to be second class citizens anymore. We demand equal rights."

Lutvak pushed himself up from his chair. Twenty Board members, six of them women, waited for Lutvak's response.

"Equal? Did anybody ever hear me say women were less important than men? Different, yes. You are different, and I thank God for the difference. Such a boring world this would be without the difference."

"So why do you object to giving us *aliyos*?" Rochelle Feld took pains to pronounce the Torah-honor correctly this time.

Lutvak stayed calm, rather unusual for the old man when contradicted. "Because women are different, so you got different responsibilities."

Anita Beck, past Sisterhood president, demanded the floor. Everett yielded. "With all due respect, Mr. Lutvak please tell us what in your judgment our responsibilities are, in this day and age?"

" The same as it was in your momma's and grandmomma's age, to raise a family, to make good Jewish homes so that our children and grandchildren will grow up to be Jews who care about the synagogue and Judaism. That is a woman's responsibility."

"Again, with all due respect, Mr. Lutvak, that is not enough for today's modern women."

"Not enough?" Lutvak raised his hands in mock bewilderment. "You are wrong, Mrs. Beck, and excuse me for contradicting such an intelligent lady. That is a bundle of responsibility. From some of the results I see, I'm sorry to say, more than most modern women can cope with. And that is why we have big beautiful synagogues that are empty for most of the year. Because you modern women are more interested in getting *aliyos* than raising your children to be good Jews."

The room erupted. Russel rapped for order. Maurice Cline clamored for the floor. "Mr. Lutvak, such an attitude is uncalled for. Our women are an asset to the congregation. We couldn't manage without their contributions of time and money. And they are to be congratulated for producing such fine Jewish homes. I agree. It's time to seriously reconsider our present policy regarding women's participation in religious services."

Lutvak wrinkled his brow. He didn't wait to be recognized by the chairman. "Alright, Mr. Maurice Cline. We got fine women. They produce wonderful Jewish homes. So I ask you, Mr. Cline why, on Shabbos, in a congregation of six hundred families, we get no more than, thirty, forty Jews to services, and many a Shabbos we have to wait around for the tenth man?"

Anita Beck exploded. "Maybe if you showed women the proper respect and allowed us to make up the quorum of ten you would improve attendance and not have to wait for the tenth Jew."

"You think, Mrs. Beck, that if the Board voted tonight to give the women *aliyos*, they would all come running to services?"

"I think maybe a lot more would."

"Maybe the Messiah will come tomorrow."

Everett rapped for order. Al Shakter raised his hand. The chairman nodded for him to speak.

"This is a ritual matter," Al shifted in Tali's direction. "Shouldn't we ask the rabbi's opinion?"

"Thanks Al, for nothing," Tali muttered under his breath. He would have much preferred to table this question, for the next ten years, at least.

Everett said, "Would you care to say something, Rabbi?"

Tali cleared his throat. "This is a complex question. I'd need at least a half hour just to explain the legal background. The hour is late. Maybe we ought to table the question for a future meeting?"

Rochelle Feld waved her hand. "No! We refuse to accept any more delays. There's been enough talk. We want the matter settled now."

The lady doesn't get up till noon, Tali said to himself. Why should she care if we're here all night?"

Again Everett rapped for order. "We'll take it to a vote. If the Board wishes to table, we'll defer the question for another meeting."

The vote: Four to table, sixteen to continue discussion.

"Rabbi, the floor is yours," Everett said. Tali braced himself for a long exposition, and for losing ninety percent of his audience.

"Let me start by saying the Talmud clearly implies that there are no

Israel Jacobs   83

legal objections to women being given *aliyot*. In fact, at one time they probably were. One commentator describes a unique situation where women must be called to the Torah, rather than the men."

For the next half hour Tali outlined the legal ramifications. To his surprise the Board followed the twists and turns. He was reminded of an admonition to the graduating class by his homiletics professor, "Never overestimate your congregation's knowledge of Judaism; never underestimate their intelligence." Tali concluded, "So you see, Mr. Lutvak, there is precedent for giving women *aliyot*."

Lutvak shook his head. "Rabbi, I still cannot accept giving women *aliyos*. She could be, and you should excuse me for talking like this in front of the ladies, unclean, in her month. To even touch the Torah at that time would make the Torah unclean."

Tali said, "That's where you are misinformed, Mr. Lutvak, as many Jews are. A Torah scroll cannot be contaminated. Of course, it must always be treated with respect. But the idea that a menstruating woman renders the Torah-scroll unclean is a folk tale. Maimonides clearly states, *A woman in her period may hold the Torah-scroll and read from it.*"

Lutvak continued to shake his head. He rose from his chair again, ever so slowly, as if he suddenly felt the burden of his years. "Rabbi, you are the authority on Jewish law. I respect your scholarship. But in my heart I feel strongly such an old tradition should not be so easily canceled. You are a young man and cannot appreciate what tradition means to old folks like me. Fifty years I worshiped in this synagogue. Never was a woman called to the Torah. I don't say any more the law does not allow it. And I don't say I will resign from the congregation if the Board votes to give women *aliyos*. But I, and the few old traditionalists left, would be uncomfortable. Only last year we voted to allow girls to be bas-mitzvah on Shabbos. Give us old people a couple of years more to adjust to that change."

Lutvak sat down wearily.

Tali turned to the chairman. "In deference to Mr. Lutvak and the others who might object to giving women aliyot I urge the Board not to vote the question tonight. I think, Everett, you should set up a committee to give the question serious study."

84   *The Convert*

Al Shakter raised his hand. "I so move."
Maurice Cline seconded the motion.
The motion to table was carried.

Al Shakter hooked arms with Tali. They strolled into the lobby.
Shakter said, "Considering how hot a potato the women's issue is the
meeting ended on a relatively peaceful note."
"I'm surprised, too, and pleased. Fact is the Board showed
maturity on this one, and consideration."
" Rabbi, temporarily you're off the hook. But the ladies won't let
it lie. Sooner or later you'll have to take a stand. I predict, sooner than
later."
"I know, Al, I know."
"As a friend, I suggest you put yourself on the side of progress.
This is predominantly a liberal congregation. You can't swim against
this current; it's too strong."
"I don't think we should cavalierly trample over the feelings of the
old-timers. I prefer to go slow on this one—very slow."
"Rabbi, I get vibrations you haven't made up your own mind yet."
"Truth of the matter is I haven't."
"I'm disappointed, Rabbi. A bright, progressive thinker like you."
"Bright or not, this issue has ramifications I need to consider."
"Such as?"
"What will the men do if women are given full equality?"
"I don't understand. We'll do what we've been doing all along."
"That's what concerns me. Pretty soon the women will take over
lock stock and barrel. Why? Because the men are more than happy to
pass the buck. When Mr. Lutvak calls for a tenth to make up the
quorum for services, the men will send their wives. You fellows are just
too eager to shift your responsibilities to the women. The synagogue
might well become a feminine institution. It's happened to other
religious denominations. It's happened to the teaching profession. The
men bow out."
"Never thought of it in that light. I guess it could happen. Still, at
the risk of beating the same bush, you can't put the ladies off much

Israel Jacobs 85

longer. Not in a liberal congregation like this."

Tali waved good night to several Board members. "Al, it's comforting to know I've got so many enlightened progressive liberals in my congregation. I might have to lean on you liberals for support one of these days."

Al Shakter affected concern. "Rabbi, what mischief are you contemplating?"

"Who knows, Al, who knows?"

"Our enigmatic bachelor rabbi. Well, whatever it is, enjoy." Shakter elbowed Tali playfully.

"To change the subject," Shakter grinned roguishly. "I never had a chance to compliment you on your last sermon."

"Which sermon? I haven't preached in a month. Not since June."

"That's the sermon."

Tali realized he was taking bait. "Thanks, Al. Nice to know I'm appreciated."

"Only jesting, Rabbi. Actually, you've delivered some fine sermons. Not always. But more often than not."

"Al, you are an inspiration."

"I try, Rabbi, I try. Anyway, in appreciation, I've got something you may be able to use."

"More encouraging words?"

Al laughed. "Something more substantial. I've been treating this patient. Says he's a ticket broker, ticket scalper is more like it. At any rate, he offered the synagogue a block of forty tickets to the Sox-Cardinal game. Maybe the kids in the youth group would like to go."

"That's a generous patient you have."

"I think the man's trying to buy himself a seat in heaven."

" Most of the kids are out of town. Off to camp, or traveling with their parents. I don't think there are anywhere near forty around."

"Be a shame to let the tickets go to waste."

"Wait a minute," Tali scratched his chin. "On second thought, I could use them. Sure Al, I'll be happy to take them off your hands."

"They're yours, Rabbi. I'll have my secretary drop them off at the synagogue office tomorrow."

"Thanks, Al. I appreciate you thinking of me." Tali headed for the door. "And tell your patient he's got a forty point down payment on his seat in heaven."

Tali fingered the tickets. How should he play this? He weighed options. A direct assault? Suicidal. She'd waste him on contact. He needed an ally. Someone to front for him. To soften the target. Who? Yes, of course! He should have thought of him right off. Devious? Maybe. The reverend won't enjoy being used, but who else is there? It's for a good cause. Sometimes laudable ends justify questionable means.

Chapter Thirteen

Malcolm Wood contemplated the blank space on the requisition form. He debated with himself what amount he should write in. He needed more money; the present budget he was forced to work with was woefully inadequate. The O.E.O operation had mushroomed beyond expectation. He might not get all he asked for, but an election was coming up. Politicians counted votes. He could deliver a respectable number from his district. Downtown could not afford to ignore him.

The front door squeaked open. Gunner Adams poked his head in.

"Afternoon, Reverend Wood. Classes over yet?"

"Ten more minutes, Gunner. Come inside and wait."

"Thanks, Reverend. It sure is a sweat out there."

Since early July, Gunner arrived each Wednesday at about closing time, ostensibly to walk his sister home. Tali would greet him warmly; Gunner would make a show of disinterest. Malcolm found this behavior puzzling. He thought it best not to ask for explanations.

A scream suddenly blasted into the office. Followed by shrieks, howls. Bedlam! Malcolm, with Gunner in pursuit, bolted into Tali's class. The youngsters were gyrating in the aisles, pounding on desks with books and pencils, stomping their feet. Angela raced in from her room. Tali sat at his desk grinning, his chair tilted against the back wall.

"What happened?"

Tali cocked one ear. "Can't hear you."

Malcolm shouted above the racket. "What's going on?"

Tali gestured for quiet.

The tumult gradually moderated. "What set them off?"

What set them off, Tali explained, was his announcement that through rabbinical connections he had acquired forty tickets for next Wednesday's game. Sox versus Cardinals. "Would the class like to go?" Would Romeo like to kiss Juliet?

Malcolm trudged back to his office, shaking his head. Five minutes past the usual closing time Tali's students scattered into Lincoln Street. Tali sauntered over to Malcolm's desk.

"Malcolm, about next week. Would you do me a favor?"

"If I can, sure. What is it?"

"I'll need help to chaperon the kids. Would you ask Angela if she's available?"

"You want me to ask Angela to go to a ball game? With you?"

"With the kids," Tali said straight-faced.

"Why don't you ask her yourself?"

"Well, you and Angela are on better terms."

"You're asking me to walk through a minefield. That's asking too much."

"You're more familiar with the territory. Besides, you're the Director. She's less likely to turn you down. It'll be a shame to have the tickets go to waste. The kids would be disappointed."

The light clicked off in Angela's room. She stepped into Malcolm's office, waved goodbye and headed for the door

"Just a minute, Angela. We have a bit of a problem."

Angela stepped back into the office. She stared suspiciously at the two men. Gunner stayed close to his sister, squinting sideways at Tali.

"The rabbi's got a block of tickets to next Wednesday's ball game. Enough to take both classes. He needs help chaperoning the children. I'd love to go, but I'm due to appear before the Task Force Committee next week. Can you fit it into your schedule?"

"Ball game? Next week...?"

Malcolm said, "I think it's a great idea. Can you make it? We'll have to cancel if you can't."

Gunner tipped the scale.

Israel Jacobs

"I sure would like to see that game."

Malcolm felt guilty for laying this dilemma on Angela. The rabbi had backed her into a corner. Accept and spend an afternoon with the rabbi. Refuse and the children lose out on a ball game. He didn't appreciate being maneuvered into being the rabbi's point man. Like it or not, he was impressed by the rabbi's tactics.

Wednesday arrived. Both classes recorded perfect attendance. Tali led the way. Angela took up the rear. The subway roared into the station. Tali braced himself against the door until the last of the children boarded. They rode the first car to Metropolitan Avenue, emerged and walked the two blocks to the stadium without incident, or comment from Angela. Tali presented the tickets; the children scampered inside.

The sun shone bright in a clear sky. The hotdogs were delicious, the soda-pop sparkled. They sat in the lower bleachers with a clear view of the field, Tali on one end of the bench, Angela on the other, and thirty-five ecstatic pre-adolescents in between.

During the seventh-inning stretch it suddenly occurred to A. Naphtali Zeig—he hadn't had a migraine all month.

Chapter Fourteen

Whatever her feelings regarding the excursion she had been inveigled into, Angela kept them to herself. She coasted through the morning silently. For the children, memories of the ball game lingered. They relived the day, replaying every inning. The children's enthusiasm inspired Malcolm Wood with a brilliant idea: Get them out of Upper Chelsea for a day. To Deer Park Mountain. For these youngsters Deer Park Mountain's fresh water lake, baseball fields, picnic grounds, boating would be a dream come true.

The project expanded in his mind. Siblings and friends would be invited to join. Give them all a chance to escape Upper Chelsea's grimy heat. Malcolm solicited Tali's opinion.

"For such a marvelous idea, Malcolm you get a *yasher ko-ah*."

"I'll need you for the entire day. Can you make it?"

"Count me in."

"Thanks, Tali. I appreciate it. By the way, what does yasher whatever you call it, mean?"

"It's hard to translate exactly, congratulations, more power to you, right on. All rolled into one."

"*YASH-KOO-AH*. Do I have it right?"

"Close enough, and gesundheit."

Malcolm broached the idea to Angela. Surprisingly, though not bubbling with joy at the prospect of spending another day with Tali, neither did she resist. Malcolm went to work on the logistics: reserving a field, chaperons; five in addition to Tali and Angela. One problem

Israel Jacobs 91

defied a solution. Transportation. Deer Park Mountain was seventy miles upstate. A parade of automobiles was impractical, even if he could commandeer enough. Fare by bus or train came to ten dollars per passenger. Too much for these kids.

Tali suggested chartered buses.

"At three hundred dollars a bus, not counting, who knows how much for a driver? My budget can't carry it."

"Call the Task Force office. They might provide them free."

Malcolm considered. "It's a thought. Our program has been getting good press lately. Downtown might just be ripe to throw us a favor."

"Try it. What've you got to lose?"

Malcolm called the Mayor's Task Force office.

A secretary answered. He detailed the plans, stressing that his request was for Upper Chelsea's disadvantaged children. He required three buses to transport some hundred-fifty children to Deer Park Mountain for a day's outing. The secretary listened patiently then suggested he call Mr. Thorndyke who was in charge of school transportation. A switchboard operator connected him with Mr. Thorndyke's secretary. Again Malcolm spelled out the particulars, emphasizing that the buses were needed to provide a hundred-fifty underprivileged children a day's outing at Deer Park Mountain. Mr. Thorndyke's secretary listened sympathetically, adding that she thought the project wonderful. But Mr. Thorndyke was on vacation and was not due back for another week. If Reverend Wood called back tomorrow and asked for Mr. Hill, assistant to Mr. Thorndyke, he might be able to help. Promptly at ten the next morning, Malcolm called. He was connected to Mr. Hill.

Malcolm replayed his story. Three buses to make it possible for a hundred and fifty underprivileged children to escape the city's searing heat for a day. His constituents would be forever grateful if the Mayor's Task Force office would make it possible by providing three buses.

"Great idea," Mr. Hill waxed enthusiastic. "But I don't have the authority to release the buses. I'll take it up with my superior. Call my office at ten tomorrow. I should have an answer by then."

92 *The Convert*

Ten sharp the next morning, Malcolm called. Mr. Hill's secretary put him through."

"Reverend Wood, I'm happy to report that I relayed your request to the transportation department and they approved it. Three buses will be at your disposal, with drivers of course."

Bless Rabbi Zeig for thinking of the Task Force office.

Mr. Hill was still on the line. "Our office has put the necessary forms into the mail. You should be getting them tomorrow. Make sure to fill them out correctly and mail them to my office right away."

As promised, the forms arrived in the next morning's mail. Malcolm meticulously filled them out, in triplicate. To make sure the letters would not go amiss, he personally hand-carried them to the post office.

Deer-Park-Mountain day arrived. With the mercury already hitting the mid-eighties and climbing, the promise of shaded parks, a silver lake and cool upstate breezes seemed especially fetching. This one day's escape from Upper Chelsea would have to last these kids all summer. But one day was better than none. Malcolm ambled out to check on the buses. They should be arriving about now. More than a hundred youngsters crowded the sidewalk, playfully throwing punches at one another, jockeying for first position in the lineup, fumbling with towels and bathing suits tucked under sweaty armpits, swinging brown paper bags into which they had packed lunch. By eight-thirty most who had signed up were in front of the O.E.O. office ready to go.

No sign of the promised buses.

Eight-forty-five, no buses. Nine, still no buses. Malcolm waited with growing apprehension. Perspiration glued his shirt to his back. Nine-fifteen; the space reserved for the buses remained empty. The children began to fall out of line. Malcolm pushed through the crowd to his basement office. Angela ran after him with Tali in hot pursuit.

Malcolm snatched the phone off the cradle. He dialed School Transportation.

"I've got one hundred-fifty kids waiting to board those buses."

Malcolm's woe elicited a "Sorry about that. Wish I could help

Israel Jacobs 93

you."

"What am I supposed to do with these children," the reverend wailed into the phone. A pause on the other end. Then Malcolm again, "Mr. Thorndyke is back? Could you let me speak to Mr. Thorndyke?"

A long moment's wait; then Malcolm near hysteria: "That's impossible. You must have gotten the forms. I filled them out myself. I personally dropped them off at the post office."

Mr. Thorndyke knew nothing about Malcolm's buses. He suggested that Malcolm call the Task Force office. Malcolm shuttled from one office to another. From each he received the same, "Sorry we can't help you." He threw up his hands. Tali saw the desperation on Malcolm's face.

Angela's eyes sizzled like twin coals. "Damn, damn them all. They wouldn't do this to white kids." She threw daggers at Tali, as though he was responsible.

Tali said, "Let me try."

Malcolm sagged into a chair. "It's no use."

"Give me the mayor's Task Force number," Tali insisted.

Malcolm scribbled the number on a pad and dragged himself to the window. The din outside had turned strident. "When them mother-fuckin' buses gonna get here?" floated through the window.

Tali dialed. "This is Rabbi A. Naphtali Zeig. Would you please connect me with the mayor?"

Malcolm listened, mesmerized by Tali's ecclesiastical baritone. He lost most of the reply coming from the other end; he heard enough to fill in the blanks: "The mayor is busy, not in. Can I help you?" Tali spelled out the catastrophe-in-the-making on Lincoln Street. From Tali's scowl Malcolm divined that the rabbi was getting another, "Sorry we can't help you."

"In that case," Tali snapped "I insist you connect me with the mayor." Silence. Tali drummed on the desk with his fingers. A long pause.

Tali: "Since we will not be able to make it to Deer Mountain Park without the buses your office promised, we will picnic outside the mayor's mansion—with picket signs."

94   *The Convert*

Silence again.

Tali exploded. "And to make sure your blundering indifference to the needs of these underprivileged children in Upper Chelsea does not go unnoticed by the citizens of our city I will call the vice president of my synagogue, Miles Shepley, who I'm sure you are aware is the publisher of the *National Press*, to send down reporters and photographers, so this will be on the record for the public to see."

Another silence. Measurably longer than the previous pauses. Tali cupped one hand over the mouthpiece. "They're consulting."

Back to the party on the other end. "You will call transport personally? No later than ten-fifteen. Very good, sir. Thank you. Yes, I will remember you to Mr. Shepley."

Malcolm gaped. "Miles Shepley is vice president of your synagogue?"

"Born Morris Shapiro. Changed his name about the time he became publisher of *National Press*. Actually, he's vice president of Temple Sinai in Shoreview, the town next to Pineville. Shepley is also a big wheel in the 'Allied Temples of America.'"

The reverend raised an eyebrow.

"No, it isn't a lie. According to the Talmud, all Jews are responsible for one another. If Miles Shepley is vice president of one synagogue, he's vice president of every synagogue." Tali pinched an ear. "Of course, if you insist on quibbling over technicalities..."

Ten-forty, the buses rolled into Lincoln Street. Malcolm wagged his head at Angela. "My dear, we have just been rescued by the infamous Jewish Hoozpah."

Tali laughed. "*Hutzpah*. Pronounce the first sound as if you're gargling."

It happened, as Tali, with Angela's assistance, was dispatching the children to board the buses. Malcolm stood within earshot. He could hardly believe what he heard.

"I've got to hand it to you, Zeig; you are an operator. That was one hell of a performance. You got those damn bureaucrats to move their asses."

Israel Jacobs   95

For a moment A. Naphtali Zeig looked as if he had been hit by a stun gun. A compliment from Angela? He quickly recovered his wits. "You want to see a performance, come see me on my pulpit."

Angela smiled. "That sure must be a sight to see."

Tali put his hands to her waist, venturing to help her board the bus. She turned partly toward him. For a short moment their faces almost touched.

"Dear Lord," Reverend Malcolm Wood whispered a prayer. "Your wonders never cease to amaze me: Sending a rabbi to Upper Chelsea so that a black girl might be reborn. Thank You, Lord."

Chapter Fifteen

Tali shoved the debris of textbooks, chalk, pencils, paper into the closet. He checked the time. Twelve-fifteen. It would be a mad scramble to catch the professor. Like the tide, Arthur Teitlebaum waited for no man. Tali had asked for the conference to finalize the professor's approval of his thesis. He slammed the closet door shut, picked up his briefcase and headed for the door. Horace Clay, the youngster who had taken the lead in the sit-in, stood in the aisle awkwardly scraping the seat of his ill-fitting denims.

"Anything the matter, Horace?"

The boy's eyes shifted to the floor.

"Something troubling you, Horace?"

Horace danced nervously side to side. Tali said "You want to tell me about it?"

"She knocked up. Gonna have a baby."

Tali speculated. Horace couldn't be the father. Not a ten-year-old!

"Does she know who the father is?"

Horace spat to the floor. "Shit, she know."

"Who is he?"

Horace sent another stream of spittle to the floor. "Her old lady's cocksuckin' sonnabitch boy friend knocked her up."

"How old is the girl?"

"She sixteen."

Tali heard Angela's class file out, then her footsteps clicking toward Malcolm's office. A troubled silence followed. Tali weighed the

Israel Jacobs 97

situation, should he pursue this further on his own, or call in Malcolm. He decided to go it alone. For whatever reason, Horace had come to him for help.

"Shouldn't the girl's mother be told that her boy friend is having sex with her daughter?"

"She know Francine gettin' it from the sonnabitch."

"Why doesn't she put a stop to it? Throw the bum out?"

"She scared he gonna beat the shit outta her if'n she say anything."

"She can go to the police."

Horace shook his head vehemently. "She go to the pigs, he gonna cut her up for sure."

"Tell me how I can help your friend."

Horace sucked in a deep breath. "You know where she able to get an abotion. She don' wanna have no baby. Ain't right what they fixin' on doin'."

"What is that?"

"Same as they done las' time."

"This isn't the first time the man's made her pregnant?"

"Ain't the first time."

Tali felt his stomach go sour. "What did they do then?"

"After she have the baby I seen 'em drown it in the bathtub. They put it in a box an' threw it out like it was garbage."

"Oh my God!" Tali seized Horace by the arm. "Who is the girl?"

Horace stared at him with frightened eyes. "You gotta swear you ain't gonna tell nobody I tole you. If'n he finds out, he gonna slice me up."

Tali shook the boy hard. "Who is she?"

"You gotta promise me."

"I promise."

"She my sister."

Over and over again Tali reassured Horace that his secret was safe. Under no circumstances would he violate the boy's confidence. Finally, Tali persuaded Horace to bring his sister in. While waiting, Tali remembered Professor Teitlebaum. Breaking an appointment with

Arthur Teitlebaum was no small matter. He would have a hard time explaining. Most likely it would be a month, at least, before he could wrangle another appointment.

Forty-five minutes later Horace returned with his sister. She cowered at the door. Tali forgot Professor Teitlebaum. The desolation imprinted in the girl's eyes pushed the professor out of mind.

Francine Clay barely reached her brother's chin, a thin frail wisp of a teenager, she appeared to have stopped growing at eight, as if she had been sponged dry years ago. She wore sneakers, wrinkled dungarees, and a ragged basted-blue blouse covering a chest as flat as a boy's. Only the heavy rosette-shaped lips, which she licked nervously with her tongue and the finely arched brow hinted at her sex. Tali approached her slowly.

"Hello, Francine."

She stared ahead, mute as the dead.

Gently, Tali put his arm around her shoulder. She recoiled as if touched by a hot iron. "I'd like to help you."

Francine cringed. Tali said, "Do you want me to help?"

"Talk to the man," Horace prompted.

Francine nodded. She appeared to be in a panic, or possibly retarded. Tali raged inwardly, wanting to strike out at someone, to make someone pay for the suffering he read on this child's face.

"Alright, Horace. We'll get your sister the help she needs. I'll talk to Malcolm; he'll know what to do."

"You said he ain't gonna tell anybody 'bout me," Francine caterwauled. She wasn't retarded after all. Fear had knotted her tongue. A greater fear had loosened it.

"It won't go any further than Malcolm. I promise."

Horace shouted, You done promised you ain't gonna tell nobody."

"Alright, Horace, I'll keep to my promise. But Malcolm knows his way around Chelsea better than me. He'll find help for Francine right away."

Horace wavered. "Can't you help without tellin' Malcolm?"

"Maybe, but it'll take me longer than it would Malcolm. The quicker this is taken care of the safer for your sister."

Israel Jacobs   99

"Don' let him tell Malcolm," Francine pulled at Horace's shirt-sleeves. Her lips quivered. "Malcolm gonna tell Mamma. Miguel is gonna kill me if'n he finds out I tole anybody."

The helplessness in the child's plea sprayed Tali like a dark stain.

"Okay, Francine, trust me. We'll take care of this ourselves."

Francine sighed.

Looking into the girl's frightened eyes, Tali judged she no longer knew how to trust; this fear-ridden child was in a perpetual state of tension.

Before leaving for home, Tali extracted the information he needed from Malcolm. The reverend was full of questions. Why had Tali stayed so late? Why the sudden interest in Chelsea's abortion clinic? Tali gave half-hearted explanations.

Malcolm had the information at his fingertips. The story that so shocked Tali was an oft repeated tale to the reverend. The reverend knew, too, when to stop pressing a man evading answers.

It required a week of prodding and shouting before Tali managed an appointment to have Francine examined by the clinic physician; another two weeks after her pregnancy was confirmed to steer through the tangle of bureaucratic and legal obstacles. Tali waved his clerical credentials. He warned the attending doctor that Francine was suicidal. If the doctor didn't act soon, he might have a dead girl on his conscience. Fortunately, Francine was in her first trimester. The abortion would be a simple procedure. Early Tuesday morning Tali drove into the city, picked Francine up outside the O.E.O. office and drove her to the clinic. Within half an hour she was assigned a cubicle where she would be prepped for surgery.

"Don't worry, Francine, you'll be just fine."

She looked up trustingly, for the first time not shrinking at his touch. Tali reached for her hand. She clasped it to her chest. "Thanks, Mr. Tali."

A heavy-set nurse, dressed in a spotless white uniform, led Francine down the corridor. Tali glanced at his watch: eleven o'clock. He sagged wearily into a bench and closed his eyes.

100   The Convert

A tap on his shoulder startled him upright. A female attendant leaned over him. "Rabbi, Francine did fine. You can take her home."

Groggily, Tali searched for his watch: one p.m.; he had slept two hours. Francine sat in a wheel chair. She smiled weakly at Tali. The attendant wheeled her to the clinic entrance. Gingerly, Tali tucked Francine into the Mustang. "Okay, Francine, I'll drive you home."

Tali led her to his car. "Where do you live?"

"Don't want you to take me home."

"Why not?"

"Ah'm afraid Mamma or Miguel gonna see me ridin' wid you."

"Where do you want me to take you?"

"Lincoln Street. Horace'll be waitin' for me there."

Horace circled the fireplug, staring up and down the street. The Mustang turned into Lincoln. Horace raced to the door. Wordlessly he helped his sister to the curb. Tali slid from behind the wheel.

"It's over, Horace. Francine is fine."

Horace put a protective arm around his sister. She searched Tali's face with somber eyes. "You an okay white man, Mr. Tali."

Horace grinned. "Yeah, you is okay, Teach."

Francine clutched her brother's hand.

A familiar painful despair assaulted Tali. What had he accomplished? A temporary reprieve for one pathetic adolescent. Next week, next month, she might be raped again—and there was nothing he could do. Nothing.

Chapter Sixteen

This year Rosh Hashanah and Tabernacles would fall on Tuesdays and Wednesdays. Tali gave notice he would be absent the next four weeks. Malcolm hired a temporary to substitute. By the second session the students were grumbling

"Tali quit?" One student worried.

Malcolm tried to reassure the class. "He did not quit; he's definitely coming back."

"When will that be?" Horace demanded.

"Soon as the Jewish Holy Days are over."

Horace was not satisfied. "When that be?"

"Two weeks." Malcolm made a note to check a Jewish calendar.

In Pineville, summer yielded to autumn. Suburbia was transformed into a montage of beige and gold. The leaves surrendered their hold and fell to the ground in bunches, where they were raked into mounds then vacuumed by village trucks. The weather turned crisp, and clear as a bell. Tee-off schedules at the Pineville Country Club tightened in expectation of the cold and snow that would blanket the fairways in another month. Vigorous north winds gyrated over the shimmering emerald-green North Bay, emboldening the more diehard sailors to cast off one last time before dry-docking for the winter months. Tali rabbinated through the Holy Day season. He supervised the opening of the Pineville Jewish Center Religious School, established curricula for the Adult Studies program, working at being a rabbi with half his mind in Upper Chelsea.

In Upper Chelsea the change in season was marked by a slowdown in garbage collection, and the threat of a full strike if union demands were not met. Entire slices of pavement disappeared under the pileup of refuse. At irregular intervals a token fleet of sanitation trucks rumbled through Upper Chelsea, carting away some of the stink, but leaving more than they took.

But it was autumn. Sanitation slow down or no, Malcolm Wood was grateful to have survived Upper Chelsea's stifling heat.

Tali returned the first Wednesday in November. Angela did not roll up a red carpet for Tali, but neither did she go out of her way to be disagreeable. To Malcolm's mind that signaled progress.

Morning sessions at public school necessitated a shift in schedule to the afternoon. Tali now worked mornings on his thesis. Afternoons he and Angela conducted remedial reading sessions. Angela occupied the rear room, while Tali used the room adjoining Malcolm Wood's office.

At three-thirty Gunner loafed into the office.

"Classes about over, Reverend?"

"Just about, Gunner."

"I come to walk Angela home."

"Didn't see you the last few weeks."

"I been busy."

"Well, I'm sure Angela appreciates it whenever you come for her."

Tali's voice rumbled into Malcolm Wood's office. Gunner asked, "Tali's come back?"

"Yes, he has. Would you like to wait for Angela in his room?"

Gunner assumed a nonchalant pose. "Guess it's just as easy sittin' in the honkey's room as standin' here."

"True enough," Malcolm agreed. "You may as well go in."

Gunner sauntered past the reverend's desk into Tali's room. Tali hailed him cheerfully. "Glad to see you, Gunner. How've you been?"

"Been okay," Gunner eased into a chair.

Tali returned to the class. One student, a wiry package of skin and bones wearing a tattered sweater and oversized denims, called out

Israel Jacobs 103

belligerently. "I wants to ask you somethin'."

"What's on your mind, Bruce?" Tali asked.

"Why've you been out four weeks?"

"You noticed? Thanks. At least somebody missed me."

Bruce did not buy Tali's flippant reply.

"You been sick, or somethin'?"

"No, I haven't been sick."

"So why've you been out?"

"Sorry if I've inconvenienced you, Bruce. The Jewish New Year fell on a Tuesday and Wednesday this year, and some other Jewish holidays. I'm a rabbi, so I had to conduct services. It's how I earn my bread."

Bruce had more questions on his mind. "What's a rabbi?"

"It's something like a minister or priest, though not exactly."

Horace Clay bounced into the aisle. "Man, why you Jews do things different? Why ain't your New Year in winter, like our's is?"

Tali took the remainder of the hour to explain Rosh Hashanah, Yom Kippur, the Feast of Tabernacles. The class continued to toss questions at him. He stole a glance at his watch.

"Sorry I gotta run now. If you want to know more about the Jewish religion, I'd be happy to give you books on the subject."

Gunner, too, had a stack of questions. He started to raise his hand, then let it drop, not wanting to be too closely identified with eight and nine-year-olds. A girl, sitting up front, called out. The girl was new to the class. Tali remembered seeing her before he took off for the High Holy days. She wore a baggy skirt several sizes too large, and a hungry look on her thin face.

"Could you save your question till next week?"

"I wants you to answer me now."

Tali yielded. "Okay, ask away."

My mamma is always cussin' at the lan'lord. She say they all fuckin' Jews. Is you a lan'lord?"

"What's your name?"

"Jane."

"No, Jane, I'm not a landlord. I don't even own the house I live

104   *The Convert*

in."

Tali dismissed the class. The children scattered, each racing to reach the door first, except for Gunner, who tarried at the desk.

"You coming, Gunner? I have to close shop."

"Right behind you, man."

Tali hastened through Angela's room. He stopped a moment to bid Malcolm Wood a quick, "See you next week." Angela was waiting outside for Gunner.

"Good afternoon, Angela," Tali tipped an imaginary hat. Angela moved out of his way.

Lincoln Street had come alive since the change in weather. A gust lifted Angela's skirt to thigh-level. Tali studied her legs with a broad smile. Angela diligently ignored him. The gust picked up debris from open garbage-cans, scattering the overflow into the street. Loose newspapers swirled along the sidewalks. People bunched near alleyways and on stoops talking and arguing in loud voices. A tow truck rumbled past, pulling a smashed Oldsmobile. Children darted between cars. Across the street a knot of pre-adolescents battled shrilly for next turn on a skateboard, ignoring a drunk curled up half in, half out of the hallway. A burly very dark-skinned man emerged and pushed the drunk out of his way with one foot. A lean-looking woman with disheveled white hair yelled down from a second story window. "Git that drunk outta here. He's been sleepin' and pissin' in the hall all night."

The man pushed the drunk into the street.

Tali started for his car. An abrupt downshift in the tumult distracted him. Tali looked across the street. The ruckus over the skateboard had ceased; it squeaked into the gutter unattended. Several people, a moment ago clustered in a group arguing, suddenly pulled apart. They were staring as one at something happening up the street.

The gang vaulted into Tali's angle of vision. It took a moment for him to make the connection between the sudden freeze in activities and the swaggering youths. They charged his way, coming on tough and arrogant four abreast, hogging the sidewalk, plucking lids off garbage cans, kicking at them and sending up a howl when one tipped over and rolled into the street spewing refuse in all directions. They strutted down Lincoln Street like ghetto sovereigns, their hands twirling and bodies tilted in a kind of side-lean. They wore bright colored trousers and high-topped shoes. The four of them were outfitted with long-sleeved yellow sweat shirts with COBRA emblazoned in red letters across their chests.

The tallest of the gang—his high Afro-cut giving him an additional two inches of height—caught sight of Tali. The youth looked to be about eighteen, tall and wiry, giving the impression of black quicksilver. He stopped in his tracks. The other three Cobras halted a pace behind him, as if waiting for instructions. Tali surmised the youth in the vanguard to be the leader. He had a soiled yellow kerchief wrapped around his forehead, which curved inward like a convex half-moon. The lower part of the kerchief met the bridge of the youth's very broad and flat nose. A wide belt with heavy silver buckles circled his waist. He minced between Tali and the Mustang. Tali tripped backwards, almost losing his balance. He caught himself in time and retreated a step. The youth leered at Tali, obstructing his passage to the Mustang. The youth's cronies danced in closer, their heads rocking from Tali to their leader and back. Angela, at Gunner's side watched grim-faced. The Cobra-chief, his eyelids squeezed to half closed slits, inspected Tali, all the while snapping his fingers to a nerve-racking rhythm.

"Where yuh from, big man?" The chief hurled his question at Tali with the contempt of the native for the alien-born.

"Pineville," Tali said.

"Pine-nee-veel," Cobra chief mimed. He made an exaggerated half turn, shuffling one foot and flexing the other knee, hop-skipping between Tali and the Mustang. "Any you cats evah been to fuckin' Pine-nee-veel?"

The trio chanted in unison, each trying to outdo the other in making stupid faces, "Ain't none o' us heard 'bout no fuckin' Pine-nee-ville, Leroy."

"Where's Pine-nee-veel at, big man?" Leroy sent a gob of spit to the sidewalk. That ain't in Brookline?"

106   *The Convert*

Tali stared at the soggy glob pasted to the sidewalk, an inch from his left shoe. "No, it's not in Brookline."

"Lucky for you, big man. Cause if you was from Brookline, we'd done shit on yo' head." Leroy tucked both thumbs into his belt. "Where is fuckin' Pine-nee-veel?"

"About fifty miles east."

"Fifty miles east? Now ain't that some fuckin' trip?" Leroy scratched under an armpit. His three comrades bobbed their heads in short circles, grinning like chimpanzees.

Leroy curtsied to the Mustang. "No wonder you gotta have such a fuckin' nice ootomobeel." He flicked imaginary dust off the hood. One of the Cobras, a fat-lipped bruiser with bulging biceps, jumped backwards onto the fender. The front-end groaned under his weight.

"Careful how yo' set yo' fuckin' ass down on that shiny ootomobile, Falco. Yo' might hurt it bad, an' big man won' have no ride back to fuckin' Pine-nee-veel."

Falco double-thumped the Mustang.

"That ain't nice, Falco." Leroy grinned malevolently .

Leroy resumed the finger-bop dance, shuffling within arm's length of Tali. "How 'bout you loanin' us yo' shiny ootomobille, big man? We would sure appreciate a spin around the block."

Tali kept silent. Leroy broke off the bop and dance routine. He pointed a finger at Tali. "I'm talkin' to you, big man."

Tali blinked. He retreated a step, out of arm's reach.

"You lost yo' tongue, big man? I asked you for a ride. We been nice to you so far. You on our territory, an' nobody shit on you—yet." Leroy snapped his fingers. Falco leaped off the fender. The four Cobras flanked Tali, two on each side. Angela stepped forward, as if to intervene. Gunner clutched her wrist, pulling her back to the basement gate. She made a weak effort to struggle free. Gunner hung on tightly, fright showing on his face. Tali made a quick assessment of the situation. Leroy's arrogance infuriated him. He considered shooting a karate kick to the Cobra-chief's groin. But there were the other three, probably carrying knives. It would be insane to make himself a dead hero for a car. He reached into his pocket and pulled out two keys

Israel Jacobs 107

dangling on a locket chain. Leroy spread his palms. Tali let go; the keys jangled into Leroy's hand. He showed his teeth to Tali, an uneven row of dull white, set in bulging gums.

"We thank yo' indeedy, big man." Leroy's eyes galloped past Tali, foraging for Angela. "How 'bout you joinin' us, girl?"

"Chase your ass."

In a swift unexpected movement, Leroy shoved Tali aside. He grabbed her by the arm, yanking hard and pulling her from Gunner's side. She missed a step, tripped and tottered for the sidewalk. Leroy broke her fall. He spun her around into his arms. Angela struggled to free herself. She pummeled at his back and shoulders. Leroy held on firmly, breathing hot into her face.

"Come on, baby, be nice to me. Big man is loanin' us his car. Let's go for a ride."

"Get your stinking hands off me." Angela flailed at him, trying to sink her nails into his neck. Leroy locked her hands tightly behind her back, forcing her to arch toward him. He pressed his stiffened phallus against her abdomen, while cupping his free hand over her breast. Gunner jumped to his sister's aid, landing a kick on Leroy's shin.

Leroy yelped. "Get that fuckin' sonnabitch."

Falco backhanded Gunner across the face, spinning him hard into the basement gate. The collision ripped away a loose-hanging bar. It clinked to the sidewalk.

"You god-damned bastard," Angela kicked helplessly at Leroy.

"Let her go."

Leroy's head jerked up at Tali's command. Surprise plastered his face.

"You gonna make me, yuh white fuck?"

"I told you to let her go."

Angela tore from Leroy's grip. Gunner dashed to her side. Leroy's mouth curled. He snarled, crouching like a cat ready to pounce on its prey. People collected on the sidewalk and street, watching from a safe distance. Women looked down on the scene from upper stories. A child ventured in close; his mother dragged him away with a sharp warning. Leroy began oscillating, rocking from side to side, both arms extended, his left palm open, beckoning, inviting Tali to approach closer. Leroy's fist opened; the keys Tali had surrendered dropped to the sidewalk. Suddenly, Leroy's right hand leaped to a back pocket. A swift upward motion. His thumb pressed into a green cucumber object that had materialized in his hand as if by magic. The cucumber sprouted gray steel. Tali fell back, inching toward the iron bar that Gunner's impact had loosened. The blade flashed in Leroy's hand. The three Cobras advanced. Leroy motioned them away; he intended to carve big man all by himself. Angela shrank into the gate. Leroy flashed the blade, rocking in close to Tali. The space between them narrowed. Leroy jabbed at the air, advancing within cutting distance. Tali side-stepped the thrusts, dodging and circling in tight sparse movements, his eyes glued to Leroy's shoulders. The blade reflected beams of afternoon sunlight as it pitched closer to Tali's chest. Several spectators who had skimmed too close fell back. A tense silence dropped onto Lincoln Street.

Tali lunged for the iron bar, scooping it up in a swift movement. He rammed the point into Leroy's midriff.

Leroy doubled over, gasping. Tali pounded the bar into Leroy's arm. The Cobra chief emitted an animal-like screech; the knife flew from his hand. He rolled to the sidewalk groaning. Leroy's three confederates surrounded Tali, one waving a long-bladed knife. Tali slashed out, flailing at them wildly, feeding on his rage, forgetting caution, the odds, blind to the spectators, experiencing a savage frenzy, an acute need to feel the iron bar bite into these animal faces. He caught the knife-wielding Cobra in the ribs, sending him crumpling to the sidewalk like an empty sack.

"Pigs!" Falco bellowed the alarm. The other Cobra still on his feet veered sharply. The two looked down the street. They raced off in opposite directions.

"Watch out, Tali!" The warning came from Gunner. Tali pivoted. Leroy squatted on one knee. A knife flashed in his hand. Tali kicked out. The knife clattered to the sidewalk. Leroy clutched his wrist, moaning, manifestly in excruciating pain. The Cobra chief's face began to swim before Tali. The contours of his body blurred. The black youth

Israel Jacobs 109

congealed into an ugly malignancy, a black disease. It had to be smashed. Battered into oblivion, out of existence. Tali raised the iron bar as
high as his arms could reach.

Gunner, still nursing the bruise inflicted by Falco, shrieked, "Kill
the sonnabitch! Bash his fuckin' head in."

Leroy cringed, terror stricken. "Man, don't! Please."

Leroy's face came into focus; it took on human form again. Tali's
stomach knotted, bringing on sudden nausea. He had come a hair's-
breadth near to killing Leroy. "My God!" The iron bar fell from his
hand. He staggered to the car, gulping in deep breaths.

Two patrol cars screeched to the curb, their sirens wailing.

Tali steadied himself against the Mustang, panting, visualizing a
battered corpse lying in the street. Through a haze he saw the two
policeman dragging Leroy and Falco in his direction.

An onlooker said, pointing to Tali, "They tried to knife him."

Tali did not quite understand what the policeman was saying, "You
want to press charges?"

Tali's head began to clear. Leroy's right arm hung limply at his side.
Falco was painfully clutching his rib.

"I... No... It was a misunderstanding..."

"These two have given us trouble before. The street would be safer
if we put them away for a while. You sure you don't want to press
charges?"

"Yes, It's alright, officer. I'd just like to head for home."

Tali searched through his pocket for the car keys.

"You looking for your keys?" Angela walked toward him, carrying
the keys to his car, "I found them on the sidewalk." Angela pressed the
keys into his hand, not letting go for a long moment.

"Thanks." Tali took the keys. He felt weak, as if his knees would
buckle any moment. He opened the car door and slumped behind the
wheel.

Gunner pushed between Angela and the car. "You gonna be
comin' back next week?"

Tali smiled feebly. "Yes... God willing... I'll be back next week."

Chapter Seventeen

Happenstance and initiative made Gunner Adams an entrepreneur.

One morning, while Chuck was preparing for the breakfast crowd, the oven exploded, hurling Chuck through the back door, and ripping a gaping hole in the roof. The Fire Department condemned the diner, effectively putting Angela out of work.

Early the next morning, Angela, accompanied by Gunner, went job hunting. By four o'clock Gunner's legs were giving out.

"Let's go home, Angela, I'm beat."

It was fast growing dark. Homeward-bound crowds were scurrying through the streets, pushing, shoving, gruffly colliding with one another. Angela, too, looked bone-tired, and discouraged.

She hooked her arm into his. "Okay, let's quit for the day."

They started for home, dodging traffic and surly pedestrians. Gunner realized that their situation was desperate. Either Angela found a job, or by Monday they wouldn't be eating. Gusts slashing through his thin mackintosh and the cold drizzle made him too miserable to care. They turned into Seventh Avenue. Gunner broke into a trot. Two more blocks and home. Even their one-room hovel looked inviting. He craved to set his tired wet body down anywhere, so long as it was out of the damp cold. A store-front caught his attention. He scanned the discolored script on the dimly lit window. Pieces of lettering had rubbed off the name DESI. Two letters of DELICATESSEN were completely gone, leaving a slice of glass through which he could peek inside. A sign propped against the window read, HELP WANTED AFTERNOONS. Gunner shouted, "Angela, Look!"

Israel Jacobs 111

Angela crossed to Gunner's side of the street. "Okay, let's try it."

The delicatessen, a ground floor wooden building, was wedged between a six-story tenement on one side and a gutted warehouse on the other. Gunner rattled the door open and surveyed the store before entering. The gloom inside made Gunner feel as if he had stepped into a catacomb. Plaster was peeling off the walls. A serving counter ran the store's length. Sparsely stocked shelves, thick with dust, reached to the ceiling. Between the counter and shelves was just enough room for one man to maneuver. An ancient cash register sat on a square counter in front of which stood a refrigerated showcase, the only equipment not looking as if it had been salvaged from a junk yard. Gunner stayed close to his sister, regretting that he had seen the help-wanted sign.

In the rear, an old-fashioned double-hung window served as a backdrop for a swarthy Puerto Rican with a thick paunch. He hunched over a notebook onto which he was scratching figures with a pencil. He looked up, turned a page looked up again, as if annoyed, returned to the notebook and turned another page. Angela stepped to the counter. Gunner hesitated a moment then followed. Angela coughed twice to get the Puerto Rican's attention. He put down his notebook and waddled to the counter. He wore khaki trousers that fit like a burlap bag, a dirty grey sweater and a grease-streaked apron. His puffed cheeks and cold eyes made Gunner's skin creep. He chewed on an unlit cigar, transferring it from one corner of his mouth to another.

"Si, what you want?"

The greeting made Gunner feel as welcome as the mumps. His first instinct was to run. Angela pointed, "I saw your sign."

The Puerto Rican set the cigar down. "Don' want a woman."

"I can wait on customers good as any man."

"Rather have a man."

"I was a waitress at Chuck's Diner, not far from here. Maybe you know the place. I worked for Chuck almost a year. He was satisfied."

At the mention of Angela's last place of employment the Puerto Rican spun around. "So why you not stay?"

"I would have; it burned down yesterday."

"What you know about that? Too bad. Chuck's Diner not bad place to eat. Good food." The Puerto Rican scratched behind his ear. "Si, I seen you there, I think. You serve me couple of times."

"Can I have the job?"

"I don' know about a girl."

"I work as good as a man."

"You gonna have to lift boxes an' crates. They pretty heavy."

"I'm strong."

"Okay. I try you for week. Fifty dollars a week and groceries at cost. You work from three to seven, Monday to Friday."

"It's a deal," Angela agreed. Too fast, Gunner said to himself.

"Who the boy?" Angela's new boss awoke to Gunner's presence.

"My brother."

The Puerto Rican grinned, showing teeth the color of his cigar. "My name is Desi. If you smart boy, maybe I find work for you, too."

Angela fared better at her new job than she had expected. She found clerking in a delicatessen less fatiguing than waiting on tables in a one-girl restaurant, trying to satisfy hungry diners all grouching for service at the same time. A further plus: at the delicatessen, Angela was protected from horny hands by a counter that ran the length of the store. Early afternoons were generally slow. Angela made herself busy, trying to prove to Desi that she earned her salary. She swept, polished the counter, dusted shelves. Desi acted as if he couldn't care less. He kept to the back of the store scratching numbers and names on a pad, or checking stock in the rear pantry. About four-thirty business perked up, mostly students on the way home from school and tired women stopping off after work. Except for a select group of non-communicating, peculiarly behaving individuals whom Desi personally served, Angela attended to the store's clientele.

At first, Desi's customers behaved curtly, as if they resented the change behind the counter. Gradually, they accommodated. Angela invited conversation. Both the students and adults lingered after making purchases. One pleased customer drew another. Desi's delicatessen picked up new business. Eventually Desi noticed that business had

Israel Jacobs 113

doubled. He then hired a full-time male clerk, but kept Angela on two afternoons a week, at reduced salary. Most of the day he kept to the rear of the store. When his special clientele entered, he would put down his notebook and shuffle to the counter.

Gunner usually stopped over at five o'clock to help with the heavy items, lugging crates, and transferring cans, bottles, containers to the shelves, carrying out garbage and emptying it into garbage cans outside. Desi's Delicatessen began to look like a clean well-stocked store.

About six o'clock, there usually was a final flurry of customers, who picked up sandwiches they had ordered in the morning or previous evening. Angela learned to shred cabbage for cold slaw and use the meat slicer, even make a mouth-watering potato salad. Things were going well, better than at Chuck's. At the end of the day, Angela had more energy. Desi proved generous with groceries, often not charging her at all. At the end of the week Angela even was left with a few dollars to spare for minor luxuries. Should a full-time position at P.S. 413 come through, she felt they would be doing grand.

Gunner and Angela fell into a comfortable routine. Gunner came in regularly to assist his sister, staying on till closing time. Occasionally, Desi paid him for the time he put in helping Angela, which boosted his self-image. After several weeks into the arrangement, the customers Desi insisted on personally serving piqued Gunner's curiosity. No matter how busy it was up front, Desi would sit in the back, marking figures into a notebook, or munching on a sandwich.

Except, when his special customers came in.

For them, Desi interrupted his scribbling and hastened to the counter. If Angela got there first, he would brush her aside, or send her off to do some chore. Gunner came to recognize Desi's favored clientele. They would stand at the counter muttering they wanted Desi. Once, Desi had locked himself in the bathroom when one of them staggered into the store. Angela knew better than to serve him. The man leaned on the counter tight-lipped, his skin stretched like starch and riddled with pock marks. He drummed nervously on the counter-top. He waited five minutes; when Desi failed to show, he scurried out. Half an hour later he was back, shaking like a pennant in the wind. By

114   *The Convert*

then Desi had finished in the bathroom. He came out, hooking up his pants, and saw the man trembling at the counter. He waddled to the rear pantry, snapped the lock open, reached inside and shuffled to the front with a grocery bag. He stuffed a container of milk and a pack of cigarettes into the bag. The man put down three twenty-dollar bills and quickly exited. Gunner wondered at the price. Sixty dollars for a quart of milk and a pack of cigarettes?

Gunner noticed, too, that the grocery items varied—milk, bread, a jar of pickles—not the cigarettes, which were a staple. Invariably, Desi retrieved the cigarettes from the rear pantry, although the front shelves were stocked with name brand cigarettes.

One wet Tuesday at about five-thirty, Gunner sloshed into the delicatessen. An emaciated white boy with caved in cheeks fidgeted to the counter. Desi did not, as was his usual habit, respond immediately. The white boy appeared as if he was about to panic. Angela tried to calm him. He began to shudder. Angela signaled Gunner to fetch Desi. Gunner skipped to the back room, finding Desi munching on a ham sandwich.

"What you want?"

Gunner pointed to the front. "One of your customers."

Desi slammed the sandwich down. "Damn! Don' get a chance to eat."

He pushed himself up and unlocked the pantry. Gunner saw the cigarette cartons neatly stacked in high rows on the shelves inside. Desi stood on tiptoe and slid off a pack. He panted to the front, forgetting to snap the lock closed. Gunner waited till he saw Desi behind the counter. Quickly, he slipped one hand in and groped. He snatched two packs off the top and stuffed them hurriedly into his pocket. Desi lumbered back. Gunner picked up a trash can and rolled it to the back door. Desi followed him with suspicious eyes, but said nothing. He reached up and snapped the padlock shut. Gunner trudged outside to dump the garbage.

That evening Gunner waited impatiently until Angela left for the library. The moment she stepped out the door he inspected the packs, noticing immediately they had been tampered with. The lids had been

Israel Jacobs 115

neatly cut, then bonded with scotch tape. He tapped one pack against his wrist. A cigarette slid out, then another. He tapped again.

Fifteen reefers fell to the table.

Gunner picked up the second pack. This pack was king-sized. He tapped again. One cigarette popped out. The king-sized cigarette was only half a cigarette. He thumped the pack with the back of his hand. The contents scattered on the table. Each cigarette was snipped in half. Gunner rummaged inside the pack with two fingers. He felt a packet inside. He pulled and extracted the cellophane bag.

Gunner stuffed the loot into his pockets. First thing tomorrow he would show his catch to Geronimo.

Geronimo was impressed. He wasted no time in introducing Gunner to Upper Chelsea's drug market. Gunner proved an eager student. In less than two hours he had unloaded his wares and netted two hundred dollars.

Geronimo asked, "Can you get more stuff?"

Gunner nodded, "Maybe."

"Get it, man, and we both be rich."

The following morning Gunner cut school and jogged to Desi's. The store was empty. Gunner leaned against the counter. He put on a brave face. Desi trudged to the front.

"What you doin' here so early?"

"I wanna buy some cigarettes."

Gunner forced himself to look directly into Desi's eyes. For a moment Desi seemed rattled. He stretched to the shelf behind the counter.

"Not those." Gunner waved three twenty dollar bills. "What you keep in the back."

Desi wheeled around. His eyes widened, darting from Gunner to the three twenties. Gunner slapped the bills to the counter. Desi glared at the money. His lips twitched menacingly. Gunner became alarmed; the idea of going into partnership with Geronimo had looked good yesterday. He had second thoughts. Who knew what this greasy character might do? He might have a knife or gun stashed under the counter. Did Desi suspect that he had looted the pantry? He should have come with Geronimo. Together they would have stood a better chance. Slowly, the tense lines pulling Desi's mouth into a threatening scowl relaxed. Desi grinned.

"You smart boy, Gunner. How you like to work for me steady?"

Gunner made his first connection. At the time he was barely eleven and a half years old.

Chapter Eighteen

Gunner, with Geronimo as tutor, swiftly graduated from apprentice to seasoned pusher. Angela, preoccupied with preparing for classes at the O.E.O., her job as receptionist at Dr. Porter's office, and afternoon clerking, had little time to supervise Gunner's activities. Gunner thrived on his new-found independence. The business flourished. It was a seller's market. He had no problem finding sources or customers. The neighborhood was rife with junk. Stuff was processed in tenement factories throughout Chelsea. Dope, horse, junk, scag, smag, crack, by whatever name, flowed like an open faucet. If you built a credit rating, you could buy a bundle on your word and pay out of profits. The pusher's talent, Gunner learned early in the game, lay mainly in not getting your throat slit by the competition.

The junk business exhilarated Gunner. He would strut along to school, not to attend classes, there wasn't much he could learn from teachers. Sitting behind a beat-up desk in P.S. 204 would get him nowhere fast. Gunner came to school to give, not receive. He pranced through the school yards and halls with his bag of largesse like Santa Clause. The "dudes" would crowd him, most of them years older, with wet eyes and dripping noses. They would ask, "You straight? You got stuff?" Gunner would reply, "Dynamite stuff." Then he would deal. In no time his bag was empty and his pockets full.

In more sober moments the fear that Angela might discover he was dealing made him nervous. She and Malcolm regularly agonized over what they called the addiction plague. They pored over charts,

118   *The Convert*

read statistics, bitched about drugs being Chelsea's cancer. He shuddered to think what would happen if she learned he was part of the cancer. Then he put the fears aside. She was too busy to pay him attention. And, any way, it was all talk. The statistics, the sociological and psychological shit, Talk! Talk! Talk! Why did so many sisters and brothers get hooked? Who was to blame? Poverty. Frustration. Ignorance. Loneliness. The system. The police. The Mafia. Day after day Gunner heard them beat the same drum. It was in the nature of grown-ups to bitch. Out in the streets it was action that counted. The cat who dealt grew rich. Shit, man. His was not to question why. His was to supply.

He did. And the money rolled in. Some weeks, as much as five hundred dollars. Gunner did not get hooked, as many pushers did. Earning the "bread" provided sufficient happiness. On occasion he smoked a joint. A couple of times, to be sociable, he sniffed horse. Once, out of curiosity, he skin-popped. But something held him in check. A trumpet sounded in the back of his head, warning him to keep the needle at bay.

Geronimo heard no such trumpet. Gunner's partner began to shoot up regularly. The cost of all that joy mounted up to big money. Fifteen, twenty dollars a day, and growing. Geronimo's skyrocketing habit came out of profits. He slacked off his end of the partnership, nodding through most of the day, coasting from one fix to another. He ceased carrying his weight. He become a liability. Gunner was torn between profit and friendship. It had been Geronimo's connections, his knowledge of the drug business that had launched Gunner on his career. Geronimo was a soul-brother. Gunner felt duty-bound to stick with him. It hadn't been mere profit that had attracted Gunner to the drug trade. A dealer was somebody. It was not solely the material reward. It was the spiritual uplift.

And despite Geronimo's habit, Gunner raked in more profit than he knew what to do with.

And there lay the irony to Gunner's success.

He could enjoy no more than a fraction of the "bread" he earned. He didn't dare spend it on himself. There were things he yearned to

Israel Jacobs 119

buy: One of those leather trench coats, a pair of high-topped shiny leather shoes the older "dudes" were sporting. Gunner would have liked to own a watch, maybe a ring. Gunner ached to shower Angela with gifts, dresses, jewelry. He longed to prove his manhood by paying the rent, maybe move to a real apartment. He could afford it, but he didn't dare. Angela would ask questions Gunner preferred not answering. To have little is a sorrow; to earn a bundle and not be able to spend is maddening. Each night Gunner counted what was left after paying for Geronimo's habit, and stuffed the cache in a hole behind the sink. His success bought him glory, and the thin hope that someday he would be able to put his fortune to use. Neither the glory nor the hope kept the cockroaches from tickling his toes, nor put heat into the radiators on icy winter nights. But the recognition and the notoriety were enough reward to keep him going. "Cats" who had never given him a second thought now showed respect. He was consulted on subjects ranging from girls to "garbage." "You think she let me stick it to her, Gunner?" "This bag gonna bring me up, Gunner?" He drank it all in, contemplated his secret cache, and kept his mind off tomorrow. Mornings, when he tumbled out of bed, he had something to look forward to. A place to go; productive activity with which to fill the empty spaces in the long day.

Without having to venture further than P.S. 204, Gunner continued to rake in the "bread." Rain or shine, summer or winter. Weekdays, when classes were in session, or weekends, mattered little. Gunner's product sold in all seasons. He had no overhead. He needed no salesmen, filed no tax return. What happened in the world outside Chelsea hardly affected Gunner's line. Inflation, recession, price control, unemployment, war, peace. Democrats, Republicans; it was all the same. Junkies hungered for a fix, and he was there to feed their hunger.

Conscience? Yes, he had a conscience. He carried Geronimo, didn't he? Did he turn anybody on? No! He satisfied demand; he didn't create it. For sure, Angela wouldn't see it his way, but why should he feel guilt? He knew dealing was illegal, that if he were busted, terrible things would happen to him. That was not the same as guilt. He sold a product "cats" demanded. He provided it. He did not dilute; he dealt stuff that to the best of his knowledge was not polluted. He never shafted his customers. If he stopped dealing, it would not make a dent on the supply side. Bad conscience? He had no reason to whip himself. For what? For selling junk to junkies begging and willing to pay for it? Had Christ himself, at that point in Gunner's career, accused him of wrongdoing he would not have understood the nature of his sin. In Gunner's circle, sin did not include pushing junk. Sin was not paying his source, not supplying his customers, passing polluted stuff as pure. Most of all, sin was getting caught by the pigs.

After a profitable afternoon dealing around the school yard, Gunner started for home; he wanted to check the accounts before Angela returned.

"You got stuff?"

Gunner turned to the tap on his shoulder. It was Geronimo. His habit was beginning to irk Gunner. Geronimo was shooting the profits into his arm about as fast as Gunner earned it. But Geronimo was still a friend. To hold out on a friend, to let money stand in the way of friendship; that would be a sin. Besides, all he did with the money was bundle it into a cigar box, which was already crammed to the full. To hold back because he might someday be able to spend, would be doing evil to a friend. Gunner poked through his pocket. He pulled out two cigarette packs; one regular, the other king-sized.

"Horse," Geronimo ordered.

Gunner handed him the king-sized pack. Geronimo zipped it open; he fumbled for the bag inside.

"You're a friend, man. Ain't never gonna fo'get you helpin' me out."

"That's okay, man."

Geronimo's hands shook. There was no use warning his friend to cut down on the junk. Geronimo was past listening.

A couple strolled by holding hands, shot glances at them and hurried off. Several older folks passed, threw them disapproving looks and moved on. From the corner of his eye Gunner saw the patrol car

Israel Jacobs 121

wheel down the street. It cruised in their direction. Geronimo didn't notice. At the moment nothing existed for him but the need to explode the "dynamite" into his veins. He veered right and trotted smack into the path of the oncoming patrol car. The driver slammed the brakes. Geronimo leaped backwards, realized who had almost flattened him and raced for the nearest alley. Gunner swallowed his breath, forgetful that he was still clutching the cigarette pack Geronimo had rejected. The patrol car began a U-turn. Gunner collected his wits. He began to walk down the street, forcing himself not to run. The patrol car completed the turn. Gunner quickened his pace. The patrol car moved faster, pulling slightly ahead of him. Gunner saw the cop on the passenger side roll down the window. Gunner made a sudden about-face and ran; ran as fast as he could.

Instinct propelled his legs to Lincoln Street. He burst into Malcolm Wood's office. Angela and the reverend were studying a chart tacked to the far wall. Tali was pecking at the typewriter with two fingers. Gunner's frantic entrance froze his fingers in mid-air.

"What's the matter?"

The answer stormed in—two policeman with drawn guns.

Gunner dashed past Tali. The cigarette pack! He suddenly remembered. He dropped it next to the typewriter and sped to Angela. She made herself a shield between Gunner and the police.

The cop in the lead, big and ruddy complexioned, grabbed Gunner by the shoulder. Angela tried to wrest the hand away. The cop shoved her to the side. She stumbled toward the desk, catching a corner in time to break her fall. Malcolm Wood squeezed between Gunner and the policeman. The burly officer of the law strong-armed him out of the way. The reverend slammed into the rear wall with a painful thud. The second policeman, who had raced into the office an arm's length behind his partner, dragged Gunner to the door. Gunner resisted; the policeman held tight. Gunner kicked at the cop's shins. He released Gunner with a loud yelp. The other cop quickly closed in. He slapped Gunner's face hard. Gunner heard chimes ringing in his ear.

"You sonnabitch mother fuckin' pig."

The policeman wound up for another slap.

"Touch that boy again, and you'll regret it."

Tali's threat aborted the policeman's swing. For a moment both lawmen looked startled. Tali stationed himself in front of the door, legs set apart, his eyes blazing at the revolvers leveled at him. Gunner scrambled back to Angela's protective cover. The cop who slapped Gunner waved his gun.

"Who're you?"

Tali stared the lawman down. "Put those guns away before you kill somebody."

The cop's eyes roved the room, as if he expected a black army to attack. At a nod from his partner the two holstered their guns.

"Who're you?" the older and apparently more stable of the officers asked.

Tali stepped back to the desk. He glanced obliquely at the pack of cigarettes Gunner had dropped in flight. Hot flashes chased inside Gunner's chest. He felt Tali's knowing stare gnaw at him. Tali slid the pack into his shirt pocket. The senior lawman's eyes narrowed.

"Empty your pockets please."

"Do you have a search warrant?"

"I can pull you all down to the station."

"You do that," Tali said. "But I suggest you have already caused us more than enough distress. For no cause you burst into this office with drawn guns, unmercifully slap a boy, push around a man of the cloth, and this young woman," Tali pointed to Angela. "And now you threaten to drag a rabbi down to a police station like a common criminal."

The policeman's eyes opened wide. "You a rabbi?"

"Yes, I am a rabbi. I am the spiritual leader of a large and well known congregation in Pineville."

"What're you doing here?"

"I am here to make my small contribution to help these unfortunate people retrieve a measure of dignity and self-respect." Tali slanted his chin upwards, piously invoking the ceiling. "God, I can understand why the black race is in revolt. The very servants of the people sworn to protect and defend their rights demean them." Tali glared at the

Israel Jacobs 123

policeman. "You can be sure that in Pineville, where I serve as rabbi, the police would not be so quick to burst into a citizen's office."

Gunner stayed glued to Angela's side. Malcolm Wood hadn't moved since being shoved into the wall. The three listened, mesmerized by Tali's performance. It was a repeat of how he had bullied the mayor's Task Force to make good on the buses they had promised.

"Gee, Rabbi, I'm sorry... We saw this kid passing a package to another kid... he started running... we figured him a pusher... You know, the kids out here are pushing junk all over the—"

Tali cut the policeman short. "Sure he started running. He has good reason to run. They all have good reason to run when they see a policeman. They can be peacefully walking the street, or talking to a friend, and the law assumes they are criminals."

"I'm sorry I slapped the kid," the younger policeman said. "Let's forget the whole thing."

"Yes, you will forget the whole thing. Just like that." Tali snapped his fingers. "For these people it won't be that simple."

It will. It will, Gunner screamed inside his head.

As if he had heard Gunner's silent plea, Tali softened his tone. "We would appreciate it if you would just leave."

The policemen turned to the door and left quietly.

Relief, for Gunner, quickly turned into an anxiety attack. The police had gone. The cigarette pack was still tucked in Tali's shirt pocket. Gunner waited for Tali's next move, hoping against hope that, by some miracle, what he expected to happen would not.

Tali toyed with the cigarette pack, studied it slowly, turned it over twice. Finally, he tapped the bottom. Two cigarettes dribbled out, falling next to the typewriter. Gunner went rigid with fear. Tali hit the pack again. The reefers tumbled out two, three at a time. Fifteen all told, scattering helter-skelter over the desk. Tali pyramided them into one pile, slowly counting, tapping each one with agonizing deliberation. Gunner closed his eyes. The reefers bore through his eyelids, wriggling in his head like clinging caterpillars. He pried one eye open; the real thing couldn't be worse then fear of the unknown. Tali lifted one reefer to his nose. He sniffed it with one nostril than the other. Angela stared at the pile incredulously. Gunner watched with mounting dread. Angela was choking to get the words out. Her eyeballs seemed to enlarge. She sucked in a deep breath. Gunner braced himself for the onslaught.

"Moron! Imbecile. Idiot. You stupid jackass," Angela shoved him down the I.Q. scale till he felt himself excluded from the human family. Her contempt ebbed and crested in a wild crescendo of maledictions. "They could have put you away for years. They should have. How could you?"

Gunner wanted to protest. Having a few reefers on his person didn't call for such hysteria. He never got past the thought. Angela seized him by the neck and shook him with such venom he felt as if his eyes would fall out of their sockets.

"If ever I catch you near that stuff, I'll personally call the cops."

She released him, panting in anger. He jumped out of reach, fearing she would have a go at him again. He rubbed his throbbing head. Did she mean what she said? Would she really turn him in to the pigs? Angela? Do that to her only brother? She didn't sound like she was making empty threats. He gave silent thanks that Geronimo had picked the king-sized pack. Lord! If she ever found out he was peddling hard stuff! He would have to quit. But it was a sorrow. A waste. Angela had sweated for years to earn a college diploma. For what? She was spitting together runs in her stocking so they would make do till next pay day. Worrying each month how she would pay for that one room hovel they shared with a nest of giant roaches and rats. Looking into the mailbox every day, hoping that some fuckin' white principal would hire her. And he with two grand stashed in a cigar box. And the connections to make more in a month than Angela could in five, even if she got lucky and one of her applications hit pay dirt. Gunner yearned to tell her that he had the solution to their financial woes. He backed off telling her anything. Afraid, not of her threat to sing to the pigs. That threat, spat out in rage, Gunner upon reflection, did not believe she was capable of carrying through. Afraid of forever losing her smile. It wasn't worth the risk.

Tali pondered the reefers on the desk. He shook his head. "Gunner, I thought you were too smart to get mixed up with grass."

Israel Jacobs 125

A deadening silence brooded over the room. Gunner's mind began to click. What was he to do now? The money he banked would go fast if he continued to bear the cost of Geronimo's habit. He didn't have the heart to turn his back on a friend. Geronimo would die if he couldn't get junk, or he would kill somebody to get it. And the junk route? What would become of it? Even as Angela glared at him with malevolent eyes, Gunner calculated options. Maybe he'd cut Fish-ears into the partnership. Maybe together they could keep the route alive without Angela the wiser.

Angela transferred her attention to Tali. She looked at him quizzically, as if undergoing an inner struggle to fathom who this white rabbi was, what he was all about. After a long moment she said, "Rabbi Zeig, I'm puzzled, real puzzled. I'm not sure what drives you to come here week after week to help black children. Maybe you sleep better at night for thinking you're making a contribution to an underprivileged race. Maybe you're genuine. The reasons don't much matter to me anymore. The facts are you're helping black kids. They take to you, even more than me. I admit at times that upset me. That's over with, it's not important. What you just did, though, muddles my mind. You risked your neck for Gunner. If the cops had called your bluff, you would have been in a heap of trouble. And, ever since that Cobra shithead tried to force me into your car I've been trying to figure you. You didn't care about him taking the car, but when that shit manhandled me, you came to my rescue like Sir Galahad. You could have been cut up bad. I didn't properly thank you. Those bastards terrified me so I couldn't speak. Then you refused to press charges. The cops practically begged you to get that insect off the streets. I didn't get it then, I still don't. What makes you tick, Rabbi Zeig? I need to know."

Angela had not opened to him at all before. It had been belligerence, bravado. This was a different Angela. No edge to her tone, almost pleading, almost tender. He hardly recognized her. He was at a loss to respond. He said, "Angela, do me a favor, drop the 'rabbi.' It makes me uncomfortable."

"Okay. Tali. Why? I think you do care. Maybe you didn't want to press charges because you didn't want to get involved with those hoodlums. But Gunner. Why? Tell me, Please."

Tali searched those dark eyes. They were moist. She was fighting back tears. Was it disappointment with Gunner? Frustration? Was he somehow the cause? He longed to take her in his arms and comfort her, tell her all will be okay. This was not just sex he was experiencing. He was in love with this black girl. What's his next move to be? He said softly,

"Gunner is your brother."

"Yes, he's *my* brother, not yours. If he weren't my brother, I'd have turned him in. What he's been doing is despicable."

"*Vayinatzlu et Mitzrayim.*"

The words flowed from Tali like as if pushed by a deep sorrow.

"And the Hebrews plundered Egypt."

"What are you talking about, Tali? I don't understand."

Tali shifted to Malcolm Wood. "The reverend understands. He knows his Bible. Those Hebrews, who stripped the Egyptians of their gold and silver were my ancestors. Maybe it was not the proper way to collect a debt. Non-Jewish Bible scholars condemned my ancestors for plundering Egypt. Well, it was payback time. Their former task masters were not about to volunteer back wages. For more than two hundred years Egypt exploited my ancestors, enslaved them, beat them, killed their children. And every Egyptian, who ever worshiped in a temple built with Hebrew blood, slept in a house built on their suffering, ate a kernel planted by their sweat, every Egyptian, man woman and child owed them."

Malcolm invaded Tali's retrospective of past history. He jostled him back to the present reality. Reverend Malcolm Wood thundered across the room, pointing an accusing finger at Gunner like a prophet of wrath. "That boy did not plunder Egyptians. He PLUNDERED BROTHERS."

Chapter Nineteen

HE PLUNDERED BROTHERS!

Reverend Wood had stripped him naked, had mercilessly shot down every alibi he had concocted to justify ripping off his brothers.

What would he do if Angela decided to dump him? With Malcolm Wood calling him the worst kind of traitor, Gunner feared it a real possibility. He would be alone in a lice-filled grubby uncaring world. Who the fuck gave a damn about him? Him, as a person; not for the junk he peddled. Who in this shit-house of a world gave a care for him? Maybe Geronimo, before he got hooked; now he was too far out to think of anything but the next fix. Nobody but Angela cared. Minus Angela what would he have left? Who could he turn to? Nobody. Shit, it wasn't worth it. He had to split the whole drug scene. All of it—smoking, buying, selling.

Except for Geronimo. He could not find it in his heart to abandon Geronimo. The price came high, fifty, seventy-five, a hundred a week. Why this compulsion to feed Geronimo's habit? In the back of his mind Gunner sought penance. Bankrupting himself squared accounts. Reverend Wood had branded him a traitor. He needed to be purged.

And Angela's horrified disbelieving look. Her brother? The one she loved more than anything had betrayed her, had gone over to the enemy. She had made him feel like a vampire sucking her life-blood. Penitence demanded that he rid himself of this blood-money. Only respect for the talent and labor that had gone into earning the small fortune restrained him from putting a match to it, or dumping it down

128   *The Convert*

the nearest sewer. He considered contributing to Malcolm Wood's Head Start Program, but deemed it wiser not to reveal how deep into dealing he was. The reverend was too sharp not to make the connection. Feeding Geronimo's habit seemed the only fitting way to wipe the slate clean.

Gunner trudged homeward-bound from school. A biting wind slashed at him, pulling tears from his eyes. Strong gusts picked up snow clouds from the streets and hurled them at pedestrians crouching to protect their faces against the cold. Icy sludge overran his shoes, trickling inside and oozing between his toes. Home afforded only partial refuge. The erratic bursts of steam provided by the landlord were no match for the damp chill which cut right to the bone. It was a cold January with temperatures held down to the low teens. He yearned for warmth, physical and emotional.

His days dragged. School, which he attended religiously, under threat of excommunication, pulled him down even further. He missed the bustle and purpose to a day, the ego-trip pushing junk had provided. He fell into a dark rut, dwelling morbidly on the cold, the monotony, the futility of it all. While preoccupied with his junk route, he had barely noticed the winter cold or summer heat. Each day took care of itself. Now the hours stretched like years. Life had become a gloom. One cheerless day followed another. He forced himself from a scratched desk in P.S. 204 to the hovel he and Angela called home. Back to school, to home again, in an endless boring routine.

Adding to his depression was the lean-assed teacher-preacher he had to listen to crapping about all the opportunities this great country provided. The shit just poured from the lady-fart:

"Do your best, work hard. In this wonderful land of opportunity and freedom we all have the same chance to make good."

It inflamed Gunner's guts to hold still for the shit she was putting down. He wanted to tell her to try heating her white ass in a freezing tenement while waiting for better times. But he was in enough trouble. He didn't need the principal calling Angela.

What he needed most at the moment was a friend. A soul brother

Israel Jacobs 129

to whom he could pour out his ache. Geronimo.

Why Geronimo's friendship still rated high was not entirely clear to Gunner. Most of the day Geronimo was stoned, in a private paradise that numbed him to the world. But in the rare moments when the old Geronimo made a brief appearance, he could still be a comfort. Before the "garbage" fouled his brain Geronimo had been advisor, protector, father-confessor.

Geronimo boarded in a six-floor walk-up with a grandmother, several aunts, and a brood of cousins.

Once, Gunner went uninvited to his partner's apartment.

At the time, he had reconnoitered several hallways and alleys but had been unable to locate Geronimo at his usual haunts. Feeling especially hungry for companionship that day, he decided to try Geronimo's tenement. He climbed the six graffiti-filled, foul-smelling flights on the chance that he might be home. The top floor stank worst of all, as if all the stink in the building had floated to the top. Gunner picked his way through the dismal litter-strewn hall. He missed seeing the broken crate, stumbled over it, striking his knee. He cursed the crate then groped for the door. The last one to the left, according to the number scratched on the mailbox downstairs. Gunner rapped three times. One of Geronimo's cousins opened the door a crack. He stood at the rutted doorsill staring at Gunner from eye sockets bulging out of wrinkled cheeks. It looked like a fifty-year-old face mistakenly grafted on a seven-year-old body. The face poked out a little further, recognized Gunner and opened the door wide. Gunner stepped into the apartment and stopped dead in his tracks. Trash was dumped all over the floor, rotting leftover food, rags, slop under and on the kitchen table. Empty beer cans, whiskey bottles, cracked dishes piled high in the rusted sink. Ripped linoleum floors. Holes in the walls large enough for a man to crawl into. Water dripping from a hole somewhere in the ceiling into a pail that ran over and formed a dirty pool. One naked light bulb threw an eye-squinting light. The urine stench mixed with a pile of decomposing garbage made him pinch his nose. He fought off nausea. In the next room two mattresses were lined end to end on the floor. A tiny shriveled woman lay half-naked. Next to the woman, a man in tattered underwear sat on his haunches with his back to the door. He tightened a rubber strip around his biceps and jabbed a needle into his arm.

Gunner asked, "Geronimo in?"

"No, he ain't," the wizened face answered.

"Know where he's at?"

"Geronimo never tell nobody where he's goin'."

Gunner had scrambled down the six flights into the street, hungrily gulping fresh air.

He never knocked on that door again. He would go as far as the second floor and yell. If Geronimo didn't curse down that he was coming, Gunner would search the streets, or park on the stoop and wait for him to show.

The last months Geronimo had spent less time at home. Finally, he had split completely. From the brief glimpse Gunner had caught of Geronimo's kin, they could hardly have missed him. If they did, it probably was with relief at the extra space. Where Geronimo slept, or ate, how he existed became an ever deepening mystery. He favored two or three hallways, where Gunner often found him nodding off. Occasionally, Geronimo would disappear entirely, sometimes for days at a stretch. After much prodding Geronimo confided his most recent address, first exacting a promise that Gunner would keep this information private. On hearing where Geronimo now lived, Gunner told himself he should have figured. What else was available to Geronimo? But as difficult as it sometimes got for him and Angela, they never sank so low as to not care, to where nothing mattered anymore.

Gunner searched the hallways Geronimo usually haunted. His friend was nowhere to be found. Feeling low, and shivering in the cold, Gunner headed home. He considered making a stop at the Head Start office. He turned left at the next street, then backtracked. The wounds were still too fresh. He and Angela had worked out a truce; he had to swear on their parents' graves he wouldn't go near grass again and faithfully attend classes. In return, Angela granted him limited freedom to rove on his own. But feelings were still tender on both sides. He

Israel Jacobs 131

wasn't ready to face the three of them. He might screw up the courage to look Tali in the eye. Possibly, Reverend Wood. Despite the raging, he was a forgiving pastor. But the three of them in combination were more than Gunner could handle. Gunner retraced his steps and plodded through the slush, bending into the damp wind. The depression worsened. He desperately needed to talk. He headed for Geronimo's private hideaway.

The first two floors of the condemned building were sealed with knotted planks. Gunner craned to the top floor, estimating the climb. From the upper levels gutted windows gaped down like eyeless sockets. He scrambled to the alley entrance, braced his shoulder against a loose board, carefully stuck his head through the opening and groped for the latch. He pushed hard against the door. It groaned open. He allowed himself a moment for his eyes to accommodate. Slithers of dim light fanned through chinks in the boarded windows of the ground floor, offering just enough light to illuminate the rubble. Only a deep need for a sympathetic ear could have made him enter that tomb. He stepped inside and pulled the door shut after him as per Geronimo's instructions. He picked his way through the crushed cans, smashed crates, an inverted rusted radiator, against which he banged his shins. Battered chairs lying on their sides, a table with two legs missing leaning against the wall, broken bottles. A cavernous breach in the wall up ahead exposed a giant cast-iron furnace, now dead and cold as the tenement it once heated. Carefully, Gunner threaded his way toward the decapitated staircase to the right. Sections of the bannister were missing. He could make out some of the broken planks sitting ominously on the steps like daggers. Potholes had been gouged out of the stairs, as if hungry animals had feasted on them. Cautiously, Gunner tested his weight on the first step. It creaked but held firm. He peered ahead into the shadows, worrying what lurked upstairs. He climbed to the first floor. He half-turned to examine his location. He decided the visit had been a mistake. Something pulled him to the next landing. On the third floor slightly more daylight sifted through. A gust twisted through a half-boarded window, caught a door dangling loosely on one hinge and sent it smacking against the wall. He jumped at the impact.

132

Clawing sounds pitter-pattered over his shoes. He kicked violently. The fat ugly rat chased across the floor.

It was time to go home.

He groped for the steps. A moan wailed down from the upper floor. Muffled as it was, he heard it. He culled it from the creaking boards, the squeaking doors, the wind whistling through the cracks. He heard it above his thumping heartbeat. It thrust fright, disgust aside. He sprinted up the stairs, pumping his legs at maximum speed, puffing hard from the exertion, hearing only the groans gurgling from the top floor. With each step the fear of what he would find mounted. He reached the top, panting. He knew even before he saw Geronimo sprawled across the bed.

Yellow tufting poured through slits in the mattress, as if the bed had, long ago, vomited its guts out. Geronimo's left arm hung limply over the side, his fingers grazing the floor. His eyes were open circles, staring without sight at the hole in the ceiling. On his chest another pair of eyes. They pierced into Gunner, daring him to move closer. For a moment he froze, recoiling in horror. The abomination roosted on Geronimo's chest, fat as a well fed kitten, defying him, caterwauling hostility. The rat moved; its movement broke the spell. Gunner picked up a loose board and swung it at the plague. He swung a second time before it surrendered its perch and fled.

"Geronimo!"

No response. Gunner elevated the limp arm. He pushed, pulled, slapped Geronimo's hands, his face. Nothing. No recognition. His pupils were shrunken pinpoints, seeing nothing. Suddenly, they rolled back into his head. A rasp scraped from his throat. Gunner lifted him part-way off the bed. Emaciated as he was, Geronimo's dead weight was too heavy to negotiate the staircase. He shifted his friend back to the bed and chased down the five flights. He ran as fast as he could whip his legs, forgetting guilt, embarrassment. Ran to the only people he could count on. Headlong into Reverend Malcolm Wood.

"What's the matter, son?"

"Geronimo! On the top floor... he's dying... I found him... I had to leave him... too heavy to carry..."

Israel Jacobs 133

The horror in Gunner's head scrambled out faster than his tongue could organize the words.

"Who is dying? Where?"

Malcolm tried to make sense out of the boy's raving. Gunner's hysteria pulled Tali from his class. The disturbance ripped into Angela's room. She raced into the office.

Tali ordered Gunner to take a deep breath. "Now, slowly, tell me where you left him."

"The house on Crawford Street... I couldn't carry him... top floor."

"Okay. We'll get in my car, and you'll show me exactly which house. Can you do that, Gunner?"

Tali didn't wait for a reply. he tugged Gunner to the door. Angela raced after them. The three slammed into the Mustang, leaving a bewildered Malcolm Wood to tend the office.

Tali blasted through the streets, his horn screaming pedestrians and cars out of the way. The Mustang screeched to a halt in front of the condemned tenement.

"How'd you get into the building?"

"The alley. A back door. It opens from the outside."

"Show me."

Gunner pointed to a slanted plank covering the door. "There it is. Pull the board up. There's a knob underneath. You gotta reach in and turn it."

Tali kicked the door in. "Where is he?"

"On the bed... upstairs..."

"What floor?"

"Top... fifth."

Tali vaulted into the gloom, stopping a moment to probe for the stairs. He found them and catapulted up the steps three at a time. Gunner chased after him. He could hear Tali thumping two floors above. Gunner panted to the fourth floor, the fifth. Tali emerged from the doorless doorway cradling Geronimo's limp body. Gunner feared to ask whether his friend was alive. Geronimo's arms were swinging like the arms of a disjointed doll. Tali shoved through, pressing Gunner against the wall. He hurtled down the staircase. Gunner followed, not quite able to catch his breath. Angela waited in the alleyway. A small mob had gathered, hurling questions. Angela stood tight-lipped. She cleared a path to the Mustang. Tali eased Geronimo into the back seat. Angela climbed in to the back and cushioned Geronimo's head on her lap. Gunner pushed into the front seat next to Tali. He turned to check if Gunner was breathing and met Angela's grim face.

Tali sprinted into Crescent Memorial bearing Geronimo in his arms. He raced the limp boy to the emergency room. The receptionist, a heavy-set black woman in a starched white uniform, looked at him, looked at the unconscious boy. There was little doubt that the boy was a breath away from death. She didn't turn a hair. Her face registered no shock. To her, Geronimo was a tale told a thousand times over. A thousand repetitions had built a solid wall around her emotions. Live through enough tragedy, Tali had learned from personal experience, and you drown or grow immune. The trick is not to become heartless. Tali didn't know into which box to fit this woman. She motioned him to a seat as she spoke into the phone on her desk. Tali heard her say something about Geronimo's condition. A slender young black, dressed in white ducks and a collarless shirt passed through the door marked EMERGENCY. He pushed a rolling cart in their direction. Tali surrendered Geronimo. The intern deposited Geronimo on the cart, probed his eyes with a pencil flashlight, and rolled him away.

Comforting the mourner, visiting the sick, constituted major parts of Tali's daily routine. He was no stranger to cemeteries or hospitals. He had sat many hours in Pineville Hospital with congregants who were fearfully waiting to learn the results of tests or an operation on a family member. Crescent Memorial Hospital was unlike anything he had experienced in Pineville. He found it more depressing than a cemetery. In a cemetery the dead are quiet. Their agony is over and done with. You can't see them or smell them. Six feet of earth separate the living from the dead. In Crescent Memorial's waiting room there was no partition between visitors and the sick. Its corridors were

Israel Jacobs 135

crammed wall-to-wall with the ailing, the infirm, the incurable. There was no escaping their moans, their smell. They sat on long benches—octogenarians hoping to stave off the grave, young people and children wrestling with death's angel. Women with crying infants in their arms, women with the yet unborn swelling their bellies. The lame, the bandaged, the bleeding, internally and externally. They waited submissively, their eyes darting after the interns and nurses hastening to-and-fro, in and out of doorways, pushing complex medical equipment along the corridors. The figures in white flitted back and forth like superior beings. Every fifteen minutes or so a name was called. Someone rose and shuffled away. Two, three, four standees rushed for the vacant seat. It went on and on in an endless assembly line. Hour after hour they arrived, with canes, on crutches, on stretchers.

Gunner sat motionless, near to choking by the misery filling the corridors, and by guilt exploding inside of him. He had been Geronimo's major supplier. He was responsible. The hours dragged on. Six-fifteen, by the corridor clock, the intern who had taken charge of Geronimo, returned.

One more move for Geronimo. To an eternal home. The wind, the cold, the rain couldn't touch him anymore. Geronimo would never again have to search for a place to lay his head down.

Gunner raised wet eyes to Angela. The finality, the utter finality penetrated. The dam burst. He cried and let the tears roll down.

Angela gently stroked his forehead. "Let's go home. It's all over."

Gunner wiped his dripping nose. He searched his sister's face, hunting for comfort, for exoneration. It was all there; all he so desperately needed. Soft, forgiving. His fear of her cutting him off had been groundless. Not her; she couldn't no matter how much he deserved it. On the spot he swore to himself: come what may, whatever it took, he would never again disappoint her. He had leaned on her too long without appreciating what a weight he was. Someday, somehow he would make it up to her.

Angela hooked her arm into his. Tali stepped ahead and pushed the door open. Solemnly they walked out of Crescent Memorial Hospital.

136   *The Convert*

A bright half-moon peeked between the hospital towers. Ordinarily, a cheerful sight. Not this evening. The night seemed to spit gloom. Two men in flapping coats, white uniforms showing underneath, were sliding a stretcher from an ambulance. They loaded the body on a cart and glided the sheet-covered human bundle into the hospital building.

"Would you take us home please, Tali."

Tali nodded gravely. He opened the car door, motioned Gunner to climb into the back, then slid behind the wheel next to Angela.

He drove at a funereal pace, feeling as he did when in a cortege following a hearse. The quiet weighed down ponderously. Crescent Memorial Hospital faded into the distance. Tali made a wrong turn, backtracked then lost the green light and had to wait for it to switch from red to green again. Gunner observed his weary face reflecting in the rear-view mirror. Angela, too, seemed to be monitoring Tali's mood. The Mustang pulled up in front of their tenement. Tali shifted to park, letting the motor idle. He opened his mouth as if to say something. He let the words go unspoken. Angela broke into the quiet.

"Would you like to come up? I'll make us a pot of coffee."

Tali trudged up the four flights, immersed in his own gloom, only peripherally conscious of the dankness, the shouting matches screaming into the halls from behind doors lining the hallway. He slouched in the chair Angela had pushed at him, brooding at the scarred Formica table. Gradually, he awakened to the apartment. An antiquated sink resting on four pitted chrome legs was packed tightly between a refrigerator and a two-burner stove that required several ignitions by scratching wooden matches against the stove's burners before the flame caught. In addition to the kitchen table, two chairs and a wooden crate that doubled as a third chair and cupboard, the room consisted of two folding cots stacked against the front wall. A lace curtain covered the one window. A faded print of a pastoral scene represented Angela's futile effort to upgrade the bleakness. The bathroom, Tali surmised, was to the left of the refrigerator. Gunner had slammed past it on entering the apartment, bumping his shins and cursing. Tali heard the trickle, then a sigh of relief followed by the flushing toilet. This was what Angela and her brother called home. One room, hardly larger than the downstairs foyer in his house.

"Here's your coffee. You want sugar with it?"

Tali reached for the plastic mug. He curled his fingers around her hand. He shook his head.

"From day one that poor kid never had a chance. Not from the day he was born."

"Geronimo's not the first to overdose. He won't be the last. You live in these parts you get used to it."

"I know. It's not right. God, I don't understand."

Angela pulled her hand away. "You're a rabbi. Don't you have a direct connection to God? Aren't you supposed to understand? Isn't that what your congregation pays you for? To explain why God does what He does?"

She mouthed the words bitterly. Immediately, as she saw the pain in his eyes, she regretted the attack. Why had she charged at him? For the space of a heartbeat she had moved to take his face between her hands, to soothe his hurt. Before she could act on that impulse, she experienced the old fears: Court House Square in Redford. The Confederate soldier with his rifle at the ready poking at her. The drunken white boy who squashed her parents. The white social workers. All the whites who had crumpled her life. And instead of cradling his head to her breast as her arms yearned, she had lashed out.

"Angela, I don't know why God does what He does. If my congregation pays me to explain God, they're wasting their money. My job is to help people survive what God allows to happen in this world; the hurt, the pain the sorrow. And believe you me that job is proving too much. Even rabbis need a hand to hold on to occasionally."

Angela still couldn't bring herself to act out what she felt. "I... I wish I could help you, Tali. I... I can't."

"You could help, Angela. More than you know."

Angela fought back the tears begging to be released. "How? How can I help you?"

"Two are better than one... If one falls the other is there for support. Pity him

who is alone... When he falls there is no one to lift him up."

The first tear broke through. One drop that opened the gates.

Only dimly aware of Angela's inner struggle, Tali continued. *"If two lie together—"*

Angela cut him off. "What are you quoting from?"

"The Bible. Ecclesiastes."

The one teardrop was pulling a rivulet after it. "Lord you are a preacher. Got to use the Bible even to say, I love you."

"I love you, Angela."

"Jesus, I thought you'd never get to it."

Angela bolted into his waiting arms. They embraced, clinging to one another as if afraid the moment would turn into a mirage. By degrees Angela brought her sobbing under control. She looked up at him.

"Rabbi Zeig, you bought yourself a problem, didn't you?"

"Yes, I bought myself a problem. The most beautiful, gorgeous problem I ever dreamt would be mine."

"Tali?"

"Yes."

"That verse from Ecclesiastes. You didn't get to finish it. I want to hear the rest."

Tali hunted for her mouth, "Some other time. At the moment I'm busy."

"Angela turned her face away. "Finish it, Tali."

"If two lie together, they will have warmth, but how can one have warmth alone?"

Angela rested her head on Tali's shoulder.

Chapter Twenty

Tali sneezed into the Kleenex. He wished himself gezundheit. The empty den hiked his misery a notch. And upstairs four vacant beautifully furnished bedrooms. He sipped the hot tea he had prepared for himself on arriving home from the Board meeting. It did little to alleviate his discomfort. He sneezed again, God-blessed himself again and slumped into the club chair. His head felt heavy as a bowling ball. His throat had started scratching the day after Sarah Levine's funeral. Was it Thursday or Friday? Only Wednesdays held anything worth remembering. The rest of the week passed by in a blur. He did remember the freezing rain during the twenty minute interment service. He hauled himself off the chair and shuffled upstairs, debating which bedroom to sleep in tonight. He chose the master bedroom, thinking how nicely it would accommodate a mistress.

He lay awake, staring at the ceiling. Usually, he dropped off as soon as his head hit the pillow. Tonight his mind went in circles. He heard his wrist watch ticking away on the dresser. Why couldn't he sleep? Maybe he was sicker than he thought. He sneezed again, touched his forehead, fearing that he had a fever. He could have a stroke, die, and nobody would know for days. Being sick wouldn't be half so depressing if he had someone to at least hand him a thermometer. He felt himself perspiring. A good sign. If he could build up a sweat, by tomorrow he should be fine. The ticking wrist watch unnerved him. He tossed the quilt aside, scrambled out of bed, stuffed the wrist watch into a drawer and scurried back to bed. His nose tickled, setting off another sneezing

140   *The Convert*

spell. He felt wiped out. It would be nice to have a caring helpmate give
him the tender loving care a man needs at times like these. Moisture
collected on his forehead, trickling down to his cheeks. The two
aspirins and tea were beginning to take effect. He closed his eyes and
tried to make his mind blank. Faces, events of the past weeks paraded
under his eyelids: Angela, Gunner, Angela. Malcolm Wood. Geronimo.
Angela.

No use. He could not beat himself to sleep.

He sat up, switched on the table lamp and reached for the
periodical on the night table. Maybe he could read himself to sleep. He
reviewed the title page, *New Discoveries in Biblical Archaeology.* He flipped
to the second page, read a sentence that referred back to a quotation on
the first page and realized he had skimmed the paragraph without
absorbing any of it. He thumbed back to the first page and re-read the
paragraph. He couldn't sleep and he couldn't concentrate. His mind
kept skating back to Upper Chelsea. To Angela and Gunner and
Malcolm Wood. And again back to Angela.

At first he had consigned thoughts of marriage to fantasy land. The
idea was absurd. He attributed infatuation with Angela to gonads
working overtime. As the weeks wore on, he recognized lust may have
been the starter, but it had advanced beyond sex. This beautiful black
girl had so invaded his thoughts he didn't go an hour without picturing
her. She filled his mind till he could think of little else. The way she
tossed her head, the sway of her hips, the curve to her breasts, the
contours of her lovely bronze-skinned face. Every visible part of her,
and the parts left to the imagination. She made him feel alive, made him
feel life was worth living. When he realized this was the real thing he
realized, too, that ahead of him lay a delicate courtship.

He pondered his situation, chewing it over and over again, as he
had for weeks. There was no precedent for what he had in mind.

By happy circumstance he had landed one of the plums in the
Allied Synagogue of America. Whether this was to be permanent or a
way-station to something else, he wasn't yet certain. In the meantime
these were comfortable quarters in which to decide. Six hundred upper-
middle-income families represented a solid pulpit.

And there was the added bonus. His congregants were several cuts above what rabbis found in the average synagogue. Not that his members were committed Jews. Except for a handful of about twenty tradition-oriented families, Judaism in particular and religion in general did not touch their lives very much. Their affiliation was mostly tribal, social, sentimental rather than born of conviction. But putting aside two or three ignorant vulgarians, his congregants were, for the most part, bright and well educated, as expert in their respective professions as he in his. Doctors, attorneys, academicians, judges, psychiatrists, top executives and industrialists. Once he ventured out of his field of expertise—Bible, Talmud, Jewish philosophy, Jewish theology—there wasn't a subject someone in his congregation didn't know as much or more than he did, be it politics, law, music, art. He had to be on guard, constantly check his facts, even in matters of Jewish ritual, or some old-timer was sure to correct him if he erred. His congregants kept him on his toes. Yes, they were a challenge, for the most part sophisticated and open to new ideas. But how would they react to a black rebbitzen? People were more than intellect.

And it wasn't only his job he had to consider. What of Angela? Would she fit in this picture? Would she want to?

He made another try at *New Discoveries in Biblical Archaeology*. No use. His thoughts strayed from the page. He thrust himself out of bed, hopped to the dresser, opened the drawer and checked the time. Ten past one. He climbed back into bed, taking his wrist watch with him. He laid it on the night table and followed the second handle as it made a turn around the clock-face. The quiet hung heavy and lonely. How did he get into this dilemma? At what point did he find himself out on this limb? He put little stock in suddenly getting the Call. Those who claimed to be visited by visions, in his judgment, were either unbalanced or outright frauds. Decisions that endure do not emerge out of one revival meeting. A true split from one's former lifestyle, change that goes to the core, if it ever happens, is a long painful process. He learned this from personal experience.

Tali retraced the intellectual leaps he had made the last ten years. The shifts in attitude, the certainties he had come to question. When had he moved to the other side? The changes had insinuated themselves subtly. No instant revelation. No sudden breakthrough. The cocoon that protected his faith was peeled away, layer by layer. Slowly, inexorably, he distanced himself from his Orthodox Yeshiva absolutes. He recalled Spinoza whom he had read at age fourteen. Such books were illicit. Had he been discovered reading them, he would have had to sit for a lecture on heresy, possibly even expelled from the Yeshiva. Despite the risk, he continued to probe. His high school biology teacher, challenging the biblical version of creation with Darwin's theory of evolution, traumatized him. The first time he sat in a classroom with girls. Agnostic classmates at Triton University. Sam Yin, his college roommate, opening a door to Confucius. Each experience put another crack into his beliefs. Questions roiled inside of him he refused, at first, to face. But the seeds were planted. They took root in fertile soil and sprouted into full bloom. The change carried intellectual freedom. And confusion.

He returned to thoughts of Angela. His depression began to lift. He imagined her taking his temperature. The scratching in his throat, and stuffed head might not clear up any quicker. But what a marvelous way to nurse a cold. How, when, did she become so urgent to his existence? Again he tried to pinpoint the moment he had decided to crash the religious and racial barriers. Was he captured at that first encounter in Jeremiah Yarden's home? What he did recollect was that she had impressed him as one of the most beautiful sensuous woman he had ever laid eyes on.

But love? Marriage? Family?

Catering to his libido was one thing. From the start she made him horny. But making it with a woman, white or black, is one thing. Bringing her home to mother, to Pineville, is another. He realized now it had been in the back of his mind for months. He couldn't say precisely when the notion popped into his head to present the Pineville Jewish Center with a black rebbitzen, no more than when he made the decision to apply to the Seminary, an institution that was anathema to the Orthodox world.

Introducing Angela to Pineville would undoubtedly raise a storm.

But both he and the congregation would survive, he was reasonably certain.

The way to go was to present them with a fait-accompli. No forewarning. No opportunity to call special Board meetings to debate the pros and cons. No more information than necessary. It would be a jolt at first encounter, a few would go into trauma, as they did when he introduced twelve black families from the pulpit that memorable Sabbath eve. However, after the initial shock they would come around. If Angela would have him, she was going to become Mrs. Zeig. He had made up his mind. The congregation would simply have to accept. If not, there were other ways to make a living. A heavier question weighed on his mind.

Would she convert?

Over and over again he had preached that intermarriage is a betrayal of the Jewish people. Every marriage outside the Jewish faith is another nail in the Jewish coffin. Parents of children intending to marry a non-Jew pleaded, "Rabbi, please. We understand you can't officiate. But come. At least to the reception. Give them your blessing. Show the youngsters you're not rejecting them. The bride's minister will be officiating. How will it look if my rabbi isn't even present? Rabbi, please."

He turned a deaf ear. Twelve million Jews left in the world. Not inconceivable for the Jewish people to become as extinct as the dodo. Six million Jews had been exterminated, among them the most pious and learned of that generation. The Jewish people could not survive the mounting intermarriage rate. He had stood his ground, persuaded that to yield made him a party to betrayal. His presence would sanction intermarriage.

They fumed, they bitched to the Board. They argued he was inconsistent. How could he be so liberal, so flexible on almost every other issue and so narrow-minded on this one? They didn't understand, he had convinced himself, because to them Judaism and Jewish survival mattered not enough.

Do not judge your fellow man until you are in his place.

Hillel, the second century sage who had expounded this principle, seemed to be talking to him across nineteen hundred years.

His present predicament gave him some appreciation of the dilemma his congregants faced. He began to understand the powerful emotions that might lead even a committed Jew to intermarry.

He loved Angela, and he believed she reciprocated that love. But conversion? Was he stretching a dream too far? He would face a hurdle or two in bringing home a black bride. But for him the trip to the marriage canopy would be via familiar territory. He was equipped to cope with criticism coming from his own kind. For Angela this would be a journey to another planet. Could he bring her to Judaism? If not could he give her up?

Tali's eyelids drooped. The ticking wrist watch faded. He switched off the lamp. He felt himself drifting off.

Tomorrow was Wednesday.

Chapter Twenty One

Gunner curled himself into the fetal position and drew the covers up to his ears. A vaguely familiar aroma tweaked his nostrils. He sniffed. Onion? Garlic? He sniffed again. The aroma stirred him awake. Dawn filtered weakly through the one window into the one-room apartment. He pried one eye open. Angela was fussing over the oven. Gunner sat up.

"What you doin' up so early?"

"Preparing dinner."

"What time is it?"

"Six-fifteen."

Gunner rubbed his eyes. "We gonna eat dinner before breakfast?"

"Go back to sleep."

"Can't sleep with you smelling up the place."

Angela scratched a wooden match against the burner. She tossed it into the oven. Gunner heard the muted explosion as the match and gas met inside the oven. He threw the blanket aside, rolled off the cot and shivered into his clothing.

"I gotta use the bathroom."

"Go on. And wash up while there's still hot water."

Gunner folded the cot and anchored it against the back wall. He marched into the bathroom and turned the hot water tap. Lukewarm water belched out in spurts. He splashed his face, dried himself and exited the bathroom. Angela had laid out bacon and eggs on the table. He dipped a slice of bacon into the egg yolk, leisurely savoring the

146   *The Convert*

combination. Angela sat down to coffee and toast. She nibbled on the toast then bounced back to the stove. She opened the oven door and peered inside. Gunner dawdled over his breakfast. He scraped the plate clean, rinsed the dishes, dried them and stacked the utensils into the box under the sink. Angela put on her coat.

"I've got to get an early start this morning. Make sure you get to school on time."

"You teachin' today?"

"Yes. I was called last night to sub at the Edgewood Avenue school. Remember, on your way no later than eight-fifteen."

"Yeah, don't worry. I won't be late."

Angela closed the door. Gunner heard her double-bolting the lock. Sullenly, he gathered his books and stalked out of the apartment.

After school, Gunner stayed on to shoot baskets with friends. By four the group broke up. He trudged home alone to the empty apartment. His stomach growled. He flung off his jacket and scrounged in the refrigerator for something to tide him over until dinner. Angela's school day finished at three, but she still gave the Head Start program several hours a week. On Wednesdays she rarely got home before six. He debated whether to go for the cold ham or settle for a peanut butter sandwich. He reached for the peanut butter jar. Footsteps thumped in the hall. Gunner recognized Tali's walk.

Since Geronimo's death, Tali had displaced him as Angela's escort. Wednesdays he drove her home. It had become a routine. She would invite him in, and they would talk over coffee and cake for the next hour. At first Gunner resented having to share his sister. As the weeks wore on he came to look forward to Tali's visits. Sometimes they went directly to a movie, usually taking him along. He liked that. After the movie they would go to a diner. He would stuff himself. Angela and Tali stuck to coffee and cake.

Gunner heard the key turn. Angela popped the door open, all bubbly.

"Hang yourself up, Tali. I've got a special on tonight."

"That's nice. I'm in the mood for a slice of gooey chocolate cake."

"It's not cake." Angela struck a match to the oven. It ignited with

Israel Jacobs 147

the usual coughing explosion. "Chat with Gunner while I set the table. Dinner will take a few minutes to warm."

Tali stared at the oven. He tugged a handkerchief from his pocket and mopped his brow. He shuffled toward the chair, almost colliding with Angela.

"Will you please sit down? You're in my way."

Tali sat as ordered. He stared at the oven.

Gunner studied Tali. The man was acting peculiar. Nervous as a pusher on spotting the cops. Not at all like Tali.

Angela spread their one plastic tablecloth and set for three. She beamed at Tali. He played with the utensils nervously. Angela hurried to the oven, opened the door and removed the casserole.

Tali stiffened.

Angela snipped off a piece of the loaf. She tested it on her tongue. "How do you like your meat loaf? Rare, medium, well done?"

Tali squirmed in his chair.

"Speak up, sir. How do you like your meat loaf?"

Tali loosened his collar. "Uh... medium. But I...I..."

Angela speared another piece, tasted it and strutted to the table carrying the casserole on a tray. She set it down tenderly, sliced a generous portion and ladled it onto Tali's plate. He blinked at the meat loaf.

"I... I... I'm not very hungry, Angela. Could you just give me a cup of coffee, black?"

The knife fell from Angela's hand. She lifted the casserole to her face and sniffed. "Something wrong with my meat loaf?"

"Your meat loaf's fine. I'm just not hungry."

"How come you're not hungry? You sick?"

"Yes, I... I'm just getting over a cold. It ruined my appetite."

"I've seen you with a cold before. It never affected your appetite. Why won't you eat my meat loaf? What's wrong with it?"

"There's nothing wrong with your meat loaf. I'm just not hungry."

"If it isn't well done enough, I can put it back in the oven."

"Please, Angela, don't bother. Just a cup of black coffee."

"Don't bother? Hell! I've already bothered. Six o'clock this morning I bothered to get up so I could prepare this meat loaf for you. Why won't you eat it? You afraid I'll poison you?"

Tali smiled feebly. "Angela, I'm sure you're a great cook. Really. It smells delicious. I just don't have an appetite."

"Shit, you don't have an appetite." Angela slammed the casserole dish to the table. Hot gravy spilled over the rim, splashing Tali's shirt-sleeve. He inspected the gray splotches spreading down to his cuff.

"I know why you lost your appetite. You learned our dirty secret. Blacks chop up the rats in their tenements and feed them to you honkeys."

Tali spread his hands imploringly, "Angela, I'm not allowed to eat the meat loaf."

"Zeig, you're full of crap. You're healthy as a horse. That's what I should have cooked for you. Horse meat!"

Angela's rage melted into tears. Gunner screeched. "You sonna-bitch, you made my sister cry." He wound up to belt the ungrateful bum. Tali caught the punch in mid-air.

"Angela, it's got nothing to do with health. I'm not allowed to eat your meat loaf because it's not kosher."

Angela raised the meat loaf shoulder-high, clearly intending to throw it at him. Gunner grabbed her arm. Socking the sonnabitch was one thing. But wasting a good meat loaf? That'd be a sin.

Tali hastened to explain.

"It's part of my religion. Meat has to be kosher. Otherwise, I'm not allowed to eat it."

"What's kosher mean?"

"Angela, it's complicated. I can't explain it under fire."

Angela lowered the casserole dish. "Okay, explain."

"Observant Jews may eat only the meat of a kosher animal. And the animal must be slaughtered according to a prescribed ritual. Also, we're not permitted to mix milk with meat products. We're required to use two sets of dishes. One for meat; the other for dairy."

"You're not putting me on? Kosher is really part of your religion?"

"Yes, kosher is an important part of my religion. If you have a Bible, I'll show you exactly where these dietary laws come from."

Israel Jacobs   149

"The Bible says you can't eat my meat loaf?"

Teardrops slid down Angela's cheeks. Tali thought how soft and vulnerable she looked. He wanted to take her in his arms and kiss her tears away. He didn't dare. Not at the moment. He couldn't tell whether the tears were generated by self-pity, or rage.

"No, the Bible doesn't say I can't eat your meat loaf. I can eat anybody's meat loaf, provided the meat is kosher and hasn't been mixed with milk, or made in a dairy pot."

"Is that what kosher means?"

"There's a lot more to it. If you give me a chance, I'll explain."

Angela accepted a handkerchief from Tali and blotted her face.

That evening Tali launched Angela on a course in Judaism's dietary laws. Patiently, he tried to make her see the connection between Judaism's reverence for life, it's concept of holiness, and the Jewish dietary code.

In subsequent sessions he moved deeper into Jewish law, history, the Jewish life-cycle. He advanced, step by step, giving her time to digest one concept before carrying her further. Gunner sat in on the sessions, going along as far as his twelve-year old attention span allowed.

Tali continued to shuttle between his two worlds, carefully avoiding premature proselytizing, easing into the subject as if treading on egg shells. Weeks passed. February made way for March. The cold winds began to lose their edge. Upper Chelsea's residents again took to the streets. Angela showed a growing interest. She asked questions. She asked for books on Judaism, which Tali eagerly provided. There was still a long way to go, before he dared asked her to convert. One evening she surprised him by asking, "Would it be very hard for me to learn Hebrew?"

"A bright girl like you? I can teach it to you in ten easy lessons."

"I'm not kidding. I'd like to learn."

"Actually," Tali said seriously, "I could teach you how to read and write in ten easy lessons. "Comprehension, to speak and understand the language, that would take longer. But it's not hard. It's a lot easier than

150   *The Convert*

learning English from scratch."

"Would you teach me?"

"Be my pleasure."

"Gunner said, "How 'bout me?"

"Depends."

"On what?"

Tali grinned. "Are you as smart as your sister?"

"Smarter."

"Okay, we got a deal. Two for the price of one."

Tali and Angela continued to contribute Wednesdays to the Head Start remedial program. Malcolm Wood's project was growing by leaps and bounds. He succeeded in securing a respectable sized grant, enough to double his staff and consider moving to larger quarters. Tali now commuted to the city two to three times a week. Wednesday afternoons were reserved for the O.E.O., after which he would chauffeur Angela home, stay for coffee and cake, and spend an hour tutoring her and Gunner in Hebrew. The sessions expanded in time and scope. Tali felt Angela moving closer, shedding lifetime defenses, beginning to trust in herself enough to trust him. He insisted she install a phone in the apartment, adding that he would pay the bill. When she resisted, he argued it was for his peace of mind. If she felt uncomfortable about it, she didn't have to call out. Just take his calls. He phoned her daily, often twice a day. Tali took her to the movies, to the theater, to kosher restaurants, to the Museum of Judaism. They discovered how much their tastes were alike in music, in theater, in books, even in food. They discovered how much they had to give one another.

Tali parked his Mustang in front of Angela's tenement. He hopped to the back, opened the trunk and removed a large valise. Angela looked at him curiously.

"You thinking of moving in?"

"Is that an invitation?"

"Might be if we had the room."

"Well, I'm thinking of a different arrangement."

Israel Jacobs   151

"What might that be?" Angela asked coyly.

Tali said, "We'll talk about that in time. Right now it's not me that's moving in."

"What do you have in that box?"

"Let's go up, and I'll show you."

Tali followed Angela up the four flights. She waved him into the apartment. Gunner sat at the table, a comic book propped against a peanut butter jar. He inspected the valise in Tali's hand.

"Man, if you figurin' on movin' in, you gonna have to sleep on the floor."

Tali laughed. "No need to get yourself all worked up, Gunner, I have no intention of displacing you."

"What you got in that valise?"

Tali snapped the lock. Out flowed assorted pots and pans, plastic utensils, and cuts of meat wrapped in wax paper bags. He looked sternly at Angela. "I'm tired of driving miles to find kosher restaurants. The pots, pans, utensils, the meat. It's all kosher." Tali winked at Gunner. "Think we can trust her to roast us a well-done meat loaf?"

Chapter Twenty Two

"Fabulous," Tali smacked his lips. "That meat loaf was fit for a king. Gunner, we are doubly blessed: beauty and talent in one package. Right?"

"Yeah, man, best meat loaf I ever ate. Kosher ain't bad."

Angela curtsied daintily. "Thank you, gentlemen. Flattery will get you everything." She started to clear the table. Tali untied her apron.

"What did you do that for?"

"Get your coat. We're going out."

Tali pointed to Gunner. "In appreciation of this gourmet dinner you made, I'm sure, he'll be happy to wash the dishes. Showtime is at eight-thirty."

"What show?"

"You'll see when we get there."

Gunner grouched. "You leavin' me to clean up this mess by myself?"

Tali nudged Angela to the door. He fastened the top button of her coat, pressing his palm to her chest. She slapped his hand away.

"Stop that; not in public."

"Gunner is not the public. Anyway your brother has seen it all."

Angela ignored him "It's really not that much, Gunner. Won't take you more than ten minutes. Just wipe down the table with a damp cloth. We'll be back no later than eleven. It'll give you time to bone up for your math test."

"Where you takin' my sister?"

Israel Jacobs   153

"If you must know, Mr. Big Nose, I'm taking her to a movie."

Gunner wiggled his index finger at Tali's nose. "Hah! Look who is callin' me Big Nose. Big Nose hisself," he sulked to Angela.

She said, "Would you like to come along?"

"I don't think this picture is for him," Tali objected.

"Why not? You taking me to a dirty movie?"

Tali raised an eyebrow. "Dirt is in the mind of the beholder."

"You accusing me of a dirty mind?" Angela feigned being offended.

"You are a paragon of virtue," Tali made a serious face. "And I'm not taking you to a dirty movie, not tonight anyway."

"So, why can't he come with us?"

"It's a rough picture. I don't think he's mature enough to handle it."

Gunner danced his hands high over his head, simultaneously wriggling his rump. "Here come da judge, here come da judge. Everybody rise for da judge. He gonna tell us which movies we mature enough to see."

Tali fought to keep a straight face. "Okay, smart aleck, we'll take you along." He turned to Angela. "But remember. I advised against it."

A light drizzle fogged the windshield. Tali switched on the window wipers; they traced two smudged arcs across the windshield. A bus loomed up ahead and rolled to the curb to pick up a queue crouched under umbrellas. Tali honked once, stepped on the accelerator and sped past the bus. He made a sharp left and found a parking space. The marquee announced the movie and star:

THE PAWN BROKER–ROD STEIGER

Tali pushed a ten-dollar bill to the grey-haired woman sitting inside the glass booth. She punched out three tickets and returned his change. The theater was close to empty, twenty to thirty patrons scattered in different sections. An usher beamed them to a seat in the center section.

Angela settled back, wondering why Tali had objected to taking Gunner. Very early in the movie she understood why.

As the story unfolded her stomach began to churn. The flashbacks into the Pawnbroker's horror were gut-wrenching. She cringed into her seat as the Nazi guard forced the pawnbroker to watch his wife sit naked, her eyes a blank, as she waited for German officers to take their turn at raping her. Angela died a little with her. She felt the Pawnbroker's pain as the Nazis reduced him to a living corpse, stripping him layer after layer to his very soul. In the end they stripped him of that as well. Why had Tali taken her to see this picture? She tossed him a resentful look. She tried to avert her eyes. The Pawnbroker's anguish locked her to the screen.

Recollections of stories she had read about German maltreatment of Jews came to mind. She remembered the name Adolf Hitler, the comical dictator with the half-brush mustache and hair falling over one eye. The swastika. Jews gassed in concentration camps. Pictures of skeletons shoveled into mass graves. Angela looked at Tali, sitting grimly in the darkened theater. Gunner slouched in his seat uncommonly quiet. She worried how the picture was affecting him.

She canvassed her own reaction. The picture was hitting her hard. Why did this Jew's agony so disturb her? He suffered no more than her race had endured for centuries. The barbarism inflicted on the Pawnbroker was no worse than what the white man had done to her people. Angela remembered Geronimo, and all the Geronimos turned into living corpses.

A grim-faced S.S. officer wearing jackboots polished to a high shine flashed across the screen. The scene awakened dormant terrors.

Redford's town square swirled uncontrollably in her head: the Confederate soldier with his rifle at the ready, pointing at her. She shut her eyes. The image faded. Two bodies on a slab replaced the soldier. She suppressed a scream, biting into her knuckles. She opened her eyes. Mercifully, the credits were rolling down the screen.

The lights flicked on. The few patrons in the theater stumbled from their seats into the aisles. Tali held Angela's coat. They waited for Gunner to slide into his parka and headed silently to the car. The drizzle had turned into a pelting rain. The gloom reminded Angela of the melancholy trip home from Crescent Hospital the day Geronimo died.

Israel Jacobs 155

They filed up the four flights, holding on to the silence. Angela set a glass of chocolate milk and donut in front of Gunner.

Gunner lifted the cup to his mouth. He looked up at Tali.

"Man, there' a couple of things I don't get about that picture."

"What don't you understand?"

"Why did that Pawnbroker take all that shit from the Germans without fighting back? He was a dead man anyway."

Tali mulled the question over a moment. He had often wondered himself. He said, "At first he probably didn't believe that human beings were capable of doing such horrible things. When he learned otherwise it was too late. He was crushed, there was no fight left in him."

Gunner bit into the donut. "Still can't figure why them Nazis stuck it to the Jews. They white, same as you Jews."

Angela poured two cups of coffee and sat down opposite Tali. She circled the rim of her cup with one finger.

"Tali, do you believe in God? Really believe there's somebody, some power that gives a damn about what happens to us here on earth?"

"Let's forget about God. I've got problems with God, too."

"Aren't rabbis supposed to believe in God?"

"I didn't say I don't believe in God. I said I've got problems with God. He and I have our differences. I have a long list of complaints. From where I sit it looks like God could have done better."

"Then what's the point of it all?"

"The point of what?"

"Religion, prayer, all that mumbo jumbo."

"The point of all that mumbo jumbo, as you call it, is that without God there wouldn't much worthwhile to live for."

"How does God make life worth living?"

"By giving us something to hope for, something to believe in."

"Like what?"

"That life is precious, that the universe didn't make itself, that we're more than the result of an accident, a universe that one day will go poof. Yes, there is brutality and hate, enough to make anyone wonder about God. But there's also goodness, caring people."

"You *are* naive, Rabbi Zeig." Angela was turning combative. "You may be able to forget what the Nazis did to your people. I'm not about to forget what the white world did to mine, and is still doing."

Tali reached out to caress her hand. She pulled away. Tali said, "I haven't forgotten anything. I still say, despite the misery both our people have suffered it's still possible to believe."

"I don't see how."

"I'd like to show you."

"Show me what?"

"Show you belief."

"How do you expect to do that?"

"I'd like you to meet my uncle."

"You never mentioned relatives. You got skeletons in your closet? Maybe some racist rednecks you wanted to keep from me?"

"Don't be cute. I had my reasons."

"What reasons?"

"I didn't think you were ready to meet my family."

"Why not?"

" They're not what you might expect. They're from a different world."

"How are they different?"

"Their life style, the way the dress, the way they worship."

"They're Jews, aren't they?"

"Yes," Tali hesitated, uncertain whether to press on. "But they're a different breed of Jews, they're hasidim."

"I've heard of them. Aren't they're like Christian fundamentalists?"

"Superficially it may seem like it. But, no. They're motivated by different ideologies. Christian fundamentalism is a reaction against too much liberalism. Hasidism is a reaction against too much scholarship."

"I don't understand."

Tali explained. "Judaism venerates scholarship. Study is a form of worship. For example, the Passover festive meal, the *Seder*, is a seminar about freedom. But this overemphasis on scholarship has had its downside. It's drained Judaism of passion and joy. Hasidism tries to strike a balance."

Israel Jacobs   157

"Your uncle is one of these hasidim?"

"Actually, he's the leader of a large hasidic clan."

Angela grimaced, "I don't fit into that crowd. Count me out."

"Please, Angela, I want you to meet my uncle."

"What's the point? You want to turn me into a hasid?"

"I don't expect you to become a hasid, just to meet my uncle."

"Does it mean that much to you, my meeting your uncle?"

"Yes it does. Very much so."

"I didn't bargain for hasids. I'm afraid I'm getting into something way over my head. Okay, you want this so badly, I'll go."

There was little enthusiasm in her voice. Tali worried that he was pressing too hard and too fast.

Gunner broke the tension. "Me, too, I wanna go. I'm not lettin' my sister go alone."

Gladys Bell smiled demurely at Tali. "Nice to see you again, Rabbi Zeig." Gladys was a well endowed shapely brunette, which Tali rarely failed to notice. Not today. He had more serious matters on his mind.

Gladys fluttered long dark eyelashes. "Go right in; Rabbi Heller is expecting you."

Tali stepped into the study. Sanford Heller rose from behind his elegant oval shaped mahogany desk and embraced Tali. "Good to see you."

Rabbi Sanford Heller was a head shorter than Tali, stocky with plump cheeks, double chin and a perpetual twinkle in his eyes.

"Have a seat, Tali. How do you like my new study?"

"Impressive," Tali admired the decor. "Fit for the C.E.O. of General Motors."

"My Board decided that their rabbi's study should reflect the image of the congregation. Rich. How are things going over at your end of town?"

"Good. No complaints. How is Arlene?"

"Great. She's opened her own real estate office. Got three women working for her."

"Arlene is a great lady. You're lucky to have her."

158   *The Convert*

"You can get lucky, too. If you ever decide to settle down."

"Right," Tali said soberly. "That's what I'm here to talk about."

"You're going to put on the ball and chain? Wonderful. About time."

"Well, I've got problems I need to talk to you about."

"Problems, already? If you think you got problems now wait till after you're married a few years."

"Sandy, this is dead serious. Please cut the comedy."

"I promise." Sanford Heller raised his right arm.

"Okay, this may come as a surprise, maybe a shock."

"Oh, Oh, Am I guessing right? Your intended is not Jewish."

"She's not Jewish."

"You scoundrel." Sanford Heller chuckled. "After moralizing to me about officiating at intermarriages. You're gonna marry a non-Jewish girl?"

"That's not the problem. I think she'll convert."

"Then she'll be Jewish on all counts. Nearly half of my congregants are married to converts. So what's the problem?"

"She's black."

Heller's eyes lost their twinkle. "My friend, you have a problem."

"Why should race be a problem in this day and age?"

"Tali, you are naive. I'm the rabbi of a Reform congregation. My congregants pride themselves on being super-liberal. And for the most part they are. But they would shudder at the thought of their rabbi bringing home a black bride. Tell me about her. How did you meet? Where is she from?"

Tali summarized his first meeting with Angela to the present.

"Sandy, you'll think me fishing for texts to make my case, but I've come to believe that rabbinic dictum, *Every day a heavenly voice announces: this man is meant for this woman; this woman is meant for this man.*"

"Tali, you are smitten. But if you want to throw quotes around, have a go at this one: *Matchmaking is as difficult for God as splitting seas.* Add to the normal marriage problems, bringing a black girl from Upper Chelsea to all-white upper-middle class Pineville, I think even God would hesitate. What are you gonna do?"

Israel Jacobs 159

"If she converts, which I think she will, I intend to marry her."

"What about your congregants? How will they react?"

"Que sera sera. Hopefully, they'll accept her. If not, there are other ways to make a living."

"Tali, I sincerely wish you the best of luck. You'll need it."

"Thanks for hearing me out, Sandy. One more thing. I'll need you to serve as a witness to the conversion."

"Gladly. And if you ask me nicely, I'll even be your best man at the wedding."

Chapter Twenty Three

Gunner mimicked the tired shuffle of an octogenarian. "Hey, Tali," he called, curling his mouth to resemble a toothless grin. "She looks like an old granny going to Sunday church."

Angela lifted her ankle-length skirt to her knees. "Tali, is my skirt that ancient looking? Maybe I should change skirts. Do I have to wear a hat? This thing is too big for my face."

Tali said, "Not to fret. You're gorgeous, whatever you wear."

Angela was not consoled.

"Look at it this way, Angela, one day the style will make a comeback."

Angela stamped her foot. "That's not funny."

"Come on Angela, be reasonable. We're not going to a fashion show. All that matters to these people is that you're modestly dressed."

Apprehensive about meeting Tali's family she reluctantly followed him to his car. Gunner bounced into the rear seat. He cranked the window open and poked his head out.

"Get your feet movin', Sis. If you late for the meetin' with Tali's uncle, the hasids gonna shave your head down to the scalp."

"Put your face back in the car, Gabriel, or I'll zip your mouth."

"Ain't nobody fast enough to zip my mouth, least of all you. And quit calling me Gabriel."

"You ashamed of your Christian name, GABRIEL?"

"The hasids gonna scalp you, the hasids gonna scalp you."

Israel Jacobs 161

Gunner ducked back into the car, narrowly escaping Angela's palm. He settled into the seat, belly-laughing at his sister.

Angela slid into the passenger seat next to Tali. His disregard for her fears irritated her. Easy for him to act so damn cool; he was no stranger to hasids. He may have left their life-style, but it still simmered. It isn't that simple to jettison childhood experiences; Angela knew that first hand.

And she knew Tali well enough by now to recognize that a part of him remained bonded to his former life. That was why he needed his uncle's approval. In some odd way that made him even more appealing. But could she accommodate to that part of him? She realized major changes to her life would be required of her, but she was not prepared to make herself over to their specifications, to anyone's specifications.

Her apprehension intensified. Tali had started her on the road to Judaism. It was a complex confusing journey, Kosher, Sabbath, God, Covenant, the glory and burden of a chosen people, Jewish suffering, the Holocaust, Zionism. It was much to digest. How much of the connection she had begun to feel for Judaism was intertwined with her feeling for Tali? She could live with these questions. But his family? Pictures of hasids massing for some rally or celebrating some Jewish festival appeared in the newspapers now and again. Occasionally, she encountered a hasid on the subway. She hadn't paid them heed. They seemed weird with earlocks curled around their ears, dressed in black hats and black suits.

Tali splashed through puddles flooding the streets since the previous night's downpour. The numbered signs changed to foreign sounding names: Kosciusko, Pulaski, Schermerhorn. This was Angela's first trip downtown. The names were strange, not the sights. The same garbage overflowing into the streets, the same depressing tenements as in Upper Chelsea. Tali forged confidently through the streets, as if familiar with every pothole. He turned right into Brussel Street and decelerated. The north curb was packed bumper to bumper. He searched for a vacant spot. Gunner tapped his shoulder.

"You got plenty space on the other side; why don't you park

there?"

"After nine it's illegal," Tali pointed to the warning sign:

No Parking Monday Wednesday Friday 9 a.m.–2 p.m.

"They mean it when they say, no parking. I ignored it once. They towed my car away. Cost me twenty-five dollars to get it back."

Tali circled the block. A middle-aged black man escorted a heavily rouged teenager who was wearing a tight fitting miniskirt to a maroon Cadillac. The man wore a gold pendant over his checkered blazer. A sudden gust lifted the girl's skirt above her buttocks. The man hurriedly tucked her into the Cadillac and sped off. Tali promptly backed his car into the vacated space. Two black youths, huddling in the doorway, regarded Tali suspiciously. He shepherded Angela and Gunner toward a four-story walk-up. A high stoop rose to the first floor. Below street level an iron gate, secured by a heavy padlock, guarded the basement entrance. Two taller and much wider buildings, which appeared to have been recently renovated, straddled the center building.

YESHIVA OHEV TSEDEK was inscribed on the facade of the building to the right. A large billboard fronting the left building announced in bold letters:

SAMUEL AND FRIEDA ROSENBERG DORMITORY.

Tali guided Angela and Gunner through an archway over which CONGREGATION OHEV TSEDEK was sculpted in bas-relief. They entered a dimly-lit vestibule. A slice of daylight peeked through a narrow casement window. One low-hanging light-fixture provided the main source of illumination. Two doors led off from the vestibule. A metal placard was screwed into each of the doors, which directed, *Men to the right. Women to the left.*

Tali pointed to the left, "You go that way."

Angela said, "I don't have to."

"It's not a bathroom," Tali chuckled. "That's the entrance to the women's gallery."

"We don't stay together?"

"We part company here. You'll be able to see and hear all."

Tali opened the door; he prodded Angela to enter. She hesitated.

"They won't eat you. Really, they're very friendly people."

Israel Jacobs 163

Angela appeared doubtful. Tali pushed her gently through the door. He motioned Gunner to the right. "We go that way."

Gunner poked his head into the room. "I ain't goin' in there by myself."

About two-hundred men, bearded and wearing broad-brimmed black hats and black knee-length jackets, sat around long rectangular tables arranged in horseshoe style. Fifty or so teen-age boys, some with incipient beards still in the fuzz stage, occupied one arm of the horseshoe. Long earlocks threaded down their cheeks or were draped around their ears.

"Man, they look like they all undertakers," Gunner whispered.

"Go in," Tali urged.

Gunner declined. "Man, you lead the way."

The tables were set with paper plates and white paper napkins. Plastic utensils, and dishes overflowing with nuts and sliced fruit loaded the tables. Platters of pickled and tomato herring were being passed from hand to hand. The platters rapidly emptied as the diners shoveled bountiful portions of herring into individual plastic dishes, sliced them into bite-sized chunks and chewed with much palate-smacking and tongue-clicking. A tall, heavy set man, standing at the head of the horseshoe and holding a long serrated knife, was sawing an enormous braided bread. The men poured generous doses of wine and whiskey from half-gallon flasks and pint-sized whiskey bottles into paper cups and shot-glasses. The underage crowd guzzled soft drinks, some drinking straight from bottles, their earlocks dangling as they tilted their heads to get at the last drop. Dark wine splotches soiled the tablecloths. A short stocky woman wearing a skirt and blouse that covered her from neck to ankles and a kerchief on her head had Angela by the arm. She took turns introducing Angela to one group of women then another, all similarly dressed in kerchiefs and long skirts. Other than the sound of dining and sporadic low-keyed conversation among the elders seated at the head table, the men's side of the room seemed unnaturally quiet.

Gunner murmured, "This a party or a wake?"

164 *The Convert*

"A party. Jews don't have wakes."
"Quietest party I ever seen."
"Don't worry, it'll liven up soon."

The man seated at the head of the horseshoe captured Gunner's attention. A thick red beard flecked with grey streaks, which he stroked with his thumb and forefinger, flowed down to his chest. His hat, of felt material and shaped like a helmet with a wide fur brim, was slightly tilted upwards. He wore a silk caftan that fell to his shoes. His wide forehead was smooth and so delicately white it appeared almost transparent. He darted a quick glance in Tali's direction then shifted to the side, as if not wanting to call attention to his entrance. The high forehead and flaring nostrils, the eyes that projected happiness and sadness at the same time bore a striking resemblance to Tali.

An auburn-bearded young man about Tali's age, who resembled the red-bearded patriarch even more than Tali, sat immediately to the right of the horseshoe next to the head table. He took note of Tali and grimaced. Several older men, seated in the same section, followed the young man's glare, gave Tali a cursory nod and returned to their food. The young man continued to stare at Tali with unfriendly eyes. Gunner trailed after Tali. They squeezed between the tables and found seats at the right arm of the horseshoe.

Gunner nudged Tali. "Who's the beard at the head table?"

"He's my uncle, the Sumtara Rebbe."

"The what?"

"The Sumtara Rebbe. His name is Dov Ber Zeig. Hasidim refer to their rabbi by their native city. My uncle served as rabbi in Sumtara, a city in Romania, and his father before him."

"That where you were born?"

"No, I was born in this country. My parents came from Sumtara."

"What about the dude with the red beard; the one giving us the eye? That your uncle's son?"

"Yeah. That's my cousin Heschel."

Tali dropped into a chair two tables removed from the Sumtara Rebbe and motioned Gunner to sit next to him.

Israel Jacobs   165

The wall-clock slung over the head table read ten-fifteen. Gunner hadn't had time for breakfast. The herring made his mouth water. Tali signaled it was okay to eat. Gunner speared a herring, made a sandwich with a twist roll and stuffed it into his mouth. Tali mumbled a prayer. The hasid at his side said, "Amen," and resumed eating. Tali ripped into a roll, chewed it thoroughly then jabbed at the herring.

A robust hasid, with a square black beard, strolled to the head-table carrying a large uncut herring on a platter. The Rebbe scanned one wing of the horseshoe, then the other. He settled his gaze on Tali for a moment, craned toward Heschel and said something in Yiddish to the hasid carrying the herring platter. The Rebbe cut a small slice, nibbled at it and handed the platter back to the hasid. He passed it to Heschel. The Rebbe's son snagged a piece with his fork and passed the platter on to the man at his side. The platter circulated the room, each hasid plucking a piece for himself. The plate reached Tali. He picked at it with his fingers and offered the plate to Gunner. He declined and passed it to the man next to him. Gunner watched the plate move on to the teenagers at the far end of the table. Gunner recalled a sermon his pastor had delivered about the "Miracle of the Loaves." The Sumtara Rebbe had just dittoed Jesus, with a herring.
"Why did they pass around the Rebbe's herring?"
"Hasidim think it's a great honor to eat the Rebbe's leftovers. The tradition is called, *Sherayim*."

A low-pitched wordless tune billowed from the Rebbe. It rippled from the head table to both ends of the horseshoe. At first the hasidim hummed the melody softly then lifted it to joyous, contagious beats. Lyrics were added to the melody. Gradually, Gunner made out the words, CHEERIE BEEM BEEM DYE DYE... One section sang CHEERIE BEEM BEEM BEEM. Another picked up the refrain with, DYE DYE DYE. The room exploded with song. Cheerie beems and dye dyes bounced off the walls, flowing from hasid to hasid, blending, fusing the hasidim into one rapturous body. The rhythms excited Gunner's feet to thump out the beats. He felt himself tripping into

166 *The Convert*

ecstasy. Tali already appeared to be in paradise.

The Sumtara Rebbe bolted from his chair. He gripped a polished ivory-topped cane in his left hand, tapping the floor in time to the rhythms. The hasidim made a circle around the Rebbe, clapping and stamping their feet.

The Rebbe began to dance.

He moved his wrist in tighter, faster circles, gliding and swaying from side to side. The singing and clapping picked up speed. It waxed louder. The excitement mounted. The Rebbe danced faster, twisting and dipping, tossing the cane from one hand to another, lifting it high above the hasidim, almost striking the ceiling fixture on several passes. He skipped and hopped, his cane rising and falling to the beat of the singing and furious clapping.

The hasidim interlocked arms and danced around the Rebbe, circling to the left then to the right. Tali grabbed Gunner by the hand and dragged him into the circle. A young sallow-faced hasid, with earlocks flying, locked arms with Gunner. The dancers spun around the Rebbe faster and faster. The beat whipped Gunner's feet on; they seemed to barely touch the floor. Gunner found the words; they poured out of him, as if he had been singing them all his life, CHEERIE BEEM BEEM BEEM...

Gradually, the dancing came to a halt. Heschel escorted his perspiring father back to the head table. Tali and Gunner filed back to their seats, both sweating and panting. Four women journeyed in and out from the rear room carrying trays laden with food, which they dispersed evenly around the tables. Steaming kugels and strudle and compote; dishes Gunner had never before tasted. He ate ravenously, no sooner finishing one helping then stacking another onto his plate. He pushed a fourth helping away.

"Nu! Naphtali can still dance like a hasid."

The remark, made by Heschel to his father but clearly meant to be heard by all present, stilled the room. The Rebbe drummed on the table with nervous fingers.

"It is too bad that Naphtali doesn't live like a hasid."

The Rebbe drummed harder; his eyes flashed a warning.

Israel Jacobs 167

"Tell me Naphtali, how does one dance like a hasid and live like a goy?"

The Rebbe's fist slammed to the table.

"Enough."

Heschel swerved to his father. "The sages say, 'These are the ones who will not inherit the world to come: he who denies resurrection, he who denies revelation, he who—'"

"I do not need you to tell me what the sages say," the Rebbe cut off Heschel in mid-sentence. "Let me remind you that he who shames another in public is as one who commits murder."

The Rebbe's censure produced a hush, muting even the women who had been chattering away in the ladies' gallery. In the male section the hasidim studiously avoided both Tali and the head table. Tali leaned back, evidencing little shame. He grinned at his cousin. Heschel curled his lips in silent contempt. The hasidim held their silence, most of them staring down at the tables and fidgeting with their utensils. A long sigh surged from the Rebbe.

"Has not sufficient suffering been meted to us by Israel's enemies? Need we add to our pain?" The Rebbe shook his head sadly. "For baseless hatred between Jews, the Holy Temple was destroyed."

Heschel's face reddened. "I do not hate Naphtali. But what I do feel is not without cause."

"Perhaps it is not without cause," the Rebbe conceded in a tired voice, "but it is without understanding." The Rebbe's eyes swept across the tables. They stopped at Tali and lingered tenderly.

"Naphtali is my sainted brother's son, may the righteous be remembered for blessing. Life has not dealt you the blow it has dealt Naphtali. God did not make of you an orphan. You have no right to judge another until you have stood in his place, endured what he has endured.

"And I will say one more thing about this matter, after which I do not want to hear any more from you about Naphtali."

An unnatural stillness hung over the tables. The Rebbe's fingers combed his beard, as if he was gripped by questions he had long been asking himself, to which he had found no answers.

"God's ways are not our ways. His thoughts are not our thoughts. Outside these walls, which have sheltered you, Heschel, live millions of Jews we cannot reach; we do not even know how to talk to them. Naphtali is the bridge between us. One day the Master of the Universe, blessed be His name, will unite Israel into one people again. Until then we must have a bridge, else there will be little left of Israel to reunite. That bridge is sacred. And I tell you, Heschel, for you have been spared the knowledge of it, to be a bridge between two worlds is to carry a fearful burden. The human heart longs to find a home on one side or the other."

The Rebbe slapped his palm sharply to the table. "Now I want to hear from my son, Shmuel. This is his *simba*."

A boy about Gunner's age, squashed between the Rebbe and a man with a luxurious white beard, reared up. Until the boy got to his feet, Gunner hadn't noticed him. He had dark, closely cropped hair, partly visible under his black hat, which was tilted high on his forehead. One earlock dangled to his shoulder; the other he twirled nervously around his forefinger. The men at the tables smiled up at him. Several of the younger boys at the far end of the horseshoe started up a clatter. They were quickly silenced by their seniors. Shmuel stared straight ahead, tensely licking his upper lip.

The elder at the boy's side nodded.

Shmuel rocketed into a Yiddish and Hebrew monologue, stopping only to catch his breath. The speech, delivered in a quivering falsetto, seemed to make a favorable impression on the audience. Despite the rapid-fire talk, Gunner recognized several Hebrew words, *Shabbos, tallis, shalom*. The Yiddish was totally foreign. Shmuel accentuated his Hebrew differently than Tali; the English with which he occasionally punctuated his talk was the same as any American-born white boy's. Shmuel synchronized his super-charged delivery with spirited thumb motions. He employed his thumb like a sword, thrusting and jabbing at the air to emphasize major points. In concert with his thumb maneuvers he rocked animatedly to and fro from the waist up. At several points he paused and wrinkled his brow like an old sage.

The Sumtara Rebbe beamed, his angry exchange with Heschel

Israel Jacobs 169

apparently forgotten.

Gunner nudged Tali. "What's this about?"

"The Rebbe's youngest son, Shmuel, has become a bar mitzvah. This is his bar mitzvah lecture."

"How many's he got."

"How many what?"

"How many sons does the Rebbe have?"

"Six. Six sons and five daughters."

"Man, that's procreatin'."

"Where did you pick up that word?"

"I'm not dumb. I read."

Tali chuckled. "Hasidim believe in large families."

Shmuel gave a final thumb jab. He wiped his brow and dropped into his chair, grinning ear to ear.

The Rebbe clasped Shmuel's hand. From the audience clusters of hasidim marched to the head table, congratulated the Rebbe and shook Shmuel's hand, *"Yasher koah*—well done, you made our Rebbe proud."

Shmuel's peers back-slapped him vigorously. The Rebbe waited for the felicitations to ebb. Finally, the last of the well-wishers wandered back to their chairs. The hasid at the Rebbe's side, a white bearded patriarchal figure, raised his hand for silence. Conversation ceased.

The Rebbe began to speak.

The hasidim directed their attention to the head table, taking in the Rebbe's every gesture. The Rebbe delivered his talk in a sing-song chant, sitting with palms crossed and swaying slightly. Gunner extracted the few English phrases the Rebbe tucked in between the Hebrew and Yiddish. He whispered questions to Tali hoping to get the gist, of the Rebbe's talk. After a few minutes he gave up. Strangely, Gunner felt himself picking up a message without words, a message more compelling than anything he had experienced listening to wordy preachers whose language he understood.

Precisely at noon the festivities concluded. The guests shuffled over to the head table in small groups, offered a final *yasher koah* to the Rebbe and bar mitzvah. Heschel stayed to the last. He shook Shmuel's

170   *The Convert*

hand energetically, turned, walked past Tali and exited.

An after-party stillness enveloped the room. Scores of empty platters and overturned bottles lay helter-skelter on the soiled table-cloths. The quiet contrasted starkly with the earlier raucous. The Rebbe broke into the silence.

"She is with you?"

"Yes," Tali said.

"Will she convert?"

"I think she will."

The Rebbe spoke in English, making Gunner feel a part of the conversation.

"If she converts, there can be no objection to the marriage. She will be a Jew in every respect. But what of your congregation? Your friends? God commands that all Jews live as brothers. Especially, does the law require that we treat converts with respect and love. Unfortunately, children do not always obey their earthly parents, and they do not always pay heed to their Heavenly Father. Are you prepared to face the consequences of such a marriage?"

"I love her, Uncle. With God's help I'll deal with the problems."

"What of her? Will she be able to live with the double burden of being black and a Jew?"

"Uncle, I can't guarantee how she will feel tomorrow. I don't know how I will feel tomorrow. I know I love her. I know that she's strong. Her experiences have made her strong. And I intend to be there whenever she needs me and help her every step of the way."

"What of your congregation. Will they accept her?"

"I hope so. I don't know for sure. I... I do know we'll all be the better for it if they do."

"You think a black *rebbitzen* will persuade your congregants to keep kosher, to observe Shabbos, to study?"

"I don't have that in mind."

"What do you have in mind?"

Absentmindedly, Tali played with a plastic fork. It snapped, breaking the stillness. He said, "My people are demolishing the base on

Israel Jacobs   171

which the entire Jewish structure rests—compassion, concern for others, integrity. They are fast becoming pagans. Only their own pleasures matter. They're selfish, tribal-minded. They care only for themselves."

"And because their rabbi marries a black woman they will suddenly change into sensitive caring people?"

"Who knows? Maybe it will shock them into considering that there's more to being a Jew than bagels and lox and being born of a Jewish mother."

The Rebbe stood up, rising as tall as his nephew. "I will speak to her." He gestured toward an alcove that seemed to have been added on to the room as an afterthought. A door led into the Rebbe's study. He motioned Tali and Gunner to follow.

Bookshelves lined the room from ceiling to floor. Every shelf was crammed with books. The room swarmed with books. The window ledges were piled with books. Large tomes jutted from shelves not wide enough to enclose their bulk. The Rebbe strode to a long rectangular table littered with notes and more books. He sat down and pointed to several chairs lining the opposite wall. Tali pulled two chairs to the table. He and Gunner sat down. A heavy footstep intruded into the silence.

The woman, who had earlier taken charge of Angela in the women's gallery, escorted her into the room. Her dark eyes and rotund face, her plump squat figure dramatically resembled Shmuel. She stopped at the threshold, took stock of the men, and urged Angela toward the table. She whispered to the Rebbe then retreated to the back. She dropped into a chair, firmly crossing her arms over her portly bosom. Tali gave Angela his chair and pulled up another one for himself.

The Rebbe made small circles on his brow with two fingers; his broad-brimmed hat cast a shadow over his forehead. He studied Angela solemnly. After a long moment of silence he spoke.

"I requested that Naphtali bring you here, not to pass judgment on your plans to marry. These are things for you both to decide. I wanted to meet you, to see you personally. And I thought it important that you see us, see where Naphtali was raised, his roots. Where he studied and

172   *The Convert*

grew to be an adult before he went out into the world."

Angela sat with hands folded, listening wordlessly. Not once, Tali noted, had his uncle mentioned Angela by name. Despite the omission, Tali sensed that his uncle was reaching out, that he was concerned and interested in the well-being of this strange woman his nephew intended to wed.

"Naphtali informed me that he has been giving you and your brother lessons in the Jewish faith."As he did with Angela, the Rebbe acknowledged Gunner's presence without mentioning him by name. "Is there anything you care to ask me regarding Naphtali, or our religion?"

The scene quickened Tali's imagination. It was a Solomon—Queen-of-Sheba tableau. The contrasts of light and shadow in the book-crammed study. Beautiful, bronze-skinned Angela staring across the antique table at the Sumtara Rebbe, spiritual leader of a sect that spanned a century and encompassed thousands of hasidim the world over. In the rear, his aunt chaperoning, silent as a stone.

Angela met the Sumtara Rebbe's gaze with questioning eyes.

"I love Aron Naphtali. But I don't know if I will ever understand Judaism, the demands it makes; not the ritual part, but the faith part."

At some point in their relationship, Tali couldn't precisely locate the time or specific reason, Angela had dropped her anger and come to love him as he did her. Still, he was taken by surprise. She had not demonstrated such feeling before. And pronouncing his full name! It made his skin tingle. He didn't recall telling her what the "A" stood for. He could barely control himself from taking her in his arms and covering her mouth with kisses.

"Judaism expects you to believe that God is just; that He created man in His image. I wish I could believe it was true. But everything I've experienced contradicts it. I've read some Jewish history since I met Naphtali. It's so full of pain, so much sorrow. Persecution, massacres. Jews have been damned, tortured, raped, as blacks have been. Not by wild savages, but by civilized barbarians. And yet,...yet you haven't given up on God or man. With all you've suffered you still believe. How have Jews managed to live with such horror without affecting their faith in God, in man, without abandoning the hope that it will

Israel Jacobs   173

ever get better?"

The Rebbe swayed, as if praying. His beard brushed against the page of an open tome, causing the paper to fold underneath itself. He ran his thumb down the crease and carefully closed the book.

"Your questions do not have simple answers." The Rebbe wrinkled his brow into deep furrows. "But this you should know. It is not true that our suffering has not affected us." Laboriously, he lifted himself from his chair. "I will show you and tell you something I hope you will not forget, no matter what you and Naphtali decide."

The Sumtara Rebbe removed his caftan, folded it neatly and draped it on the back of his chair. Over his shirt he wore a white woolen cloth with black stripes that fitted over his head. At each end of the four-cornered garment long thick threads were tucked under his belt. He rolled up his left sleeve and reached across the table.

"Here are the numbers they branded on me."

Angela winced.

"On millions of Jews they branded numbers, as if we were cattle. And like cattle they slaughtered us."

The Rebbe rolled back his sleeve, buttoned the cuff and put on his caftan. He stood tall and slightly stooped, the memory of indescribable torment marched across his face.

"We were not affected? You are wrong, my child. Every Jew who lived through that horror was affected. We came out, those who survived, broken in body and spirit. Yes, I, too, cried to God, 'Show Yourself. Give us to understand why. Let us know, at least, that this is Your will, and not without purpose—a world gone mad.' I heard no answer. I still hear no answer. Yes, I was affected. All of us were affected in one way or another. One death-camp Jew who survived with me, a cousin, came out with an uncontrollable urge to smash windows. My obsession was the reverse. Whenever I saw something broken—a chair, a table, no matter how old, even a useless stick, I was driven to repair it, to glue it together. This has been the Jewish neurosis since the beginning, to repair what others smash. To mend, to try to make whole what the world breaks. And, yes, you are correct. Again and again the world has tried to break the Jewish people. I cannot say

174   *The Convert*

why. Perhaps to be a fixer one must first be broken."

Angela shook her head. "There's so much to be fixed. So many broken people, so broken they're nothing but garbage. Why did God create a world filled with so much garbage, so much human gar—"

"I don't know what God has in mind," the rebbe cut her off sharply. "What I do know is that God does not create garbage. God creates man in His image. It is man who turns the Divine image into garbage."

A weariness crept into the Rebbe's demeanor. His tone softened. "But it need not be so." He removed a tome from an upper shelf, opened it and shuffled through the pages.

"Rabbi Haninah said in the name of the Holy One, blessed be He, *The human eye contains both black and white. Vision is derived from the black.* It is the dark moments of our history that have deepened our compassion. Perhaps that is why we have been destined to suffer."

The Rebbe closed the tome and regarded Angela warmly.

"How did you and Naphtali meet?"

Tali answered, "It's an incredible story, Uncle. One unbelievable coincidence piled on another."

Sorrow and tenderness mingled in the Rebbe's eyes. He said softly, looking at Tali, but directing his words to Angela and Gunner. "Naphtali, I know that you have come to question everything. I understand. We all do at one time or another. Many times in the Camps both your father and I, experiencing the horror, the depths that human beings could descend, questioned. How could there be a God that allows this to happen to his chosen people, to innocent children? Many who once believed came to the conclusion that there is no sense to anything. There is no Judge and no judgment in this world. There is only accident, coincidence as you put it. Hopefully, you will one day relearn this truth: What we see with our mortal eyes as accident, as coincidence, is the *Ribono shel olam*—the Master of the Universe— making Himself anonymous.

"Now tell me how you met."

Chapter Twenty Four

A couple dismounted from a bicycle-built-for-two and strolled to the water's edge. They stood holding hands, silently staring into the lake. The water shimmered like silver beads. In the distance, an office building skyrocketed thirty stories high, its shadow covering half the lake. Tali circled the lake slowly, steering with one hand, the other resting on Angela's lap. "Stop here for a while, Tali, it's so lovely and peaceful."

Tali pulled to the side, keeping the motor in idle.

Angela said, "Your uncle mentioned you lost your father when you were very young. What happened?"

"He never recovered from what they did to him in Buchenwald."

"And your mother?"

"She died not long after. My aunt and uncle raised me."

"Tali I have a question. You are a rabbi; your uncle is called Rebbe. What's the difference? Does it have something to do with scholarship? Age?"

"Let's see how to explain."

Angela snuggled in close. "Go on."

" Maybe the best way to describe it is, Rabbis like me preach sermons. A rebbe like my uncle is a sermon."

Angela said, "I'm ready, Aron Naphtali."

"Ready for what?"

"Ready to convert to Judaism. That's why you wanted me to meet your uncle, wasn't it?"

Tali cut the engine. "Yes, I've been waiting for you to say that."

"In all this time you haven't mentioned conversion. Why?"

"Jewish law prohibits pressuring a non-Jew to convert."

"I love you Aron Naphtali, and you've made me love Judaism. I want to convert."

Tali covered her mouth with his. His elbow hit the horn; it blasted into the quiet, startling the lovers at the lake's edge.

"Me, too," Gunner made his presence felt. "I want to convert, too."

Tali disengaged himself from Angela.

"Okay, Gunner, we'll make it a doubleheader."

Tali had summarized the conversion rituals to Angela and Gunner. He had explained that a *mikveh*—a ritualarium—is primarily used by women who have completed the requisite period following menstruation. Only after immersion in the mikveh may husband and wife cohabit. This ritualarium, Tali elaborated, was also used for conversion purposes.

The anteroom projected a quiet intimacy, a divan, two love seats, several cane-backed chairs, pretty lamps and a wine-colored rug. A trellis with climbing vines separated the anteroom from a partially visible room to the right. To the left, a glass partition allowed a view of the ritualarium's tiny office. A thin, sharply-featured woman fluttered about inside. Gunner refused to budge from his chair.

"No, I ain't gonna let nobody stick me. I changed my mind."

Tali shrugged. "Okay. If you want to back out, I'll tell Reverend Stern he can leave. He's a busy man. I can't expect him to wait around all day."

"What about Angela?"

"She's going through the conversion. As planned."

"It's easy for her. All she has to do is take a bath."

"That's the way it goes. I don't make the rules."

"That mean she's gonna be Jewish, and not me?"

"It appears that way."

Israel Jacobs 177

In his first burst of enthusiasm Gunner had assumed that conversion involved standing up in a Jewish church and making a decision for Judaism; maybe having holy water sprinkled on him. On learning what was involved his ardor cooled considerably.

"I been circumcised when I was a baby. I ain't got that much to spare."

Tali laughed. "The mohel will not circumcise you. I promise."

"Good. Then all I got to do is take a bath in the mikveh. Right?"

"No. As I explained to you the law requires a *tipat dahm*—a symbolic circumcision, drawing a drop of blood."

Gunner's hand dived to his groin. "What kind of blood-thirsty religion you rabbi of?"

"It's just a drop. You won't even feel it."

"How does he draw the blood? How big is the needle?"

Tali measured a tiny circle with his thumb and forefinger. "Just an itsy jab with a needle."

"Jab a needle into my dick? No deal. It ain't no pincushion."

"I tell you it won't hurt. One quick jab, and it's over."

Gunner conjured up a nightmare—one quick jab, and the wind would be whistling through the hole. "But why, if I already been circumcised?"

Tali had covered this ground several times. "Because, as I have already explained, the circumcision must be performed with the intent to convert. It's like becoming an American citizen. First you declare your intention by filing citizenship papers. Then you take a test. If you pass, you swear allegiance before a judge. Only then are you a citizen with all the privileges and responsibilities. Same with conversion. It's the intention that makes circumcision a religious ritual. Otherwise, it's just an operation."

"Can't I dip myself in the mikveh a couple of extra times instead, with the intention of converting? Won't that prove I have good intentions?"

"It won't prove anything, except you're afraid of a little blood. Let's forget the whole thing. Maybe you just don't have what it takes to be a Jew."

178   *The Convert*

"You saying I'm afraid of a little blood?"

"Well, you tell me. Are you?"

Gunner thrust out his chin. "I'm no coward."

"Do you want to convert? Yes or no? Make up your mind."

"I made up my mind. If Angela's gonna be Jewish, so'm I."

"Good. I think Reverend Stern is ready to do the circumcision."

Gunner felt his knees go weak. He put on a brave face and followed Tali into the circumcision chamber. The late morning sun poured though the blinds splashing a cheerful striated pattern of light and shadow on the sky-blue walls. Gunner saw neither sunshine nor sky-blue walls. He had eyes only for the table in the center of the room. It rested ominously, waist-high, on four chrome legs with black leather cushioning, just wide enough and long enough to accommodate a large-sized body.

Tali introduced Gunner to the mohel. "This is the young man I told you about. He's a little nervous."

Reverend Stern grinned down at Gunner. A gap separated his two front teeth, which pinched into his lower lip. He was slightly built, though tall, with a goatee that came to a point just above his Adam's apple. He wore a white tunic, loosely fitted and belted in the back. "No need to be nervous, young fellow. It will be over before you know it."

Reverend Stern's voice sounded exactly right for his profession, thin and slicing. Gunner watched the mohel open a sinister looking brown satchel.

Reverend Stern patted the table. "Drop your trousers and lie down."

Gunner stumbled backward. The moment of truth was at hand. Reverend Stern beckoned for him to step forward. He fumbled with his belt. His trousers crumpled to the floor.

"Now the shorts, please."

Gunner obeyed like a programmed robot. The briefs fell away. A draft scooted up his bare rump.

"Very good. Now lie down."

Meekly, Gunner lay on his back. The light fixture overhead ogled at him. His body stiffened.

Israel Jacobs

"Relax, young fellow."

The frozen grin on the mohel inched closer. Gunner felt the man's hot breath. He dug his nails into the leather cushioning. Suddenly, cold alcohol splashed between his legs. He felt a powerful urge to urinate. Reverend Stern recited a blessing in Hebrew. As from a distance, Gunner heard two voices answer, Amen. Then a slight sting. He closed his eyes.

"How do you feel?"

Gunner opened his eyes. "Okay, I'm ready. Go ahead."

Reverend Stern looked puzzled. "Go ahead with what?"

"With the circumcision," Gunner shrieked. "Go ahead before I change my mind." He gritted his teeth and shut his eyes again.

"It's finished."

"What's finished?" Gunner muttered between clenched teeth.

"The *tipat dahm*, it's done."

Gunner bolted into a sitting position. He searched between his thighs. "It's all there. In one piece. Thank you, Lord."

Reverend Stern chuckled. Tali looked on with a big smile. Gunner thought they looked beautiful. The world looked beautiful. He became aware of a stranger he hadn't noticed enter the room. The stranger stood behind the mohel, grinning from ear to ear. Gunner hopped off the table. The stranger strutted toward him.

"You were splendid, son. Welcome into the fold."

Tali said, "This is a friend of mine. Rabbi Sanford Heller. I asked him to be a witness to your conversion."

"It was a privilege."

Rabbi Heller had little round eyes that twinkled merrily. He was short, barely reaching to Tali's shoulder. He impressed Gunner as a chunky cheerful character. The rabbi pumped Gunner's hand enthusiastically.

"Am I Jewish now?"

"Almost," Tali said. "After immersion in the mikveh your conversion will be officially completed."

"Lead me to it, man," Gunner gushed, overjoyed at emerging from the *tipat dahm* ordeal intact.

180 *The Convert*

"It'll be a while yet. Angela is going in first."

"Whatever you say."

Gunner trooped after the two rabbis. The woman behind the glass partition pointed the way.

"Rabbis, she is prepared."

Tali about-faced. "Reverend Stern! Where is he?"

"I'm coming. I'm coming," the mohel sprinted into the anteroom clutching his satchel. "I had to clean my instruments."

Gunner and the three men followed the woman to a door in the rear. She disappeared inside.

Gunner said, "What happens now?"

"Angela is in the mikveh. The three of us constitute a *bet din*—a Jewish court. We have to witness the immersion."

"Does Angela wear anything when she gets dunked?"

"Not when she goes down. Nothing may intervene between the body and the water. She has to be completely nude."

"You mean, you three cats are gonna watch my sister bathe all naked? Can't you take that old lady's word that Angela's in the mikveh?"

Rabbi Heller's eyes scoffed. "A *bet din*, a Jewish court, can't take anything for granted. We have to sign on the dotted line that your sister was dunked. So we've got to personally make sure all is kosher."

"Look, Sandy," Tali growled. "Cut the comedy. I know how you feel about the mikveh. All I'm asking is that you be a witness. When you convert your people, do it your way."

Gunner said, "There's other ways to become Jewish?"

"Yes, Gunner my boy, there are other—"

Tali cut his friend off in mid-sentence. "Rabbi Heller is a Reform Rabbi. He doesn't consider this part of the ritual necessary."

Gunner thumbed at Sanford Heller. "Ain't he a rabbi?"

"Yes, he's a rabbi. But our ideas about Jewish law differ."

"So who's right? I mean, which one of you rabbis am I supposed to listen to after I'm Jewish?"

Heller barged in again, this time refusing to yield until he had his say. "That's a decision you'll have to make for yourself. After you've

Israel Jacobs 181

studied more, and had time to think about the differences. Right now it's important that you know there are differences."

"Okay, Sandy, you've made your point. Since I'm responsible for this conversion, we'll do it my way. Now let's get on with it. Mrs. Weintraub doesn't have all day. And neither do I."

The two men squared off into a glaring contest.

"Nu, Rabbis. She is waiting for you," Mrs. Weintraub reminded them in a shrill voice.

Tali shrugged and followed Mrs. Weintraub. Heller and Reverend Stern trailed.

"Wait for me," Gunner shouted, "I wanna watch what goes on."

"Yes, maybe you'd better," Tali said, throwing visual barbs at Sanford Heller. "I don't want you getting wild ideas about what goes on in a mikveh."

The alcove opened to an opaque glass door. Imprinted on the glass in cursive writing was the one word, mikveh. A white card swinging from the end of a short string announced, MIKVEH IN USE.

Mrs. Weintraub opened the door a crack and slid her head into the alcove. She gestured for the men to retreat a step, opened the door a bit wider and squeezed into the alcove. Reverend Stern threw a cuff and glanced at his wrist watch, muttering that he had another circumcision scheduled.

"All right, Rabbis," Mrs. Weintraub's shrill voice reverberated into the alcove. "She is in the water. You may now enter."

Gunner wiggled between the rabbis and peered into the brightly lit room. The mikveh was tiled in pink and white. He looked down from the narrow balcony into a miniature swimming pool. Five steps dropped to the bottom of the crystal clear water. A rail, clamped to the wall, sloped parallel to the steps, reaching almost to the floor. Gunner's view was partially blocked by a supporting column. He pressed around the post, hoping to catch a glimpse of Angela. He discovered her curled to one side wrapped in a sheet from her neck down to her toes. Mrs. Weintraub ordered her to the center.

"Rabbis, you see she is in the water?"

182   *The Convert*

Tali stepped to the ledge. "Yes, Mrs. Weintraub we are witnesses that she is in the water."

Gunner poked his head further in. Tali crouched over the railing.

"I ask you now, in the presence of this *bet din*, do you, Angela Adams, of your own free will choose the Jewish faith as your own?"

"I do," Angela answered firmly.

"Do you renounce allegiance to all other faiths and religions?"

"I do."

"Do you accept the truth that there is but one God, the creator of man and the universe, and that only He is to be worshiped?"

"I do."

"Do you pledge to abide, to the best of your ability, by the laws and traditions of the Torah, as interpreted by our sages and teachers?"

"I so pledge."

"You will now immerse yourself three times as directed by Mrs. Weintraub. By this immersion you will be spiritually reborn, cleansed of all sins and become a true daughter of Israel."

Gunner pressed close to the railing, bumping his shins against a crossbar. He let out a yelp. Angela looked up, saw him and smiled. She seemed so small and alone. Gunner hung over the railing and saluted.

"She must now drop the sheet and dip herself completely into the water." Mrs. Weintraub jostled the men back into the alcove. She pulled the door partially closed from the inside, enough to block vision, but not sound.

"All the way," Mrs. Weintraub ordered.

Gunner heard a splash.

"Now recite the blessings," Mrs. Weintraub shouted from below.

Angela's recited the blessing flawlessly, *"Boruh atah Adonoy Eloheynu meleh ha-o-lam asher kid'shanu b'mitzvotav v'tsivanu al ha-t'vilah.* Blessed are You O Lord our God who has sanctified us by His commandments and instructed us concerning immersion."

Tali said, "Now recite the blessing for life."

"... *she-he-he-yanu v'ki-y'manu vi-hi-gee-anu la-z'man ha-zeh.* Blessed are You O Lord our God, King of the universe, who has kept us in life and sustained us and enabled us to reach this moment."

Two splashes followed in succession.

Tali whooped loud enough to be heard through the partially open door, "MAZEL TOV." He turned to Gunner. "You're next. While Angela is dressing, you can take your bath. Then we'll witness your dunking."

"You mean I gotta take a bath before I climb into that tub?"

"Of course! Mrs. Weintraub isn't going to let you dirty up the mikveh."

"That's stupid. I gotta wash myself so's I can take a bath?"

Tali shoved him forward. "Get going before we decide to do another *tipat dahm* on you."

Gunner luxuriated in the water. The outsized enamel tub boasted gilt-covered hot and cold faucets which actually poured hot and cold water. Blissfully, he worked up a thick lather while contemplating the future. Angela and Tali were planning to wed soon after the conversion. He would be moving in with them. Tali had described the house, the neighborhood, the Temple. Pineville sounded like a dream come true. Leaving Upper Chelsea, out of which he had rarely ventured, to enter a white Jewish world did worry him some. Before Tali, what he knew of Jews arrived via street-propaganda that pegged Jews as slumlords, or thieving shopkeepers who would screw you every chance they got. But Tali didn't fit that picture. Nor the Sumtara Rebbe. Till now he hadn't given much thought to it, but the Yardens were Jewish. He would be an asshole to let a bunch of dumb cats talk him out of his big chance. He and Angela were gonna make it. A rap on the door interrupted Gunner's musing about the future.

"Are you ready, already?" Mrs. Weintraub demanded impatiently.

"In a minute."

"Hurry up and get dressed please. I must cut your nails before you go into the mikveh."

Gunner sloshed out of the tub, dabbed himself with a towel and climbed into his shorts.

"I am coming in."

"Gimmie a minute to get my pants on."

Mrs. Weintraub pushed through the door waving a pair of mean looking scissors.

"Give me your hand please. Right hand first."

Gunner surrendered his right hand. She locked his thumb into a vise-like grip and clipped the nail, digging in close to the skin. Gunner yelped. Mrs. Weintraub tightened her grip.

"Don't move your hands, please."

Compared to this torture, the *tipat dahm* had been a breeze.

Meticulously, Mrs. Weintraub scalped each fingernail. She released his hand.

"Your right foot, please."

Gunner stalled, searching around for an escape. There was none. Mrs. Weintraub snapped the scissors impatiently.

"Hurry up, please, and give me your right foot."

Gunner did as ordered. Mrs. Weintraub wrenched his ankle into her lap, clipped away precisely, then grabbed the left ankle. Gunner gritted his teeth. With a final expert clip she sheared his last left toenail.

"Now you go through there, please," she pointed the scissors toward the door. "The rabbis are waiting for you."

He raced past the lady, grateful that he still had all his fingers.

Gunner's immersion followed the same procedure as Angela's. Except, unlike Angela, he was not provided with a sheet. He stood stark naked throughout the entire ceremony, the three men gawking at him as if he were a fish in an aquarium. Tali instructed him to recite the blessings. Angela had urged him to rehearse it before the service. "I got a good memory," he insisted. "I don't have to go over it a million times."

His mind went blank.

Tali cued the beginning phrase; then a full line.

Nothing. He couldn't remember a word. Mrs. Weintraub shouted for the rabbis to hurry. Tali shepherded him through the blessings word by word. He felt like a naked moron.

He tramped up the five steps, chastened. He dressed and trekked into the anteroom. They stood in a half-circle all smiles waiting for him. Angela kissed him on the cheek.

Israel Jacobs 185

"Why'd you do that for?"

"For being so wonderful about the whole thing."

Gunner wiped off the kiss. "Nothin' to it."

Tali said, "Now that you're both officially Jewish let's choose Jewish names for you."

"That wasn't part of the deal," Gunner protested. "You never said nothin' about me changing my name."

"It's not absolutely necessary, but it is a tradition. You keep your family name, Adams." Tali turned to Angela. "Not you; Adams won't be your name much longer." She smiled demurely. He returned to Gunner. "But you should have a Jewish name. Usually, we select a Biblical name. It's meant to confirm that once you convert, you're as much a part of the Jewish people as a Jew who can trace his family back to Abraham."

Angela said, "That's a beautiful thought. Can I choose my name?"

"I don't see why not."

Angela reflected. "Let's see... We studied the scroll of Esther a while back for the Purim holiday. Esther, she was quite a gal. Yes... I'd like Esther."

"That's an inspiration." Tali pecked Angela on the cheek. "How about you, Gunner?"

Okay, if she's gonna be Esther, I pick, Mordecai, Esther's uncle. How's that for a switch? I'm gonna be my sister's uncle."

"Great. Esther and Mordecai it'll be."

Tali snapped a pen from an inside pocket, walked to the roll-top desk in the corner, opened the drawer and removed two manila envelopes. He slipped out two handsomely ornamented legal-sized documents.

Rabbi Sanford Heller stayed Tali's hand.

"Hold on a minute. Before you inscribe these names on the conversion certificates I suggest you give the matter further thought."

"What's the matter now?"

"Mordecai is no name to give this fine young man."

Tali's pen hovered over the conversion certificates. "Why not?"

"The man was an egotist. He almost got his people killed, all

186   *The Convert*

because he wouldn't bow down to Haman. Also, look at the name, Mordecai, from the Babylonian god Marduk. No doubt about it, he was more Persian than Jew. And Esther? From the Babylonian goddess, Ishtar. Think about it before you saddle these fine young people with names like that."

Gunner regarded the Reform rabbi with new-found admiration.

Change his name? If he's got to, he's got to. They *tipat dahm*ed him, scalped his nails, dunked him naked in holy water. He went this far; so he takes on another name. No big deal. If it makes Tali happy, Angela will be happy. A cheap way to spread joy. This put sunshine into the deal. To be called by a god's name? Marduk! Beautiful. And Ishtar? If anyone deserved to be named after a goddess, it was his sister.

"Can I change my mind about the name?"

"Yes, I suppose so."

"No Mordecai for me. If I gotta have a new name, I want the original. I want, Marduk."

Tali dropped the pen. "I never heard of a Jew named Marduk. No, you can't take that name."

"Marduk, or nothin'."

"I tell you no Jew has ever been called Marduk."

Rabbi Heller cackled. "Mordecai, Marduk. It's all in the family."

Tali swerved. "Who asked you?"

"You asked me."

"I asked you to be a member of the *bet din*. And for the life of me I don't know why."

"You asked me, my friend, because you hold me in such high esteem. Also, because all your buddies are at the Rabbinical Alliance convention. Now am I a member of this *bet din*, or not? Be careful, how you answer, Rabbi Zeig. If I'm not, you didn't have the required three rabbis to constitute a *bet din*. That means, according to your tradition, this entire conversion is null and void. So, how say you?"

Tali stared blank-faced.

"I take it then that I am a member of this illustrious *bet din*. Courts are supposed to make decisions. My decision is, Marduk, Mordecai, what's the difference? If this young man wants Marduk, let him be

Israel Jacobs   **187**

Marduk."

Tali sputtered an expletive under his breath. "Reverend Stern, did you ever hear of such a ridiculous name for a Jew?"

Reverend Stern picked up his satchel. He said, "It is not the name that honors the man, but the man that honors the name."

Tali surrendered. "If it's Marduk, you want, Marduk you get. But I'll be damned before I allow my wife to be an Ishtar."

Angela stepped between Tali and Sanford Heller. "Wasn't Esther's Hebrew name, Hadassah?"

"Yes, it was," Tali said.

"That's the name I want. Hadassah."

Tali inscribed "Hadassah" on the first certificate. He glared at Sanford Heller and penned "Marduk" on the second certificate

Rabbi Sanford Heller applauded. "Rabbi Aron Naphtali Zeig, his beautiful bride, Hadassah, and brother-in-law, Marduk Adams. You three will make quite a splash in Pineville. MAZEL TOV!"

Chapter Twenty Five

Tali centered his tie, meticulously denting a dimple with his little finger. He inspected himself. The right sideburn slanted lower than the left. He plugged in the electric razor again. The razor slipped from his hands to the counter top. Nervous? Since ordination he had officiated at fifty to sixty weddings. Not the same as playing with your own marbles. He disconnected the razor. Better leave well enough alone before he trimmed himself bald.

A year and two weeks since he met Angela—Hadassah. Her new name would take getting used to. Strange, life's twists and turns. What if he had picked a different day to visit the Yardens? Or had missed Malcolm Wood's lecture at the Seminary? Would he still be a bachelor with no prospects? Or does God direct our lives, as his uncle believes? If his uncle is right, where does that leave free will? He stretched into the closet and plucked his jacket off the hanger. No percentage in trying to calculate tomorrow with yesterday's ifs. Tomorrow he would be a married man. He studied himself in the mirror again. Dark blue tie with a splash of red. Just right for the navy-blue suit he had bought for the occasion. He flicked his cuff to check the time. Twelve-thirty. The ceremony was scheduled for three-thirty. He still had to pick up Sanford Heller, then drive into the city. He smiled at the recollection of the mikveh scene, "Mordecai, Marduk. What's the difference?" Logically, Sandy had a point. But tradition doesn't stand on logic alone.

A hunger pang nibbled at his stomach.

In deference to his uncle he had agreed to fast, as tradition requires

Israel Jacobs 189

a bride and groom to do on their wedding day, which symbolically wipes the slate clean so the couple may start afresh, pure and cleansed of all sins. He hurried to the garage, hoping to drive off without meeting congregants.

He had dropped hints that he was giving marriage serious consideration. He was reluctant to offer more details. Also, he had decided against introducing Hadassah before the wedding. A condescending reception, or a coarse remark by some boor could have dire consequences. There was bound to be a joker who would think it cute to make an out-of-order comment. He would be treading on egg shells after the wedding, but married he would be better equipped to deal with whatever problems they might face.

Tali eased out of the garage, feeling like a thief in his own driveway. As luck would have it, Muriel Shakter climbed out of her Cadillac. She waved excitedly. He waved back and stepped on the accelerator.

Sanford Heller's house was under three miles from Pineville. Tali negotiated the winding driveway with caution, remembering the time Daniel, the Heller's four-year-old, had suddenly darted from behind a tree. Miraculously, he had braked in time. Today his shot nerves were not up to sudden stops. He cut the motor, sprinted to the entrance and pushed the chime. Sanford Heller opened the door.

"You're early; it's only one-fifteen."

"Figured I'd give myself some extra time."

"Nervous groom, eh? Come in. Join me for lunch."

"I'm fasting."

Heller rolled his eyes. "You'll be too weak to perform tonight."

"Do me a favor, Sandy, cut the comedy. I'm not up to it today."

"Okay, sorry. Come in anyway, and say hello to Arlene."

"All right. But just a minute. I don't want to be late."

"What are you worried about? They can't start without you."

A petite blonde wearing an apron over tight-fitting slacks and a harried face palpitated into the foyer.

"Hi Arlene," Tali said wanly.

Arlene Heller stood on tip toes and pecked Tali on the cheek.

190   *The Convert*

"You're a handsome groom. If I weren't married to chubby, I'd marry you myself."

Sanford Heller winced. "I lost five pounds the last two weeks."

Arlene patted her husband's belly. "Dear, you've got a ways to go before we can call you slim." She returned to Tali.

"I'm sorry I can't make the ceremony. I've got both Daniel and Aviva down with the measles."

"That's okay, Arlene, I understand. Just tell this character husband of yours to behave himself."

"He will. He'd better." Arlene reached up to kiss him on the other cheek. "Congratulations, Tali. And good luck. I wish you and Hadassah every happiness. You picked a winner. Hadassah is bright, she's beautiful, she's everything a man could want."

"Thanks."

Sanford Heller followed Tali to the Mustang.

Heller said, "Want me to drive? You look kind of pasty."

"Yes, I'd appreciate it."

Heller slid behind the wheel. Tali shifted to the passenger side.

Arlene Heller waved from the doorway. "Call us when you get back."

Traffic on the expressway moved briskly. Huge trailer trucks and chartered buses pounded down the first lane, occasionally darting perilously out to pass slower moving vehicles. Heller stayed in the center lane, one hand on the wheel, and the left elbow dangling from the window. The wind blasted into the car, scrambling his carefully groomed hair. He pulled in his elbow.

"How do you get your air-conditioner going?"

"The knob is under the radio."

Heller groped under the dashboard. His fingers found the button. Cool air flowed upwards. He rolled the window closed.

"Professor Teitlebaum going to officiate?"

"The Professor's only going to deliver the wedding address."

"Whom do you have lined up to perform the ceremony?"

"Prepare yourself for a shock."

"Let's not play guessing games. Who'll be the *m'sadder kiddushin?*"
"My uncle."
"Which uncle?"
"The Sumtara Rebbe."
The car strayed over the white line, almost sideswiping a passing van.
"Watch it," Tali warned. "I've got a bride expecting me."
Heller slapped both hands to the wheel. "Your uncle is actually going to co-officiate with Professor Arthur Teitlebaum?"
"Well, technically, the *m'sadder kiddushin* performs the wedding ceremony. Teitlebaum will merely speak, maybe offer a blessing."
"Even so. The Sumtara Rebbe even stepping into the Seminary building? I don't believe it. He's really coming?"
"He said he would. I've never known him to go back on his word."
"God! The Messiah must be on his way."
Heller drove on, keeping his eye on the road. Traffic pulled in from the service roads jamming the lanes. Tali stared into the distance, as baffled as Heller. His uncle had agreed, actually in so many words asked, to be the *m'sadder kiddushin*, knowing the wedding ceremony would be held in the Seminary building, and that Professor Arthur Teitlebaum would be speaking.

Tali recalled his uncle's reaction to Professor Teitlebaum's book, *Judaism Without God.* And two years later when the professor published *God in the Image of the Semites.* According to a story in the Jewish Weekly, his uncle ordered both books burned. Tali doubted that his uncle would go that far. But Tali knew for a fact that his uncle put the books under a ban. which rendered that "unholy" work untouchable to the Rebbe's thousands of followers. In the opinion of the Sumtara Rebbe, scholars of Teitlebaum's ilk delayed the coming of the Messiah. Inasmuch as the professor didn't believe in the Messiah, he was indifferent to the indictment. The Sumtara Rebbe and his hasidim, Professor Teitlebaum had responded, belong in a Jewish Museum.
That his uncle agreed to even step into the Seminary building, which produced such heresy, was an enigma. And to co-officiate with

192   *The Convert*

his arch theological adversary, Arthur Teitlebaum!

Tali thought about the contending sects that had riddled Jewish unity over the centuries. Sadducees and Pharisees squared off in the first century B.C.E. and stoked their quarrels for a hundred years. Karaites and Rabbanites fought their theological wars around the eighth century. Now Orthodox, Conservative and Reform Jews were at each other. Fortunately, Jews did not slaughter each other over doctrine. Tali recalled a lecture delivered by his uncle about the schools of Shammai and Hillel. These schools clashed over Jewish law for about a century. They differed on weighty religious and political issues. But both opinions are faithfully recorded in the Talmud because, as the rabbis believed, "Both are the words of the living God." His uncle's lecture had been provoked by a dispute between him and the "Kotler Rebbe," who was even more to the right. The heated dispute centered over the newly-born State of Israel. Followers of the Kotler Rebbe criticized his uncle for insisting that Jews need not wait for the Messiah to emigrate to Israel. The Sumtara hasidim were chagrined to see their rebbe criticized publicly and were ready to man the ramparts. His uncle reminded them that despite critical differences between the schools of Shammai and Hillel, it never developed into animosity. "The two competing schools continued to live in harmony, and their sons and daughters intermarried." Was the Sumtara Rebbe, by officiating at the Seminary, signaling a message? Reminding the Jewish world that the ancient Temple in Jerusalem was destroyed because of unwarranted hatred between Jews? Or was it more personal? A debt Rav Dov Ber felt he owed his deceased brother, Tali's father? Or both?

Boro Bridge came into view. The line of cars to the toll moved at a snail's pace. Heller tapped the brakes. "Well, did you figure out why the professor and your uncle agreed to co-officiate?"

"I think so."

"So, tell me."

"Teitlebaum was my Bible professor; his signature is on my ordination certificate."

"What about your uncle? What's making him shatter every precedent?"

Israel Jacobs 193

"I suppose because I'm his nephew."

The Seminary chapel had been freshened with a coat of yellow paint. Otherwise, it was the same chapel Tali had worshiped in as a student, parquet floors, two sections of metal folding chairs, and a narrow carpet arrowing down the center aisle to the one-step platform that served as a pulpit. The ark, of walnut with intricate religious motifs hand-carved on its antique facing, dominated the eastern wall. Two chandeliers, each with multiple shaded bulbs, hung low from the open-beamed ceiling. A small table, covered with a white tablecloth on which a wine-goblet and bottle of wine had been prepared, stood on the pulpit to the left of the Ark. Four young men, whom Tali recognized to be rabbinical students, were on the pulpit testing the portable marriage canopy under which the wedding ceremony would take place. Three other couples, friends of Tali's from Seminary days, were waiting in the aisle.

"I've brought the *hattan*," Heller sang out. "The groom is here. Nervous, but he made it."

A tall heavyset man with stooped shoulders rushed Tali. "Ladies and gentlemen, observe if you please, while you have the chance, the last of an extinct species." The rabbi broke into a wide grin. "Congratulations, Naphtali. With you married off, it's unanimous for our class."

"Thanks," Tali said sheepishly.

The women fluttered about Tali, congratulating him and offering their cheeks to be pecked.

"The bride! Where's the bride?" Sanford Heller trumpeted.

"Rabbi Zeig."

Tali peered over Heller's shoulders for the owner of the familiar voice. Malcolm Wood waved his arms. At his side stood a solemn-faced Jeremiah Yarden. Tali pushed through the aisle toward the two men.

Malcolm Wood seized Tali by the arm. "Congratulations, Tali. This is one beautiful day."

Jeremiah Yarden extended his hand. "My very best wishes, Rabbi Zeig. I wish you and Hadassah every happiness."

"Thank you. I owe the both of you so very much. This couldn't

194   *The Convert*

have happened without the two of you."

Tali searched behind the two men. "Did you bring Hadassah?"

Yarden said, "Yes, she is with the ladies."

"She all right?"

Yarden's formal posture yielded to a smile. "Hadassah's fine. We're having a little trouble with her brother."

"He's not sick?"

"No, not sick. Just nervous. I wouldn't have thought walking down the aisle would unsettle him so."

"I thought you and Mrs. Yarden would give Hadassah away."

"We offered. But Hadassah wants to be escorted by her brother. You know how inseparable they are."

"Will he be all right?"

"Between my wife and Mrs. Wood we will pull him through."

Suddenly, the chattering subsided. The tall, stooped-shouldered rabbi said softly, "It looks as if this wedding will begin on time."

Sanford Heller gaped at the chapel entrance. "If I didn't see this with my own eyes, I would not have believed it."

The circle round Tali opened. The Sumtara Rebbe walked toward the marriage canopy, escorted by Professor Arthur Teitlebaum.

"Mazel tov," Tali's uncle embraced him. He was clad in the same silk caftan and fur-trimmed hat he had worn at the bar mitzvah of his son, Shmuel. Tali wondered why his uncle had arrived alone. To the best of his recollection, the Sumtara Rebbe never traveled without a full complement of hasidim escorting him.

Professor Teitlebaum, dressed in a pin-striped business suit, offered his hand. "Congratulations, Naphtali."

"Thank you, Professor. I appreciate your coming."

The professor nodded. "How soon can we start?"

Malcolm Wood said, "I'll run upstairs and tell the ladies we're ready."

The four rabbinical students ascended the pulpit, each carrying a gold-plated rod. They extended the telescoped rods to their full length, worked the hooks at each corner into clips attached to the satin canopy then spread apart as far as the rods allowed. They raised the *huppah—*

the marriage canopy, over their heads. Professor Teitlebaum bid the Sumtara Rebbe ascend the pulpit first. Both men took up positions facing the groom. Tali shifted his weight from one foot to the other. He bit on a cuticle, peering over his eyebrows toward the door.

Heller whispered, "Take it easy, Tali, or you'll never make it through. It's only your wedding. I've survived it. So will you."

The chapel door swung open. Marduk, dressed in a dark suit and starched white shirt, held his sister by the arm. He escorted her half way down the aisle, disengaged himself and continued solemnly to the first row. Heller nudged Tali. "Go get your bride."

Hadassah waited, holding white roses. Tali stared longingly. She wore a small pillbox hat and half-veil, and a body-hugging silk shantung suit that highlighted her figure in soft subtle lines. She smiled, a nervous shy smile. Tali felt his heart pounding. She gave him her arm. They marched slow-paced toward the huppah. Professor Teitlebaum beckoned them to approach closer.

Tali's uncle raised the wine goblet.

"Blessed are You O Lord, our God, who has made Israel holy by consecrating marriage...," The Rebbe intoned the betrothal blessings in Hebrew.

Tali accepted the goblet from his uncle; he tilted it to his lips. The Rebbe gestured for him to offer the goblet to Hadassah. Rebecca Yarden lifted the bride's veil. Hadassah sipped as instructed, glancing sideways at Tali, invoking in his mind's eye the enigmatic smile of a bronze-skinned Mona Lisa. She returned the goblet to Tali.

The Rebbe called for the ring. Heller placed it on the table. The Rebbe inspected the plain gold wedding band then raised it for the witnesses to examine. He handed it to Tali and signaled him to recite the marriage vow:

"*Harey at m'kudeshet lee...*" Tali spiraled the ring onto the index finger of Hadassah's right hand, "By this ring you are consecrated to me as my wife in accordance with the Law of Moses and Israel."

The Rebbe read the marriage contract in a steady voice. He refilled the wine goblet and chanted the concluding benedictions:

"... Praised are You, O Lord our God, King of the universe, who created man and woman in Your image... who created joy and gladness... May there always be heard in the cities of Judah and streets of Jerusalem the sound of joy and gladness, the sound of joyous wedding celebrations, of young people feasting and singing... Blessed are You, O Lord, who causes the bride and groom to rejoice."

The Sumtara Rebbe stepped aside to make way for Professor Teitlebaum. Hadassah nestled in close to Tali. Professor Teitlebaum made a small bow to the Sumtara Rebbe then faced the bride and groom.

"There are legal reasons why the wedding band must be of plain gold and have no diamond inset, which I will not enter into now. The tradition also carries a psychological truth that you would do well to apply to all human relationships. The ideal diamond contains no flaws. Once a diamond sustains a defect it is there forever and significantly diminishes its value. Gold is different. If a gold ring sustains a scratch, it is possible, with some polish, to restore it to its original unblemished state. There may be perfect diamonds, but on this side of heaven there are no perfect human beings. To believe otherwise, to demand perfection in our spouses, our children, our friends, to believe that we can find that mythical perfect partner with whom we will live in perfect happiness forever after is to invite disappointment. We all have blemishes. We all have our flaws and stains. Marriage is about exploiting the love that brings you together today, using it as the polish which erases those blemishes and enables husband and wife to start afresh every day of their lives. Hadassah, Naphtali, it is my sincere hope that you take the message of the plain gold wedding band to heart so that you may build a home in Israel that will be filled with joy.

"And now in accordance with the law of Moses and Israel, you Naphtali, and you Hadassah, are husband and wife."

Not once in his talk, Tali noted, had the Professor invoked God. Even when petitioning for the health and well-being of the bride and groom he omitted any reference to God. Yet, peculiarly, God was there, implicit in whatever Arthur Teitlebaum said and did.

The Sumtara Rebbe directed Sanford Heller to a glass wrapped in a white linen cloth. Heller whispered into Tali's ear, "Please, buddy,

Israel Jacobs   197

wait till I get my fingers out of the way." He set the glass next to Tali's right heel. Tali lifted his foot and smashed down hard. The glass shattered with a loud pop.

MAZEL TOV! MAZEL TOV!

Malcolm Wood squeezed next to Yarden. "What's that they're shouting?"

"*Mazel tov.* Good luck. They are wishing the bride and groom good luck."

"They sure will need a large dose of it. I pray to God, He watches over them. Those are two are very special young people."

"Kiss the bride," the stoop-shouldered rabbi shouted. "Kiss the bride."

Tali hesitated. Sanford Heller pushed him forward. Tali lifted Hadassah's veil.

The Sumtara Rebbe descended the pulpit. He approached Yarden. "You are Dr. Yarden?"

"Yes," Yarden said, taken aback by the Rebbe's sudden overture.

"Naphtali has spoken to me of you. Please be so kind as to tell him I would like that he and his bride visit with me soon."

"Yes. Certainly. I will give him the message."

The Sumtara Rebbe turned strode hurriedly to the chapel exit.

Malcolm Wood said, "He is a strange man."

Yarden watched the Rebbe depart. "An extraordinary man."

Malcolm Wood said, "For me this entire experience has been extraordinary. From the moment I met Rabbi Zeig at the Seminary. I remember having lunch with him, at a kosher delicatessen. He asked me, casually, whether Angela worked at the O.E.O., as if it were just of passing interest to him. He said she had a relative who was a member of his congregation. I thought it a little strange, but it didn't register. Actually, little of Rabbi Zeig registered at the time. I didn't take him seriously; a white rabbi from suburbia volunteering to teach black kids in Upper Chelsea. I invited him to come down to our office, never thinking I'd see him again. A year later he marries my best teacher, Angela!"

"Hadassah," Yarden said.

"I stand corrected. Hadassah. Extraordinary! The whole thing is not to be believed." Malcolm Wood shook his head. "You start something, thinking you've got the rules of the game down pat. The next day you wake up and discover it's a different ball game."

"I'm afraid, Reverend Wood, that after Rabbi and Mrs. Zeig set up house in Pineville they will not be playing games very long."

Malcolm ventured a hand on Yarden's shoulder. "Dr. Yarden, I do believe you worry too much."

"I sincerely hope, Reverend Wood, that my concern is unwarranted."

Chapter Twenty Six

Tali paid silent tribute to Sam Yin for introducing him to Mt. Tamalpais. Since those roseate college years, he had scaled higher mountains. The vista from the summit of Mt. Tamalpais had permanently etched itself into his mind's eye. It was a celebration of creation. He had determined then to return one day, perhaps to share it with someone, *the* someone.

San Francisco leaped from the Pacific like a reincarnation of Venus. Skyscrapers pierced the low-hanging clouds, disappearing, as if severed, and reappearing again. City and sky merged. To the east, Tiburon sat at the edge of a peninsula, jutting out like a thumb. Sausalito shimmered peacefully in the haze. San Rafael reposed, distant yet clearly visible. San Pablo, Berkeley, all linked by bridges to San Francisco like umbilical cords. The panorama moved Tali to whisper the benediction invoked by traditional Jews upon experiencing nature's wonders, "Blessed are You, O God, who created this astonishing universe."

Hadassah cuddled into his arms. "It's breathtaking."

"That it is. Admit the drive up was worth it?"

"Yes, now that we made it. I wasn't so sure we would. Some of those curves were terrifying."

Tali grinned, "Remember, what goes up must come down."

"How far is down?"

"The sign said, two thousand feet."

"Eek!" Hadassah folded herself into Tali's arms. He stroked her hair, "Nothing to worry about. We rented a solid car, and with me as your chauffeur, you couldn't be safer in your bathtub."

"Can't help worrying," Hadassah brushed Tali's lips with her fingers. "Sometimes I get vibes that behind your macho-front sits another worrier."

"What makes you so perceptive?"

Hadassah trained a coy smile upward. "Comes with experience, and knowing my man."

"Just married, and you've already stripped me to the core."

"Not to the core—yet." Hadassah pointed toward San Francisco. "Look at those clouds. It's like heaven reaching down to touch the city."

"Sometimes I think those clouds are there to hide what goes on down here on earth from God's heavenly angels. They couldn't handle it."

Hadassah nibbled his ear. "Your conscience bothering you?"

Tali shrugged. "You heard Professor Teitlebaum. Nobody's perfect."

"Not even you, lover?"

"Sorry to disappoint you. Not even me."

Hadassah locked eyes with Tali. The afternoon sun tinted her face rust-red, like autumn foliage. Tali drew a line from her cheek, to the nape of her neck, circling around her bare shoulders, descending to the upper hem of her blouse. He felt the rise of her breast under the sheer cotton material responding ever so slightly to his touch. A white-haired couple standing at the opposite end of the overlook had turned to watch them. They smiled, as if fondly recalling times long past.

Hadassah slipped one hand between Tali's roving fingers and her breast. She whispered in his ear, her breathing coming a bit faster than normal.

"We should get back to the hotel. We... we need time to pack."

"Uh... right... Let's get back to the hotel... We need time to pack."

"Let me do that," Tali reached for her blouse. He undid the three-pearl-shaped buttons, lingering at each one. The blouse floated down to the carpet. Hadassah stepped out of her skirt. He unfastened her brassiere. It dropped next to the skirt and blouse. She rolled down her panties. He spun her around slowly, stripping his clothes, his eyes never leaving her body, drinking in her nakedness. They stared at each other, hardly breathing. A verse from Genesis popped into his head, *And they were both naked, the man and his wife, and they felt no shame.* He had lost his virginity in college, and since then he hadn't exactly been celibate. But, stripping in front of a woman made him uncomfortable. Not now. No awkwardness, no embarrassment. It was as if preternaturally their bodies were created to connect.

San Francisco's striking harbor-view, visible through the picture window, blurred. The cream-colored drapes, the delicate Danish-teak furniture, the cluster of iris and jonquil on the coffee table, the lovely painting of a late nineteenth century 'Frisco scene, began to fade. The entire room faded. The street cars clanging up and down San Francisco's hills, the traffic, the people, all receded to another time, another space. He heard nothing, saw nothing but Hadassah standing, in their private time, their private space. He reached to touch her breast and stopped short, letting his arm hang suspended between their bodies, fearful that a precipitous move would dispel the magic and plunge them back to real time, real space. She enclosed his hand in hers and slowly retreated to the bed, tugging him after her. He slid one hand under her waist, gently declining her body to the bed. She lowered his face to her breast. He brushed his lips across her nipples. One, then the other, feeling them grow rigid, feeling his own erection pulsating. He lay down next to her, caressing her belly, sliding downward and parting her thighs, inhaling her moist fragrance. She cupped his head in her hands, riding him back to her breast. Their mouths pressed hungrily, lips parting, their tongues exploring, touching, stroking with fingers, lips. He rolled her on her back and raised himself over her. She lay with eyes closed emitting soft cries. She arched her body upward, coiling herself around his legs. She touched the velvet crowning his erection with one finger, then two fingers, then gripping it with her hand, guiding it downward between her thighs, circling it, teasing it around her dark-haired mound, not allowing him to enter. She glided under him, stroking him with her mouth and tongue, down, across his chest and belly, sliding lower and lower, fondling his erection, bringing it to her lips, her tongue brushing, flicking, sending exquisite tremors through his groin. Gently, he forced her to reverse positions, separating the lips between her thighs with his tongue, tasting the wetness. She trembled. She pulled him upwards. "Now, Tali, please. Put it in, hard... hard... please ." He mounted her. Slowly he slid inside her. She circled her legs around his waist, pressing herself tightly against him, making circular motions. They began to move to one another's rhythm. He thrust deeper, at first conscious, aware, in control. Then losing himself inside her, carried along by the exquisite ferocity of her momentum, her spasms merging into his, peaking and ebbing with him. Deeper... one body...one rhythm... the rhythm of Creation... spinning out of control until neither could control their ecstasy. They exploded into each other together.

Hadassah fell back into the pillow, luxuriating voluptuously in the afterglow of her orgasm. "God! That was beautiful."

Tali rolled to his side. He fondled her nipples. "Funny you should describe it that way."

"What's funny about what I said?"

"Not humorous funny. Interesting funny. Like significant funny."

"You're losing me, honey."

"That would be a tragedy," Tali said seriously. "Now that I found you, I don't think I could hack it alone anymore."

His somber tone startled her. She kissed his neck. "You won't lose me. Please explain what you meant by funny."

"After making such passionate love, I don't know that we want to make heavy conversation."

"You inspired me, my body and mind," Hadassah said. She slipped her hand between his thighs. "Go on. Explain."

Tali sat up, crossing his legs under him. "Remember the wedding service?"

"I'll never forget. It was beautiful."

Tali studied her expression. She had given him her body without

Israel Jacobs   203

reservation. There were layers to her mind he had not yet plumbed, that she was holding back, still wary of completely exposing herself. Maybe that was part of the magnetism. Maybe only flesh is meant to become one; not minds. He felt grateful to whatever power had brought them together.

He went on to explain, "Toward the close of the wedding service a benediction is chanted in which God is blessed, 'for causing the groom to rejoice with the bride.' I knew what it meant, intellectually. Now I understand those blessings. Not just with my mind. With all of me. And there is a difference. Like knowing the chemical composition of sugar, and tasting it."

"Tali, you make sex sound like a religious experience."

"Jews have always believed that under the right auspices, namely marriage, it is a religious experience. I was taught to believe that. I taught it to students in my classes. But I didn't fully understand. Not really. It took loving you to make me understand."

They embraced and dozed in each other's arms.

Chapter Twenty Seven

Hadassah snapped the valise shut. Two larger suitcases were lined up at the door. She swept a damp cloth across the table.

Tali frowned, "Why bother to clean up? You're not coming back."

"I don't want to leave a dirty apartment."

"Anything else to go?"

"That's it. All Marduk and I own."

"Where is he?"

"In the car, chafing at the bit."

"Okay, bid adieu to Upper Chelsea."

Adieu to Upper Chelsea. Now that she was actually on her way, the old anxieties intruded. Traipsing through a honeymoon, tomorrow could be blocked out. Especially in a city such as San Francisco, especially for lovers. She had surrendered herself to Tali, opening to him in ways she never thought possible. Lying in his arms, she had also surrendered her rage, her mistrust, for good, she thought. Like the view from Mt. Tamalpais, the future glowed with promise. Thrust back into reality, apprehension cast a shadow over the honeymoon afterglow.

They carted the valises downstairs. Hadassah procrastinated. The tenement looked as decrepit as ever. Foot-wide holes that made climbing the steps a hazard gashed the concrete. Cracks zig-zagged across the grimy windows overhead, some with boards making do for window panes. And behind the visible ugliness were the rooms and tenants to match. Still, she felt reluctant, almost guilty about leaving, as if she were a deserter. Whatever their apartment had lacked in creature comforts, it had been home. Familiar ground. Strange how fast memory winnowed out the bad times. She drifted back to the hallway for a final mailbox check. Nothing.

Tali rattled the hallway door, "Let's go, Rebbitzen." The title sent an alarm tingling up her spine. "I want to beat rush-hour traffic." Tali playfully slapped her on the behind. Pineville's waiting for us."

The mention of Pineville raised new fears. She felt his eyes undressing her right in the street—she's near panic and that lecher is still horny.

"Can't wait till they see what I'm bringing home. You'll knock their eyeballs right out of their sockets."

"That's what I'm afraid of."

"You afraid of being the most beautiful creature in Pineville?"

His high spirits, pretense or for real, irritated her.

"Shouldn't you have prepared them?"

"For what?"

"For me. That I'm not exactly what they're expecting. I doubt they've ever had a rebbitzen like me before."

"I've never been married before."

"You are not the first rabbi of the Pineville Jewish Center, are you?"

"No, I'm not the first rabbi of the Pineville Jewish Center."

"And the others did have wives, yes?"

"Those that were married did."

"My background is not quite the same as that of the other rebbitzens." She heard herself suddenly shouting. Her fears made no dent in his misplaced humor. He made a small circle with his thumb and forefinger. "Hadassah, don't let that worry you this tiny bit. We've got a stack of converts in the congregation. In fact Sandra Russel, my president's wife, is a convert."

"That's not what I—"

Tali cut her short. "And I did let one of my people in on the secret."

"Who?"

An extremely obese woman with a puffed face stumbled out of the doorway. "Is you gonna block this doorway fo'evah?"

Tali made way. The woman thumped down the stoop.

Hadassah put the question to him again. "Who did you tell?"

"An elderly gentleman. His name's Lutvak. Fine old guy."

"Why him?"

"Well, he's chairman of the ritual committee, and an Orthodox Jew, a rarity in Pineville. I thought it only right to assure him that your conversion was strictly kosher. When I told him my uncle, the Sumtara Rebbe, would be officiating at our wedding, that settled it for Lutvak."

"Is that all you told him? That I'm a convert?"

"What else is there to tell?"

"Hadassah stared at him with dubious eyes, still undecided whether he was play-acting or merely dense.

"That I have a permanent tan."

He veered toward her. For the first time she saw anger in his eyes directed at her. "That is relevant to nothing, as far as I'm concerned."

Marduk helped heave their luggage into the trunk.

"Anything else to go?"

Tali slammed the car trunk closed. "That's it; climb in."

Marduk bounced into the back seat. "Give her the gas, man."

They drove through smog patches hovering over Chelsea, allowing sunlight to break through only spasmodically. As they crossed Boro Bridge the sky turned a clear blue. The expressway opened to six lanes with tree-lined islands dividing east and west bound traffic. Pastel-colored frame houses, each with an attached garage and neat lawns whizzed by. Marduk kept count of the exit numbers. Thirty-six, seven, eight, passed in quick succession. Tali drove at a steady fifty-five-mile-an-hour clip. At exit sixty-four he turned off the expressway into a long downhill ramp. A sign bearing arrows pointing in opposite directions guided traffic exiting to Northville and Pineville respectively. They cruised south, passing large homes with expansive park-like lawns. Marduk rolled down the rear window, stuck his head out and inhaled.

Israel Jacobs 207

Spring exploded in a kaleidoscope of color. The lawns were splashed with red, pink, purple, yellow. An occasional mansion peeked through the shrubbery. On both sides of the lanes, branches thick with foliage, arched thirty, forty feet above them, shaping a natural tunnel over their heads.

Tali steered into the driveway marked Twenty-Four Flower Lane. He braked in front of the two-car garage. Marduk stared wide-eyed.

"How many people live here?"

"Just our happy family," Tali said.

"This whole house is just for the three of us?"

Tali chuckled, "Give us a little time, and we'll add a tenant or two, or three." He hastened to the passenger side and opened the door. "Come on gang. Let's unpack. We've only got a couple of hours to get ready."

Marduk paused to admire the azaleas lining the cobblestone path. Pensively, he followed Hadassah into the house. Tali gave them a quick tour of the lower floor.

Kitchen, breakfast nook, dining room. A room to cook in, another to eat in. A den and a vaulted living room with a wood-burning fireplace. And three bathrooms downstairs. Marduk rapped his forehead.

"Jesus! This house is big."

"Jesus doesn't pay the rent here." Tali shooed him to the staircase. "Second room to the right is yours. Upstairs with you now."

Marduk lugged his valise up the stairs. The door was ajar. He peeked inside. "Holy Jee-sus, this was his room?" He entered cautiously, taking care to step softly, as if he were trespassing. Two windows cross-ventilated the room, one of which overlooked the garden, the other provided a partial view of the ocean, which sparkled in the distance, splashing a fragment of rainbow on the wall. A wrought iron floor lamp stood close by a roll-top desk. And next to it a large screen television. And a bed! Not a cot with a caved-in mattress, but a queen-sized bed covered with a yellow tufted bedspread. Hesitantly, he shuffled to the bed and stroked the headboard. It felt smooth and expensive. He dropped down gently to the edge, his thoughts sliding over all that had happened to him and his sister since meeting up with Tali. What the hell was he doing here? Was this for real? Was he dreaming? He pressed down on the bed. The back of his hand appeared abnormally dark against the bright yellow spread. He followed the hand up to the wrist and further up to his elbow. He stretched both arms, angling them so that he had a clear view of both at the same time. His right arm seemed a darker shade than his left. Must be the light, he told himself. He pushed himself off the bed and trudged to the dresser. He dug into his pockets and dragged out the few odd pieces he habitually carried on his person. A penknife, a key chain shy of keys. Two quarters and a dime. An Israeli shekel Tali had given him. The sum total of his possessions. Ruefully, he remembered the cash-filled cigar box. Gone but not forgotten. He slid open the top drawer and stashed his sparse treasures into one corner. He stared into the beveled mirror, feeling small and out of place. His reflection stared back.

"Why the shit not?" He spoke to his face. "I'm as good as any sonnabitch."

If he could make it in Upper Chelsea, he could make it here. Didn't take a genius to learn how to live rich.

He unpacked, arranged his socks and underwear neatly in the second drawer, shirts in the bottom, found the hall bathroom, undressed and stepped into the pink-tiled shower. He fumbled with the fancy spigots till he figured out how to regulate the hot and cold flow. Warm water surged out in a jet-stream pelting his skin like a million tiny fingers. This was living, he told himself. Easy to get used to. He dried himself and draped the freshly laundered towel around his waist. The phone rang as he shuttled past the master bedroom. Tali's voice rattled into the hallway. Marduk heard him thank someone. Then a short muted argument between Tali and his sister followed by, "Thank you, I'm looking forward to meeting you, too."

Marduk returned to his room. It seemed friendlier. He changed into a tan lightweight jacket and brown trousers that Tali had bought him for the reception. He scrambled downstairs into the living room. Hadassah was already dressed. She looked beautiful—and scared.

Israel Jacobs 209

The five minute drive to the Pineville Jewish Center seemed like an eternity to Hadassah. She had chosen a powder blue skirt and high-necked white-lace shirtwaist with which to make her debut. She frowned into the rear-view mirror.

"You think I went too heavy on the make-up?"

Tali said, "You look just great, honey."

She wet two fingers and tamped down a rebellious curl. Her nerves were in a tangle. Tali backed into the space marked:

RESERVED FOR RABBI.

She twisted out of the passenger seat. Her skirt crawled up to her thighs. She tugged at it, trying to hold it below the knees. The skirt floated up again as soon as she released it.

"Tali, my skirt, is it too short?"

"He studied her legs. Not for this rabbi."

Insensitive clod. She felt like slapping his face. She didn't need a clown. She needed empathy. If he would show a little concern, she might gather courage, knowing her anxiety had a partner. His calm facade was driving her up a wall.

Marduk popped out of the back seat and strutted ahead as if he didn't have a care in the world. Her anxiety mounted. Tali held out his hand.

"Come on honey, there's nothing to worry about. They'll love you, every last one of them."

She clutched his arm. "I hope so."

The sun, still a bright red disc at seven-thirty, sprayed finger-like rays at the sanctuary facade. It towered fifty feet above ground level, sculptured out of blue marble in the shape of two convex tablets. The complex of buildings, sanctuary, social hall and religious school looked down from a knoll set back half an acre from the driveway. A sloping curbstone walk forked into three narrower footpaths with islands of shrubbery and flower-splashed gardens between them. The bronze sanctuary doors were a scaled-down version of the towering tablets fronting the sanctuary. An inscription in gilded cursive script was chiseled over the main entrance:

210   *The Convert*

SHE IS A TREE OF LIFE TO ALL WHO GRASP HER,
AND WHOEVER HOLDS ON TO HER IS HAPPY.
(Proverbs 3:18)

Tali ushered them into the lobby. Hadassah tightened her grip on Tali's arm. Deep piled wall to wall carpeting cushioned their steps. Five crystal chandeliers sparkled from the vaulted ceiling. A picture window covered one entire wall, visually carrying the outside garden into the lobby. Marduk broke into the hush.

"Wow! This ain't nothin' like Lincoln Baptist Church."

Hadassah dived into her purse. All thumbs, she tugged out her compact. She pouted into the mirror.

"I feel a mess."

Tali prodded her on. "You look great."

She wrenched out a tissue and scrubbed her lower lip. "Where's the ladies' room? I want to freshen up."

"Honey, you can't improve on perfection. Please, calm down."

Hadassah glared at him. "Don't tell me to calm down. This is not your debut. I'm the one they'll all be inspecting. I never met a soul in that room. I don't know how they'll react to me."

"Look, honey, I'm here."

"A lot of comfort you are."

Tali spread his hands. "I'm doing the best I know how."

"This isn't the way I should be meeting them. Not for the first time. Here I am, your black rebbitzen, take it or leave it. It's like you're shoving me down their throats. I should have met, at least, some of them before tonight. If I had one or two familiar faces to count on, maybe my stomach wouldn't be doing flip-flops now."

"I figured introducing you this way would be best."

"Best for you maybe. Not for me. Start thinking of my feelings for a change." Hadassah jammed the shredded tissue back into her purse. "Where the hell is the ladies' room?"

Marduk, impatient to explore further, struck out on his own. The winding staircase up ahead intrigued him. He scampered up the steps of the staircase. It terminated in an upper lobby smaller than the one

Israel Jacobs 211

on the ground floor, but furnished in the same grand style. Directly ahead double doors, brocaded in red velvet, heated his curiosity. A loud babble emanating from the other side of the doors cascaded into the lobby. He, pulled the doors open and slipped into the ballroom of the Pineville Jewish Center.

Two chandeliers hung low over a crescent-shaped dance floor. A stage with heavy red curtains spanned the width of the ballroom. Tables with wine-red tablecloths and chairs in plush red padding circled the dance floor.

Each of the tables were stacked with generous platters of smoked fish, lox, chopped herring, sliced fruits and a variety of colorful finger cakes. Traffic flowed to and from the tables. Glasses, dishes, silverware clanked and tinkled merrily. People stood in groups, some talking in loud voices, others muting their conversation. Waitresses in red and white uniforms serviced the buffet tables, filling and refilling the platters and collecting the leftovers. Two women, one a tall brunette and very tan, were ladling drinks from a punch bowl. The shorter of the two, a flashy redhead wore a flesh-colored brassiere under a see-through blouse. A half dozen men surrounded the punch bowl, swilling drinks and flirting with the two giggling women. Most of the men wore bright colored jackets and shirts. Sprinkled around the room, looking out of place, were a few elderly people conservatively dressed. Marduk's entrance attracted a few curious glances.

The doorway through which he had unobtrusively slipped into the ballroom was within an earshot of a semicircular bar. A black bartender, wearing a formal maroon jacket and bow tie, looked at him inquisitively, then returned to squeezing lemon into a tall glass for an obese man puffing on a cigar.

The bartender said, "You want it on the rocks, Mr. Kraft?"

"Yeah, throw in a couple of cubes," the fat man said.

Even in that gaudily dressed crowd, Mr. Kraft stuck out like a bugle in a church choir. He wore pumpkin-colored pants, an orange floral-patterned shirt and gleaming patent-leather pull-ons with gold buckles at the tongues.

Standing next to Kraft, a tall well-built man dressed in a solid

212   *The Convert*

brown jacket and black pants twirled the drink in his hand. He sported a mustache and long sideburns speckled with grey. He glanced in Marduk's direction, lifted one eyebrow then skimmed over the ballroom.

Two others joined the men at the bar. The first, thin and deeply tanned, was dragging his left foot. He wore a short pinch-waist blue jacket tucked into tight-fitting trousers. A tall light complexioned man with a blond crew-cut and friendly face joined the group.

"What happened to your leg, Al?" The man with the mustache asked.

"Tennis. Ran for a net shot and turned my ankle."

Kraft blew a smoke-cloud. "You have the Doc check it out?"

"Yes, he taped it yesterday." Al grimaced. "Said to forget about tennis for the next two months, at least." He spanned his waist with two hands. "If I have to sit on my ass for two months, I'll put on a ton."

The tall blond man clicked his tongue. "Too bad. Maybe you ought to take up golf."

Al reached down to rub his leg. "Not me, Everett. I'm still too young to settle for golf."

Everett said. "Listen here, Dr. Shakter, I play golf, and you're ten years my senior."

Al Shakter craned to follow a curvaceous almost bare-breasted brunette mincing by. "I may have a few years on you, Mr. President, but physically I feel ten years younger."

"And carnally," the man with the mustache laughed.

"An ogler does not necessarily a Don Juan make," Everett laughed.

Marduk noted that Mr. Kraft did not join in the small talk. He chomped on his cigar with the air of a man that had bigger things on his mind.

"In my opinion this is all wrong."

"What's eating you, Seymour?" Everett asked.

"What's eating me, Everett, is the rabbi." Mr. Kraft spat out an ash clinging to his lower lip. "The wedding should have been here in the Pineville Jewish Center, of which he is the rabbi. At the least, he should

Israel Jacobs   213

have brought his fiancee out to Pineville and introduced her to you, Everett. You are the president of this congregation. Why all the secrecy?"

Everett retorted, "Do your employees introduce you to their girl friends before they pop the question?"

"Don't compare my business to Temple business. A rabbi's wife plays an important part in the congregation. She's expected to be a role model. That makes it our business." Seymour Kraft loosened his belt. He looked at the man with the mustache. "What do you say, Maurice?"

"Well, that depends," Maurice twirled his mustache.

"Depends on what?" Seymour Kraft demanded.

Marduk pressed against the wall trying to make himself invisible. The conversation he had just audited drained his newfound self-confidence. He was at the bottom again. He became aware of a sudden cessation of clatter. The ballroom had plunged into a hush. A nattily dressed man with a square beard, who had been stroking the bare back of a lady, clearly not his wife, dropped his cocktail. He gaped at the door. Movement to and fro the buffet tables came to a halt. The clique milling about the bar were staring at the door. Seymour Kraft's cigar hung limply from his mouth. Maurice, the man with the speckled moustache and sideburns emptied his glass and swallowed hard. Seymour Kraft's double chin began to quiver.

"Jesus! Jesus Christ! She's black!"

Maurice grabbed Kraft by the lapel. "Keep your voice down."

"But... But...She... She's black!"

"Damn it, Seymour! I'm not color blind. I can see she's black."

Al Shakter stroked his chin. "God! What a beautiful creature."

Tali escorted Hadassah into the ballroom. The silence could be cut with a knife. No one moved. The ninth plague that struck Egypt leaped to Tali's mind, *Darkness descended upon all the land of Egypt for three days. People could not see one another, and for three days none could rise from where they sat.* Tali had anticipated Hadassah would be a surprise. He was right. But somebody had better defrost this crowd—and fast.

Everett detached himself from the coterie at the bar. He hastened toward Tali and Hadassah and clasped Tali's hand. "Congratulations, Rabbi, it's great to have you back. We missed you." He fixed his eyes on Hadassah. "Shaw-lome, Mrs. Zeig. I'm Everett Russel, president of the Temple. Welcome to the Pineville Jewish Center."

Hadassah extended her hand. "Shalom, Mr. Russel. Please call me Hadassah."

Everett Russel smiled. "I will, if you call me Everett."

The freeze that had held the crowd in a viselike grip melted. Al Shakter rushed to Tali and Hadassah. He pumped Tali's hand several times, wishing him well on his marriage, then gave Hadassah his full attention. "Rebbitzen Zeig, I'm Al Shakter. My sincerest congratulations and very best wishes. And if I may be so bold, you married a man with excellent taste."

Chapter Twenty Eight

Although the Pineville Chronicle's editorials often made Tali chafe, on the whole it was a well written weekly. He leafed through the local news section, giving most of his attention to Hadassah. She wore a belted robe open at the top and showing a tantalizing slice of cleavage. Marduk spooned cold cereal into a bowl.

Tali said, "Well, Rebbitzen Zeig, now that you've met our congregants, how say you?"

"For a time there, when we first walked in, I was worried. I didn't know what to expect. But, your congregants surely gave us a warm welcome. They made us feel at home. Do they often throw such lavish parties?"

"First off, Rebbitzen Zeig, I need to remind you they are your congregants as well. And yes, they don't stint, they can afford it. Also, It's not every day they get themselves a beautiful new rebbitzen."

Marduk jangled his spoon. "Wild, man, wild. First time I've been to a Jewish party. They don't drink much, but those cats can eat."

The kitchen phone jangled.

"Do me a favor, Hadassah, answer it."

Hadassah carried the phone to the table. "Good morning, Hadassah. This is Sandra, Sandra Russel. Remember?"

Hadassah tried to match the voice to one of the hundred women she had been introduced to at the reception.

"Good morning Mrs. Russel."

"Sandra. Please call me Sandra. I hope I'm not disturbing you, but

I wanted to catch you before you leave. Are you free next Sunday?"

Tali strolled back to the kitchen. "Who was it?"

"Sandra Russel. We're invited to a barbecue. Next Sunday."

"I figured the invitations would be pouring in. Did you accept?"

"I told her, depending on whether you're free, I'd be happy to accept. She sounded real friendly. I think it was nice of her to include Marduk."

"Sandra's a great gal." Tali dropped two sugar cubes into his coffee mug. "They're good people. Call her back and tell her we accept."

Hadassah said, "I can't place her. What does she look like?"

"She's a brunette. Big brown eyes. Tall, sexy looking, a wee bit on the plump side. *Zaftig.*"

Hadassah stirred her coffee. "And what does zaftig mean?"

"It's Yiddish. Closest translation—a juicy handful."

"You seem to know her real well."

Tali dunked a donut into the coffee, "I've got an eye for good-looking women, to which you can attest."

Hadassah applied a touch of lipstick. "Do the Russels have children?"

"Two boys. Kenneth, a pre-med student at State University. And David, who is Marduk's age, give or take a couple of months. Kenneth is a serious nose-in-the-book kid. A lot like his father. David is a tornado."

"I remember you telling me that the president's wife is a convert." Tali ran a comb through his hair. "From the way she's fitted into the congregation you'd never guess."

Hadassah rotated a turn. She wore navy-blue slacks and a sleeveless cotton blouse. "How do I look?"

"Beautiful as always," Tali said to her reflection in the vanity mirror. He pecked her on the cheek. "Let's get Marduk and go."

The Russel's flagstone patio offered a dramatic view of the North Bay. Power boats churned through the water, crisscrossing one another at dangerously close range and trailing high wakes after them. Off in the

Israel Jacobs 217

distance a sailboat listed gracefully port side.

Everett Russel collapsed his chef's hat and tucked it into a rack under the built-in stone barbecue pit. The coals, sizzling while the steaks were being served, had turned to grey ash.

"How about sitting around the pool?" Everett said.

The two couples moved to lounging chairs arranged in a semi-circle at the shallow end of the pool.

"Let me freshen up your drink, Rabbi." Everett started to rise.

"No, don't bother. I've still got a way to go on this one."

"How about you, Hadassah?" Sandra Russel asked. "Want a refill?"

"That's enough for me, Sandra. Thanks. Another one and Tali will have to carry me home."

"I don't think he'd mind."

"I wouldn't mind. But how would it look? A soused rebbitzen."

Everett laughed, "Might be cute."

Tali swished the ice in his glass. "You did those steaks just great, Everett. They were darn good."

"And strictly kosher," Everett said.

Tali chuckled. "I'd never think to question it. Not with Sandra running your kitchen."

David Russel panted to the patio, sweat pouring down his face. Marduk followed equally in a sweat.

Sandra inspected the youngsters. "What were you boys doing?"

"Throwing baskets," David said between pants. "Marduk can really play basketball. Mom, can we go for a swim?"

"Yes, I guess so," Sandra said. The sun still hit the pool area with an eye-squinting light, though a cool breeze was blowing in from the bay. Sandra tucked her son under the chin. His face was smudged with dark dirty lines. "How did you get your face so filthy?"

David shrugged. "I dunno."

"It looks like you've been rolling in the charcoal. Get yourself into the bathroom and wash that shmutz off your face before you go into the pool."

"Okay, Mom."

"And check the bath house. "I'm sure we have a bathing suit that

218 *The Convert*

will fit Marduk."

Both boys scrambled into the bath house.

"I'm glad they hit it off so well," Sandra said.

Hadassah noted a mid-western twang occasionally creeping into Sandra Russel's speech. "You're not originally from the East, are you?"

"Not originally," Sandra smiled. "I was born in Boise."

"Where is that?" Hadassah said.

Sandra laughed. "You easterners think civilization ends in the East. Boise is the capital of Idaho. That's where I met this hunk of man."

Everett put his arm around Sandra. "Would you believe it? A Jewish boy from the Bronx making off with an Idaho WASP?"

Sandra looked up lovingly, "Well, in that major's uniform you didn't look very Bronxish, or Jewish." She turned to Hadassah. "Frankly, I don't remember ever meeting a Jew before Everett. What I knew about Jews and Judaism you could have scratched on a thumbnail. There is a small Jewish community in Boise, but we just didn't move in that circle. It was that major's uniform that swept me off my feet."

Tali grinned. "From what Everett's told me he didn't know much more about Judaism either. And I venture to guess that he never would have known more, if he had married a nice Jewish girl from the Bronx."

"Maybe," Sandra said pensively. "I'm glad he found me."

Marduk and David whooped out of the bath house, popping towels at each other. Marduk wore one of his new friend's bathing trunks. It circled his waist with room to spare, requiring him to hold on to his trunks with one hand while swinging the towel with the other. They galloped to the pool. "Race you," David challenged. They lined up at the deep end. David counted off. "Ready, set, go." They raced the length of the pool. David easily outdistanced his guest. The two boys splashed merrily back to the deep end.

Tali inquired, "How is Kenneth doing?"

"Good," Everett said, eager to talk about his son. "He's working at Camp Olami as a swimming instructor."

Israel Jacobs 219

Tali asked, "This is his final year at State University, isn't it?"

Sandra answered. "Yes. Then on to medical school, hopefully."

Everett frowned, "What do you mean, hopefully? Any medical school will be more than happy to get a kid that bright."

"Sorry for doubting our son, dear," Sandra lowered her eyes in mock contrition. She cast a sideways glance at Hadassah. "Kenneth's the apple of his father's eye. Daddy's pride and joy."

Everett said, "He's your son, too."

"Yes, he is. And I hope he's accepted. For your sake as much as for Kenneth. I don't think you could take a rejection."

"I admit I would be terribly disappointed. But I'd still have you." Everett kissed his wife on the lips.

Tali detoured around the bay. Dusk dropped leisurely over the horizon, reflecting red and orange colors in the water.

"So, how did you and David get along?" Tali spoke over his shoulder, cautiously negotiating the narrow winding lanes.

"Great. We had a great time," Marduk yawned, dog-weary after an afternoon of sun and water. "I'm goin' over tomorrow. He invited me to meet some of the other guys."

"That's just fine," Tali said.

"They're real people, the Russels," Hadassah said.

"I thought you would like them."

"What does he do?"

" He's a vice president at Aerospace."

"Sounds like an important position."

"It is. Last year the government awarded his company a two-billion-dollar contract to build part of the space shuttle."

"My, that is impressive."

Tali eased into the garage and cut the motor. "Not half as impressive as the fact that he rose to the top in a field dominated by WASPs. And he never once compromised his integrity as a Jew, or as a man."

Tali reviewed the chapter headings for the textbook he intended

220   *The Convert*

to use for the fall-term confirmation class. He leaned back, thinking how well things had turned out. Three years as rabbi of the Pineville Jewish Center had given him an education in the convolutions of the suburban American Jewish psyche: materialistic, spoiled, selfish, parochial. Guilty on all counts. But not racists. Nevertheless, he had not been as confident as the front he showed. Anything could have happened. Had Hadassah received a lukewarm welcome, she might well have interpreted it the wrong way. All the worrying had been for nothing. The congregation had come through with flying colors. They had welcomed both Hadassah and Marduk with open arms.

The Russel barbecue proved to be merely a starter. Invitations kept pouring in. As a bachelor, he was the awkward odd man at a party. He was rarely invited for a social evening by congregants. Now the phone rang off the hook. He and Hadassah were pulled into the summer social stream. Hostesses vied to capture them for an evening. They were wined and dined in a dizzying round of parties. He wished they would ease up on the invitations. The pace had become too frantic for both him and Hadassah. She needed time to digest it all, and he needed a rest. But they were insistent, and gracious.

Seymour Kraft was the fly in the ointment. Tali did give him credit for consistency. Kraft was consistently a boor. He was the first to come running with tales of anti-Semites attacking Jews or Israel. Seymour Kraft had adopted the motto, "Give bigotry no sanction" as his own, but only as applied to Jews. Other victims of bigotry were not his concern. Whenever their paths crossed, Seymour Kraft made it a point to throw a sauerkraut look. The man never came out and said so, but left the distinct impression that as far as he was concerned Tali was a traitor to his people and his calling. The law of averages, Tali consoled himself, requires that in every crowd there be a bigot, even in a Jewish crowd. Thank the Lord for the Russels in this world.

Tali picked up the Pineville Chronicle for a close read. He gasped. Hadassah's picture was plastered on the front page:
PINEVILLE JEWISH CENTER'S RABBI BRINGS
BLACK BRIDE HOME TO HIS CONGREGATION.

Israel Jacobs 221

If Hadassah had seen the article, she made no mention of it. For his part, he thought it the better part of discretion to keep it from her, if possible.

The study phone rang. He picked up the receiver.

"Yes, Maurice. We're both doing just fine."

"Rabbi! Are you aware of what's happened?"

The lawyer's tone set off an alarm. When Tali had left his office in the afternoon, all had seemed well. He feared an accident, possibly to a member in the congregation. He forced calm into his voice.

"No, Maurice, I don't know what happened. Tell me."

"Your marriage put the Pineville Jewish Center on the front page."

"Is that right?"

"The B'nai Kodesh, The American Jewish Alliance, even the N.A.A.C.P.," Cline raced through the list. "Your marriage is precedent-shattering, they say. They're praising us to the hilt. John Dorsey, of the Chronicle, wrote an editorial about your marriage. The man rarely waxes ecstatic, especially when he writes about Jews. I don't have the exact quote in front of me. But he applauds the Pineville Jewish Center for accepting the marriage of their rabbi to a black woman. He says our example will go far in breaching the walls between Jews and blacks."

"How did the newspapers and all those organizations get wind of our marriage so fast?"

"Well, you know, reporters. They have a nose for news."

"You don't think a congregant leaked the story?"

A brief silence on the other end. "Why would anyone do that?"

"For the publicity."

"Well, whatever the reason. It didn't hurt the Pineville Jewish Center, nor the Jewish community. Listen to this quote from the BLACK ECHO, "Jews recognize black is beautiful; why don't we?" Coming from that black separatist paper it's quite a concession."

"I've got to go, Maurice." Tali slammed the phone down.

Maurice Cline, shrewd counselor, sidetracked him. He tried to untangle the anger he felt. Why did Cline's call make him so hot under the collar? The fact of the matter was that Tali never did care for the attorney, his impressive credentials notwithstanding. Cline was first vice president of the Pineville Jewish Center and senior partner of Cline, Block and Reich, one of the county's top law firms. Tali suspected Cline was the culprit. Knowing Cline, he also suspected that when the lawyer first saw Hadassah, the night of the reception, he had second thoughts about spreading the news. But events had outdistanced Cline's misgivings.

Maurice Cline saw to it that his altruism, legal or otherwise, never escaped public attention. He was a master at public relations.

"We are duty-bound to provide every citizen the full protection of the law," Cline would posture to the press whenever "altruism" moved him to take on a case pro-bono. The Pineville Chronicle frequently featured him on its front page. Cline, while defending a rapist-murderer, had even made the front page of the New York Times. Tali gnawed inside, thinking how Cline exploited his marriage to Hadassah, after he recognized its publicity value.

On the other hand, Tali reconsidered, for whatever reason, the hypocrite was drumming up good will. Why not accept? Why tear apart the man's motives? Whose motives are pure? Self-interest prompts almost every altruistic act. Ecclesiastes, that pragmatic cynic, had long ago concluded: All that man does, his every enterprise, is motivated by envy.

Human nature being what it is, why not exploit even its darker side for a worthy purpose?

Hadassah and Marduk had bridged the divide between Upper Chelsea and white suburbia. They appeared happy. The congregation had embraced them. From his vantage point, the future looked bright. Why nit-pick?

Tali returned to the Chronicle. It suddenly struck him—the Yardens had not been at the reception, nor any of the blacks. He wondered why.

Chapter Twenty Nine

August floated in on a heat wave. July's frenzied tempo had slowed to a crawl. Tali was grateful to be off the social merry-go-round. He dawdled on the front patio, languidly contemplating the weeping-willow drooping over the front lawn. An occasional breeze puffed in at intervals from the bay, but offered scant relief from the heat. The little morning shade provided by the elm trees contracted as the sun spiraled higher into the azure sky. He idled into the house and stripped off his jacket and tie.

"That you?" Hadassah called from upstairs.

"Nobody but."

"You're late."

" Had to wait for the tenth man so we could say the Mourner's Kaddish. Seems like everybody is away. Can't say Kaddish without ten men."

"I set breakfast on the patio. I'll be down in a minute."

Marduk had already dug into breakfast. The sun lifted higher. A haze began to spread over the bay. The kitchen radio blared the weather forecast, "high in the nineties; winds ten to fifteen miles an hour." Hadassah carried a tray laden with coffee, two fried eggs and a platter of Danish pastry.

"I just had a bowl of corn flakes," Tali said.

"What am I supposed to do with these eggs?"

Tali slid the eggs toward Marduk. "You want eggs?"

"Already had two scrambled eggs."

"Okay, I'll eat them. Waste not, want not."

Tali finished the eggs. He patted his belly. "I'm growing a rubber tire."

"Comes from good living," Hadassah laughed.

Tali yawned. "What's your schedule today, honey?"

"Sandra's driving me down to Bay Park. She's going to help me choose material for the living room drapes."

"Why don't you put drape shopping off for a rainy day? Let's all hop down to the beach. Today will be a scorcher."

"I can't. We've arranged to go today. And I want to get those drapes hung before the holidays. Sandra will be here in a few minutes."

Tali selected a prune Danish. He shoved the plate to Marduk. "What have you got planned for today?"

"Nothing much. I was thinking I might bike down to David's house."

"How would you like to go sailing?"

"Man, I would like that."

"Ever been sailing before?"

"No, but I learn fast."

"Okay. get yourself into a bathing suit."

Marduk stuffed the last of the pastry in his mouth.

"Also a shirt and a pair of shorts to change into later."

Marduk raced upstairs. He made a quick trip to the bathroom, then whipped into swimming trunks. He stuffed an extra T-shirt into an airline bag and started back to the patio.

The tranquil family scene had changed into a shouting match. His sister was fuming at Tali.

"I don't want him to go. In fact, I don't understand how you can go. Don't you have any pride?"

"What's pride got to do with it?"

"The only reason you've got docking privileges at the club is because Cline forced you on them."

"What do I care? All I do is use their facilities to save myself the trouble of dragging my Sunfish down every time I want to sail. It's an honorary membership. Doesn't cost me a dime."

Israel Jacobs 225

"Some honor, "Hadassah scoffed. "Well, you just go sail by yourself."

"But it'll be a great experience for him. He should learn."

"So far, he's managed to survive without learning how to sail."

"Hadassah, you're overly sensitive. Not everybody has got to love us. So they don't pull out the red carpet for me. So what? I go down, do my thing and come home. You're making a big deal out of nothing."

"Don't you tell me I'm making a big deal out of nothing. I've had experience with honkeys who can't abide our kind."

This was not the first squabble Marduk had witnessed. They had squared off for a husband-wife duel before. But nothing like this. He hadn't seen his sister so hostile since Upper Chelsea days. He shrank into his chair.

Tali blocked Hadassah's exit. "I wish you wouldn't use that word."

"Why not?"

"It upsets me."

"So you're not completely insensitive, after all. How come those bigots at the club don't upset you?"

"I'm not married to them. What they think of me doesn't matter."

"Does what I think matter?"

"You know it does."

"Good. Then forget the whole thing. If you must sail, go by yourself."

Tali bit his lip. "You're being irrational about this, you know."

Hadassah swerved. "I may be new to Pineville, but I've been here long enough to know that the Pineville Yacht Club doesn't cotton to Jews or blacks. To them, my brother and I are untouchables. Maybe you can hide your Jewishness, we sure can't hide that we're black."

"Now look here, Hadassah," Tali bellowed. "You know damn well that everybody at the yacht club is aware that I'm a rabbi. And for that matter they know that Maurice Cline is vice president of the synagogue. Whatever faults Cline may have, hiding the fact that he is a Jew is not one of them."

"Tokenism," Hadassah shouted.

"Phony pride," Tali yelled.

226 *The Convert*

Hadassah pivoted to Marduk, as if looking to him for support. He felt safer in neutral. She returned to pound at Tali.

"I don't care what the hell you call it. My brother's hide isn't as thick as yours. I don't want him hurt."

"Why would he get hurt?" Tali seemed bent on taking this argument to the limit. Marduk couldn't stay neutral any longer.

"Yeah, why would I be hurt?"

"You keep out of this," Hadassah warned.

"You talkin' about me bein' hurt, ain't you?"

"He's right," Tali countered. "Let him decide whether he wants to go."

Marduk opted for sailing.

Hadassah slammed out of the house.

Marduk rolled his wrist. "Boy, is she mad."

Tali caught the screen door on the second rebound. He grinned sheepishly at Marduk. "I better bring you back in one piece."

Tali ruminated over the squall he had raised. Hadassah was right, he had to concede. Maurice Cline was the yacht club's token Jew. Barely three months in town, and Hadassah had already been primed. God! These women are like a computer network. What one knows, the others learn fast. Cline's qualifications for token-Jew were impeccable— distinguished attorney and vice president of the Pineville Jewish Center. The Pineville Beach and Yacht Club couldn't have chosen better. Here was exhibit number one, proof that the club did not discriminate.

The xenophobic little minds sitting on the club's board of directors were no strangers to Tali. He was acquainted with their foibles, their vices, their petty—and grand—larcenies. Before Cline, no Jew had been invited to join. The restrictive-covenant effectively limited membership to white Christians. The club came in for criticism when the application of a prominent Jewish judge, who had been sponsored by a Christian friend, was rejected. The criticism made no impact. It was a private club, and they intended to keep it that way. When Cline broke into the club they exploited his membership. "How can you accuse us of discrimination," they protested, "the vice

Israel Jacobs 227

president of the Pineville Jewish Center is a member." And Cline didn't mind being exploited. He had reasons, he claimed.

At a Jewish Center meeting, though no one asked, Cline felt that it behooved him to explain why he had joined the club. "Someone has to show those WASPs that Jews don't have horns."

After the meeting Lutvak, the ritual committee chairman, filled Tali in on how it came about that the yacht club made an exception of Maurice Cline.

Cline had been knocking at the doors for years, but the Pineville Beach and Yacht Club could not be pried open. The lawyer owned a sixty-five-foot Sea-Craft, and mooring a yacht of that size at the public marina with the common folk didn't look right. Club membership would provide his million-dollar boat a fitting home.

Lutvak added, with a knowing shrug, "More than a little it can also help him win the Republican nomination for a seat on the State Supreme Court, which is Mr. Cline's number one dream for this life."

Opportunity knocked in the woes of Brian Conset, president of the Pineville Trust Company. Conset had set up a dummy corporation and lent himself funds to buy land adjoining Continental Avenue. As a member of the Town Council, Brian Conset was privy to information that the state planned to widen the avenue into a major artery, which would feed into the expressway. This guaranteed that the land would quadruple in value. The Homeowners Association fought the proposed widening, and won. The state decided to widen Brian Avenue two miles south instead. The change in plans left Conset with assets he could not liquidate, and his bank with a half-million-dollar shortage that Mr. Conset could not explain.

"How Cline kept those embezzlers out of jail," Lutvak scratched his head in the telling, "is more than an honest layman can understand." Lutvak speculated, "There are rumors that Seymour Kraft helped. That multi-millionaire has almost every politician in the county in his pocket. Anyway, Conset was, and is still, a director of the Pineville Beach and Yacht Club."

Once in, Cline made his presence felt. He learned that Tali sailed. He had seen him haul his Sunfish down to the public marina on a trailer. Cline arm-twisted the membership committee. He persuaded the committee that it would be a noble ecumenical gesture to offer Rabbi Zeig an honorary membership. After all, how much space does a Sunfish take up? The committee, chaired by Brian Conset, went along. Next, Cline pressured Tali into accepting. He argued, "It's your duty to accept, Rabbi. Between the two of us we have an opportunity to break down WASP prejudice. Besides, it's an insult to the Jewish community not to have its rabbi represented, what with all the other clergy in town having been given honorary membership. It makes us Jews look like second class citizens."

Cline could have spared himself much wasted breath. Tali couldn't care less what the WASPs at the yacht club thought about Jews, one way or the other. But it was a nuisance to pack his Sunfish on a trailer and haul it down to the marina every time he wanted to sail. If the club volunteered a home for his Sunfish, why not? When Cline produced the offer of honorary membership, Tali let him run through all the reasons why the rabbi should accept, then to the lawyer's surprise said,

"Okay. When can I bring my Sunfish down?"

A narrow booth guarded the entrance to the yacht club. Inside, a thin red-faced man sat with his head propped up on one elbow. He squinted at the decal on the windshield and waved Tali on. The clubhouse, a long low-slung wooden building, was situated at the bottom of a steep hill. Tali poked the Mustang into one of the freshly marked spaces. Several exotic looking foreign cars were interspersed among the dozen Cadillacs and Lincolns parked in the first row. Most of the parking spaces beyond the first section were unoccupied. He wiggled out of his slacks. Underneath he wore orange swim-trunks. He kicked off his loafers and slipped on a pair of thongs.

"I should have told you to bring thongs."

"I don't have any," Marduk said.

"The sneakers will have to do. Except, you'll get them soaked."

"Can I sail barefoot?"

"Yes. The thongs are just to walk the boat out. Underneath, the sand is mushy. And there are rocks."

Israel Jacobs 229

"I don't mind."

"Okay. Let's go."

They headed for the beach. Women, mostly middle aged and up, lounged on private verandas, rubbing on screen lotion, doing their nails, chatting over the cabana rails. Several toddlers splashed merrily in a kiddy-pool under the watchful eye of a counselor. At the deep end of the Olympic-sized swimming pool, a pretty teenager perched nervously on the high diving board. She pinched her nose and leaped feet first.

Tali led the way to the beach. Marduk winced as the hot sand made contact with his bare feet. He hopped to the water's edge. A dock poked out about fifty yards into the bay. Sleek power boats, schooners, sloops, and one magnificent two-masted ketch were lashed to the dock. A bald athletic looking man cast off his line to an attendant standing on the dock. The yacht pitched forward, its motors churning the water like giant egg beaters. Off at a safe distance, two boys, waist high in the water, poised to leap on a small flat-bottomed sailboat. One weighted the boat down while the other nimbly leaped aboard. His partner followed with equal expertise. He drew the mainsail taut with one hand while working the tiller with the other. A gust caught the sail. It fluttered aimlessly then puffed out, forcing the craft to heel port side. In a moment the boat straightened and sailed crosswise into the wind.

"Beautiful sight, isn't it," Tali said.

"Yeah, they sure know how to sail."

"You ready to try it?"

"Yep, I'm ready."

"Okay, Skipper. Let's go." Tali pointed to a line of racks, each holding two Sunfish. "There. That's my yacht."

Marduk shielded his eyes from the sun's glare. Tali's Sunfish was painted a deep blue with a white line running down the center.

"How do we get it into the water?"

"We push."

Tali unlocked the crossbar; the boat coasted from its rollers onto the sand. He tugged, guiding the stern toward the water. Marduk put his back to the fore. The Sunfish glided over the sand with surprisingly

230 *The Convert*

little effort.

Tali said, "Before we go any further, you'll find two life preservers in the well. Throw me one and strap the other on."

They waded into the water. Climbing aboard had looked simple. Now, with the Sunfish bobbing and the waves breaking against his chest, Marduk was less confident. He pushed himself off the bottom. Tali held firmly to the other side. Marduk's hand slipped on the wet surface. He tumbled face first into the water. He surfaced, several feet off, coughing up water.

Tali laughed. "Try again,"

On the second jump he made it aboard.

"There's not much of a wind, so we won't be sailing too fast. It should make it easier to teach you the basics."

Overhead, a few clouds, no more than scattered feathers, dotted an otherwise clear sky. Near shore, the water was emerald green. Further out, where the horizon and bay met it shaded into silver. Tali directed Marduk to the centerboard.

"When we get a little speed up, you push the centerboard down. I'll let you know when."

Marduk crawled in close to the centerboard. The Sunfish tilted sharply. Water lapped over the stern. He retreated in haste.

"Not so fast. You have to be careful shifting weight."

Marduk inched his way back to the centerboard.

They tacked parallel to shore. Marduk began to get the feel of sailing, shifting and balancing in concert with the boat's bob and sway. More craft crowded the bay. The ten a.m. ferry crossed their stern, creating a wake that jostled their Sunfish like cork. Sea gulls circled overhead; every so often one dived toward the water, skimmed the waves then arched back into the sky. Behind, a sailboat on a parallel tack overtook them. It carried a huge bell-shaped sail in addition to the mainsail.

Tali shouted into the wind, "That's a spinnaker. With that kind of a sail you ride like a motorboat."

Cumulus clouds blowing in on an easterly wind clustered overhead.

Israel Jacobs   231

The sun went under, darkening the water. A sudden gust tilted the Sunfish starboard. The port side lifted far out of the water. Marduk leaned back as far as he could. The Sunfish straightened itself out.

"Good boy. You saved us from tipping." Tali gripped the tiller firmly. "Where did that gust come from?"

The sun peeked from under the clouds, brightening the bay again. The water stayed choppy.

"How about you taking over the tiller?"

Marduk shimmied over the flat surface. They exchanged places.

"I'll handle the mainsail until you get the feel of the tiller."

Marduk held to the same course. Land was still in sight, though the beach looked small and distant, the clubhouse no more than a dot. The waves were breaking higher and choppier with deep troughs. Off to starboard the ferry, its stacks smoking, cut through the water on the twelve-noon run back to the mainland. Marduk handled the rudder confidently.

"Ready to come about?"

"Right on Cap'n."

A power boat charged full throttle. Marduk swung hard to starboard. The wind caught the Sunfish astern, pitching it crazily in the same direction. The boom hit water. Marduk felt himself sliding, sliding helplessly down into the waves. Tali flailed the air on the upended edge. Marduk bobbed up a few feet from the Sunfish. It lay on its side like a wounded bird. Tali surfaced, spitting water from his mouth like a spigot.

"You alright?"

"That sonnabitch looked like he was gonna ram us for sure."

"Don't get excited, Skipper. He was more than fifty feet to port. This is your first dunk. Probably won't be the last."

"Whatta we do now?"

"Stay where you are. When I tell you, push on the boom. Your life preserver will buoy you up." Tali pressed one foot down on the centerboard while holding to the edge. Marduk pushed up. The boom climbed high, pulling the mainsail with it. They shimmied back on deck.

Marduk sailed on. Twice more he capsized while changing tack.

232 *The Convert*

After an hour of handling the tiller, he mastered the coming-about skill. Tali handed him the sheet.

"Here. I think you're ready to take over. Try to keep us on this tack."

Marduk wound the sheet around his right hand and worked the tiller with the other. Stronger gusts drove in from the east, propelling them at motorboat speed through the water. Marduk exhilarated in battling wind and waves, riding the Sunfish like a bronco as it crashed into troughs and bucked high up on the crests. They were about a mile from shore. The clouds to the east thickened. The sun began to play hide and seek The temperature had dropped ten degrees in the last few minutes. Marduk felt a chill on his back. Water-caps bubbled on the waves. Tali scanned the horizon.

"Those clouds look threatening. We may get some rain, maybe a thunder shower. Better head for shore."

Marduk came about expertly and started on a long tack for land. The wind picked up speed, blowing spray into his face. Holding course became a battle. The mainsail cut into his hand. His lower back began to ache. He felt cold. An ominous purple-gray limned the clouds. The Sunfish crashed deeper into the troughs and rose higher on the crests. Marduk felt the boat sliding dangerously to starboard. The water took on a menacing appearance. It began to rain, first a light sprinkle, which turned into a downpour beating a staccato on the hull. The Sunfish seemed too puny to survive the elements. Tali crawled toward the tiller, balancing cautiously on the wildly pitching surface.

"Let me take over."

Marduk relinquished the helm and held on to the mast for dear life. The rain poured down in a fury. Water and sky merged into a gray wall, making it difficult to tell where the sky ended and the bay began. Suddenly, the sky exploded, lighting up the horizon. Marduk huddled under the mainsail. The wind pushed them furiously toward the beach. Marduk could see the tree-tops behind the clubhouse rocking violently. The dock and beach were deserted.

"Grab hold of the centerboard," Tali ordered.

Marduk crawled aft, his teeth chattering from cold and fright.

Israel Jacobs   233

"Pull up, quick."

Marduk felt the plate underneath the hull bite into sand. The Sunfish pitched backwards.

"Pull!"

He yanked with all his might. The centerboard came up. Tali collapsed the sail. They hopped into the water. Working swiftly, they tugged the Sunfish onto the rack.

"Come on, let's get into dry clothing."

They raced through the downpour to the car. Marduk grabbed his bag. Tali pointed to the clubhouse.

"Run. We'll change in the locker room."

After experiencing his first storm at sea—Marduk had feared it would be his last—the locker room felt snug and secure. It was a long room all carpeted in orange, and a ceiling almost low enough to touch if he stood on his toes. Rows of wooden benches were strung end to end. A man in the next row was having difficulty zipping his fly. He cursed under his breath, slammed his locker and stalked out, paying them no notice. Marduk peeled off the wet T-shirt, which the rain had glued to his back. He changed into dry clothes, wrung out his trunks and T-shirt and stuffed them into his bag. He felt a tickle crawling inside one nostril. He sneezed. Tali looked at him with alarm.

"I hope you're not catching a cold."

"Nah, it's just my nose tickling a bit."

The tickling wandered to the other nostril. Marduk exploded into a sneezing fit, spraying a shower from his mouth. Tali rubbed his arms and back.

"That feel better?"

"Yeah, I'm okay now." Marduk swung the bag over his shoulder.

"Tell you what," Tali wiggled into his loafers. "Let's have lunch here at the club. You can order a sandwich and hot chocolate. Maybe by the time we finish eating the rain will let up. How's that sound?"

"Great. All that sailing's given me an appetite. I am hungry."

They strolled into the dining room. Small round tables with white tablecloths were arrayed around a core resembling the spokes of a wheel. Six bar stools stood evenly spaced alongside the bar rail, polished to a high shine. A large window offered an unobstructed view of the bay, still showing a darkly belligerent face. Except for two women conversing animatedly, the dining room was empty. A hostess, wearing a tan skirt and blouse, directed them to a table near the window. They pulled in chairs. Immediately, a waitress wearing a frilly pink apron put down place settings for two, and two glasses of ice-water. She entered their order in a notebook: Tuna fish salad and coffee for Tali. Same for Marduk with hot chocolate instead of coffee.

Tali played with his fork. "So, how did you like it, Skipper?"

"It was great. Except for the rain."

"That's a sailing hazard. Weather is like a woman, no telling when she'll change her mind. Would you like to go out again?"

"Sure," Marduk said. But he wasn't so sure.

"Maybe we'll try again next week. We'll pack slickers, just in case. That way if it comes down like it did today, we won't get soaked."

Marduk nodded, thinking to himself that getting soaked worried him less than drowning, or being hit by a bolt of lightening.

A buxom, smartly coiffured woman in her fifties walked into the dining room. She caught sight of Tali and marched up to the table. A small diamond-studded cross sparkled on her ample bosom. She was stout, but tall, and carried her weight elegantly. Tali rose as the woman approached.

The woman smiled, showing even white teeth. "How are you, Rabbi Zeig. It's always a pleasure to see you here at the club."

"Thank you, Mrs. Conset. Always nice to be here."

"Don't let me keep you standing, Rabbi."

Marduk stared sullenly at Mrs. Conset, resentful of the way she had barged over to their table uninvited, as if she owned the place. She smiled down at him with big eyes.

"Who do we have with us?"

Marduk gathered Mrs. Conset meant him. His dislike for the lady grew a yard each time she opened her mouth.

"This is Marduk. He's my—"

Israel Jacobs 235

"How compassionate of you, Rabbi, to give so much of your time to those less fortunate." Mrs. Conset fingered her diamond-studded cross. "How do you like our club, young man?"

Marduk put on a wide grin that showed his teeth to the molars. "Why I jus' loves yo' boo-tee-ful club mos' awful ma'am." The drawl cackled out a little thicker than he had intended. Tali threw him a dirty look.

"My, what a nice boy. Do bring him again, Rabbi."

"That is very hospitable of you, Mrs. Conset. Thank you." Tali sent Marduk another silent warning. "I'll take you up on it, being he is my bro—"

Again Mrs. Conset sliced Tali off in mid-sentence. "Rabbi, I haven't had a chance to tell you. Your lecture at our church last May was just marvelous." Mrs. Conset fluttered her eyelashes. "As chairperson of the committee I should have sent a thank you note. I do feel remiss. But my husband and I were leaving for Tokyo. In fact, we just returned Monday."

Tali made a little bow. "Thank you, Mrs. Conset. And how did you enjoy the trip?"

"Wonderful. It wasn't our first trip, you know. We have been to the Far East before. My husband and I travel extensively."

Marduk stared hard at Mrs. Conset, hoping she would travel to another table. The waitress returned, carrying their order on a silver tray. She set it down and left.

"Oh, and that reminds me. I am ashamed of myself. Here it is August, and I never thanked you for that lovely Brotherhood service. I thought it a marvelous idea for the clergy to exchange pulpits."

Marduk's stomach growled. He lifted the tuna sandwich to his mouth and ripped into it with his teeth, thinking that he could starve waiting for this lady to shut her gums. The sandwich oozed with mayonnaise, just as he liked it. If only Mrs. Conset would shove off.

"Your sermon on brotherhood was a delight." Mrs. Conset winked, "And it gave Reverend Perkins and the congregation a little vacation from each other."

A thin severe looking woman marched into the dining room. The

236

The Convert

hostess hastened to greet her. She escorted the woman to a table secluded in a niche at the far end of the room.

"Oh, Maude Perkins just walked in. You know Mrs. Perkins, Rabbi, don't you? Maude is our minister's wife."

"Yes, Mrs. Conset. I've had the pleasure of meeting Mrs. Perkins."

Mrs. Conset waved daintily with the tips of her fingers.

"Well, it's been nice chatting with you, Rabbi. We must do it again sometime." Mrs. Conset turned in the direction of the minister's wife. She pivoted back to the table.

"Oh, I forgot to congratulate you, Rabbi. I just heard the fabulous news yesterday. What lucky girl finally caught you?"

A lump of tuna became trapped in Marduk's throat. He grabbed the chocolate milk and swallowed hard.

"Is she a local girl?"

"No, my wife is from the city."

"Really?"

Tali took advantage of the pause. "This is my brother-in-law."

"Your what?"

"My brother-in-law, Marduk Adams."

Mrs. Conset stared incredulously. "Your brother-in-law?"

"My brother-in-law. My wife's brother."

Mrs. Conset regained her composure. She raked Marduk over with cold eyes. She said, "You did notify the membership committee."

"What about, Mrs. Conset?"

"Well, that you now have a family."

"Why should that be of interest to the membership committee?"

"It is their responsibility to keep tabs on how many members we have. Our club is becoming overcrowded. The facilities are not unlimited, as you know. Some of our members feel that we have been too liberal in extending invitations to join the club."

Tali's mouth set in a grim line. "I believe I understand what you mean, Mrs. Conset."

"I'm sure you do, Rabbi Zeig." Mrs. Conset's fingers stroked the crucifix on her bosom. "You'll excuse me. I see Maude is getting impatient. We have some important matters to discuss."

Israel Jacobs 237

Tali slammed himself into the chair. He stabbed his fork savagely into the salad. Marduk peered over his sandwich, silently appraising the drastic change in his brother-in-law's mood. Tali signaled the waitress. She computed the bill and set it face down on a plate next to Tali. He paid with a ten dollar bill, plus three singles for the waitress.

"You finished?"

"Yeah."

"Let's go home."

Hadassah stacked the dinner dishes into the dishwasher. She said to Tali. "I'm sorry I got so steamed this morning. I guess you're right. I am oversensitive. How did the sailing go?"

Marduk said, "It was great. I took over the helm. I'm really learning how to sail."

"I'm glad you enjoyed it. Hadassah looked at Tali. "I left my car in the driveway. Your Sunfish is blocking the garage. How come you brought it home?"

"The keel needs painting," Tali said blandly.

Chapter Thirty

Indian summer delivered ideal sailing weather. Tali and Marduk sailed weekly—from the public marina. Tali registered Marduk in the synagogue's religious school. By late September the family had settled into a routine. Sandra Russel tutored Hadassah in the intricacies of congregational life. Hadassah was drafted to serve on Sisterhood's social action committee. At first, all the committees, grandly listed on Sisterhood's elegant stationary, awed her. She learned quickly that the primary function of committees was to provide a rostrum for the officers.

Shirley Stoner, Sisterhood's social action chairperson, stood regally behind the lectern. She wore oversized tinted glasses and a blue dress sprinkled with delicate white flowers. She was in her mid-forties, plump, but attractive in a matronly way.

"It's criminal the way the East End farmers exploit those poor migrant workers. They live in shacks with no sanitary facilities. They are paid slave-wages." Shirley waved notes, from which she had been reciting statistics on black unemployment, the population explosion, children who go to bed hungry every night and the degrading of the environment. She looked sternly at the audience of fifty or so meticulously groomed women in the audience.

"As Jews we have an obligation to show concern for all people, regardless of race or creed."

Shirley Stoner allowed several moments to acknowledge the

Israel Jacobs   239

applause.

Rochelle Feld, Sisterhood president, tapped her gavel daintily.

"Thank you, Shirley, for your comprehensive report. Before we move on to the next item on our agenda, decorating the powder room, any questions or comments about Shirley's report?"

Hadassah's hand went up.

"Yes, Hadassah," Would you like to speak on the report?"

It took a moment for Hadassah to realize she had been recognized.

"Well, not on the report. But it concerns social action."

"Go right ahead," Rochelle said cheerfully.

Hadassah studied the faces staring at her. She had second thoughts about speaking. The ladies waited.

"I... I think there is a worthwhile project right in our own county about which we can do more than talk. We can really make a difference."

Rochelle's bright smile faded. "What do you have in mind?"

"Well, I've been following the fight for low-cost housing in Bedford Village. We could get up a petition, or start a letter writing campaign to our congressmen, telling them we support the idea.

Sandra Russel sprang to her feet. "I think that's a grand idea. Here we are trying to change the world, and there are people in need of decent affordable housing in our own county."

"I didn't recognize you, Sandra," Rochelle rapped her gavel. "But, if the ladies think we should involve ourselves in this project, we can take it up under new business. After we vote on the powder room."

Sandra idled the Cadillac in neutral. She shifted sideways to Hadassah. "You put some spice into the meeting tonight."

"I don't know what got into me. One minute Rochelle is calling for comments on Shirley's report; the next thing I know I have the floor."

"I'm glad you spoke. Your idea was just what we need. Real projects to sink our teeth into."

"I hope the women didn't think me cheeky. You know, I'm a newcomer to Sisterhood. They might resent me giving them advice."

240   *The Convert*

"Nonsense, it was good advice. And you're the rebbitzen. That gives you special privileges. Any other ideas percolating in that head of yours?"

"Sandra, I think that was more than enough for the time being."

Tali plunged into the High Holy Day season, while Marduk tackled a double load: public school in the morning and religious school three afternoons a week.

Marduk's first experience with High Holy Day services left him with mixed feelings. Five hour services? Way too long to warm a seat. By the second day of Rosh Hashanah he learned how Jews got through those marathon services. The majority arrived two to three hours late. Then they promenaded in and out whenever the spirit, or nature's call, moved them. Few, beside the rabbi and cantor, and a few elderly gents such as Lutvak, sat through it all. For the sermons and certain high points in the service, the ushers closed the doors and everybody stayed put. The rest of the day it was a walkathon, a constant march up and down the aisles. By Yom Kippur, Marduk felt sufficiently at home to join the parade. At times he found more congregants congregating outside the sanctuary than inside.

Cantor Bindel, in Marduk's judgment, should have been backed by a guitar instead of a weepy organ. That might have held his interest longer. Even so, Marduk found portions of the service enjoyable. Cantor Bindel, short and round-faced with a pot belly, had a pleasant tenor voice. Every so often, he jazzed up the congregational melodies and plucked him out of his daydreams. The afternoon Martyrology service on Yom Kippur almost moved him to tears. In somber voice Tali narrated the grim story: ten sages tortured to death because they refused to submit to the Roman edict banning the study of Torah and ordination of rabbis. Tali sat in a tall red-cushioned chair. Periodically, he would step to the lectern and announce pages, lead in responsive readings, or explain different prayers.

Hadassah took special interest in Tali's performance, thinking that whether in Uptown Chelsea teaching black kids to read, or in pontifical garb, skipping from pulpit chair to lectern, his style was the same—informal, conversational, as if he were personally addressing each congregant.

And more than a thousand came to the High Holy Day services. They poured into the synagogue, men, women, children; the women dressed to kill. Hadassah recalled a remark Tali made in jest, but like most comedy it contained an element of truth:

"Some come to services to close the eye; others to eye the clothes."

During the sermons most every pew was occupied. For the Yizkor Memorial Service, the sanctuary was filled to overflowing, with dozens forced to stand. Following Yizkor, the sanctuary emptied, leaving no more than a hundred diehards to continue the services. About half an hour before the conclusion of *Yom Kippur* the sanctuary filled up again, the congregation waiting expectantly for the sounding of the *shofar*—the ram's horn, signaling that the fast was over.

Autumn embraced Pineville, sprinkling trees and shrubbery with variegated shades, first painting golden tints to the edges, then worming its way to into the core of every leaf. Suburbia became a montage of rust-reds, yellows, deep brown and golds. The leaves began to drop seriously, first in singles, then in ever increasing clusters, clogging gutters, and carpeting the lawns and driveways. Winter was in the air. Spaces between berths in the marinas grew wider as boats were dry-docked. The days grew shorter and colder. Clocks were reset to standard time, and by five-thirty p.m., when religious school classes were dismissed, night had already blanketed Pineville.

Tali riffled through the one-hundred-year calendar. It was a slim hard-covered book with rows of numbers running across the pages. The first seven columns marked off the civil year; the second half of the page showed the corresponding Hebrew dates. Because the Hebrew calendar follows the lunar cycle, while the civil year is calculated on the earth revolving around the sun, the two rarely coincide. Tali thumbed down the columns. Marduk slouched in his chair, staring at the oil

242   *The Convert*

painting of Moses carrying the Tablets down from Mt. Sinai. Tali circled a date in February.

"Okay, we'll schedule your bar mitzvah for February the sixteenth. That will be the twenty-sixth day of the Hebrew month, Shevat."

Marduk stacked his books on Tali's desk. "What do I have to do?"

You'll meet with Cantor Bindel once a week after religious school classes. He'll teach you how to cantillate the *Haftorah*, which on your date is Jeremiah, chapter twenty-four."

"You telling me I gotta go an extra hour every week?"

Tali closed the calendar. "That's the way it is, if you want to be bar mitzvah. Remember, I'm not forcing you."

"Maybe you ain't, But my sister is. Do the other kids go for bar mitzvah lessons after classes?"

"Yes, they do. As a matter of fact, the brighter kids also read selections from the Torah. And that takes a bit of doing."

"Whatta you mean, the brighter kids? I'm as smart as any of them."

"I didn't mean to question your I.Q., but the other kids do have a four-year head start on you. However, if you want to put in the extra time, I suppose you could do the same." Tali stroked a pencil against his chin. "Of course that means you would have to meet with Cantor Bindel twice a week."

Marduk doodled circles in his notebook. "I'll stick with the *Haftorah*."

"Okay. but I want you to read the English translation of both the Torah portion and *Haftorah*."

"What for?"

"So you'll understand what you're saying. That's a must for every bar or bat mitzvah candidate."

Marduk shrugged. "If I gotta, I gotta. How many chapters I gotta read?"

Mishpatim, the Torah portion for your date, runs from Exodus, chapter twenty-one, through chapter twenty-three."

"What about the *Haftorah*?" How long is that?"

"The entire assignment is only eighteen pages. And you've got

Israel Jacobs 243

more than three months to work on it. So don't give me that long-suffering look."

Marduk leafed through the first three pages of Exodus. He stared glumly at the fine print. "How come you have to read from the Torah and the prophets every Sabbath?"

"There is an interesting history to that tradition. Want to hear it?"

Marduk nodded. He worked himself up to a comfortable position. Large raindrops began to tap against the window.

"It started about two thousand years ago, after Rome conquered Judea. The Romans issued a decree forbidding Jews to study Torah, on pain of death."

"Like in the Yom Kippur Martyrology service?"

"Yes. And to the Romans, Torah meant the Pentateuch—the first five books of the Bible. They stationed guards at the doors of every synagogue to make sure that the Jews would not read the Torah during services, as was the custom. The decree was a major tragedy to the Jewish people. Without the Torah, they believed, Judaism could not survive. They continued to study Torah secretly, knowing that any Jew caught violating the decree would be crucified, which was how Romans executed criminals. The Jews never lost hope that one day the Roman tyrants wold be overthrown. But they worried that the traditional cycle of Torah readings might be forgotten. So the rabbis did a clever thing. They substituted readings from other parts of the Bible, not included in the Roman ban. And the chapters they selected had a tie-in with the subject matter of the Torah portion that should have been read on that particular Sabbath. That way, they hoped, later generations would remember the correct Torah assignment for each Sabbath."

Marduk leaned over the desk. "Jews don't need to worry about Romans any more. How come we still have to read the *Haftorah*?"

"Good question. I suppose the answer is that once a tradition takes hold, it tends to stay on, even when the reason why it started no longer applies."

Marduk made a sour face. "Because of those sonnabitch Romans I got to study a double load."

Tali laughed. "Here's what I want you to do. When you've finished

244   *The Convert*

reading the assignment, write a short essay on the connection between the Torah and *Haftorah*."

"You expect me to figure out the connection by myself?"

"Didn't you say you're as bright as the other kids in the class?"

"Yeah, but like you said, I'm new to this jive."

"Alright, I'll start you off. Read the first two verses in *Mishpatim*."

Tali flipped to the opening verse of Exodus, chapter twenty-one, *These are the laws you shall set before them: When you acquire a Hebrew slave, he shall serve six years; in the seventh year he shall go free, without payment.*

Marduk asked, "The Hebrews had slaves?"

Tali nodded. "Yes, the Torah did not prohibit slavery. What it did was to limit the master's power. If the Torah had ordered slaves to be set free outright, no one would have obeyed. But the Torah introduced a new idea: slaves had rights. A slave could not be treated as a non-person. He had to be properly fed, housed, clothed. A cruel master was subject to severe punishment. The most important right of the Hebrew slave was that in the seventh year he automatically went free."

Marduk shook his head. "That still don't sound right. But I guess it's better than being a slave all your life."

"Right. Now let's look at the *Haftorah*."

Marduk flipped to Jeremiah, chapter thirty-four. Tali continued, "Jeremiah lived about twenty-five-hundred years ago. The Babylonians had laid siege to Jerusalem. It looked hopeless. Zedekiah, the last king of Judah, persuaded the Hebrew slave owners to swear that if God would deliver them, they would free their slaves, in accordance with the law in Exodus that you just read. Owing to a threat from Egypt, the Babylonians abandoned the siege. Immediately, the Hebrew slave-holders, now that they were saved, reneged on their oath to free their slaves."

"That was a sonnabitch thing to do."

"It sure was," Tali agreed. "Now read what Jeremiah has to say about that broken promise."

Marduk read aloud,

You have profaned My name... Therefore, these are the words of the Lord. You did not obey Me to proclaim liberty for your kinsman; So, I will proclaim a deliverance for you: A deliverance to the sword, to pestilence and to famine. And I will make you repugnant to all the nations of the earth. You have disregarded my Covenant and have not fulfilled the terms which you yourself had pledged... I will give you up to your enemies and to those who seek your lives, and your bodies will be food for birds of prey and wild beasts.

Marduk whistled. "Those Hebrews got what was comin' to them. It ain't healthy to mess with the Lord."

"No, it isn't," Tali said soberly.

Chapter Thirty One

Marduk examined the invitation, hand-written on deckle-edged paper,

Dr. and Mrs. Albert Shakter cordially invite you
to the reception honoring their daughter Vanessa
on the occasion of her Bat Mitzvah.
Please respond on or before January fifth.

The invitation evoked carnal visions. In religious school classes Vanessa grabbed his attention by squeezing a finger into her bra, or running the rubber tip of a pencil along her tongue. If she caught him staring, she would further titillate him by coy sensuous smiles. Vanessa featured in his dreams. One night she chased him around the classroom giggling wildly while his classmates egged her on. Panting, he collapsed into a chair. She bounced into his lap, wiggling her bottom between his thighs and shrieking to Rabbi Kroner, their Hebrew teacher, "Marduk's gotta be TIPAS-DAHMED!" He had awakened in a fright to find his pajamas wet.

Marduk checked the "I-will-attend" box. On the way to religious school classes, he dropped the response card into the corner mailbox.

Hadassah crouched behind Tali and Marduk, bracing herself against the wind slashing at her face. They ran for the synagogue lobby. Hadassah said, her eyes tearing from the cold, "I need the ladies' room."

Marduk looped his coat around a hanger, wondering why women had to run to the john so much. He headed for the stairs. Al and Muriel

Israel Jacobs 247

Shakter were conferring in the upper lobby.

Marduk tipped his skullcap. "Shabbat Shalom."

"Good Shabbos," Al answered mechanically, as in a fog.

Muriel whined to Al, "I hope the family gets here before it's all over."

"Stop worrying. It's only seven-thirty. The roads are probably clear by now." Al gnawed on his thumbnail. The snow plows been working all day."

"I hope you're right. After what this weekend is costing. God!"

Marduk selected a pew in the third row, close enough to get an unobstructed view of Vanessa, yet not so close as to make his ogling obvious. Tali and Vanessa were conferring on the pulpit. Marduk flipped the pages of a Bible trying to appear indifferent. Vanessa wore a pale-blue silk miniskirt with a matching silk jacket and white blouse. She looked all soft and pretty.

"My mother picked the dress; blame her," Vanessa protested.

Marduk guessed she was being reprimanded because of the miniskirt. Tali had lectured the girls time and again about proper dress on the pulpit. The girls listened docilely, and when he was out of hearing would snicker, "If the rabbi doesn't like miniskirts, he oughtn't to look."

Tali dismissed Vanessa. She hopped down the two pulpit steps and swayed provocatively toward Marduk. He busied himself with turning pages.

"He doesn't like my dress," Vanessa pouted, lifting the hem, to display more pink thigh. "You think it's too short, Marduk?"

"It's okay," Marduk forced himself to sound casual.

"Gee, I'm nervous." Delicate worry lines creased her brow.

"You got nothing to worry about," Marduk tried to comfort her.

Vanessa twirled a strand of hair curling her forehead. A lot of people will be coming. Relatives and everything. I'm afraid I'll screw up."

"Aw you'll do okay."

"Suppose I goof."

"So what if you do? They gonna shoot you?"

"That's not funny," Vanessa pouted. Marduk's heart skipped a beat. He craved to stroke the worry from her face. He retrieved his nonchalant posture. "It's stupid to be nervous. Even if you do goof, who'll know except for Cantor Bindel and my brother-in-law? And they won't tell nobody."

A little of the anxiety went out of Vanessa's eyes. Marduk felt the hero at having cheered her a bit.

Tali pressed through the pulpit doors dressed in his black robe. He signaled Vanessa. She grabbed Marduk's hand and squeezed. Her touch sent an exquisite shock up his arm. She ascended the pulpit, sat down next to Tali and stared ahead with glazed eyes.

Guests plus the regular Sabbath attendees began to fill the pews. Vanessa's uncle and aunt solemnly ascended the pulpit and opened the Ark, giving the congregation a full view of the plush wine-red curtains.

"Please rise," Tali announced.

Cantor Bindel pushed his three-cornered pulpit hat to a rakish angle and blew into his pitch pipe. Vanessa opened the service with the "Sabbath Prayer" from *Fiddler On The Roof*. The amplifier magnified the quiver in her voice. Marduk feared she would freeze. Midway through the song, she picked up courage. She came through stronger, her delightful soprano voice ringing clear as a bell. Marduk breathed easier.

"Be seated," Tali directed. "Please turn to page three-hundred-six. Vanessa, our bat mitzvah this Sabbath eve, will lead us in the responsive English reading."

Vanessa began in a confident voice,
Throughout the ages You have blessed us, O Lord,
with women who tended the altars of our faith.
The congregation responded,
Through these noble women Israel was redeemed;
because of them Israel has survived.

Services concluded at nine-thirty. Vanessa had outdone herself. She was a source of pride to Tali and to her parents.

Tali eased into the parking lot. He glanced at the dashboard clock.

Israel Jacobs 249

"Seven-thirty, Honey. We'll stay half an hour or so, congratulate the Shakters then take off to the Heller's anniversary party."

"Won't the Shakters be offended if we leave so soon?"

"I can't worry about that. The Hellers are good friends."

Hadassah turned to Marduk. "Will you get a ride home?"

Marduk said, "I told you, I'm gonna sleep over at David's house."

Hadassah gaped. A life-size three-dimensional cardboard replica of Vanessa, stood at the lobby entrance, so realistic looking she almost congratulated it. With Tali at her side she stepped into the reception hall.

Waitresses clad in skimpy skirts were serving hors-d'oeuvres. White lace over damask covered the smorgasbord tables. Silver bowls filled with flowers served as centerpieces. Small trees strung with colored lights lined the walls at evenly spaced intervals. Gleaming platters of china and gold-plated silverware were stacked in neat piles within easy reach. Waitresses crisscrossed the room with trays of stuffed mushrooms, miniature franks and meatballs. Waiters stood at the ready to refill the steaming chafing dishes with pepper steaks, stuffed cabbage, crepe suzettes. Three chefs stood behind tables slicing turkey, dispensing lamb chops and veal upon request. On and on it flowed. Never had Hadassah seen such a variety of food, and in such abundance. And this was the reception, with dinner yet to come. Liquor cascaded from three bars like Niagara Falls, giving the lie to the idea that Jews don't drink much. Several guests were already staggering. An eight-piece orchestra blared on the stage. Couples squirmed and twisted over the buffed parquet dance-floor. Hadassah watched Al Shakter dip his hand under Rochelle Feld's low cut gown; she slapped his hand unconvincingly. Muriel was being pawed by another man.

"I'm gonna look for David," Marduk said.

"Okay, go on," Tali said. "We'll be leaving soon."

Hadassah checked Marduk's exit. "You going to be alright?"

The orchestra broke into a fast Mambo. Tali shouted over the tumult. "What are you worried about? He's in good hands. Let him enjoy himself." Tali waved Marduk off. "Go on, have a good time."

250   *The Convert*

Marduk found David ladling punch from a huge crystal punch bowl. He ambled over. Shortly, several peers from his Hebrew school class joined them. The group increased to a dozen adolescents. They loitered around the punch bowl watching the adults carry on.

Marduk said, "I don't see Vanessa around."

"I saw her go up to the sanctuary with the photographer," David said.

Kevin Sharf, scheduled to be bar mitzvah the following month, screwed up his face. "Why didn't they take pictures during the services?"

David waved the ladle under Kevin's chin. "Stupid, don't you know you're not allowed to take pictures on the Sabbath?"

Kevin scratched his head. "Oh, yeah. I forgot."

Marduk took the ladle from Kevin. He dipped it into the punch bowl. "If she don't get back soon, she'll miss her own party."

"No, she won't. This party's hardly started." David looked at his friend. "You got hot pants for her, don't you?"

Marduk swirled the ladle around the punch bowl several times.

"You're wasting your time. Vanessa's nothin' but a cock-teaser."

Marduk filled his cup and downed the contents in one swallow. The spiked drink seared his throat. "Aw, she don't mean nothin' to me."

"Yeah," Kevin challenged, "so why're you asking about her?"

The M.C. hopped onto the stage. He was stocky, with shiny, long black hair and a wrinkled face. He wore a black tuxedo over a ruffled red shirt. Lights flashed on and off; the orchestra stopped playing. The vocalist, a tall fleshy blond in a maroon pants-suit and low-cut blouse that advertised her hills and hollows, stepped away from the microphone.

"Ladies and gentlemen." The M.C. took over the stage. He warbled into the microphone, "Your hosts, Dr. and Mrs. Shakter, invite you to the ballroom for dinner. Please go right to your tables. Also, will Vanessa's young friends please remain in the reception hall."

Marduk said, "Don't we get dinner?"

Israel Jacobs 251

"Yeah," David said. "But first the M.C. lines us up in size places and marches us in together."

"Why can't we just walk to our tables like everybody else?"

"That's the routine. This M.C. likes to put on a show. We're part of it. He thinks it impresses the guests."

"Screw the M.C." The husky voice intruding into the conversation startled Marduk. "And shit on making an impression. Let's go to our tables."

Kevin Sharf turned. "Hi, Melody."

Melody Karp, the oldest of the group, had been bat mitzvah six months ago. She was taller, almost by a head, than her peers. Her red hair was pulled back in a French knot. She wore a gold-belted sleeveless royal blue satin blouse and skirt. She had large interesting eyes, and a rebellious mouth. She was as flat-chested as a boy. Her gruff diction and behavior gave the impression she would have preferred to be male.

The M.C. scurried off the stage, mopping his brow with a soggy handkerchief. He clapped his hands. "Okay, kids, let's line up for the processional. "You, kid," he ordered Marduk to the front. "And you," he pointed to Melody. "You take up the rear."

"Screw you!" Melody gave him the finger. The others followed her lead, each giving the M.C. a finger at the as they tramped past him. The M.C. staggered into the ballroom. He keened to a passing waitress, "Why did I pick this profession to make a living? I should have been a funeral director."

David rested his head on the table. "Boy, am I tired."

Marduk yawned. "Me, too."

Melody ambled toward them with a bored look. "Let's split."

David lifted his head. "Where to?"

"Any place is better than this shit party," Melody said. "Let's get the rest of the gang."

They found Kevin dozing in a corner then traversed the ballroom heading for the lobby, bumping into tables and guests. They stopped to gather up Vanessa. She lay sprawled across two chairs. Melody poked her shoulder.

252   *The Convert*

"Whassa matter?" Vanessa opened one eye. She looked like a worn-out Raggedy-Ann doll. A putrid smell wafted up from her mouth that tasted like vomit. Marduk backed away.

"Hey, Vanessa, It's not polite for the guest of honor to sleep through her own party."

Vanessa forced herself up on one elbow.

Melody's eyes burned with an idea. "Why don't we quit this shit party and have us a party of our own?"

David said, "Where?

Kevin suggested timidly, "We could use one of the classrooms."

"Hey, you're not so dumb, after all, Kevin."

Three more girls and two boys joined the group. They clumped into the religious school building, their footsteps echoing in the darkened corridor. David opened the door to classroom five. He reached for the light-switch. Melody pulled his hand away.

"Don't put on the lights. The custodian might be around."

Marduk said "What're we gonna do here in the dark?"

No one answered.

They sat down on the floor in a circle. Melody snuggled up to Marduk. She felt and smelled more like a girl. He prepared himself for a kiss. She put something into his hand. He brought the object close to his face. It was a cigarette.

"You ever smoke a joint, Marduk?"

"Where did you get that?"

Melody chuckled. "I get all I want. And junk, too."

"From who?"

"David's brother, Kenny. He's got connections at college. I buy from him. Guaranteed good stuff."

A thin shaft of light poked through the window from the parking lot. Marduk saw David Russel grinning proudly.

Chapter Thirty Two

Jeremiah Yarden stepped up to the reader's lectern. At a nod from Tali, he began the Musaf service. Zalman Lutvak had led the earlier Shaharit service. Cantor Bindel was down with the flu, which Tali regretted. But there was a silver lining to Bindel's indisposition. Every so often Bindel got carried away and stretched recitatives beyond Tali's patience. Dr. Yarden's unpretentious tenor was a welcome change. And the service would conclude at least a half hour sooner.

From his pulpit chair, Tali studied the Sabbath regulars, thinking what amazing changes had been wrought. Lutvak, Isidore Hirshman, his entire contingent of traditionalists gave no second thought to the fact that a black Jew led Sabbath services, as if it had always been that way. They stood, sat, read responsively, bowed, paused, said amen at the required places, prayed in silent devotion. They seemed oblivious to Jeremiah being black.

Astonishing, how malleable the human brain is. It learns and unlearns. It can be conditioned and de-conditioned. One year narrow lapels, slim ties, tapered slacks and miniskirts are in. Madison Avenue decides it's time for a change, next fall slims are dead, trousers flare and skirts scrape the sidewalk. Pavlov was right. Anybody can be made to salivate at the gong. People adjust to change. To the point where they believe it's always been that way. Even black Jews worshiping side by side with white Jews.

Shortly after being voted in as members, the blacks switched from the eight o'clock Friday evening service to Sabbath morning services.

The Barnetts became Sabbath morning regulars and brought their bouncy three-year-old daughter Hannah. The Sabbath morning regulars did not fuss over decorum.

"You just bring Hannah," Lutvak reassured Mrs. Barnett. "So what if Hannah makes a little noise? Believe me, she won't disturb God."

Sarah Walker stayed home with her new born twins, but Peretz came with the other four Walker children. Gever Silvano arranged for his manager to take charge of the pharmacy on Saturdays. Mira Carter dragged Tom to services every Saturday morning. Jeremiah Yarden switched office hours so he could join Rebecca and Jonathan.

The Sabbath morning worshipers were mostly retired. Zalman Lutvak and Isidore Hirsch were octogenarians. These Jews were committed to the synagogue, to Jewish law and tradition. They required no gimmicks, no exciting sermon-titles, no choirs to lure them to synagogue. They came because they believed that Jews were obligated to attend synagogue services on Sabbath mornings. They rarely attended late Friday evening services. For these traditionalists, the Sabbath began well before sunset Friday, and extended to well after sundown Saturday night. They deemed Friday night services a concession to the uncommitted element in the congregation, for whom a twenty-five-hour Sabbath was too much. They conceded a need for this "watered-down" service. "Something is better than nothing," Zalman Lutvak granted. But it was not for him. God created Friday night for Jews to spend at home, quietly, peacefully. A leisurely Sabbath evening dinner with family, *zemirot*—Sabbath table songs, Sabbath conversation, study and early to bed. And if the flame still burned, fulfillment of the commandment, *Be fruitful and multiply*. Saturday morning was made to linger in the synagogue.

By strict Orthodox standards, the Sabbath morning service was not traditional. No partition separated the sexes, microphones were permitted, both of which were anathema to strictly Orthodox Jews. To encourage the younger and less knowledgeable set, who on occasion attended, Tali pulled a few concessions from Zalman Lutvak. He persuaded the ritual committee to omit some of the repetitive liturgy and substitute responsive English readings. He cut parts of the lengthy

Israel Jacobs

scriptural readings to allow time for discussion of the assigned Torah text. The Sabbath morning worshipers were happy with the status quo. They allowed no interference from the liberal element who were content to let the traditionalists do their "thing."

Zalman Lutvak was *Gabbai*—the man in charge of parceling out the honors: who was to be called to the Torah, who to open the Ark, who to lead the *P'sukey d'zimrah*—the introductory psalms. Zalman Lutvak was eighty-two years old, stocky, broad-shouldered, with a bullish neck and personality to match. Until age seventy-five, Zalman Lutvak owned Pineville's one and only kosher butcher shop. Over the years shrewd investments had made him a rich man. Nevertheless, he refused to relinquish the butcher shop. He felt it his duty to personally certify that there be no chicanery, as he knew was prevalent in the kosher-butcher business. He took on more help and eased up, coming in later and leaving earlier. But until age seventy-five, he held the reins. Finally, it became too much even for Zalman Lutvak. When a younger man, of impeccable integrity who came highly recommended by Tali's predecessor, offered to buy the butcher shop, Zalman Lutvak retired. He sold the business, glad to turn his butcher shop over to a man he could trust. Since retirement, he devoted full time to the synagogue. On questions pertaining to *kashrut*, Zalman Lutvak spoke with the same authority in the synagogue as he had in his butcher shop. And even regarding ritual matters, Tali often deferred to Zalman Lutvak.

In his butcher shop Zalman Lutvak never vacillated. Either a chicken was kosher, and he sold it at a fair price, or it was *trayfe*—not kosher, and he would not sell it to a Jew at any price. He remained as single-minded in synagogue protocol. One is a Jew, or is not a Jew. If a man is Jewish, you bid him, "Good Shabbos." You make him feel at home. If he's in the synagogue for the first time, you honor him with an *aliyah*.

The first Sabbath morning the blacks attended services Zalman Lutvak distributed five of the eight Torah honors to them. They would have gotten all the honors, except for the fact that the first two honors are traditionally reserved for the Kohen and Levite—direct descendants of the ancient tribe of Levi. *Maftir*, the last honor, required extensive preparation. Lutvak usually gave that honoree a week's notice.

Tom Carter, because he and Mira had taken seats in the back, came to Lutvak's immediate attention. He steered directly toward them, passing several dozen half-empty rows. From his pulpit chair, Tali heard Lutvak's Sabbath greeting, especially reserved for those electing rear seats, "Good Shabbos. The seats up front cost you the same price."

Tom's muffled reply did not reach Tali. He saw Lutvak hand Tom an *aliyah*-card. Tom shook his head. He had as yet to learn that you don't turn down an honor when it is offered by Zalman Lutvak.

Roger Barnett, a long-faced solemn teenager and eldest son of the Barnetts, opened the Ark. He pulled the tassels, removed the Torah and marched down the aisle, leading the processional. Tali saw the boy's father break into a wide grin. Tali reviewed the scriptural reading assigned for that Sabbath. Two of the regular worshipers were called to recite the benedictions for the first and second Torah honors respectively.

"Shlishi, please," Lutvak shouted. "Who has the third honor?"

Tali saw Mira nudge her husband into action. He hastened to the reader's lectern. Lutvak showed Tom the proper way to brush the Torah-scroll with the fringes of his *Tallit*—prayer shawl. Tom intoned the benediction from the card-prompter.

"A little louder please," Lutvak urged. "If we can't hear you say the blessing, we can't answer, 'Amen.'"

Yarden and Gever Silvano were honored with the fourth and fifth *aliyot*, respectively. They recited the blessings in faultless Hebrew. Lutvak was clearly pleased by their performance.

Two more honors were parceled out to the newcomers. Lutvak tendered each man a hand-crunching *yasher koah*. As the honorees returned to their pews, the Sabbath regulars offered handshakes ranging from vigorous to limp. A few stared into their Bibles as the blacks filed past. Tali understood their reticence. Black Jews were strange creatures. They had never met a black Jew; they were confused. Over the years each of the Sabbath morning worshipers had carved out a niche for himself; where to sit, who got what honors, and how often. Order, routine provided an island of security in a fast-changing world. Suddenly, they were challenged by strangers, who appeared to them like aliens from another planet. They felt threatened.

By and large, the Sabbath morning worshipers were wary of liberals, which included freethinkers, radicals, Jewish atheists, communists, Jews who called for change. Once a Jew gives an inch on religious matters, they argued, he is on the road to apostasy. And they held fast to this conviction, despite the fact that their own "traditional" services had wandered a distance from the old forms. But now the rites they observed had, for them, become traditional, and they brooked no further change. Black Jews required a mental readjustment for which they were unprepared.

Time and proximity transformed the aliens into kinfolk. The Sabbath regulars became comfortable with the blacks. Kiddush after services helped bridge the racial divide. A jigger of schnapps, a slice of sponge cake tended to open communication between Jews. As time wore on, the Sabbath regulars paid less attention to the skin pigment of their fellow worshipers. A Jew is invited to recite the Torah benedictions, is called for *hagbah*, or *gelilah*—raising or dressing the Torah scroll, he opens the Ark, leads the Torah processional or recessional. He leads the congregation in prayer. He sits behind you, in front of you, at your side, chanting hymns you have been chanting most of your life, and your father and grandfather before you for generations. You become so accustomed to seeing both him and his family in synagogue, the shade of his skin becomes irrelevant.

The congregation rose. Jeremiah Yarden bowed slightly, intoning in Hebrew, "We bend the knee and worship, acknowledging the King of Kings, the Holy One, praised be He..."

Yes, Tali reflected, time and proximity brought marvelous changes. But there was more to the conversion. Deeper primal instincts inscribed in the Jewish conscience were working their magic. He recalled Leviticus 19:33:

When a stranger resides with you in your land, you shall not wrong him.
The stranger who resides with you shall be to you as one of your citizens;

you shall love him as yourself, for you were strangers in the land of Egypt. I the Lord am your God.

These traditionalists might concede a custom here, a ritual there. But a law so definitively stated in the Torah, by God Himself, brooked no deviation. Another year, at most, Tali was convinced, and there would be no memory of aliens at Sabbath morning services.

Several troubling questions clouded his optimism. The blacks, initially punctilious in attending Friday evening services, had dropped out. When Tali tactfully asked why, Jeremiah explained that the children found the hour too late. Also, after a day's work, the men were tired. They preferred to spend Sabbath eve at home with their families. The explanations lacked conviction. Tali sensed other influences at work, which Jeremiah Yarden did not care to elaborate.

And Tali still could not put out of mind, even after all these months, that not a single black had attended the reception welcoming Hadassah to Pineville. What interpretation did she give to their conspicuous absence? He felt apprehensive about broaching the subject. But the questions persisted.

Chapter Thirty Three

Daylight burrowed through the slats, casting stripes of light and shadow on the ceiling. Tali drew the Venetian blinds. Newly fallen snow coated the back lawn. He tucked the morning newspaper under his arm and strolled into the dinette.

"How is Marduk feeling?"

Hadassah pampered two eggs into the frying pan. "He says his throat still feels a bit sore. I think I'll keep him home today."

"No school? That should make him feel better."

"The cough really sounds bad. He isn't faking."

"I guess you're right. With his bar mitzvah less than two weeks off there's no point in taking chances."

Tali, with Hadassah's encouragement, had decided on a simple bar mitzvah. Sabbath services, followed by a modest kiddush: wine, choice of rye, scotch, bourbon. Then a buffet lunch of lox, smoked fish, egg salad, tuna, coffee and cake. Figuring on an attendance of three hundred, Tali estimated the total cost to be in the neighborhood of about two thousand dollars, a modest sum compared to bar mitzvah receptions held at the Pineville Jewish Center. Everett Russel had suggested that the synagogue defray the cost. Tali thanked Everett for the thought, but insisted on footing the bill himself. To play safe, he ordered the caterer to prepare for four hundred. Friday night he and Hadassah would host the *Oneg Shabbat*—the Fellowship Hour. In January the announcement went out to the congregation via the synagogue bulletin,

Marduk Adams, brother of Mrs. Zeig, will be called to the Torah as a bar mitzvah Saturday morning, February sixteenth. Rabbi and Mrs. Zeig invite the congregation to the Kiddush-luncheon following services.

Marduk, in red flannel pajamas, hunched over a cup of hot chocolate. He puckered his lips and slurped the chocolate drink.

"Will you please tone down that music," Tali grumbled through the newspaper.

"It's hot," Marduk keened.

"So blow on it."

Marduk puffed out his cheeks and exhaled. The hot chocolate billowed over the rim into the saucer. He licked the sides clean.

"You don't let anything go to waste, do you? Wipe your nose; it looks like you gave it a chocolate bath."

Marduk dried his face with a napkin.

Hadassah drifted into the dinette, carrying the morning mail. She extracted an envelope, puzzled over the return address, then handed it to Tali.

"You've got a letter from your uncle."

Tali set the newspaper down. He pried the envelope open. His eyes darted down the page.

"He wants to come!"

"He wants to come to what?"

"To the bar mitzvah. My uncle wants to come to Marduk's bar mitzvah. He asks if we've got room to put him and my aunt up for Shabbos."

"Did you send him an invitation?"

"No. It never occurred to me he would accept."

"How did he know about the bar mitzvah?"

"He must have read it in the synagogue bulletin. I once mentioned to him that I write a monthly column. He said he'd like to read it. I had the office put him on the mailing list. I'd forgotten all about it."

"I think it's marvelous that he wants to come. Write him that we have plenty of room. No, wait, there's not much time. Call him and tell

Israel Jacobs 261

him we would love to have them."

"But I can't invite him to the Pineville Jewish Center."

"Why not?"

"You don't understand."

Hadassah carried the coffeepot to the table. "No, I don't understand. Exactly what is the problem?"

Tali chewed on a hangnail. "My uncle won't worship in a synagogue with mixed seating. In Orthodox synagogues women sit in the balcony. We use a microphone on the Sabbath. And the services are abbreviated. I can't invite the Sumtara Rebbe to worship in a Conservative synagogue."

"He says he wants to come. You can't refuse him."

"Right. And neither can I invite him. This is one heck of a dilemma."

Hadassah poured herself a cup of coffee. "I see he wrote you several pages. What else does he have to say?"

"He asks about you and Marduk. He's concerned about how you made the adjustment. How the congregation has received you. He is especially interested in Marduk's progress. Whether he will continue his religious studies after his bar mitzvah. He asks if I've shown him how to put on the phylacteries. He hopes we are all well, and writes that he is looking forward to seeing us. He seems genuinely interested in coming."

Hadassah spooned sugar into her coffee. "The first time I met your uncle he impressed me as one of the most caring men I ever met. More than that. There was something extraordinary about him, deep, almost mystical, yet aware of everything going on around him, and concerned. Call him today, and tell him we would be delighted to have him and your aunt stay with us."

"But what about the mixed seating? In his circles mixing the sexes is a serious violation of Jewish law."

"Convert the synagogue."

Tali gave Hadassah an odd look.

"For Marduk's bar mitzvah, convert it into an Orthodox synagogue."

262   *The Convert*

"How in heaven's name can I do that? Our sanctuary was not designed to segregate the sexes. We don't have a women's gallery."

"Partition the sanctuary. Sisterhood does it when we want to close off part of the auditorium for small parties or meetings. Run the partitions down the center aisle. Tell your ushers to direct the women to one side, the men to the other. Voila! The Pineville Jewish Center is an Orthodox synagogue."

"And the abbreviated services? I could ask Bindel to chant the full traditional service. But what about the microphones?"

Marduk intervened. "I don't need a microphone. I've been rehearsing without a microphone. Cantor Bindel said I come over loud and clear."

Tali scratched his chin. "It might just work. I could promote that Sabbath service, as a special hasidic Sabbath. It's the in-thing nowadays, Hasidism, Mysticism."

Hadassah made a wry face. "Always fishing for the gimmick. Can't you trust your own people to understand? Tell your ritual committee straight out that your uncle, the Sumtara Rebbe, is coming, that out of deference to him you want to have this one Orthodox service. They'll go along, I'm sure. Especially, the Sabbath morning regulars."

Tali pondered a moment. He stretched across the table and kissed Hadassah on the tip of her nose.

"Rebbitzen Zeig, you are a genius."

The Rebbe had written that he expected to come by train and taxi. Tali would not hear of it. Friday, the morning before Marduk's bar mitzvah, he drove into the city to pick up his uncle and aunt.

Hadassah smoothed down the floral-patterned bedspreads on the twin beds. She gave the guest room a final inspection. The doorbell chimed. She called down. "Marduk, will you answer the door, please."

Marduk yelled up, "Okay, I'll get it."

Hadassah hastened downstairs. Tali stood in the vestibule with a valise in each hand.

"Where are your aunt and uncle?"

"My aunt? Uncle?" Uh... in the car."

"Don't you think you ought to invite them in?"

"Right. I'll go get them." Tali started for the door.

Hadassah checked his exit. "Since you already brought their luggage in, why don't you leave it here, and go get your aunt and uncle?"

"Oh, yeah. Good thinking." Tali dropped both valises. They thudded to the floor. One opened. Shirts, underwear, socks flooded out.

"What is the matter with you?" Hadassah gathered up the apparel. Carefully, she folded them back into the valise. "Will you please bring your aunt and uncle into the house. They must be freezing."

Tali veered to the door and tripped over the other valise. Marduk caught him by the elbow. Hadassah shrugged.

"Marduk, maybe you'd better go and get them. Your brother-in-law is not all here today."

The bell chimed again. Marduk skipped to the door. The Sumtara Rebbe stood in the doorway, his beard fluttering in the wind. Tali's aunt stood at her husband's side, solemn-faced and bundled in an ankle-length coat. Hadassah hastened to the door.

"Shalom! shalom!" She ushered the Sumtara Rebbe and his wife into the house. "Naphtali, take your aunt and uncle's coats. Marduk, bring the valises upstairs then come down and show the Rebbe and Rebbitzen to their room." Hadassah barked orders like a drill sergeant. Marduk lugged the valises upstairs, settled the guests in their room, then hustled downstairs. In the excitement he had forgotten his stomach. Now it growled. He trooped into the kitchen. Tali and Hadassah were talking in whispers.

Tali said, "Did she bring food?"

"No, she did not," Hadassah said.

"What will they eat?"

"They'll eat what I serve them."

But they never eat out. They only eat Glatt kosher."

"I know all about Glatt kosher."

"You do?"

264   *The Convert*

Hadassah nudged Tali aside. She opened the refrigerator and passed a container of milk to Marduk. "You'll find chocolate crackers in the pantry."

"Who told you about Glatt kosher?"

Hadassah showered him with a superior smile. "Soon as I knew for certain that they were coming I called your aunt and asked if there was anything special I should prepare."

"You called my aunt?"

"Yes, I called your aunt. She explained about Glatt kosher. You never mentioned there are different degrees of kosher. Your aunt gave me the number of the butcher shop where she buys her meat. They delivered it Tuesday."

"All the way from Brussel Street to Pineville?"

"There are people who will go to the ends of the earth for your uncle. One of his hasidim delivered it. I had to fight the man to pay the bill. Your aunt had already paid. I wouldn't let him go until he took my money and promised to credit her."

"You did all that on your own?"

"Sure did. The meat has your uncle's seal on it. What do you call it? Hashgahah?" Hadassah reached into a cabinet drawer. "I saved one. Here it is." She waved a small tin button with Hebrew letters imprinted on it under Tali's nose. "See?"

Tali's benighted demeanor since his uncle and aunt's arrival began to clear. He grinned.

"Hadassah, you are not only beautiful, you are absolutely remarkable."

"Well, one of us has got to keep a head on her shoulders." She shooed him aside. "Now get out of my kitchen. I've got a roast in the oven."

The Sumtara Rebbe glanced anxiously at the dashboard clock. "Shabbos is in fifteen minutes."

"It's less than five minutes to shule, Uncle."

Worrying Tali more than arriving before the Sabbath began, was whether Zalman Lutvak had managed to assemble a minyan. Not until

Israel Jacobs 265

the previous night did it occur to him to arrange for a traditional sundown service. Collecting ten men for a five o'clock service on a Friday afternoon required someone who wouldn't take no for an answer. Tali had phoned Zalman Lutvak for help. The old man assured him, "Don't worry, Rabbi, I will see to it that there is a minyan." Tali worried if even Zalman Lutvak could scrape together a quorum at that hour. His uncle would be distressed if he had to forgo worshiping without the required quorum. And he, Tali, would be humiliated that in all of Pineville ten Jews couldn't be found to make a minyan. He cut into the synagogue parking lot. Marduk scrambled out first and proudly assisted the Rebbe from the car. The Rebbe tilted his head up, tracking the fifty-foot facade soaring above the sanctuary. He clutched his wide-brimmed hat.

"This is your shule?"

"Yes, Uncle," Tali said, haltingly.

"It is impressive."

Tali led the way to the main entrance. They shed their coats and climbed the stairs to the sanctuary. The Rebbe stopped to examine the lobby.

"Naphtali, you must have very rich people in your congregation to build a shule like this."

Knowing the Sumtara Rebbe was not impressed by material opulence, Tali speculated that his uncle was diplomatically asking, "Was this synagogue built to glorify God, or its builders?"

Marduk opened the sanctuary doors. Nervously, Tali followed, hoping that Lutvak had succeeded in gathering a minyan.

The first twelve rows were filled. There were at least a hundred men in the sanctuary. Lutvak had corralled every male Sabbath regular, including the blacks. Also, a dozen other men, whom Tali hadn't seen in synagogue since the High Holy days. Evidently, Zalman Lutvak did not deem a bare quorum sufficient to welcome the Sumtara Rebbe. Tali made a mental note to write Lutvak a thank-you note. He escorted his uncle down a side aisle. Partitions to separate the sexes had already been put in place. Yarden and Lutvak were in a spirited debate; whatever the issue, Lutvak as usual seemed to be winning the argument.

266   *The Convert*

Yarden's hands were spread out in a gesture of surrender. Lutvak looked in their direction, saw the Rebbe coming his way and immediately rose. Jeremiah Yarden turned and stood up. Before Tali had escorted his uncle halfway down the aisle, the entire congregation had risen.

Tali did not want for respect from the Sabbath regulars. He knew some did not agree with many of his innovations. Still, they respected him as a modern university-trained American rabbi who, on the whole, did have a traditional bent. And, a rabbi whatever his views, is to be respected. If not for himself, then for his position. But no American trained rabbi could transport these traditionalists back to the old country, to memories of the shtetl, to a life that was no more. Tali felt a twinge of envy at the awe his uncle inspired by his mere presence. The old-timers surrounded the Rebbe, showering him with Sabbath greetings. Tali waited for each man to shake his uncle's hand, then escorted him to a front pew. The congregation remained standing until the Rebbe sat down.

Lutvak signaled Jeremiah Yarden to ascend the pulpit.

"Dr. Yarden, I think it is time to begin the *minhah* service."

Tali surmised that was the reason for the debate between Yarden and Lutvak, he had noted upon entering the sanctuary, Lutvak had drafted the doctor to lead in the afternoon service. Yarden had declined. Lutvak, true to his obstinate nature, refused to accept no for an answer.

Yarden ascended the pulpit, shuffled the thick leather-bound pulpit prayer book and intoned the brief afternoon service in a meticulous Sephardi accent, articulating every word. Tali observed the close attention his uncle paid to Yarden. The Sumtara Rebbe was obviously impressed.

Cantor Bindel rose to lead the *Kabbalat Shabbat* service—the traditional Sabbath eve service. He wore a woolen tallit in place of the formal ornate pulpit robe he usually bedecked himself in when conducting services. Tali noted, too, that Bindel had dispensed with his pitch pipe. Also absent, Tali noted, were the usual theatrics. Skillfully, Bindel wove hasidic refrains into the service that carried Tali back to

Israel Jacobs 267

boyhood days in the Brussel Street synagogue. The Rebbe prayed with his eyes closed, gently swaying, joining with the congregation in the traditional choral refrains.

Tali had assigned Marduk to chant the *Kiddush*, and *Yigdal*—a poetic rendition of Maimonides' *Thirteen Principles of Faith*, which traditionally concludes the Sabbath eve service. Marduk chanted the final verse in a confident fortissimo and returned to his pew next to Tali.

The Rebbe extended his hand, *Yasher ko-ah*. Marduk was sufficiently familiar with synagogue protocol to know that the Rebbe was congratulating him for his performance.

The Sabbath regulars again clustered around the Rebbe, each shaking his hand and bidding him a "Good Shabbos." Jeremiah Yarden approached the Rebbe. "Shabbat Shalom. We are honored by your presence."

The Rebbe nodded. *"Yasher koah.* I very much enjoyed the way you *davened Minchah.* Dr. Yarden, you *daven* with much feeling. I have read your father's book, so I understand from where comes the spark."

Tali guided his uncle out of the sanctuary via the side aisle. Marduk followed a pace behind. The Rebbe halted at the last row.

"Why do you have those dividers in the aisles?"

Tali held the sanctuary doors open. "You mean the partitions?"

"Yes. What is their purpose?"

Gently, Tali nudged his uncle to the door.

The Rebbe would not be diverted. "Why the partitions?"

"They're to separate the men and women for tomorrow's service."

A rich shule like this uses partitions for a *mechitzah?*"

Tali had not expected that the partitions would escape his uncle's notice. But he had hoped that his uncle wouldn't ask.

"Actually, Uncle, we don't have a *mechitzah.*"

"No? Men and women sit together in your shule?"

"Yes, Uncle. We put the partitions up for this Shabbos only. So you would *daven* with us."

The night air was frigid but dry. The Rebbe walked erect, taking long easy strides. The walk from synagogue to home took twenty-five minutes. Hadassah welcomed them at the door.

"Shabbat Shalom, Shabbat Shalom." She hurried them out of the cold.

"Gut Shabbos," the Rebbe's breath made small vapor clouds. Hadassah closed the door behind him. He rubbed his hands together.

"That was a good walk. Here in the country it is a joy to walk."

"I enjoy it, too," Tali said. "Except, sometimes on Shabbos it rains buckets. Then I wouldn't mind living closer to the shule."

"And your *ba-aley-batim*—the members of your congregation? What do they do when it rains?

Tali searched for an answer. "Well... Some come... Some stay home."

Hadassah steered them into the dining room. She wore a high-necked blouse and pleated skirt that fell well below the knees. Tali's aunt had changed into a dark tweed dress. She wore a kerchief on her head. Her round face was scrubbed to a shine. She greeted her husband with an energetic, "Gut Shabbos," then Tali and Marduk.

The Sabbath candles, the spanking white tablecloth and sparkling silverware beckoned warmly.

Friday nights were a rush. Rush through dinner. Rush to dress, rush to make the eight o'clock service. All the rushing robbed Sabbath eve of its purpose. Having a service at sundown enabled Tali to relax and enjoy Sabbath dinner, as it was meant to be enjoyed. His uncle and aunt brought an added measure of family and holiness to the Sabbath table. And the dinner Hadassah had prepared for the occasion gave Tali cause to wonder. Where had she learned to make gefilte fish? Probably from Sandra Russel, Tali guessed. But where had Sandra learned? The more he experienced the enthusiasm with which both women had embraced Jewish ritual and the Jewish cuisine, the more convinced he became that what the synagogue needed was a larger dose of converts. They better appreciated what native-born Jews took for granted.

After the gefilte fish, Hadassah served matzah-ball soup, *kugel*, stuffed derma. Tali's aunt admired the consistency and color of the

Israel Jacobs 269

stuffed derma.

"Very good, the way you made the stuffed derma." She smacked her lips. "You are a *ta-ye-reh balabuste*."

Hadassah shrugged at Tali. He explained, "*Balabuste* means mistress of the house. *Ta-ye-reh* means precious. My aunt thinks you are a treasure." Tali bent to peck her cheek.

Hadassah accepted the kiss frigidly. Too bad the compliment didn't come from you, she thought to herself. Tali's aunt had snagged on to a thorn that of late had been needling Hadassah. Here she was remaking herself body and soul, changing into a person she hardly recognized anymore. She deserved a little applause for her efforts. Fitting into his world, learning to run a Jewish kitchen, playing hostess to his congregants. At the beginning she would wake in the morning to anxiety attacks, afraid that she could never bridge the cultural divide. And if not for Sandra Russel, she might not have pulled it off. Her husband rarely noticed. Too involved counseling everybody else. He had a tough job, she acknowledged. A six-hundred-family congregation constantly making demands. But she, too, had needs. Why wasn't he paying more attention to her needs?

The Rebbe leaned back in his chair.

"Nu, Naphtali. The Talmud says, 'If three people have eaten at one table and spoken words of Torah, it is as if they have eaten at God's table.' The women have done their share to make this a *ta-ye-reh* Shabbos. Now it is time for us to do ours."

Much of the Torah discussion, carried on in a blend of Hebrew, Yiddish and English, went over Hadassah's head. But she caught the gist. Uncle and nephew were debating the limitations of freedom. The inspiration for the debate, as she gathered, was the chapters assigned to be read from the Torah the following day, which dealt with a Hebrew sold into servitude. The Rebbe pyramided quotations from the Talmud to support his opinion that the only freedom man has is the freedom to choose his master. Tali dissented. He quoted Deuteronomy, *I have set before you a blessing and a curse, therefore, choose life*, which, he argued, proved the Rebbe wrong. Hadassah was impressed by the give and take.

Tali revered his uncle, nevertheless, they debated as equals. Tali conceded a point; the Rebbe made one, Tali made one. At the conclusion, the questions remained unresolved. The discussion seemed to be more important than conclusions. The Rebbe turned to Marduk.

"Nu, Mordecai."

Tali had not informed the Rebbe that his brother-in-law preferred to be called Marduk. No one at the table corrected the Rebbe, including Marduk.

"Did you study the Sidra for this Shabbos?"

Marduk exchanged glances with Tali. "Yep, I did."

The Rebbe combed his beard with two fingers. "And do you remember the law regarding a Hebrew slave?"

"He automatically goes free on *shemitah*—the seventh year."

"Good. And if the slave does not want to go free? If he says that he is happy with his master, he loves the wife his master has given him, and the children he has fathered with her, what is the law?"

Marduk fired back the answer. "The Torah says they bring the slave to a doorpost and pierce his ear. Then he can stay a slave if he wants to."

"And why did the Torah require that a slave who doesn't want to go free have his ears pierced at a doorpost?" The Rebbe chanted the question in a sing song voice.

"Because the doorposts were witnesses that when the Angel of Death passed over the Hebrew houses, God had told them He didn't want the Hebrews to be slaves to nobody but Him. So a slave who don't want to go free gets his ears pierced at a doorpost."

Marduk squinted at the Rebbe. "It's only an earlobe. Doesn't hurt much, Tali told me. Less than a *tipat dahm*."

Marduk looked pleased with himself at having the answers at his fingertips. The Rebbe chuckled. "Very good, Mordecai. You have done well. And I must give a *yasher koah* to you, Naphtali. You are a good teacher."

Hadassah was sure she saw moisture film Tali's eyes.

The Rebbe continued. "I have one more question I would like you to answer for me. Not from the Torah, or the commentators. I would

Israel Jacobs 271

like to hear your own opinion."

Marduk leaned over the table. Hadassah watched her brother's face beam, clearly flattered that the Sumtara Rebbe was interested in his opinion.

"What do you think of a man who would rather have a master, even a good master, than be free?"

Marduk pondered the question with a grave face. "I don't know about anybody else. I don't want to be a slave."

The Rebbe stroked his beard. "And what about being God's slave; would you want to be God's slave?"

Tali went taut. The Rebbe's wife leaned forward in her chair straining to hear Marduk's answer, as if a cosmic issue hung in the balance. Hadassah, too, seemed caught up in the dialogue. The Rebbe rocked from side to side, one hand tugging at his beard, the other supporting his forehead. Marduk considered the question at length.

"No I don't want to be God's slave either. Nothin' personal. I dig God. But when I mind Him, I wanna mind Him like a free man, not a slave."

Hadassah let her breath out, *From the mouth of babes...*

The Rebbe smiled, breaking the tension. Tali relaxed. The Rebbe began to tap a rhythmic beat with his fingers. He rocked back and forth in time to the beat. The tapping snared Tali first, then Marduk. Tali's aunt began to sway from side to side. The beat caught Hadassah. It was as if they all heard a tune playing in the Rebbe's head. Hadassah wasn't sure when the melody became actual sound. It flowed from the Rebbe's head to their ears, softly at first, then gaining momentum, louder and joyful, different and yet akin to soul music she remembered from childhood.

Chapter Thirty Four

Despite Hadassah's rosy prediction, Tali had misgivings about separating the sexes. He feared a rebellion, especially from the militant females in the congregation. They had demonstrated that they would not blindly submit to authority. He worried about them kicking up a fracas at the door: Rabbi is turning our Temple Orthodox; we insist on sitting with our husbands.

Originally, the Pineville Jewish Center, founded by Orthodox Jews such as Lutvak and Hirschman, was an Orthodox synagogue. Most of the members had little memory of those early years, and would fiercely oppose turning the clock back. Apprehensively, Tali watched the members file in.

Not ten o'clock and close to four hundred men, women, children, were rapidly filling the pews. Sandra Russel sat next to Hadassah, giving her moral support. Tali observed Muriel Shakter glide into the sanctuary, waving a kiss to her husband, as if they were going on separate vacations. She joined Rochelle Feld, Sisterhood president, in the female section. Tali appraised the sea of blue skullcaps and *talesim*, worn by the men, and the women seated to the left of the partitions speaking in whispers. Thus far no protests, no incidents. The congregation seemed to accept the novel seating arrangements in good spirits. Hadassah had correctly gauged the congregation. Remarkable, how women can size up a situation intuitively. He tended to analyze, examine the pros and cons before acting. Women cut to the heart of

Israel Jacobs   273

the matter and usually come up on the right side.

Tali directed his attention to Cantor Bindel. He again had dispensed with his formal pulpit robe and instead wore a large woolen *tallit*—the traditional prayer shawl, over a navy-blue vested suit. His pitch-pipe had vanished. No trills or prolonged recitatives. He led the service like a hasid in ecstasy, introducing exciting hasidic melodies. The congregation enthusiastically joined in the cheerful refrains. Cantor Bindel had scratched the veneer of these sophisticates and liberated the hasid underneath.

Tali asked the congregation to rise. Bindel chanted Marduk's name, Mordecai ben Avraham.

Marduk hesitated. His confidence seemed to have wilted. Below, in the first pew, Hadassah stiffened. Sandra whispered into her ear. She smiled nervously. Marduk walked to the lectern haltingly. Bindel prompted him to begin.

He chanted the first set of blessings, "*Borhu et Adonoy ha-mevorah...* Blessed be the Lord who is to be blessed."

Weak but no errors.

Cantor Bindel gestured for him to continue. He delivered the second set of benedictions in a stronger voice. The congregation rose on cue for the ritual dressing of the Torah scroll, then resumed their seats. Marduk started on the *Haftorah*. Once on his way, he regained his aplomb. Midway he unglued his eyes from the text and looked boldly around the sanctuary. He stumbled on a phrase. He stuttered the next two verses and chanted on. For the remainder of the *Haftorah* he kept his nose buried in the text. From his vantage point on the pulpit, Tali observed his uncle, flanked by Lutvak and Hirschman, straining not to miss a verse. Marduk chanted the final lines with his bravado restored and returned to the pulpit chair next to Tali.

Tali clasped his hand firmly. "*Yasher ko-ah.* You did well."

"I goofed a couple of verses, didn't I?"

"Not really. All in all, you did a fine job. We're proud of you."

Bindel led the recessional with Marduk proudly carrying the Torah scroll. The Cantor chanted from Proverbs:

The Torah is a tree of life to those who take hold of it;
happy are those who support it.

The Torah scroll was returned to the Ark. Tali asked the congregation to be seated. He waited for quiet, then announced, "My uncle, the Sumtara Rebbe, will deliver the bar mitzvah charge."

There was a brief outbreak of whispers, then quiet again.

Tali sat down, telling himself how incredible this entire weekend was. Out of courtesy he had asked his uncle if he would like to deliver the charge, never expecting that he would agree. He did, eagerly, as if he had been waiting to be asked. His uncle had shattered precedent by co-officiating with Professor Teitlebaum at the Seminary. That strained credibility. But the wedding had been a private affair with few in attendance. This was a public appearance with more than four hundred present. True, for this one Sabbath the Pineville Jewish Center had been converted into an Orthodox synagogue, no mixed seating, no microphone, a full traditional service, an unabridged scriptural reading. But his uncle understood that on the following Sabbath all would revert to normal. The partitions would go, the microphones plugged back in, and the services radically cut. When word got out, as it surely would, that the Sumtara Rebbe had worshiped, in fact, had preached in a Conservative synagogue, he would be in for a load of criticism from the Orthodox world. It didn't seem to trouble him.

God had sent Jonah to preach to Nineveh so that the people of that wicked city might mend its ways and be saved. Was this what his uncle had in mind? To save these Jews? Tali doubted it. His uncle was not so naive as to think the Pineville Jewish Center would turn Orthodox. But neither did the Sumtara Rebbe make a move without a grand purpose in mind.

The Sumtara Rebbe folded back the upper part of his prayer shawl, uncovering the large skullcap and long earlocks underneath. Zalman Lutvak hastened to his side, escorted him to the pulpit, then returned to his pew, looking as if he had escorted the Messiah. A hush settled over the sanctuary. Not a murmur, not a cough. Tali prodded Marduk toward the lectern.

Casually, as if he were picking up the thread of an interrupted

Israel Jacobs 275

conversation, the Rebbe led into a question.

"Mordecai, if the *Ribbono Shel Olam*, the Master of the universe were to reveal to you His *Shechinah*—His Divine presence, how would you feel?"

Marduk licked his lips. The Rebbe didn't mean to rap with him now? Not in front of all these people? He dared a look up and waited for the Sumtara Rebbe to tell him how he should feel if God suddenly came calling.

"How would you feel?" the Rebbe repeated. Marduk shifted his weight. He hooked one thumb into a pocket, then the other. His palms began to sweat. The Rebbe wasn't fooling. He expected an answer.

"Gee! I...I... don't know. I guess I'd be scared stiff."

"Mordecai, you remember last night we talked at the Shabbos table?" The Rebbe spoke softly, soothingly. The congregation faded. The two of them were alone. Back home at the Sabbath table, discussing Torah. The Rebbe pressed down gently on Marduk's shoulder.

"Do you remember, Mordecai, what *Moshe Rabbenu*, Moses our teacher, did after he came down from Mt. Sinai?"

"I think so. He told the Hebrews about the laws. The Hebrews promised to obey. Then Moses wrote it down for them. Afterward, they built an altar and sacrificed some oxen to God."

"Yes, yes," the Rebbe urged him on. "Then what does the Torah tell us happened next?"

The final verses had blown from his memory. He drew a blank.

"Afterwards," the Rebbe cued. "When Nadav and Avihu, the sons of Aaron, the High priest, and the seventy elders went up to the mountain with Moses. What does the Torah tell us they saw?"

The answer rocketed into his head. "They saw God."

The Rebbe twirled an earlock. "Correct. They saw God's *Shechina*. With human eyes they looked upon the Divine presence. A vision few mortals are granted. Do you remember that verse, Mordecai?"

Marduk nodded. The Rebbe had nudged the verses back into his memory. That part of the story had seemed weird. He had meant to ask Tali about it. But with Bindel pressuring him to rehearse, Tali pushing

276 *The Convert*

him to finish the essay, public school, Hebrew School, it had slipped his mind.

"What did Moses and the Elders of Israel do while in the presence of God's Shechinah?"

"They ate and drank."

Tali began to see connections, to understand what his uncle was driving at. And to understand as well why the Sumtara Rebbe was acclaimed to be one of the world's great hasidic leaders. His grasp of the secular and holy, his genius in harmonizing the two, in his writings, his lectures, and most importantly, in his life, reflected the essence of Judaism. Tali perceived, as never before, what his uncle was about. He perceived as well the effect the Rebbe was having on the congregation. It was a unique moment—a black boy being bar mitzvah. The spiritual leader of a world-wide hasidic sect preaching in a Liberal synagogue. The last time the sexes were separated in the Pineville Jewish Center happened decades before his tenure, in the old building, at that time called Kenesset Israel. Few were still around to tell of those years; Zalman Lutvak and two or three old-timers. Since then, the name of the congregation had been changed to the Pineville Jewish Center. The congregation had quadrupled its membership, prospered and evolved into a typical upper-middle-class suburban congregation. Services, in form were Jewish, in spirit Protestant. Black pulpit gown, *shulhan*—reading table moved from center to front, professionals leading the service instead of laymen. The congregation stood up and sat down on signal, turned pages as directed, read responsively when told to, and departed when dismissed. Spontaneity, fervor, Jews collectively worshiping as individuals, were foreign to the average Conservative Jew. The focus of a bar and bat mitzvah had moved from synagogue to catering hall. It had all been Americanized—services to please grandma and grandpa. Then Saturday night orgy.

And he was part of the system. More. He was the hub around which it all circled. He, as rabbi, sanctified the system.

A Sabbath service, the likes of this, had never happened in Pineville, and probably never would again. They were already behind schedule. At this hour, Bindel usually was leading the congregation in *Adon Olam*, the final hymn. No one seemed impatient to depart. For the moment, his uncle had mesmerized four hundred Conservative Jews. He continued,

"To eat and drink in the presence of God's Shechinah! How did Moses permit this? And not only did he permit it, he himself ate and drank." The Rebbe leaned one elbow on the lectern. "Does this not seem disrespectful?"

Marduk touched his brow. "I did wonder about it. With God right there, it don't seem right to eat dinner."

"Mordecai, strange as it may seem, the Torah did not think it disrespectful to eat and rejoice in God's presence." The Rebbe turned full face to the congregation, then locked eyes with Marduk again.

"Last night, at the Sabbath table, we ate and drank, and we sang Sabbath songs. We talked Torah. God was there, Mordecai. We may not have seen him, as did Moses and the Elders. But God was with us last night, as He is here in this synagogue now. As He is everywhere. There are religions that believe God wants man only to fast, to mortify the flesh, to suffer. They believe this world is evil and that man is born in sin. Our faith insists that man is born pure, innocent. When God created the world, He said: *Behold it is good.* And so it is, Mordecai, if you and I and mankind will it. Everything God created is waiting. Do you know for what it is waiting, Mordecai? It is waiting for us to make it holy. That is what the psalmist meant, *What is man that You are mindful of him; yet You have made him little less than divine.* We have been granted the power to desecrate God's world, to make it ugly, dirty. Or, we can make it beautiful, holy. Eating, drinking, all of life, all of God's world is waiting for us to make it holy. Do you understand, Mordecai?"

"I... I think so."

It was hardly possible, Tali thought. Bright as Marduk might be, no thirteen-year-old could comprehend such abstractions. Yet, the expression on his face, the light that shines when comprehension cracks open an enigma, indicated that he did understand. His uncle had touched the boy via a truer conduit than the intellect, as he seemed to reach out to the congregation. Not by communicating in words, as

278 *The Convert*

much as by transmitting a presence.

The Rebbe elaborated a few moments more on the theme of holiness and joy. He concluded, "This Mordecai, is your obligation as a Jew. To make the world holy."

Tali stepped to the lectern and escorted his uncle to a pulpit chair. Cantor Bindel resumed his place at the lectern. Ten minutes past one, an hour and fifteen minutes later than usual. The congregation joined in *Adon Olam*, then rose on cue. They remained standing, as was customary, waiting for Tali and the guest rabbi to march down the aisle for the traditional exchange of Sabbath greetings,

Zalman Lutvak bolted to the pulpit.

"Gut Shabbos! Gut Shabbos, Rebbe."

Tali understood what made Zalman Lutvak jump the gun. He smiled to himself. The old man knows protocol, when in the presence of a Rebbe, the likes of the Sumtara Rebbe. The Rebbe wait at the door for the congregation to file past? Such a custom might be fitting for an American rabbi. Zalman Lutvak was not about to allow the Sumtara Rebbe to march down any aisle. The Rebbe doesn't come to you; you go to the Rebbe. And God forbid! What if a woman tried to shake his hand?

Hirschman scurried to the pulpit, leading a rush of old-timers.

The crowds of well-wishers made his head reel. A four-hour service; then table-hopping from one end of the ballroom to the other, taking pains not to offend a member by failing to personally say, "Shabbat Shalom, I'm so glad you came, I hope you enjoyed the services. Did your table have enough to eat?" He was exhausted. He would have to forgo his Sabbath nap. Hadassah seemed to hold up under the strain much better than he. Tali noticed that Dr. Yarden, Peretz Walker and Isaac Barnett were huddled around the head table talking to his uncle. The black members had wandered over to the head table shortly after the luncheon began, presumably to say Shabbat Shalom and leave. But his uncle had detained them. They had been deeply engrossed in conversation with his uncle since, and that was about an hour ago. Tali wondered what they were talking about.

Chapter Thirty Five

Four to six inches of snow had been predicted. The stained glass windows, normally splashing bright rainbow hues into the sanctuary, were lifeless this morning. Lutvak tugged into his coat.

"Good Shabbos, Rabbi. I think I'll skip kiddush this morning. It looks like any minute we will have a snow storm. For a change the weatherman was right. I want to get home before it starts coming down heavy."

"Anybody staying for kiddish?"

"Most everybody already left."

"Have a good Shabbos, Mr. Lutvak."

Zalman Lutvak trundled past the four remaining blacks. He stopped to extend Sabbath greetings. "Good Shabbos, Dr. Yarden, Mr. Silvano, Mr. Barnett. And to you, Mr. Carter."

An awkward silence pressed down on the sanctuary. Yarden stared at the Ark, as if trying to avoid eye contact with Tali. Overhead, the Eternal Light cast dim orange rays. Silvano braced himself against a pew. Isaac Barnett stood nervously at his side. Tom Carter was his usual taciturn self. Tali folded his *talit*. He smelled a problem.

"All is normal again," Tali said, forcing cheer into his voice. "The microphone is back, mixed seating, short service. Cantor Bindel made record time this morning. It's only eleven-thirty."

"Do you have a few moments, Rabbi?"

"Sure, Dr. Yarden."

Jeremiah Yarden seemed ill at ease.

"Anything the matter, Dr. Yarden?"

Tom Carter moved to the fore. Silvano put an arm out, blocking him. Carter sulked back. The lights flickered and went out. They flickered again, went on and stayed lit. Yarden shifted his coat from one arm to another.

"This past Tuesday evening we met to discuss our membership in the Pineville Jewish Center. We voted to resign. I felt you should be told before we submit our resignation to the membership committee."

"The four of you intend to resign. Why?"

Yarden shook his head. "Not just we four. All of us."

"All of you?" Tali searched each face for an explanation.

"Please understand, Rabbi Zeig, we have no quarrel with the synagogue. Considering the circumstances, you have accommodated to us, and we to you remarkably well."

Tali said, "I thought we were long past that. There is no you and us in the Pineville Jewish Center. Only Jews."

"Perhaps. In any event that is not what prompted our decision."

"Then why?"

Dr. Yarden removed his glasses. He took several moments to polish them with his handkerchief. Tali sensed the gesture was a pretext to gather his thoughts. Yarden replaced the glasses. "Some of us want to make a deeper commitment to Judaism. In order to facilitate—"

"Wonderful," Tali cut Yarden off. "That surely is no reason to resign."

Gever Silvano said, "Hear Jeremiah out, Rabbi, please."

The sanctuary felt oppressively warm. During services something had gone askew with the thermostat, driving the heat up uncomfortably. Zalman Lutvak refused to permit repairs on the Sabbath. The custodian had switched the oil burner on and off manually every half hour. He had evidently not bothered to turn it off. Tali motioned Marduk to open a side vent. He sidled through a row to one of the stained glass windows and pushed the bottom half out. A freezing gust slammed into his face. The noon sky had become ominously dark. Large snowflakes drifted past the window, adhering and building white mounds on the sill. A car skidded out of the parking lot, barely missing a lamppost. Marduk cut back across the pews.

Yarden looked at Barnett. "Why don't you tell him yourself, Isaac?"

Isaac Barnett, a huge hulk of a man with thick red lips and protruding ears had impressed Tali as a good-natured uninhibited extrovert. One Sabbath, during the Fellowship hour, he had unabashedly suggested to Hadassah that she and the rabbi should raise a large family.

"We're considering," Hadassah had said.

Isaac had loosed a hearty belly laugh. "Considering won't do the job. God intended for a man and woman to raise a large family."

"What makes you think so?"

"My six kids. They keep me sociable and my wife young. Sure to do the same for you and the rabbi."

Today, Isaac had trouble speaking his mind. He chewed at his lips, studied his shoes a long moment.

"Partly, you are to blame, Rabbi."

"Me? Did I do something to offend you?"

Barnett shook his head. "No, nothing like that."

"What is it, then?"

"It all started with that first sermon I heard you preach. You said that Judaism is a do-it-yourself religion. That nobody can pray for you, or study for you, observe Jewish law for you, honor your parents for you, or honor the Sabbath for you. That sermon made an impression on me."

Tali remembered that Sabbath evening. Not the sermon. What had stayed etched in his mind were the "amens" the blacks had showered him with. And the effect on his stolid congregants.

Barnett continued, "At that time what you were saying touched me in a kind of general way. Later, weeks and months later, it dawned on me that you and your wife and Marduk never drive to the synagogue on the Sabbath. No matter the weather, you walk. I mentioned it to Mr. Lutvak. He explained that though you are liberal about many things, when it comes down to observing the law, you're traditional. And according to the law, Mr. Lutvak said, driving on the Sabbath is

282 *The Convert*

prohibited. He told me that's why he lives within walking distance of the synagogue, even though his wife is not happy with the neighborhood. I thought about it a long time. The deeper I went into what the Sabbath is about, the better I understood why you won't drive on Sabbath. I discussed it with Peretz Walker; he would have been here, but Sarah is down with a bad cold. Peretz said he had noticed the same thing. We have a rotating adult-study group that meets bi-weekly at different homes. Peretz brought the subject up, and surprisingly, a few other families, including Gever here, also had been giving it thought. We tossed the subject around for months. Some of us began to question whether driving on Sabbath, even if only to synagogue, is right. It seems to detract from the Sabbath sanctity. Tom revived the idea we had shelved when we joined the Pineville Jewish Center, of building, or maybe buying a large house, and starting our own synagogue. Jeremiah insisted we tell you before we finalize the decision."

"So that's it," Tali said, looking somewhat relieved.

"Yes, we've been batting the idea, of building our own synagogue, around for quite a while."

"Tell me, my friend," Tali snapped, "Did my uncle have anything to do with finalizing your decision?"

"Well, we... we were heading in that direction. I...uh... did put the question to him at Marduk's bar mitzvah last week."

"You did, did you? And what did my uncle have to say?"

"Well, he suggested it might be better to pray at home than drive to the synagogue on Sabbath."

"Only suggested?"

"I...I... suppose it was a bit stronger than that."

"Yes. More like telling you that driving on Sabbath, not only voids a Jew's prayers, but makes a mockery of them."

Barnett fidgeted uncomfortably. "Those were not exactly his words."

"But close to it?"

"Well, to be honest, close to it, yes."

"It's easy for him and his hasidim to condemn," Tali snapped. "But what other ties do most of my congregants have to Judaism?

Discourage synagogue attendance, and the last link is gone. They would have nothing. And believe me, if my congregants didn't drive to synagogue, they wouldn't stay home praying. Here at least they get a feel for the Sabbath. It's not much, but it's better than nothing. And my uncle is well aware of it."

"Your uncle understands the dilemma," Silvano leaped to the Rebbe's defense. "He did not intend to criticize you. We discussed our situation only. He merely advised us to look for alternatives to driving on the Sabbath."

"Gentlemen, I'm not disputing that there is merit to my uncle's point of view. But you have to be realistic. It isn't that simple to establish a synagogue. For starters, you don't have enough families to carry that heavy a load. Even if you manage to scrape together enough money to buy or build, what about a rabbi? Let's say you do without a rabbi, what about a religious school for your kids? How will you staff it? Congregations able to pay the freight have enormous difficulty finding good teachers. You're buying yourselves more headaches than you can imagine."

"I did point those problems out, "Yarden said. "Peretz and Isaac both teach at Northville High School. They are excellent pedagogues and have volunteered their services."

"Volunteers, no matter how dedicated, seldom work out. You'd be fooling yourselves, and cheating your kids out of a good Jewish education. We've been up the volunteer road. Forget it."

Jeremiah Yarden was uncharacteristically silent, as if he supported the decision, but for reasons he preferred not to discuss.

"Dr. Yarden, the Sabbath is not all there is to this resignation?"

"You heard Isaac. Of all people you, as rabbi, should appreciate that the Sabbath is sufficient reason for our decision. I remind you of what Ahad Ha-am said, whom you have quoted on a number of occasions, *More than Israel kept the Sabbath, the Sabbath has kept Israel.* You should be pleased that Isaac and Peretz want to put into practice what you taught them."

The good doctor was overreacting. There was more to this than met the eye. Tali believed he knew the core reason for the resignation.

284   *The Convert*

He had suspected it all along. And he didn't like it.

"What about you, Dr. Yarden? You haven't turned Orthodox, have you? You don't intend to stop driving on Sabbath?"

"No."

"Then why are you resigning?"

"If we go ahead with our plans, all of us will have to pitch in, financially and otherwise."

"True enough. You'll need all the help you can get, and more. I'll tell you what I think, Dr. Yarden. I think you're afraid of upsetting the apple cart. That's what really is behind this decision. At least as far you're concerned."

"What do you mean by that, Rabbi?"

"I mean, accepting a dozen or so black families who know enough to make themselves inconspicuous is one thing. My bringing a black rebbitzen to the Pineville Jewish Center is quite another. You're afraid for Hadassah. You've been worried ever since she's come to Pineville."

"I never said any such thing, or given any indication."

"No, you haven't. But you are apprehensive about it. Level with me, Dr. Yarden. That's why none of you showed at the reception to welcome Hadassah to the community. I wondered about it at the time, but I didn't pursue it. You attend services, you pay your dues. Otherwise we never see any of you. In all the time Hadassah's been in town, not once have you visited us. Hadassah is your niece. I know how much you and Mrs. Yarden care about her. In fact, that's the problem. You love her, and you're afraid she'll be hurt by too much black exposure. Well, Dr. Yarden, you're not being fair. My congregants have their faults. But they are not racists."

"I never for a moment accused them of being racists."

"In that case, I propose an alternative. How many are involved in this Sabbath problem?"

"There is Isaac, Peretz Walker. One or two others."

"So, we have two definite and two maybes. I suggest that those families who prefer not to drive on Sabbath move to walking distance of the synagogue. Since the defense plants have downsized, quite a number of families are relocating. There are more "For Sale" signs

Israel Jacobs 285

around town than ever. It's a buyer's market. It sure will be a lot cheaper for all of you than building and maintaining your own synagogue."

Silvano stared at him with sad eyes.

"Okay, I know you will run into some opposition. But if ever an idea has found its time and place, this is it. Even if you have to trample over a few bigots. And you won't stand alone. The entire Jewish community will stand with you. It'll be our fight as well."

Tom Carter chuckled cynically. "Whites put themselves on the line for blacks? Hah!"

"Yes, we'll put ourselves on the line. You're Jews. Locking you out of this community isn't only racism; it would be anti-Semitism to boot."

Silvano asked, "You prepared to load us on your people?"

Tali swerved to Silvano. "I said it to Dr. Yarden, and I'll say it to you. There is no you people, or us people. You're Jews as much as any white Jew; more so than many I have to deal with. If a bigot assaults you, he assaults me. When you're denied your rights, it's a Jew being denied his rights. That makes it doubly our fight. What's open to me, to any one in my congregation, must be open to you as well."

Silvano sighed. "If you try to push blacks on this all-white community, if you insist on making our fight yours, what has been opened to you may very well shut in your faces, too."

"That's a risk we've got to take. Otherwise, the Pineville Jewish Center is one big expensive farce that's not worth my time, or any rabbi's."

Tom Carter stared at Tali quizzically. "Man, are you for real?"

Silvano said, "You don't realize what you are getting into, Rabbi."

"Maybe yes, maybe no. In any event, you're not putting up a building overnight. We have some hot-shot real estate people in the Pineville Jewish Center. I'll talk to them. We'll find decent housing within walking distance of the synagogue, for any of you who want to move."

Jeremiah Yarden asked, "And what of Hadassah? We'll be putting her into the middle of this battle. She's had more than enough. I'm

286 *The Convert*

concerned about what another battle would do to her."

Tali said softly, "I share your concern, Dr. Yarden. Hadassah is my wife. I love her. If there was any way to spare her, believe me, I would. But, can you imagine if all of you resign? She'll figure out the reason. I'm afraid to think of what it would do to our marriage."

"You could explain to her about the Sabbath problem."

"Come now, Dr. Yarden. You know Hadassah. She's not a naive little girl. She'll know."

"Very well, Rabbi, I concede. You have a point. Any direction we take puts all of us at risk, one way or another. Let's give the congregation the benefit of the doubt. It's the only way, I suppose, to find out to what extent Jews are prepared to stand on principle."

Jeremiah Yarden paused. "Rabbi, on another matter, before we leave. You were clearly irritated by the advice your uncle gave us regarding driving on the Sabbath. Although he did not initiate our consideration of the problem, he confirmed it was the correct decision. You probably are aware, nevertheless, it bears repetition. Your uncle is an extraordinary man. He is gifted with profound insight into human nature. No, it goes beyond insight. As a physician, trained to think scientifically, I hesitate to say this. The Sumtara Rebbe, I can't help but believe, is prescient. Not that he can predict the future in detail. But, he sees the larger picture as few men do. He has a vision of what tomorrow should be like. Do not underestimate his wisdom."

"Dr. Yarden, I never have."

Chapter Thirty Six

March stomped in with a vengeance. Fierce gusts piled up mountainous snow-drifts, bringing the county to near paralysis. The snow converted to slush. Pelting rains washed the residue into catch basins that backed up and bubbled like geysers. Miniature lakes covered the roads and lanes. A welcome spell of clear skies permitted the county to dry out. The sun rose higher and brighter each day. Mellowing winds and spring rains massaged the landscape into life. Trees, stripped bare by the unusually frigid winter, began to sprout buds. Hedges filled out. Forsythia and azaleas splashed the acres of lawn in bright pastels. Lilacs bloomed purple and fragrant. Gardeners, professional and amateur, weeded, trimmed, fertilized, seeded. House painters sponged Pineville homes inside and out with fresh cheerful colors.

The homeowners, without exception, stayed white.

"For Sale" signs, in abundance in past seasons, had vanished. Potential black buyers were shown no homes by any of the town's real estate agents. Several leads Tali had suggested they follow through had led to dead ends. Tali began to suspect these real estate agents had no intention of showing a house to blacks. Yarden didn't press him. Silvano, Barnett, the other blacks, stayed off the subject. He read into their silence. The sudden shortfall of homes for sale was no more than they had expected. They were waiting for him to admit failure. April was half gone. Still no offers to show a house, and none in sight. He was being played for a fool. He personally knew of houses, ideally

288   *The Convert*

located, and priced right, that had changed ownership. A Jewish couple with three children had bought one of those homes. He made his usual house call. They appeared to be amiable people. Still, he had to swallow hard when he tacked the mezuzah on their door in the traditional home-dedication ceremony. His resentment was irrationally directed to this new family. Though strangers to the community, they had been eagerly accepted. All the character references they needed were a down-payment and a credit rating. Isaac Barnett, Peretz Walker, any black, no matter his education, financial rating, qualifications as a human being, could not get a foot in the door. An ugly thought took hold. Hadassah's ticket of admission was his coattails. On her own she would have been blacklisted.

He continued to pester every real estate agency in town, peppering them for news. Roger Kern, a synagogue trustee, listed dozens of homes. His was the largest real estate agency in town. Nothing from Roger Kern. Doggedly, he persisted, with ever mounting fear that time was running out. Yarden became distant, withdrawn. When asked by Lutvak to lead in services, he declined. No amount of prodding by Lutvak helped. The old man realized there was a problem and stopped asking. Relations became strained, conversation held to a minimum. A formal "Good Shabbos," and that was the extent of communication. Tali guessed that Yarden was having a difficult time trying to buy a few more weeks. Tali could smell resignation in the air.

He had concluded it best, in Hadassah's presence, to avoid the subject, until at least one house had materialized. But, she could not long be kept in the dark. The subject hung heavy at home. He sensed her coiling up inside, withdrawing from congregants. And in small ways less responsive to him.

Suddenly, an idea struck, like a bolt from the blue.

"Hadassah, do you have the Heller's phone number handy?"

"Yes, isn't it kind of late to be calling them?"

"This is important; they won't mind."

Tali dialed the Hellers. Rabbi Sanford Heller answered.

"How are you, Sandy?"

"No, Sandy, I don't need rabbinical counseling. At the moment I

Israel Jacobs 289

need to speak to Fran. I have a problem I think she might be able to help me with."

"No, Sandy, that is not my problem. Please stop horsing around and put Fran on."

Why didn't he think of Fran Heller sooner? It might be a cliché, but nonetheless true: necessity is the mother of invention. She, even more than her husband, was a torrid civil rights advocate. If there were a conspiracy afoot to prevent blacks from buying homes in Pineville, she would expose it.

And he was in an excellent position to feed her leads. Families considering relocating frequently asked him to check out synagogues and religious schools before putting their homes up for sale. Often he knew, before the real estate people did, which families in the congregation were planning to buy a larger house and intended to put their present house on the market. Or the reverse. Older couples, after their children had married and left the area, finding themselves alone and unable to cope with a large house. He might be accused of exploiting his position. Well, Roger Kern and company had been given sufficient opportunity to do the job they were in business to do. He was operating in that murky grey area where, on occasion, the ends justify the means. If exploiting his position as rabbi was not exactly ethical, a conspiracy to lock out blacks from a community was illegal. You fight fire with fire.

In June Tali learned that a congregant, Rose Shapiro, widowed two years ago, had bought a condominium in Palm Beach, Florida. Sam, her late husband, had died after a painfully lingering illness. Following the funeral services, Tali had tried to console her. Rose Shapiro's children were devoted to their parents. They had flown in from the West Coast to stand vigil at their father's bedside. During *shiva*—the seven days of mourning—they were a comfort to their grieving mother. They made an all-out effort to persuade her to sell her house and move in with one of them. Rose Shapiro rejected all the well-intentioned offers. To her mind, Sam was not gone. The memories were too vivid. She wanted to die in this house in which she and Sam had lived for most of their married life. The children could do no more. They scattered back to their own homes and families. They phoned regularly, wrote post cards, sent pictures of the grandchildren, and on occasion flew in for a visit. They appealed to Tali to look after their mother. By degrees, he succeeded in getting Rose Shapiro to accept her husband's death. At fifty-seven, he drummed into her, she was too young to consign herself to the grave. Sam wouldn't have wanted that. There was still much happiness in store for her. She had devoted children, grandchildren to enjoy; she had her health.

It was a Sunday evening when Rose Shapiro called to tell him the good news.

She had met this very nice gentleman, a widower. They had been corresponding for months. He had proposed. She said yes. The happy couple planned to move South right after the wedding.

Tali hastened to offer his congratulations, in person. Rose Shapiro's house was ideally located, about half a mile from the synagogue. Rose Shapiro was not a money-hungry woman, and if she wanted to sell, the price would be reasonable. Tali wished her every happiness. Rose Shapiro planned a small study wedding, just for the immediate family. She asked Tali to officiate. He had been at her side in sorrow, now she wanted him to share in her *simha*. The date would be set as soon as she found a buyer for her house. Tali informed her that she could set the date immediately. He knew of a fine Jewish family that wanted to move closer to the synagogue. Rose Shapiro was thrilled. How lucky to have a rabbi and real estate agent rolled into one.

It was only one house. But, he had broken through; he had proved it could be done. He waved Rose Shapiro a cheery good night and skipped to his Mustang, whistling, *Is This the Little Girl I Married.*

"Hadassah, we did it. It's only one house, but it's a breakthrough. First thing tomorrow I'll call Fran. She'll work out the details and set a closing date." Hadassah did not look convinced. She went upstairs, leaving a trail of silence. She undressed and slipped under the covers. Tali climbed into bed. She submitted to his love making as if it were a chore.

Israel Jacobs 291

Marduk pushed himself up against the headboard. Pencils, crumpled paper, a compass, protractor lay strewn about. He closed the geometry book, telling himself it was hopeless. In one night he wasn't going to make up for three months of goofing off. He yawned and stretched out across the bed. The downstairs phone jangled into his room. He shifted to his right side. The rings grated...four–five... He decided it would be easier on his nerves to answer. Swearing at the walls that he was becoming a damned answering machine, he loped downstairs and clipped the receiver off the hook on the eighth ring. A woman's voice quivered at the other end.

"May I speak to the rabbi?"

"He's not in. Can I take a message?

"Who is this?"

"Harry, the telephone horror," he had a mind to answer, but thought better of it. He gave the caller back her question. "Who is this?"

A long moment of silence, as if the lady didn't care to identify herself. Then hesitatingly, "This is Mrs. Shapiro."

"Oh, Mrs. Shapiro," Marduk said into the phone, glad that he had not acted the wiseacre. Mrs. Shapiro was a nice old lady. He didn't want to cause her any grief. He made a special effort to be pleasant. "This is Marduk. The rabbi's out. Won't be back till about ten. You want him to call you back?"

No answer on the other end. If not for her heavy breathing, he would have thought that Mrs. Shapiro had deserted the phone. Finally, "Yes, Marduk. Please have the rabbi call back. Anytime up to eleven o'clock."

He trudged back upstairs to untangle the mysteries of isosceles triangles, forgetting Mrs. Shapiro and pledging that next semester he would pace himself better. Study, do his work during the term so that he wouldn't have go through this end-term torture again, the same pledge he had made the term before. But this time he meant it. Two hours of grueling concentration passed. He heard the door slam. Footsteps tramped into the vestibule. Angles, axioms, theorems danced behind his eyeballs. He slapped the geometry book closed. Hell, he wasn't going to stuff any more in his head tonight. He tossed the book aside and shuffled downstairs. Tali was chuckling over a comedy routine in the feature film they had just seen.

"Hi, Professor, how is the math coming along?"

Marduk made a wry face. "These problems are ball-busters."

Hadassah threw him an angry look. "If you did a little studying during the term, you wouldn't have to slave away the last minute."

"That's me," Marduk grinned. I do my best under pressure."

"Any calls while we were out?"

Marduk scratched behind his ear. "Oh, yeah. One. Mrs. Shapiro called. She wants you to call back."

"She say what she wanted?"

"No. But she sounded kinda shaky."

Tali went to the phone. When he returned, Marduk could see that he was shaking.

Hadassah came into the den, wearing a robe. "What happened?"

Tali's mouth was set in a grim line. "Rose Shapiro backed down. She won't let Fran's agency handle the sale of her house. Somebody threatened her that if she does, she'll have a lawsuit on her hands."

Hadassah stormed, "That's a lot of crap. Fran is a licensed real estate agent, isn't she?"

"Yes, but I'm afraid that's not what this is about."

"What is it about?"

"About selling her house to a black family. She must have found out who the buyer is. I know she wouldn't have backed out on her own. But she's afraid. She's had enough trouble as it is. Someone got to her."

"Some white son of a bitch."

Alarmed by the outburst, Tali watched Hadassah's face contort. The no-longer-to-be-denied conspiracy to blacklist her race had flushed up the old hate. A hate he had believed exorcised had been lying dormant, waiting to be triggered. He felt a glob in his throat. "She wouldn't tell me who threatened her, but I damn well am gonna find out."

Israel Jacobs 293

Finding out was easier said then done. Try as he might, Tali could not pry the information from Rose Shapiro. When he called, she was either out, or on the way out. Frustrated though he was, he empathized with Rose Shapiro's dilemma. She was a woman alone, a widow who saw another chance at husband, home, happiness. A chance to live once more, an opportunity she had thought would never again come her way. She was afraid to stand up to whatever threats were made. Tali understood. Who would threaten Rose Shapiro? He suspected Roger Kern, the real estate broker, had turned the screws on Rose Shapiro, or had passed on the information to someone else, who put the heat on. But he had no evidence. The one time he cornered Rose Shapiro at home and demanded to know who had threatened her, she turned white as a sheet. Rose Shapiro was too frightened to talk.

Meanwhile, the blacks were growing restive. Yarden still had them in check, insisting they allow the rabbi more time to explore a few other possibilities. Tom Carter protested that nothing would come of it. They had given the rabbi more than enough time. He conceded that the rabbi was doing his best, but the conspiracy to keep Pineville free of blacks confirmed his libeling distrust of the white man. Maybe Rabbi Zeig was the exception. And exceptions, Carter argued vehemently, do not convert a community that has been conditioned to look down on the black man as less than human. Tom Carter had his eye on a piece of property in the black section of Northville that was well suited to their purpose and within the price range they could afford. It was time to stop waffling.

Tali continued to clutch at straws. He knocked on doors of members he heard were contemplating a move, he followed up rumors. In one instance, he knew for certain that the house was for sale, and he knew the asking price. When he came to inquire, the owner told him he had a change of heart. The house wasn't for sale. Two weeks later Tali learned the house had been sold to a white family relocating from Detroit. In another instance, when he came to look at a house, he was informed that the price had scooted up thirty thousand dollars. He went through the motions, beginning to think that it was futile, but unable to surrender. He had been certain that with Fran's help he would desegregate Pineville. And his congregation would surely support him. He had only to lead the way. Together, he and the congregation would cut the ground out from under the bigots. He wrestled with the turn his crusade had taken. Where did his congregation stand? They had taken to Hadassah with no problems, or so it seemed. They had accommodated nicely to the twelve black families he had thrust on them. He had believed he was on solid ground in expecting the congregation to follow his lead. Could he have been mistaken? How far did their liberalism go when the chips were down?

Marduk scraped through his exams, sure that he passed them all, not by much, but passed. The afternoon of the final exams he stayed on at school to shoot baskets with a few blacks he had befriended. Of late, his friendship with the kids in the congregation had turned lukewarm. He would have been hard put to say who lowered the burners; he or they. There had been no tussles, no arguments, nothing specific to cool the friendships. He had simply slipped into a camaraderie with the few blacks in school, to the exclusion of his erstwhile white buddies. The last few weeks David Russel pretty much ignored him, and Marduk let it be. He also noticed that his sister and David's mother were no longer as thick as they used to be. The phone calls, the visits back and forth had stopped. He sensed that the adults, too, were staying out of each other's way. He had overheard Tali and his sister discuss the matter. Tali had put it down to personal problems the Russels were having.

"I hardly see them at services anymore," Tali had said. "And Everett's got a hangdog beaten look about him. Something is troubling the Russels they don't want to talk about."

Hadassah had listened stone-faced, unimpressed by Tali's explanation.

Along about five o'clock Frank Willis said he had to cut out. Willis worked three afternoons a week at a car-wash. He called for Marduk to return the basketball. Marduk dribbled the ball in a circle around Willis.

"Let's shoot a few more baskets."

Israel Jacobs 295

"Man, I gotta split. My boss warned me if'n I come late again, he gonna fire me. I need the bread." Willis held out his hand for the ball. Marduk flipped it into the air.

"Come on man, I gotta go."

Marduk dribbled the ball around Willis in the direction of the basket. He arched a one-handed push-shot upwards. The ball rimmed a full circle around the hoop and dropped off to one side. The two boys leaped for the ball. Willis, taller by several inches, snatched it first.

"See you tomorrow," Willis called over his shoulder.

The other players dispersed. Marduk ambled home alone, feeling down for no reason he could explain. He let himself in with his house-key.

Tali was slouching on a club chair in front of the television set, waiting for Hadassah to come home. Marduk dropped to the sofa next to Tali. Dr. Terrence Simeon had sliced a long cut into beautiful Anadine Starr's chest, opening up a wide cavity. He cut further, snipped and sawed with steady rubber-gloved hands. Two masked nurses mopped his brow. The camera panned to the screen monitoring Anadine Starr's heartbeat. The crest and troughs were narrowing dangerously into a straight line. The front door slammed.

Hadassah stormed into the den. She charged directly to the television set and yanked the knob. The screen went blank.

Tali lurched to the television box. "Hey, why did you do that? I have to see if he puts her heart back in time."

Hadassah blockad his path, her eyes ablaze.

"It's those white bitches! They're the reason why a black can't buy a house in this town."

"What are you talking about?"

"I finally wrung the lousy dirty story from Sandra. She said she hadn't told me because she didn't want to hurt me. Crap! She's turned out to be no better than the rest of them."

"Will you please calm down and start from the beginning?"

"Our neighbors," Hadassah spat the word between clenched teeth, "they've organized to keep the town black-free. Marduk and I are already more than they can tolerate. They've collected every racist in town, of which there is no shortage, and formed a committee, 'The Pineville Concerned Citizens Committee,' they call themselves. Sandra said Mrs. Conset asked her to attend. Conset is the bitch heading the committee. She thinks Conset started the campaign to keep blacks out."

Marduk remembered being introduced to Mrs. Conset at the yacht club. She was wearing a diamond cross and a big mouth.

Hadassah raged on. "Sandra went to the meeting not knowing, or so she claims, what it was about. She said fifty women showed up, all hysterical that you're turning the neighborhood black. They're having nightmares of blacks shooting up drugs, burglarizing white homes, raping white women."

Tali asked, "Why was Sandra invited to the meeting?"

"Because she's Everett's wife. She was told, in so many words, to bring the message back to Everett. As president of the Pineville Jewish Center, he'd pressure you to quit your crusade."

Tali fumed, "Nobody's gonna pressure me to quit anything."

"It'll amount to the same thing if the congregation fires you. That'll get me and Marduk out of town, too."

"Don't you believe for one second that a few bigots can influence Jews to fire their rabbi."

In the face of Tali's outburst, Hadassah's fury subsided. "The worst of it is, Sandra sounded so damn neutral."

Tali heaved himself out of the chair. "We'll find out how damn neutral everybody is."

He dashed to the phone.

Chapter Thirty Seven

Tali eased his car into the space marked, "Reserved for Rabbi." He made a fast count; fifty cars in all. The nearly empty parking lot did not bode well. He hastened to the auditorium, expecting to politick before the meeting got started. Hadassah would be arriving shortly in her own car, probably with Marduk. He wanted to nail down enough votes so as to cut the wrangling to a minimum. The less exposure Hadassah had to synagogue politics, the easier he would breathe, particularly on this issue. He had urged her to pass up this meeting, promising a blow-by-blow description when he got home. She insisted on coming, and on bringing Marduk; why, he couldn't figure. Maybe it was only his imagination working overtime lately; she had turned sullen, moody, keeping to herself, barely speaking to him. Hopefully, after tonight she would defrost. Until this was over, he thought it best not to argue.

He resented having had to arm-twist members to attend this meeting. Particularly distasteful was canvassing congregants for votes. The Catholic Church had the right idea. They operated by clerical fiat, sparing their priests for the real work of the priesthood. Electioneering for projects he was convinced were vital to Jewish life, and to which his members were indifferent, was both undignified and physically draining. Unfortunately, rabbis had to play the political game. Otherwise, nothing would get done.

The moment he entered he was hit by a premonition of trouble. Yarden, Silvano, Isaac Barnett, Peretz Walker, Tom and Mira Carter were present, in addition to three other black couples. They sat, bunched together, in the middle of the auditorium. Ten empty rows separated them from the white contingent. Self-imposed segregation had returned to the Pineville Jewish Center. Zalman Lutvak was surrounded by his coterie of Sabbath morning regulars. Another group of twenty, or so, hovered around Seymour Kraft and Maurice Cline. Silvano, sitting at Yarden's side, gave Tali a curt nod. Tom Carter sat next to Mira, as if quarried out of a sullen mountain. Sourly, Tali contemplated the rows of unoccupied seats. Five hundred members had turned out to debate which caterer should be granted an exclusive franchise. For this special meeting he had personally made dozens of phone calls. On his instructions a mailing went out to the entire membership, spelling out the purpose of the meeting, "Jewish families are being denied the right to move into Pineville because they are black. We dare not sit idly by in the face of this violation of the basic rights of members of our congregation. We must do whatever it takes to end this blatant bigotry."

He brooded at the lame turnout. Despite his best efforts a scant hundred members thought the issue of sufficient importance to attend. Something was rotten in the town of Pineville.

Tali pressed past Zalman Lutvak, who acknowledged him with a slight bow. Everett Russel, pale, and seeming to have aged ten years since Tali had seen him at services a month ago, was quietly but animatedly gesturing to Maurice Cline. Janet Plotkin, wearing a tight miniskirt, sat next to Everett. She crossed one leg over the other and ruffled through a notebook. The auditorium doors swished open then closed with a soft thud. Hadassah marched hurriedly down the side aisle with Marduk trailing close behind. She wore a half-sleeve high-necked sweater, light tan skirt and oversized dark glasses. Tali motioned her to join him up front. She shook her head and tugged Marduk to sit with the blacks. Everett Russel tapped his gavel.

"I call this meeting to order," Everett announced in a tired voice. "Since this is a special meeting called at the rabbi's request, we can dispense with the minutes of the last meeting." Everett waved the gavel at Tali. "Rabbi, you have the floor."

Tali pushed himself up slowly. He stood a long moment taking stock of the attendance. Hadassah stared blankly ahead, as if deliberately avoiding locking eyes with him.

In a loud voice that carried to the back row Seymour Kraft jeered, "What a waste of electricity."

Tali's eyes narrowed to angry slits. "I agree, Seymour. It's a waste of electricity. Maybe putting up this fancy building was a waste."

Kraft looked as if he had swallowed a scream that was choking him. Maurice Cline seized the floor. "Rabbi, You've got your meeting. At your request a mailing was sent to the congregation. And I understand you personally phoned members. There's no call to be sarcastic. You can't force people to attend meetings."

Tali arched toward the lawyer. "Something tells me that the membership was encouraged by certain parties to sit this meeting out."

Cline chewed on his lip, "Let's not get paranoid, Rabbi. You may find this difficult to believe, but not everything dear to you has the same priority for others in this congregation."

"Priorities? Five hundred members turn out to decide whether this or that caterer be given an exclusive. And practically an empty auditorium for what is on tonight's agenda."

Everett Russel hit the table again. "Rabbi, we need to make do with what we have."

Tali crisscrossed the auditorium with his eyes, scanning the faces looking up at him. "Okay, we've got enough interested parties here to deal with the problem, and maybe find a solution—if we really have a mind to."

Kraft found his voice. "I didn't know we had a problem, Rabbi."

"It figures, Seymour. And when Hitler was cremating Jews, people like you didn't think there was a problem either."

Kraft paled. He stared open-mouthed, as if disbelieving his ears. Everett rapped the gavel again.

"Seymour, there is no need to provoke the rabbi. And, Rabbi, would you please get to the subject at hand."

"Yes, I'll make it short. Anyone not aware by now of the whole miserable story is either unconscious, or doesn't want to know."

Tali glared at Kraft, who was gnashing his teeth, as if ready to commit murder.

Tali continued, "Several families, four or five presently, want to move close to the synagogue so they wouldn't have to drive to services on the Sabbath. They're not welfare cases. They're not looking for charity. They are willing and able to pay a fair price. But because they're black, every dirty trick in the book has been pulled to deny them this basic right, to choose where to live. So far, not one black family has been shown a house, and there have been plenty available. You and I know it's illegal, and they could take this to the courts. But they don't want to go that route. They are members of the Pineville Jewish Center. It's our obligation to do something about it, to publicly and officially express our indignation. That's the long and short of what I have to say, and why I called this meeting."

Albert Shakter raised his hand.

"Al," Everett Russel said. "You have the floor."

Shakter posed thoughtfully. "Rabbi, You're right. We are aware of what has been going on. But, what can we do? The Jewish Center is here to sell religion, not houses. Personally, I have no problem with blacks moving to Pineville. But I don't see us promoting the idea to the gentile community. You tried. You really tried. You even went into the real estate business, I hear." Mock laughter interrupted Shakter. He signaled for quiet, waited a moment for the laughter to subside then continued. "I admire your perseverance. You put yourself on the line for your convictions. But facts are facts. You've discovered for yourself that it's tilting at windmills trying to fight the community on this issue."

Tali brooded for a moment. "That's why I called this meeting, Al. I can't fight this battle alone. I realize that now. But together we have a chance. At the least, we'll force the bigots out into the open."

Cline raised his hand. The chairman recognized him.

"Rabbi, you're being naive. Alone or together, it makes no difference. What do you expect this congregation to do that you haven't already tried?"

Zalman Lutvak rose. He leaned heavily on the chair in front of him, appraising Maurice Cline with a sour face.

Everett Russel asked, "Do you want to speak, Mr. Lutvak?"

Cline sat down.

Lutvak sighed. He pressed himself up to an erect position and faced the chairman with a sad expression. "Yes, Everett, I want to speak. I am ashamed of the congregation, and of myself. Yes, we all knew what was happening, and we let Rabbi Zeig knock his head against a stone wall. The truth is, we all expected that after a few knocks the rabbi would realize that his head is not stone, and he would give up. Inside my heart I also wished he would give up."

Lutvak spoke his mind, passionately recounting how the blacks had knitted into the Sabbath morning services. How they rarely missed a Sabbath. Cold, rain, snow; they came. How they contributed to the services by their presence. How he gave them aliyahs, how proud they were to accept the honors. He described how beautifully Dr. Jeremiah Yarden often led the services with his fine tenor voice.

"These are genuine Jews. I, especially, should have respected them and supported their decision not to drive on the Sabbath. Instead I, too, let the rabbi fight alone. So, I am ashamed. But, we have a God who forgives, who gives us a second chance. The rabbi came to my house and made me see how, by keeping silent, I violated what the Torah says, *You should not stand idly by when your neighbor's life is in danger.* If I still close my eyes to this sin, I have no right to expect God to forgive me when I sin."

Cline interrupted. "You're exaggerating, Mr. Lutvak. Nobody's life is in danger. Most of us drive to synagogue on Sabbath."

Lutvak shook his head. "You are wrong, Maurice. Jewish lives are in danger. Maybe not physically. But the Jewish *neshamah*—the Jewish soul, is in danger. Tell me honestly, Maurice, would you be so neutral if white Jewish families were denied the right to live in Pineville?" Lutvak jabbed a finger at the lawyer. "No, Maurice, you would not be neutral. You would scream: Bigotry! You would call the A.D.L., the A.J.C., the whole alphabet of Jewish organizations. You would sue, you would fight all the way to the Supreme Court. I know you for a long time, Maurice." Lutvak's voice broke. The intense emotions provoked by the congregation's apathy to an injustice perpetrated on fellow Jews

302   *The Convert*

coupled with personal guilt was draining the old man. He paused to catch his breath.

"Maurice Cline, you would be one angry Jew if the gentiles stopped a white Jew from buying a house in Pineville. I know how you felt when the yacht club turned down your application to join. You pushed until you got in. And why did you make such a big fuss about becoming a member of the yacht club? So that your boat could have a garage?"

Cline squirmed in his seat. Lutvak snatched off his glasses and pointed to the black section.

"Well, Mr. Cline, these Jews want to buy houses in Pineville so they can honor the Sabbath. If we don't support the rabbi, we say to our children that living a Jewish life is less important than membership in the yacht club."

Lutvak wiped his glasses and fitted them back to his nose. Sol Blum, a tall thin red-complexioned man with an imposing red mustache, asked to be heard. Blum, a past president of the Pineville Jewish Center, was senior partner in the accounting firm of Blum, Frank and Tyler.

"Mr. Lutvak, none of us objects to our fellow black Jews living near the synagogue, or anywhere in Pineville they choose to live."

Blum spoke in a monotone, yet he managed to rivet everyone's attention. The few times Tali heard Blum speak up at Board meetings, the man impressed him as a master at redundancy. He would repeat the obvious, yet leave his audience with the feeling that he had said something momentous. Blum continued in the same monotone.

"We did not interfere with Rabbi Zeig's crusade to integrate Pineville. I am certain our fellow black Jews appreciate the fact that our rabbi has worked so diligently on their behalf. What more can we do?"

Lutvak had remained standing, quietly massaging his chin during Blum's diplomatic rebuff. He waited for the accountant to finish.

"Sol, I'm glad you asked that question. A few of us have met privately, and we have come up with an idea."

Tali noted Kraft questioning Cline. The lawyer shrugged, looking puzzled. Blum fingered his mustache, checked with Cline, who shrugged again.

Israel Jacobs 303

Lutvak continued, "I own a half acre lot about a fifteen minute walk from the synagogue. Mr. Kastner—," Lutvak canted sideways to acknowledge a fragile looking man with wisps of white hair curling around his ears. "Mr. Kastner owns the lot on Maple Court, about half a mile from the synagogue. And the synagogue owns two acres that Sam Shapiro, may his soul rest in peace, willed to the synagogue. That also is walking distance. So, this is what I propose…"

Lutvak proposed that the Pineville Jewish Center finance the building of four homes on these lots. If the Board agreed, he and Mr. Kastner would donate the land they own to the synagogue. Lutvak calculated that four very nice homes could be built for seventy to seventy-five thousand dollars each. The synagogue would sell the homes to the blacks, and might even realize a modest profit. The retired butcher dropped slowly back into his chair; he finished his presentation while seated.

"It may not take care of everyone who wants to move. But like the Talmud says: You do not have to finish everything you begin; but you have to make a beginning."

A great Jew, Tali thought to himself. He glanced at Yarden; there was no reaction from the doctor. Hadassah sat like a statue, her eyes fixed on Everett Russel. The next voice Tali heard was Blum's monotone.

"Mr. Lutvak. That is a generous offer. And I'm sure I speak for all of us when I say that you and Mr. Kastner are the kind of Jews we can take pride in. However, we should not leap hastily into this project. As I indicated before, none of us are bigots. We would gladly welcome blacks as neighbors, and it doesn't matter whether they're Jews or gentiles. But do we have a right to impose our standards on others who do not feel as we do?"

"We not only got a right; we got an obligation!"

Mr. Kastner had bounced up from his chair, all five feet of him, waving a fist at six-foot Blum. The accountant had roused a sleeping tiger.

"I do not like what you said, 'it doesn't matter they are Jews.' It matters to me even if it doesn't matter to you, Mr. Solomon Blum."

Cline interceded. "Please, Mr. Kastner. You're putting the wrong interpretation to what Sol is saying."

"So let him explain."

"If you don't mind, Sol, may I explain what you meant?"

"What's the matter? Sol can't speak for himself?" Kastner's ire now boiled at Cline. "He needs a lawyer to speak for him?"

Blum appeared to have had enough. He sat down, leaving the field for Cline to fight it out with Kastner.

"Certainly it matters to Sol that they are Jews," Cline chose his words carefully. "That is why it is such a delicate problem. As it now stands, this whole business has become a Jewish question. We're on a collision course. Us against them. We're a tiny minority. We can't afford to antagonize the entire WASP establishment. They could make things mighty uncomfortable for every Jew in town."

"Maybe that is our trouble," Lutvak shouted from his chair. "We have been living so comfortably in this town for so long, we turn our backs on Jews who don't have it so good."

"That's not fair, Mr. Lutvak," Cline said indignantly. "We contribute to the United Jewish Appeal. We hold rallies for Soviet Jewry. We..."

Lutvak sliced the lawyer off in mid-sentence. "That's all very nice. But charity begins at home. While you are improving the world, Mr. Cline, maybe you could spare time to make things a little better right here in Pineville."

Lutvak's zealots broke into applause. Cline's faction demanded an apology. Everett Russel banged feebly for order.

"Let's try and conduct this meeting like adults."

The skirmish quieted down. Rochelle Feld waved her hand. The diamond-studded bracelet on her wrist sparkled in the overhead light. She wore a low-cut summer blouse that displayed a generous slice of cleavage. Everett called on the Sisterhood president.

"I feel terrible that blacks can't buy houses in this neighborhood," Rochelle squeezed out a sigh from deep inside her bosom. "I sympathize with them. I really do." Rochelle heaved another sigh. "But you know, we've been on such good terms with our neighbors all these

Israel Jacobs   305

years, it would be criminal to split the community. I mean, look how we're fighting among ourselves. We could start a civil war. It's been such a nice place to live. Why spoil it?" Rochelle heaved another sigh and wiggled back into her chair.

While speaking, Rochelle Feld had cut Tali's line of vision to Hadassah. He now could see her shooting visual daggers at Everett, who seemed to have turned to jelly. There was a dramatic change in Everett's behavior. He had never lost control of a meeting as he had tonight. Everett gave the impression of a beaten man.

Seymour Kraft took the floor. "We took the blacks in. They've been coming to our synagogue a year now. Did you hear anyone complaining? No. We voted them in as members. What else do they expect from us. Blood? If we force blacks on this town that's what you'll see. Blood. Our blood. The goyim will burn crosses on our lawns. How would you like to see a cross burning in front of the synagogue? They'll crucify us. We gotta live with the goyim; it's their town."

Tom Carter was the first to leap up. He yanked Mira by the arm and bumped past Yarden, overturning a chair and sending it cracking to the floor like a rifle shot. He stomped into the aisle without looking back, pulling Mira after him. Gever Silvano picked up the chair and caught up with Tom and Mira. The others followed, quietly heading for the exit in single file. Dr. Yarden stepped into the aisle, cast a sad glance at Tali, turned on his heels and trudged out of the auditorium.

"You should be ashamed of yourself, Mr. Kraft."

Lutvak's roar pulled Tali's attention back to the meeting. The old man had leaped to his feet and was brandishing a gnarled fist at Seymour Kraft. If Kraft experienced shame, Tali saw no evidence of it. Kraft smirked at the chairs vacated by the blacks.

Kraft and Cline had lived up to expectations. Everett Russel's behavior raised a dark enigma. Why had he gotten no support from the president? Not through this entire fiasco. And Sandra hadn't even shown for the meeting. It didn't tally with the man he knew. Everett Russel, a man, who had climbed to the top of a billion-dollar corporation, afraid to stand up to these cretins?

Isidore Hirschman demanded to be heard.

On the rare occasions that Lutvak was absent Hirschman reigned at Sabbath morning services. Hirschman was more to the right than Lutvak. He would have liked to turn the Pineville Jewish Center back into the Orthodox synagogue it originally was. Lutvak would not have minded, except that having lived so long in Pineville, he knew what was possible and what was not. He had accommodated to the compromise. Isidore Hirschman, a dress manufacturer for thirty-five years, had until retirement belonged to an Orthodox synagogue. His son, Dr. Joshua Hirschman, a neurosurgeon with a highly successful practice in Pineville, feared for his parents' safety in the crime-ridden city. After repeated urging the elder Hirschman reluctantly agreed to settle in Pineville.

Everett gave Mr. Hirschman the floor.

"I think we have argued enough," Hirschman said. "If it is in order, I wish to make a motion."

Everett said, "A motion is in order."

"I move we accept, with thanks, Mr. Lutvak's and Mr. Kastner's generous offer. I further move that the Pineville Jewish Center finance the building of two houses on the property we own. And when the houses are completed we offer the houses for sale at cost, to those black members of our congregation who wish to move closer to the synagogue for religious reasons." Isidore Hirschman adjusted his skullcap, a familiar habit he had when arguing a point of ritual with Lutvak. "This is not part of the motion. But while I have the floor, I wish to announce that if the motion passes, I will increase my High Holiday pledge to the synagogue by five thousand dollars."

Kastner's pledge triggered a round of applause from the traditionalists. Three of Hirschman's comrades announced that they, too, would increase their contributions. Lutvak stood up, smiling for the first time that evening.

"Yes, Mr. Lutvak," Everett said.

"I second the motion."

Cline signaled that he wanted to speak. Everett waved him on.

"We've argued the issue enough. It's time we voted the question. But before we do, I'd like to hear the chairman's opinion."

Israel Jacobs 307

Al Shakter called for the floor. "The chairman is supposed to chair meetings, not offer opinions."

"The chairman may relinquish the chair if he wants to speak," Cline persisted. "And in my judgment, he should. Before I cast my vote, I would like to hear what Everett has to say."

Tali remarked to himself, Cline needed Everett Russel's opinion like the serpent needed Eve to tell him about the apple. Something ugly was in the works. Everett was being set up. For a brief moment Everett hesitated, his eyes angry and defiant. It appeared he would refuse to cede the chair. The moment passed. Everett let the gavel fall to the table.

"The chair is yours; you can have it."

Cline strode to the table. He brushed shoulders with Everett. There was a whispered exchange. Tali caught one word from Everett: Bastard!

Cline plucked the gavel from the table, fingering it lovingly. "Go ahead, Everett. Tell us how you feel about the motion."

Everett Russel writhed like a man standing barefoot on hot coals. "The Pineville Jewish Center is not in a position to force integration on this town. Much as I admire the good intentions behind Mr. Hirschman's motion, I can't support it." Everett Russel sat down. Tali was stunned.

Cline assigned Al Shakter to tally the votes. "All those in favor of the motion." The Sabbath regulars raised their hands as a bloc.

Al Shakter counted hands. "Forty-one in favor."

"Against," Cline rapped the gavel once.

Shakter counted the nay votes. "Fifty-six."

Tali winced. He knew it was over when Everett surrendered the chair. Why? What hold did Cline have over Everett? Tali's rout was complete. Kraft and Cline, with Everett's collaboration, had clobbered him. Cline smacked the gavel firmly to the table. "This meeting is adjourned."

Everett bolted to his feet, stalked past Tali without a word and pushed through the exit doors.

Seymour Kraft hitched up his trousers. Cliques formed in the rear

308 · The Convert

of the auditorium. Kraft whacked Cline playfully on the shoulders.

"Maurice, you make a great chairman. Congratulations. I think you put an end to this crap once and for all. And it's a good thing you did. I've been watching things. Their kids and ours were getting too chummy. How'd you like, one day, your kid brings one of them home, and you got yourself a black son or daughter-in-law?"

Tali lunged toward Kraft. He glared into the pugnacious beady eyes, thinking how satisfying it would be to blacken them. "Don't worry about a black son or daughter-in law, Seymour. They wouldn't touch you with a ten-foot pole. You're not fit to shine their shoes." Kraft and Cline gawked wordlessly at Tali. As through a haze he became aware of Marduk sitting alone in the middle of the auditorium. The chair beside him was empty. He tore across the rows.

"Hadassah! Where's Hadassah?"

Chapter Thirty Eight

Tali crunched the transmission into drive. The engine caught, then stalled. He churned the ignition again. The Mustang lurched forward, sideswiping a rhododendron bush. He banked sharply out of the parking lot, racing to beat the light at the end of the driveway. The yellow light switched to red. He slammed down on the brakes. Marduk plunged toward the dashboard.

"Man, the way you're drivin' you gonna kill us both."

Tali drummed on the wheel. The light changed to green. He shot across Main Street, ignored a stop sign and careened into his driveway on two wheels. He screeched to a stop inches behind Hadassah's new Chevy.

Her car was parked askew, crowding the rose bush garden. Only blind rage would make her ram into her roses. He sprinted to the side entrance and thumbed the doorbell. The chime sang three times; he could hear it ringing inside the foyer. Marduk stood on tiptoe, peering through the foyer window.

"There's nobody downstairs. You gonna have to use your key."

Tali searched through his trouser pockets. "Damn it, they're in the car."

Marduk jogged to the car; the keys dangled from the dashboard. He jiggled out the keys and raced back. Tali grabbed them, fumbled to isolate the house key and jammed it into the latch. He pushed the door in.

One floor lamp glowed dimly in the living room. The refrigerator

310 *The Convert*

whined into the foyer. It shut off, leaving an ominous quiet in its wake. A thud, from upstairs, erupted into the silence. A second thud followed. Footsteps, interrupted by drawers rattling and slamming shut, clicked back and forth. Tali hurtled up the stairs two at a time. The door to the master bedroom was partially ajar. Tali pushed the door open wide.

One bulging valise and an overnight bag sat on the king-sized bed. Hadassah's back was to the door. She crouched over a second valise, pressing her full weight down on the lid. Tali stopped short.

"What are you doing?"

Hadassah managed the lid closed and clamped the lock shut. Tali thrust into the room. He twirled her around.

She turned full face. Her eyes were bloodshot. Smudges stained her cheeks. Wads of tissue paper were strewn every which way on the bed.

"Will you please tell me what this is all about?"

"First thing tomorrow we're leaving."

"Where, may I ask, are you going?" Tali followed her to the bed. A box of Kleenex lay aslant on the pillow. She wrenched out a tissue.

"I don't know. Back to Chelsea maybe. Anywhere, so long as it's away from here."

"And how long do you expect to be gone?"

Hadassah blew into the tissue. "Permanently."

"Just like that!" Tali snapped his fingers.

She snapped back. "Just like that."

"What about him? Did you ask Marduk what he wants to do? Maybe your brother wants to stay."

Hadassah looked inquiringly at Marduk, as if she had not considered that possibility. "Do you want to stay?"

Marduk hovered near the door. His eyes danced from Tali to the luggage, not daring to meet his sister's look. What could he say that would change anything? He felt whipped about by dreadful conflicts. He couldn't let her take off without him. If it would help, he'd do anything to persuade her to stay, to end talk of returning to Chelsea. From past experience, he knew when she was in that frame of mind nothing could make her budge. It suddenly dawned on him why she had brought him to that shit meeting. She figured the congregation would vote against the brothers. She wanted him to see it for himself. Well, he did, and he was mad, but not enough to forget Chelsea's cold winters, the choking summers, the rats and the stink. The winos pissing and shitting in the graffiti-littered cracked hallways. Why should she want to drag him back to that shithole? When he had known no other way of life, it had seemed the natural order of things. Not anymore. He had a clean room of his own, not a stinking hole. A bathroom that ran hot and cold needle showers. He lived in a house with a lawn and a garden. Never cold anymore, or hungry. The thought of returning to Chelsea petrified him. Why should he go back? Because the congregation didn't want to buy houses for the brothers? It wasn't as if they had no place to live. How would him creeping back to that shithole in Chelsea help them? He felt like a traitor to his sister, to his race. But he couldn't bear going back. He would rather die.

"No! I ain't never going back to that shithole."

Hadassah stared at him. Her eyes filmed with moisture. Marduk could feel the pain he was causing her. She walked to the bed and zipped the overnight bag closed.

"What will you do now?"

"What I said. I'm leaving first thing tomorrow morning."

"By yourself? Without your brother?"

"With or without him. Tomorrow morning I'm out of here."

"Hadassah, it doesn't make sense. To walk out on me, on your brother. Because one congregational meeting didn't go our way?" Tali circled her waist. Her breast felt warm against his arms. For a moment she seemed not to resist. He fondled her hair, her face, thinking she had a change of heart. She broke out of his embrace.

"I won't stay."

He seized her ring-finger and forcibly pushed it upwards. "Doesn't this mean anything to you?"

The tears ran down freely. "Yes, it does."

"Then how can you stand here and tell me you're leaving? How can you just pack your bags and walk out on me?"

She popped another tissue and blew her nose. "I'm not walking

312   *The Convert*

out on anybody."

Tali struck a fist against the valise on the bed. "What do you call this?"

"You're free to join me, both of you. Anytime you decide." She had reverted to steel.

"Running won't solve anything."

"I don't give a damn what you call it. I've had it with this town. They're all cut out of the same hate-nigger cloth. WASPs, Jews."

"Jews are not racists."

"I heard a nigger-hater tonight. Loud and clear."

Tali recoiled, as if she had drawn blood. She had still been there when Kraft spewed his poison. He steadied himself against the bed.

"It's not fair to condemn a whole congregation because of one sick mind. It's just not right."

"One sick mind! Is that so?" Hadassah crumpled a tissue into a ball. "Explain the vote tonight. Explain why ninety percent of the congregation stayed home. Explain why everybody's been avoiding us these past couple of months. They make me feel like I'm dirt, like blacks carry some filthy disease.

"Maybe it's true of WASPs. It's not true of Jews. They're afraid. They're conditioned to quake every time a gentile barks at them. That's cowardice maybe, it's not racism."

"Crap. There's no difference."

She was back in Upper Chelsea. At the O.E.O., disgorging the old bitterness against the white world. She was at war with the white man again. With every white man, indiscriminately, him included. He dogged her to the closet and back, desperately trying to stanch the rage pouring out.

"Look how the congregation accepted our marriage."

"Crap!"

"Crap is no answer." Tali spread his arms, entreating her. "If they were racists, they never would have adjusted to their rabbi marrying a black girl."

She thrust out her chin. The tears were gone, replaced by hard contempt. "I'm the token black for your phony liberals. Like Cline is the token Jew at the yacht club, with which, as I remember, you had no problem."

Tali pleaded to her back. "You're so damn angry you can't think straight. "I admit I was wrong about the yacht club. But that doesn't make me a racist. Dumb, maybe, but not a racist. And neither are my congregants."

Hadassah tossed her head defiantly. "Looks like you don't know your congregants. They sure proved you wrong tonight."

"It was not racism, I tell you. It was fear, cowardice. But can't you see it isn't racism? They're afraid to take on the whole town. They're terrified. They think the WASPs will roll over them. I hate that yellow streak. I know their faults: selfish, self-centered, cowards. Guilty. But I tell you, except for one or two miserable bigots, they are not racists."

Hadassah whirled, all the rage at the white world written large on her face. "And I tell you again, crap! When Jews want to, they can put up a damn good fight. Cline managed to beat the yacht club's no-Jews-wanted policy."

"Honey, it hasn't always been that way. Not so long ago Jews were afraid of their own shadows, and many still are."

"When were Jews afraid? I don't see any trace of it. I don't see Jews living in fear and trembling."

"How could you see it? You've just come into the picture. You can't know their ghetto mentality the way I do."

"I know enough to make me puke."

"Listen a minute. Just hear me out."

Tali held a firm grip on her arm, forcing her to look at him.

"As a kid, there was this Catholic church right around the corner from my yeshiva. One Easter week, sixteen of us were playing stick-ball during recess, and another ten, at least, stood on the sidelines. Three Irish kids—they had just been to Mass—came swaggering into our street, putting on the tough-guy act. They broke up our game and threatened to beat us "Jew boys" up. Would you believe it? Twenty-six Jewish kids swallowing crap from three snotty juvenile anti-Semites. These people at the meeting tonight are still carrying the fear habit. They're still conditioned to tremble when a gentile looks at them

314   *The Convert*

crossly. That's why they voted the way they did. They're afraid to stand up to the goyim. They're still reliving the pogroms their parents suffered in the old country. Can't you understand that?"

Hadassah broke away. "Your long-suffering history makes me weep all over. Jews afraid? Crap! Three million Jews have been whipping the asses of eighty million Arabs for the last twenty-five years. When Jews fight for their own, they don't turn tail."

"It's not the same thing. Please understand. The Israelis have no choice. Their backs are up against the wall. They have nowhere else to go. They're fighting to survive."

"And what do you think we've been fighting for," Hadassah punched back. "But that would be too much for you to understand. Black lives don't add up the same as white lives, to any of you."

"A life is a life to me; black or white, and you know that. But the fight isn't the same. Blacks can afford to lose one battle, two, three. You can go on fighting. You can look forward to winning the next one, or the one after that. And sooner or later you will win. We Jews lose once, just once, and it's all over for us. Finished. We'd be slaughtered, every last mother's son and daughter. It happened in my parent's lifetime, and it could happen again. They would rape, burn, torture. They would slit every Jewish throat." Tali piled atrocity on atrocity in a last-ditch effort to make her understand. "Genocide is what we're talking about if the Arabs win, even one battle."

Hadassah looked at him coldly, clinically. "Genocide, Rabbi Zeig, is the name of the game for blacks. Two hundred years your white world ground us down, lynched our men, raped our women, snatched mothers from children and sold them on the auction block, separated husbands and wives, broke up our families. Deliberately kept us illiterate. Your white world turned us into animals. We don't want to lose any more battles."

Tali sighed. "You don't understand."

"I understand better than you think. I made a mistake. I'm through playing black rebbitzen to white Jews. I've had it."

Tali let himself drop onto the bed. He felt barren of arguments. "You really mean to walk out on me?"

Israel Jacobs 315

He thought he detected a break in her determination, a softening. The doubt in her eyes passed. "I'm walking out of this nigger-hating town and nigger-hating congregation. Any one cares to join me is welcome."

Tali felt spent, empty; he had no more strength to argue. "What about Judaism? You mean to walk out on that, too?"

The question hung between them a long moment. She answered in a tired voice. "Right now all I want to do is get out of Pineville. I've had enough of Jews, at least white Jews. As far as Judaism is concerned, I... I don't know. I need time to think abut it."

"You can't separate the two, Hadassah. You can't give up on Jews; black or white, and still hold on to Judaism. That's exactly what the congregation is guilty of."

Hadassah transferred a skirt still hanging in the closet into her overnight bag. "If that's the way it works, I suppose I'll have to walk out on Judaism, too. It doesn't seem to have made Jews more caring or sensitive to anybody but themselves."

Tali leaned against the bureau. He felt an almost forgotten malaise coming on. Spots shimmered inside the corner of his left eye. A familiar pain throbbed at his temples.

The doorbell played a discordant merry tune, startling Marduk. He glanced at the digital-clock on the bureau. Ten-thirty. Late for anybody to come calling, even to a rabbi's home. Hadassah brushed past Tali. For a moment she hesitated, then climbed the stairs, stepped in to the master bedroom and slammed the door. The doorbell chimed again. Tali stared vacantly at Marduk.

"Do me a favor and see who that is."

Marduk chased downstairs and pried open two slats in the Venetian blinds. A Cadillac was parked behind Tali's car. The quarter-moon shed enough light to make out two stooped figures standing in the walkway. He switched on the outside light. Amber flooded the portico. He pulled the blinds open all the way. The two men in the driveway stepped closer. Marduk recognized Kastner and Hirschman. The party at the doorbell pressed again and moved back into Marduk's line of sight. It was Lutvak. What the heck were they doing here at this

316   *The Convert*

hour? He opened the door. The three men crouched in the doorway.
The amber light cast eerie shadows on their faces. Lutvak and Hirschman wore snap-brim hats. Kastner hadn't removed the skullcap he had
been wearing at the meeting.

Lutvak spoke. "Can we speak with the rabbi, please?"

Yeah, sure." Marduk stepped aside. He closed the door behind
them.

"Who was it," Tali called from above.

Marduk named the visitors.

"Who?"

Marduk shouted their names up again. Tali lumbered downstairs.
Isidore Hirschman doffed his hat; underneath he wore a black skullcap.
Lutvak and Kastner stood silently at his side. Tali greeted each man
with a brief handshake. A dull hammer pounded behind his right eye.
He looked at the three men through an overlay of bursting bubbles.

Hirschman shifted his hat from one hand to the other. "Rabbi, we
are sorry to intrude on you so late. We came to apologize for what
happened tonight. We are ashamed. I speak for all of the Shabbos
morning worshipers. We did not want this night to go by without
telling you our feelings."

Tali heard Hirschman out in silence. The throbbing in his right eye
became a sharp pain. He winced at the sound of the grandfather clock
in the living room pealing the half hour. Lutvak pressed forward.

"Is the rebbitzen still awake?"

"Yes, I think so."

"We would like to apologize to her personally. To tell her how
sorry, how ashamed we are. Can we speak to the rebbitzen?"

Footsteps padded down the stairs. Tali made a half-twist away
from the night visitors. Hadassah crossed to the foyer. She had changed
into flat shoes and a flaring robe that billowed out as she walked. Her
hair was swept back and piled high like a tiara. Lutvak made a formal
bow.

"Rebbitzen Zeig, we are here to apologize for the disgraceful
behavior of our congregation tonight, especially for that sorry vote. I
want you to know that. Perhaps we lost a battle, but the war is not

Israel Jacobs 317

over."

Hadassah came to a halt near the foyer entrance. She posed frostily under the archway.

"It's over for me, Mr. Lutvak. When I was preparing for conversion, I remember my husband teaching me that your Torah commands Jews to treat the stranger kindly, to love him as yourself. He neglected to tell me that this does not include black strangers."

Lutvak spread his hands contritely. "What can I say, Rebbitzen Zeig? We have been acting like Jews who have forgotten their Torah. I, too. I am ashamed that I and my friends did not come forward sooner to help the rabbi fight this battle."

Hadassah stared coldly at the octogenarian. "If after all those centuries Jews can so conveniently shunt their Torah aside, it doesn't say much for Jews or their Torah. Does it?"

Kastner tapped Lutvak aside. "Rebbitzen Zeig, if you will excuse me, I know how you feel—maybe not a hundred percent. But please! It is not the Torah's fault that Jews do not always live up to the commandments. God made Jews human, like everybody else. Many times we act badly. That is why we have a Yom Kippur. To ask forgiveness from God. But before we can expect God to forgive, we need to have forgiveness in our hearts."

The mild censure dispensed with, Kastner retreated diffidently, as if regretting what he said. He had come to apologize and forgot who the aggrieved party was. He shook his head. "One day, when they think back to what happened tonight, a lot of Jews will be sorry, and a-shamed."

Hadassah took Kastner's measure with unforgiving eyes. "From what I saw tonight all those "sorry" Jews lined up with that hypocrite president of your synagogue. With a man like that for a leader, I don't expect your Jews will ever weep over a black man's troubles."

The three men exchanged knowing glances. Hirschman nodded to Lutvak, as if asking permission to speak.

"Rebbitzen Zeig, that was not Everett Russel you saw tonight. He was not himself. He hasn't been for more than a month."

"If it wasn't Everett Russel, it must have been his twin brother

318   *The Convert*

who turned the vote against us."

"That was a frightened father, in panic about his son."

Tali seized Lutvak by the arm. "What do you mean?"

Lutvak winced. "Please, Rabbi. You are hurting me."

"I'm sorry." Tali released the old man. Lutvak massaged his arm, looking very wrinkled and spent. Through the pounding in his head and his own weariness, Tali perceived the toll on Lutvak. He asked the visitors into the living room. Marduk turned up the three-way floor lamp. Lutvak dropped into a club chair. Of the three elders he appeared the most worn.

"It is a nasty business, a very nasty business. I repeat it to you only because I want you to understand why Everett Russel spoke the way he did." Lutvak paused, as if trying to collect his thoughts.

"Everett's older boy, Kenneth, is in trouble with the police." Lutvak coughed. "They charged him and some other crazy college boys at the university with selling drugs. Can you believe it? Kenneth Russel a drug dealer? Did he need the money? How can you explain such a thing?" Lutvak rocked his head back and forth.

Tali listened, incredulous that this could happen without his having an inkling of what was going on. That explained the change in the Russel family. Everett shuffling around with that pinched haggard look. The Russels' steep fall off in attendance at synagogue services. Sandra's remoteness. Tali tried to focus on Lutvak through the bubbles swirling behind his eyelids. The throbbing in his head took a turn for the worse.

Marduk heard Lutvak out with little surprise. Except for the fact that Kenneth got picked up by the police this was last year's news. Cops don't bust rich suburban kids like they do in Chelsea. But Chelsea or Pineville, junk was peddled all over. Rich white kids are not supposed to do drugs. They have no reason. So parents are blown over when their kids turn out to be no different. Then he remembered Angela's hysteria when she found out he owned a few joints. She never learned the full story. Thank the Lord!

Lutvak continued "You can't imagine what this did to the Russels. That their son would do such a thing?"

Marduk could well imagine.

Israel Jacobs 319

"The shame! And if they found Kenneth guilty, that meant the end of his dreams to become a doctor. No medical school would accept someone with a police record. To make a long dirty story short, the Russels asked Cline to help their boy.

"Maurice Cline's got a reputation as a criminal lawyer. He is smart, but it takes more than smart to get a dismissal on a drug charge. It takes connections. And Cline has connections. One of his connections is that *momzer*, Seymour Kraft. A *goniff* first class. I know. I did business with him. I don't know whether he personally hates black people, or he acts like he does because he thinks the goyim expect him to. Probably it is some of both. Whatever the reason, behind the vote tonight is Seymour Kraft. When he saw you for the first time, Rebbitzen Zeig, he almost had a heart attack. Maybe one Jew should not hope this for another, but I wish he would have, at least a mild one. Maybe it would take his mind off from making so much *tsoros* for other people.

"Seymour could find nothing to say against you, though you can be sure, he tried. After the congregation got over the shock that they now had a black rebbitzen, they accepted the marriage. Especially, we traditionalists. Maybe you don't know this, but even traditional Jews have children married to converts. To us you and the rebbitzen are an inspiration. You proved that a convert can be a good Jew, sometimes a better Jew than those who are born Jews. Seymour could not stop the congregation from voting in Dr. Yarden and the other black families. The Christians have black members in their churches. It hurt him, but Seymour had to keep a lock on his mouth. When the rabbi talked about helping blacks buy homes in Pineville, Seymour decided things had gone too far. This he would stop one way or another. When Kenneth was arrested, he saw his chance. He knew that Cline is Russel's lawyer, and he knows also that Cline is aching to be State Supreme Court judge. He convinced Cline that if the congregation, of which he is vice president, builds houses for blacks in Pineville, he should forget about being elected judge. Seymour said he would use his influence with the district attorney to allow Kenneth to plead guilty to possession instead of dealing. As a first offender he would not be sentenced to jail.

"The price was for Cline to persuade Everett to oppose the rabbi,

320   *The Convert*

to publicly announce that it is dangerous for Jews to force black families on the goyim. When the rabbi called tonight's meeting, Seymour was ready. I thought, maybe, we could still beat him. But after Everett spoke it was a lost cause. Yes, that *momzer*, Seymour, is shrewd. He knows how to use people."

Lutvak sank into the club chair, exhausted by the long narration. "Everett Russel had to make a choice. His son, Kenneth, or fighting to integrate Pineville. He chose his son." Lutvak looked up at Hadassah with eyes pleading for understanding. "It is hard to blame a father for trying to protect his son."

"God! these are synagogue leaders? They're animals!" Hadassah turned sharply and raced upstairs.

Geronimo!

He hung in Marduk's nightmare, a gaunt upright corpse, waving him into the gutted tenement. Marduk retreated in terror. Geronimo beckoned with skeletal arms. His cracked lips grinned and groaned simultaneously. Marduk felt his hair being yanked at the roots. Angela brooded over him. She dragged him up the stoop into the piss-drenched hallway. Rats! Thousands of rats scurried in feces, clawing at the excrement-splashed walls. He opened his mouth to scream. Angela swung at him in slow motion. He spat teeth to the floor. He wrestled himself out of the nightmare. Geronimo's dead eyes began to fade. His pajamas had mangled around him like a corkscrew. He focused on the bureau mirror. A sweaty disheveled face stared back at him. Slowly, the fear abated. He drew the curtains and let Pineville's sunshine pour into the room. It was a beautiful morning. A good day to live, to swim, to sail. He opened a window and inhaled the clean fragrant air. Blue sky, fresh morning breeze, the perfumed dew-covered lawn. Lilacs keeping company with wisteria. It was all a nightmare—Geronimo, his sister threatening to leave. It would all work out. He checked the bureau clock. Nine-thirty. A shame to waste such a day indoors. He clumped into the bathroom and washed up. His mood soared straight up. He tugged sneakers over his socks, squirmed into a polo-shirt and bounced downstairs. Instantly, his upbeat mood vanished. Tali was sitting at the dinette table, his head shored up by an elbow, staring blankly into an empty coffee mug.

"Where's Hadassah?"

Tali barely stirred.

Marduk fell back into panic. "Where's my sister?"

Tali pointed to the door.

Chapter Thirty Nine

"Shit! You just gonna sit there and do nothin'?" It was like screaming at a corpse. He jiggled Tali's arm. "You gotta get her to come back."

Tali stared with empty eyes. "I don't know where she is."

"Whatta you mean, you don't know. Man, you gotta know."

"I...I fell asleep on the couch. When I woke up she... she was gone."

"With her clothes and valise and stuff?"

"I...I guess she took her things. I haven't been upstairs."

"How do you know she ain't upstairs sleepin', or somethin'?"

Tali handed Marduk a note, crumpled at the edges. It read, "Couldn't take it anymore. Will notify you where I'm staying soon as I relocate."

He dashed upstairs. Hadassah's two valises were gone. Under the bed, nothing. Several skirts still hung in her closet, but he could tell from the bare hangers on the crossbar that most of her wardrobe was missing. He yanked drawers open. All empty! His mind conjured up horrible scenes. Maybe she'd had an accident, maybe she'd kill herself. Frantically, he sprinted downstairs, looking for Tali. He found him stretched out on the living room couch. Marduk tried to shake him upright. Tali brushed him away, covering his eyes with both arms. Marduk abandoned the effort, confused. How could he just lie there? Maybe he figured she was only trying to throw a scare into them. That was it. Sure! Soon as she saw nobody running after her, she'd be back.

Israel Jacobs 323

She wouldn't desert her own brother. Then he recollected the beaten look on her face when he said he's staying. No, she wasn't coming back. She had split for good. Why should she come back? Not for him. He had sold out. What would become of him now? He should have left with her. No! He couldn't go back. Not to that shithole. Upper Chelsea battered at his memory: the rats squeaking in the walls, the rotting garbage, the cold winters without heat, the stinking heat in summer. She had no fuckin' right to expect him to go back to that shit. Why did he feel guilty? He hadn't run out on her. She had skipped. His mind rocked back and forth, from remorse to self pity, to guilt, to anger. Shit on his sister. He slammed out of the house, leaped on his bicycle and rode off aimlessly.

He stumbled through the day, and the next, and the one after that, Worried, angry, guilt-ridden. He had recurring nightmares: Geronimo, his sister dead, mutilated, crushed in an accident. At times she attacked him with hate in her eyes. The nightmares pounded him awake in cold sweats. The house became a morgue. He ate breakfast alone, slapped sandwiches together for lunch, occasionally broiled a hamburger. For the most part, he lived on eggs, cheese and cold cereal. Tali sagged around the house, hardly speaking.

Tuesday morning, after six days of waiting, a post card arrived. It had lain on Tali's desk with other unopened mail. Had Tali read it? There was nothing on the post card, other than his sister's name and an Upper Chelsea return address. Marduk read it aloud,

c/o Madeline Bates
829 Seventh Avenue

Marduk turned the card over. "She don't write nothin' about what she's doing, how she's feeling. How we're doing. Just an address. Don't she care anything about us anymore?"

"I don't know. I'm driving into the city tomorrow to find out."

Marduk said hesitantly, "You want me to go with you?"

"No. I'd better go alone."

"You gonna bring her back ?"

"If I can talk some sense into her."

324   *The Convert*

Marduk moped the day away. Dusk cast long shadows on the lawn. He heard a car pull into the driveway. He ran to meet it. The passenger seat next to Tali was empty.

"She ain't comin' back?"

Tali shook his head.

"Where's she at? What's she doing?"

Wearily, Tali switched off the headlights, throwing the homes across the street into obscurity. "She's staying with a girl friend."

"She ain't sick, or somethin'?"

"No, she's not sick." Tali stroked small circles on his left temple. His eyes were bloodshot. He shuffled into the house and lay down on the couch.

Marduk twisted awake from the same nightmare. Geronimo. His sister furiously hammering at him, hate in her eyes. The shithole tenements. He sat up. Dawn filtered into his room. He rehearsed the wreckage of the last few weeks. Maybe he should ask Tali to drive him into the city. Maybe he could talk her into coming home. He rejected the thought, fearing that if he failed, Tali might decide to leave him stranded. Despite the loneliness, the guilt, Upper Chelsea still loomed as the larger evil. So long as he remained in Pineville there was hope she might change her mind about coming back.

Tali kept to himself, speaking in monosyllables, when speaking at all. Weeks passed. Tali drooped through August like a widower unable to shake his grief. He fumbled about the house listless, apathetic. Each day that passed heightened Marduk's conviction that his sister wasn't coming back. Around Tali, he masked his depression for fear that if Tali abandoned hope of her returning, he might be sent packing. How long can a cat sponge on his brother-in-law after the man is convinced his wife has split for good? Not long, Marduk feared. Adding to the worry of finding himself cast adrift was the ache of separation from his sister. He missed her. Shit! He hadn't realized how glued he was to her. Yet, he didn't dare contact her. Vivid recollections of Upper Chelsea's stench immobilized him.

September brought another post card from the city. The card

Israel Jacobs 325

listed a different address, "Chelsea Arms Apartments." In addition to a return address, she had scribbled lines across the card:

In case of emergency you can reach me
during school hours at P.S. 89.

She had printed the address and phone number of the school in clear block letters. The post card was signed, "Angela."

Marduk pried his eyes open. Sunlight drenched the room. He stumbled out of bed. He hated the mornings even more than the nights. All of Sunday ahead of him, and no one to talk to, nothing to do. Tomorrow the same. And the day after, and the day after that. It was another sonnabitch fuckin' day he didn't want to greet. He closed his eyes. An image of his sister bubbled behind his eyelids. He tossed from side to side, unable to find a comfortable position. He threw himself out of bed and drifted downstairs. He fixed himself a bowl of milk and Cheerios. The milk tasted sour. He finished half and poured the remainder into the sink. It was too much. He couldn't carry this load by himself anymore. He wandered into the den and rifled through Tali's desk, hunting for the membership list. He found it lying loose in the top drawer. He thumbed down the roster:

"Dr. Jeremiah Yarden: 24 Jericho Ave...Northville,...843-2600."

He lifted the phone and dialed the first two numbers. The phone felt cold, unfriendly. He set it back on the cradle. He needed an ear attached to a face to hear him out. He felt skittish about announcing himself in advance. That would commit him to visit. If he still felt the urge to talk after biking to Northville, he'd ring the bell. If not, he kept the choice of turning back.

Rebecca Yarden touched his shirt. "My goodness, you are in a sweat. How did you get here?"

Marduk pointed to his bicycle. "I biked down."

"All the way from Pineville?"

Marduk forced a smile. "Only took me twenty-five minutes."

"It's nice of you to visit us. But bike riding on a sweltering day like this? You could get yourself a sunstroke." Rebecca closed the door,

326 *The Convert*

shutting out the heat. "Next time ask your sister to drive you."

"She's run off."

Rebecca seized Marduk's arm. "What are you saying, son?"

"She's not living with us anymore. She left the morning after the synagogue meeting. Hasn't been back since."

"Oh, my God!" Rebecca Yarden pulled him into the den. Jeremiah lounged in a club chair. One arm dangled over the side. His eyes were closed. Rebecca shook him awake. He rubbed his eyes open.

"Marduk! Good to see you, son."

Rebecca continued to pump his arm.

"I'm up! I'm up!" What on earth is the matter?"

"Hadassah! She ran off. She's gone."

"What!"

"She left the rabbi. After that horrible congregational meeting. I had a premonition something was wrong. We should have called her." Rebecca kept tugging at her husband. "We let that poor girl face those awful people by herself. I told you we should have—"

"All right, all right. Let's calm down." Jeremiah disengaged his arm from Rebecca's grip. "We'll get her to return. But first we must know where she's gone to. Marduk, do you know where she is?"

Marduk stared at Jeremiah, suddenly feeling his mouth dry. An ache crept from his stomach to his chest. His eyes misted. A damp line, tasting of salt dribbled from his nostrils. He held his breath, trying to stem the sobs pushing to emerge. His eyes began to gush tears like a faucet. He couldn't stop crying. He didn't want to stop. Heavy weights had pushed him into the pits, so far down he couldn't feel the sun any more. Somebody was about to lift the weights from his back. He wasn't alone anymore.

"You poor boy. What you must have been going through." Rebecca cuddled him in her arms. "Let me get you something cold to drink. And some cookies." She hurried into the kitchen. She returned, carrying a tall glass and a batch of home-baked oatmeal cookies. He drained the glass, biting gratefully into the thick cookies between sips.

"You feel a little better?"

Marduk nodded. Jeremiah nudged him to the sofa.

"Now tell me, Marduk. Do you know where Hadassah is?"

"Yeah. She's sent us post cards." Marduk apprized Jeremiah of the Chelsea Arms Apartments address. Also of P.S. 89 and the contact-in-case-of-emergency line. "That means she's got a job and won't be comin' back, don't it?"

"I don't know, Marduk. But she is evidently concerned about you and the rabbi. Have you been to see her?"

"Tali has. Twice I know about."

"What about you?"

Marduk squirmed. "No."

Jeremiah said, "I should not have allowed the rabbi to push integration on Pineville. It was a mistake. He and Hadassah didn't need this."

Marduk grimaced. "Yeah. They sure gave Tali a bad time. They're all the same. Pineville Jewish Center honkeys ain't no different."

Jeremiah raised a warning finger. "Remember, Marduk, the rabbi is also a white man. And he's married to your sister."

"Yeah, Tali's white. But he's different."

"How is he different?"

"I... I don't know exactly, but he is." Marduk scratched behind his ear. "He sure as hell don't act like those other Jew honkeys."

Jeremiah regarded Marduk pensively. "Aren't you Jewish, too?"

The question rattled him. He let it roll around his head for a while. "Yeah, I guess I am. I had *tipat dahm*, and got dunked in the *mikveh*."

"Do you want to remain Jewish?"

The grilling threw him into a muddle. He turned back the question. "How about you and Aunt Rebecca? You two gonna stay Jewish?"

"Yes. We intend to remain Jews."

"They stuck it to you, and you ain't mad?"

"They didn't really stick it to us, Marduk. They merely didn't want to get involved in our battles. They worried how the gentiles would react. There is a difference between being a bigot and sitting on the sidelines."

Marduk scowled. "I bet if we was white, they wouldn't be sitting on the sidelines. They wouldn't worry about the gentiles."

"I suppose that's true."

"That proves white Jews are no different. They won't go to bat for us because we're black. Right?"

Rebecca said, "Jonathan is out in the yard. I want to check on him." She left the den. Jeremiah let the question hang in the silence.

"Marduk, you were bar mitzvah a few months ago. That means you are a man. So, I'll speak to you like a man."

Marduk settled into the club chair.

"It is true that many Jews find it hard to see us as equals. Jews, too, have their prejudices. How could it be otherwise? They live in a country dominated by white Christians. It would be unrealistic to expect Jews not to be influenced by the conduct of the majority. Still, Jews are different. White Jews may feel uncomfortable with us. But, Marduk, Jews could not lynch a black man. They haven't gone that far downhill. Most Jews still hold life sacred, black or white. Yes, they will not put themselves at risk for a black man as they would for a white Jew, they may even fear us a little. They've caught some of the native bigotry. But twenty centuries of conditioning are not easily discarded. The Torah, Jewish history, the Jewish experience have thus far held Jewish bigotry in check. Jews may not be excited about living next to us, but they would not actively deny us our rights. And there are Jews like Mr. Lutvak and his friends, who firmly believe that the Torah commands all Jews to be responsible for one another, whether they are black or white. And they are willing to stand by those beliefs, no matter the consequences."

"Are you saying, Uncle Jeremiah, we should give them Jews medals because they don't lynch black people?"

Yarden regarded him mournfully. "In these times, Marduk, when men slaughter one another on the slightest pretext, it is no small thing to hold on to one's belief that life is sacred. Even we blacks are prone to violence. I see it happening. The looting, rioting, gunning down the innocent with the guilty. Aunt Rebecca and I want to remain Jews because the Jewish heritage makes no distinction between people. All men are created in God's image."

"But the Jews in Pineville don't want us there."

"Not all of them."

"Most of them don't want us around. That's why my sister ran away. I don't feel good about staying where I'm not wanted, either."

"Then go where you are wanted."

"Where is that?"

"The Sumtara Rebbe."

Marduk looked at Jeremiah in bewilderment. "What's the Sumtara Rebbe want with me?"

"He wants you to be a Jew, who understands what being a Jew means. He has invited us to send our children to his Yeshiva until such time we are in a position to establish our own religious school. Beginning this autumn, some of our families will be sending their children to dorm at the Sumtara Yeshiva. When Jonathan becomes of age, Aunt Rebecca and I intend to send him along with the other children."

The notion struck Marduk as absurd. He pictured himself in a black caftan dragging to his ankles, a black sombrero on his head and earlocks curling down his cheeks. The image seemed ridiculous.

Jeremiah put his arm around Marduk. "More important for the moment, it isn't right that you haven't seen your sister all this time."

"I didn't walk out on her," Marduk protested.

"You must go see your sister," Jeremiah repeated firmly. "She loves you, and she must be hurt."

Jeremiah had hit a tender spot. He had no choice. There was no putting it off. He had to see his sister. The idea frightened him. What if she had decided to split with Tali for good? That would put him forever back in the stinking tenement. He felt the old panic rising.

"What about Tali and my sister? You think they gonna make up?"

"I don't know. Your sister and the rabbi will have to work that out by themselves."

Chapter Forty

Traffic crawled in fits and starts toward the toll booths. Five lanes merged into three, provoking hazardous jockeying by chafing horn-tooting drivers. Yarden eased across the lane feeding into the exact change toll booth. He tossed three quarters into the bin. The arm jerked up, then swiftly dropped behind the Chrysler. Chelsea came into view. Glumly, Marduk surveyed the spectacle from the upper roadway: trailer trucks, buses, taxis competing to beat the lights. Factories belching astringent smoke clouds. A hodgepodge of tenements, expensive co-ops, skyscrapers thrown together within a few square miles, as if a deranged architect had designed the city. It looked wilder, grimier than ever. They rolled off the down ramp and were forced to a standstill by stalled traffic. The light changed three times. At the first intersection Yarden dodged off Boro Boulevard and cut into parallel streets heading downtown. Double-parked cars barely allowed passage. A stray tiger cat suddenly pounced in front of the Chrysler. Yarden hit the brake. Marduk pitched forward, his head coming to a stop inches from the dashboard. The cat scurried under a parked car. Yarden shifted to low drive, carefully negotiating the narrow streets. Youths slouching in doorways followed the car with sullen looks. A squat disheveled woman dragging a bucket waddled out of a doorway. She emptied the bucket into a trash can filled to the brim. The slop spilled over the sides onto the sidewalk. The garbage, the dismal tenements, the stench tied Marduk's stomach into knots.

They drove deeper into the city. By degrees Marduk accommo-

Israel Jacobs   331

dated to the sounds and smells. The streets took on a familiar face. School girls jumping rope, chasing each other on roller skates. Kids kicking at garbage cans, tossing a ball in the middle of the street, cursing at cars for interrupting their game. Open hydrants gushing torrents into the gutters.

Yarden turned into Brussel Street. He back-parked between two derelict cars, slid out from behind the wheel and locked the doors. A gangly black youth, wearing purple trousers and a sleeveless shirt, leaned against the lamppost in front of OHEV TSEDEK. He cast inhospitable glances their way. Marduk trudged up the short stoop. They filed into the vestibule. The entrance to the Sumtara synagogue seemed to have changed little. A narrow window slicing sunlight into the hallway, and the whitewashed walls were as he remembered them. Marduk remembered the placards. He located them, tacked to the doors in the same position. Men to the right; Ladies to the left. At the time both he and his sister thought they were directions to the bathroom. Now, familiar with the Orthodox tradition of separating the sexes, he knew what they were for and could read the Hebrew text. Yarden, it seemed, also knew his way around. This was clearly not his first visit to Brussel Street. He pushed open the door marked Men and beckoned Marduk to enter. The long room and walnut-stained backless benches triggered a replay of his first visit. How long ago? Queer how it felt like both last week and like a million years ago. He remembered Shmuel, the Sumtara Rebbe's youngest son, blasting off his bar mitzvah talk. Heschel, the Rebbe's eldest, bad-mouthing Tali, and being warned by the Rebbe to button his lip. The wild, happy dancing that had pulled him, body and soul, into the circle of ecstatic hasidim. The Rebbe himself dancing. That had all happened right here in this room, in happier times. Now it was so quiet he could hear himself breathing.

Marduk whispered, "Where's my sister?"

Yarden pointed to the other end of the room. "Knock on the door. The Rebbe is probably waiting for you."

"You comin' in with me?"

"No. The Rebbe wants to see you and Hadassah alone."

"You won't leave till I'm through?"

332   *The Convert*

"I'll wait. You needn't worry."

Marduk vacillated. Yarden gestured for him to knock. He rehearsed how to greet his sister, "You feelin' okay? What you been doin'? Real glad to see you." It felt stupid, but he could think of nothing more appropriate. He rapped softly, pushed the door open and stepped into the Rebbe's study. It was as if no time had passed since that first interview with the Rebbe. The room was as he remembered it—shelves, rising from floor to ceiling and spanning the room's width, jammed with books. Volumes piled on the two windowsills. A bronze plate with the word *Mizrah*—East, the direction of Jerusalem, hung on the one bare spot between two book shelves. Several smaller volumes lay in a jumble around a huge tome on the Rebbe's table, which Marduk recognized as a tractate of the Talmud. The Rebbe sat at an angle to the door, wearing a black felt hat, one hand supporting his forehead. His sister's back was to the door. Tucked into the far corner, the Rebbe's wife sat on a straight-backed chair, her lips moving silently as she bent over a black leather-bound volume. Marduk wondered by what name his sister now went. Was she still Hadassah, or had she switched back to Angela? He decided that in the Rebbe's presence it would be the proper thing to stick with her Hebrew name. He rattled the doorknob.

Hadassah turned slowly then jolted upright upon seeing him. She wore a long-sleeved blouse and navy-blue skirt that dropped well below the knee. She gripped the back of her chair with both hands. Marduk waited near the door, tongue-tied. She stared soulfully across the room.

"How are you, Marduk?"

The strain in her voice tore at his insides. He wanted to run to her, touch her, embrace her. Embarrassment, confusion immobilized him.

"Okay," was all he could muster.

An awkward silence filled the space between them.

The Sumtara Rebbe frowned, darting disapproving glances from Hadassah to Marduk. "Brother and sister have not seen one another for so long, and they greet each other like strangers?"

Hadassah rushed him. She threw her arms around his neck and squeezed. She sniffled, cradling his head between her hands and rumpling his hair. He ached inside for her, thinking what a sonnabitch

Israel Jacobs 333

he had been. For a soft mattress, a few lousy comforts he had scrapped her, the only family he really could count on. Even had been ready to disown his race. He felt lower than a basement. Whatever the upshot of this meeting, he knew one thing for sure; he would never desert her again. She walked him to the table, clutching his hand and holding on until they both sat down.

The Rebbe embraced them with his eyes. "I am pleased you came, Mordecai. How is my nephew, Naphtali?"

Marduk made a wry face. "He's not doing good. Most of the day he mopes. He don't go out, except to the synagogue. Just drags himself around the house. Like nothin' matters since Hadassah left."

It is not good for man to be alone, the Rebbe quoted from Genesis. "A man without a wife is incomplete."

"My husband doesn't seem to think so," Hadassah said, with an edge to her voice.

"That is not true," the Rebbe snapped. "You know that is not true; you just heard from your brother how much he needs you."

"Well... here I am, and he's in Pineville. Evidently, being rabbi of the Pineville Jewish Center means more to him than I do."

The Rebbe regarded her with stern eyes."You have thrust upon your husband an impossible dilemma. Whatever he chooses he must lose a part of himself. He is unable to make a decision. So he chooses to do nothing. He stays and languishes. The symptoms Mordecai describes, are that of a man in deep depression."

"I can't go back. I just can't go back to those people." Hadassah dabbed at the moisture filming her eyes. Marduk put his arms around her. All these weeks he had been busy feeling sorry for himself. Even now, he had tried to milk her conscience, hoping that worry for Tali would change her mind about returning to Pineville. He hadn't given a thought about how she felt. The time had come for him to stop being a sonnabitch. The decision to stay firmed in his mind. If she stayed, he'd stay. Nothing would separate them again. She needed him, and he intended to be around for her to lean on.

"I'm not goin' back either."

Hadassah squeezed his hand. He felt a mile tall.

334   *The Convert*

The Rebbe turned back to him. "And what will you do, Mordecai, if you do not go back?"

Marduk shrugged. "I don't know. I haven't thought about it."

The Rebbe stroked his beard. "You can stay here with us. Live and study at our Yeshiva."

Marduk recalled Jeremiah having made the same suggestion. It figured. The idea came from the Rebbe. Jeremiah Yarden was the middleman.

"I don't fit in here. I don't even own the right kind of clothes."

The Rebbe smiled. "What you are wearing now, Mordecai, is fine."

"What about the...the..." Marduk tapped behind his ear.

"*Payos?*" The Rebbe's eyes twinkled.

"Yeah. Those long sideburns. And those long black coats. And black hats. They're not my style."

The Rebbe coughed lightly into his hands. "You do not have to grow payos. Although sideburns, as you call them, and beards are in style nowadays everywhere. Mordecai, our Yeshiva students are like boys everywhere. They play ball, they quarrel, misbehave. Except for one thing: they study Torah. And that makes a difference."

City noises invaded the room. A truck lumbered by, rattling the windowsill so violently it loosened a book hanging precariously on the edge. Marduk bounded to the floor and retrieved the book. He replaced it carefully on the sill. The Rebbe thanked him. A siren wailed in the distance. Marduk returned to his seat. Hadassah was staring oddly at the Rebbe.

"Why are you taking such an interest in our problems? I understand you being worried about Tali. He's your nephew. But why Marduk and me? Not that I don't appreciate it. And it might be a good idea for Marduk to attend your yeshiva, if that's what he wants. But why are you concerned about what happens to us? Pineville is happy we're gone. And you want to hold on to us. Why?"

The Rebbe rose slowly, clasped his hands behind his back and walked, slightly stooped, to the window.

"I understand why Mordecai doesn't want to leave the suburbs. Here, except for the heat and cold, one can not tell winter from summer. We have a tree on this street. One tree. I can see it from this window. The leaves are beginning to turn yellow. In a few weeks they will begin to fall, and I will know that autumn is here. That tree is precious to me. In Sumtara, as a boy, I was surrounded by trees taller than a ten-story building, with trunks so thick it required three men arm-to-arm to encircle them. Yes, then I knew when the *Ribono shel olam* was ready to change the seasons."

The Rebbe sighed. He returned to the table and sat down, facing Hadassah. Sunlight cut two narrow paths of light into the study. Myriads of dust particles pranced in the luminous flux. The light beams crossed paths behind the Rebbe, creating the illusion of a nimbus crowning his head.

"Know this, Hadassah. Not a leaf falls to the ground, not a sparrow is born that is not the will of the *Ribono shel olam. All things are in the hands of heaven, except the fear of heaven.* Your first meeting with Naphtali may have appeared as chance. It was not. God willed that you meet."

The Rebbe's eyes glazed over. Though speaking to her, Hadassah had the impression that he had retreated inwardly, to a universe beyond her vision. He caressed his beard with long delicate fingers.

"This generation does not have the *z'hus*—the merit—of recognizing God working His will in our world. It is bereft of understanding. We are like the generation of Esther. Not once in the Book of Esther is God's name mentioned. Salvation seemed to have come from a mountain of coincidences: a foolish king drinks too much and banishes his queen; from thousands it is Esther who is chosen in Vashti's stead. By chance Mordecai overhears a plot to kill the king. This deliverance chance? Accident? So that generation believed. So they named it *Purim*—chance. Nonsense. It was God who would not permit a Haman to annihilate His people. Why could they not recognize the truth? They were not worthy. They had deserted Torah, made light of the Law, assimilated heathen decadence. Such a generation was not privileged to perceive God working His will. And we are not. Though His miracles are daily with us, though He performs wonders for us, we see only accident, only chance." The Rebbe paused; the glaze washed from his

336   *The Convert*

eyes.

"No, Hadassah. Your meeting with Naphtali was not chance. He saw you and was attracted to you. It is easy to believe this was nothing more than a young man attracted to a beautiful woman." The Rebbe cupped one hand over his forehead. "When Naphtali first brought you to me, there came to my mind the verse from Song of Songs,

I am black but comely, O daughters of Jerusalem;
Like the tents of Kedar, like the pavilions of Solomon.

"But, Hadassah, you are black. You are from a different culture. There are many beautiful Jewish women. Naphtali could have been attracted to any one of them. How did it come to pass that Naphtali, a rabbi in the suburbs, should meet and marry a black woman from the inner city? Am I to believe that this is chance? Nothing more than an accident?"

The sunlight arrowing in from the two windows swirled around the Rebbe. He seemed bathed in royal purple. His features blurred, blending unnaturally into the purple glow. For a moment she felt as if she were experiencing a mystical vision. It was an illusion, Hadassah told herself. Nothing more than lights and shadows playing tricks with her eyesight. She looked at Marduk. He sat quietly, as if entranced. Did he experience the same vision? The Rebbe's singsong waxed firmer.

"No, Hadassah, this was not an accident. There is purpose to your marriage. A purpose that goes beyond you and Naphtali. God has ordained your conversion and your marriage because Jews have lost their way. My people need your people to bring them back to God."

Jews needed blacks? Like Samson needed a haircut! Like she needed a canker! Kraft and Cline and the Russels leaped to Hadassah's mind. To these people blacks were mutants. And the feeling was mutual.

"Yes, the black people can help the Jew rediscover God and his Jewish heritage. I know such a thought is strange to you, but think. Your people, for more than two hundred years have suffered oppression and degradation, as the pharaohs of Egypt made Israel suffer over two hundred years. Suffering makes a nation cry out to God. Sometimes suffering makes people cry out against God. But whether suffering breeds tears or anger, God must listen. Like a loving father, God cannot indefinitely hear his children weep and not respond. He is compelled by His very nature to embrace the sufferer. Suffering opens channels to the Divine. Your suffering is fresh; the black people still suffer. The American Jew is prosperous, secure. He no longer suffers oppression, he is no longer persecuted. For this we should be grateful. But, our many blessings have raised a barrier between us and God."

The Rebbe began to sway, his eyes partly closed, as if in prayer, "Thousands of years ago, *Moshe Rabenu*, Moses, our teacher, predicted this would come to pass. Before the Children of Israel entered the Promised Land, he warned, *Take care—when you have eaten and are satisfied, and have built fine houses to live in; when your herds and your flocks increase—take care that you do not become haughty and forget the Lord your God.* As *Moshe Rabenu* predicted, so it happened. Over and over again. And each time Jews forgot their God, we paid dearly. And it is happening again. To this generation. We have come to believe that our own strength and our own might has brought us all these blessing. And if we are not brought to our senses, we will, God forbid, pay again." The Rebbe sat up, his piercing blue eyes tracking Hadassah. "In order for the Jew to recover the Jewish soul we need to embrace a suffering people."

Hadassah looked askance at the Rebbe. "Is that why Tali married me? Because my black experience would help Jews return to God?"

The Rebbe weighed the question. "It could have been mixed together with other feelings he had for you. Yes, without his being aware, such thoughts may have influenced his choice."

"You're saying that he was attracted to me because I'm a member of an oppressed race? If not for that he wouldn't have been interested in me?"

"It is not for me to answer such questions," the Rebbe said gently. "Only the *Ribono shel olam* can probe the human heart."

"So it wasn't me that mattered. He needed me for his Divine purpose. He needed a black sufferer to save his backsliding congregation. It wasn't love. It was need. Well, Tali can take his Divine purpose and—"

"Just 'cause Tali needs you ain't no reason to get mad."

The Rebbe gave a startled turn. His eyes converged on Marduk. He smiled, then shifted back to Hadassah.

"Listen to what Mordecai is saying, Hadassah. To be needed is a blessing. To be needed by God..."

The Rebbe left the thought unfinished.

"And Naphtali needs you for himself. Particularly now, does he need you. I spoke to him yesterday. He is torn by this separation. I do not know how he was able to conduct Rosh Hashanah services. I am greatly worried about him. In three days we will observe Yom Kippur. We shall fast. We shall ask God to forgive us our sins. We will seek to be reconciled with our Creator. I ask you for Naphtali's sake, go back to him. Do not let him spend Yom Kippur alone. This is a day when the *Ribono shel olam* and Israel are reunited. Let husband and wife be reunited."

"I want to be with him, too. I don't want to be alone." Hadassah could no longer suppress the tears pushing for release. She sobbed. "I can't... I can't go back to that house, to that synagogue. I can't. I just can't."

The Rebbe stood up. "I do not want to cause you more pain. You have had enough. Perhaps I am asking more than you can give. I understand your hurt. Then return with Dr. Yarden. Be with your uncle and aunt for Yom Kippur. I will call Naphtali and tell him I spoke to you, and where you are. At least he will know that you are close by. Perhaps that will make Yom Kippur easier for him to bear."

"And after Yom Kippur," Hadassah sighed, "what happens after Yom Kippur?"

"If it is God's will that you and Naphtali reconcile, so it will be."

Chapter Forty One

Twilight slowly blanketed Pineville, heralding *Kol Nidre* eve. The sun, a fading orange disc, peeked through the elms and pines bathing the synagogue facade in alternating light and shadow. Several cars snaked around the parking lot hunting for open spaces. Tali thrust through the lobby into the sanctuary. The pews were filling rapidly. Pre-service conversation was subdued, expectant. The men were attired in white prayer shawls and white skullcaps. The women wore white hats or white-laced head coverings. A white satin mantle veiled the Ark. Both the lectern and reading table were draped in white. Al Shakter stepped into the aisle and wished Tali a happy new year. He returned the greeting. Cline and Kraft, chatting in whispers, kept their backs to the aisle, studiously avoiding Tali. He ignored the rebuff, marched to the clergy dressing room, removed his shoes and slipped into a pair of white rubber-soled canvas shoes. He deliberated over the elaborate white pulpit robe hanging in the closet. It stared at him like a challenge. He hesitated, pulled it off the hanger and buttoned himself into it. He ran his fingers along the white four-cornered pulpit hat, debating whether to wear it or the plain white skullcap. He decided to come out in full regalia. Lastly, he draped the prayer shawl around his shoulders. He faltered at the door a moment, pushed it open and stepped to the lectern. Every pew was filled.

Except for two vacant seats in the first row.

"Please rise for the opening prayer." Tali felt his throat tighten. He coughed, allowed himself a moment, then began:

340   *The Convert*

"Amid the uncertainties, perplexities, confusions and sorrows of life we need You O God..."

His reading lost volume. He forced inflection into his voice.

"...We have ignored your commandments and reaped confusion. We have acted faithlessly and have stumbled. O God, you are near us and within us, yet You are the Eternal Mystery. You probe our innermost thoughts. Nothing escapes You. Nothing can be hidden from You. Give us the courage to confront ourselves, to audit our deeds as we audit our balance sheets. We stand before you on this night of Kol Nidre, stripped of pretense, revealed in our weakness. Turn us to You, O God. Strengthen our faltering will. Help us to put aside vanity and greed, to dismiss from our hearts the selfishness that blinds us to Your awesome holiness, that excludes us from Your presence..."

The congregation listened to the reading, soberly. Even prior to the actual recital, Kol Nidre had enveloped the sanctuary in an aura of expectant intensity. As child, as adult, as rabbi, Kol Nidre's mystique moved him as no other Holy Day. What was it about Kol Nidre that so powerfully pulled at the Jewish heart? Objectively, Kol Nidre was nothing more than a legalistic formula acquitting Jews guilty of breaking solemn promises.

"... *All vows and oaths we take, all promises and obligations we make to God between this Yom Kippur and the next... Should we forget them... be unable to fulfill them... We hereby publicly retract...*"

Tali puzzled at the effect Kol Nidre night had on him and on the congregation. Out of context it could be argued that Kol Nidre contradicts basic Jewish doctrine, that a Jew must honor his vow come what may. In this setting such arguments were irrelevant. Kol Nidre's hold on him, and on Jews throughout the world, was beyond rational explanation. Kol Nidre night was a night fraught with suspense, anxiety, of concern what the new year held in store for the Jewish people and for the individual Jew.

The fog had lifted. His mind was functioning. He could reason things out. His uncle's call had opened a clearing. He wasn't fully out of the dark, there were hard decisions yet to make. But he knew the general direction he had to travel. He believed in himself once again.

Israel Jacobs   341

He could trust his instincts. The thought had begun as a dot in the back of his head. His uncle had called him a bridge. "It is time, Naphtali, to decide. You cannot forever span the chasm. One side or the other. Else you will be torn apart. The burden of carrying two worlds will break you. Decide."

Kol Nidre! What was it telling him tonight? Not the words. The message behind the words. The ground on which the mystique rested. The power to touch Jews tied to Judaism with slenderest of threads. Commitment! But to what? To something beyond the self. Commitment to a benevolent power that desires man to survive, but will not force him to choose survival. To what was he committed? To his fifty-thousand dollar annual salary plus fringe benefits? He had manipulated Hadassah and Marduk into conversion. Subtly, cleverly, he had won them over. Why? To save their souls? They did not need to be Jews in order to be saved. He wanted Angela. So he converted her to Hadassah. Now he owed them. The congregation; he owed them too. How to reach them? Not by preaching. Preach yourself blue in the face. Preach for the next fifty years. Jews will not move an inch closer to the Covenant. They will sit on the same values, or lack of values, the same priorities. Why? Because they recognize that the preacher is cut of the same cloth, hardly different from the Krafts of the world. They sold cars and real estate and stocks; he sold religion. Both read the market, then promoted their products with half-truths. In a way he was the worse of the two. They made no pious claims; it's understood that in the corporate world the bottom line is profit and power. How does he explain away the compromises he makes? His congregants were no fools. They have eyes to see ears to hear. Small wonder their minds are like sieves. Pious platitudes may catch their attention in the short run, but will not be retained very long. What rabbis, ministers, priests say matters little. What they do make lasting impressions. His uncle rarely preached. The man himself was a sermon. That is why thousands were ready to follow his lead. Deuteronomy 22:6 reverberated in his mind:

If you chance upon a bird's nest, in any tree or on the ground, with fledglings or eggs and the mother bird is sitting on the fledglings or on the eggs, do not take the mother bird together with her young. Send the

342   *The Convert*

mother bird away before you take the young.

The rabbis caution, "He who says that the purpose of this law is to spare the mother bird the pain of seeing her young taken is to be stilled. The purpose is to condition the Jew to be merciful."

How is a Jew conditioned to be merciful? Not by listening to sermons. By *acting* mercifully. Teaching that endures after class is dismissed must be supported by doing. The act teaches.

Cantor Bindel approached the reader's lectern. He blew into his pitch-pipe. The choir members waited expectantly for their cue. Cline, now acting president, stepped to the Ark.

Tali motioned him back.

Cline appeared bewildered. Seymour Kraft craned to the pulpit, his brow furrowed like a plowed field. Tali addressed the congregation, pacing his words slowly, forcefully:

"Jewish law regards a pledge as sacred. The Torah admonishes the Jew, *Better not to vow than to vow and not fulfill.*"

Someone in the front row sneezed. In the stillness it sounded like a cannon shot. Tali gripped the lectern with both hands.

"On occasion, unthinkingly, we make rash promises, impetuous commitments. We are human. Our resources, material and spiritual, are limited. Circumstances frequently intercept our best intentions. Therefore, Judaism provides Kol Nidre, to clear channels to God that guilt obstructs."

Tali paused. He crisscrossed the sanctuary with his eyes. Again he ferreted out the two empty seats in the first row.

"There are two kinds of vows. There is the vow we make to God, *bein adam lamakom*—vows between man and his Creator. On Kol Nidre night we seek absolution for the promises we made to God and failed to fulfill. He is a forgiving God. He will absolve us of those commitments.

"And there are vows *bein adam l'adam*—commitments we make to our fellow man. Kol Nidre cannot wipe *that* slate clean. God may pardon us for breaking promises to Him. Kol Nidre, however, does not absolve us of the pain we caused our fellow man. We will find no absolution until we make amends, until we ask forgiveness from those

Israel Jacobs   343

we have hurt.

"When our ancestors stood at Mt. Sinai they committed themselves to Torah. From that day to this every Jew is pledged to speak the truth, to seek justice, to act mercifully, to defend the cause of the widow, the orphan, the stranger. This congregation has violated those sacred commitments. Because of our acts of omission and commission, because of our active and passive bigotry fellow Jews, members of our congregation, have been made to feel as outcasts. Among them, my wife and brother-in-law."

A thousand Jews seemed to suck in their breath at the same time.

"Therefore, until this congregation publicly acknowledges the wrong we have done to fellow Jews, until we pledge to make amends, to live up to our commitments as Jews—" Tali slammed his fist down on the lectern. "—THERE WILL BE NO KOL NIDRE CHANTED TONIGHT."

The pronouncement hovered over the pews like a Satanic decree.

"Get out of the way!"

Cline lunged for the Ark curtain. Tali barred the way. Cline attempted to shove him aside. Tali resisted. Seymour Kraft raced up to the Ark and yanked the curtain open. Tali gave way, momentarily caught off guard. Cline pulled a Torah scroll from the Ark and handed it to Kraft. He reached for a second scroll. Defiantly, he whipped past Tali and joined Kraft at the reader's lectern. They flanked Cantor Bindel and motioned him to begin. Tali struck the lectern with his fist again. "Until we confess the wrong we have done to our black members, THERE WILL BE NO KOL NIDRE"

Bindel shifted attention from Cline to Tali and back to Cline. "Start Kol Nidre or, as president of the congregation, I'll personally see to it that you're sacked."

Bindel raised his hands, entreating Tali, then Cline, then back to Tali. Cline repeated his threat through gritted teeth. The congregation floundered in their pews like troops without a leader. Tali whirled to Cline.

"You have no jurisdiction on this pulpit. There will be no Kol Nidre until there is a confession."

344   *The Convert*

"Start Kol Nidre, Cantor, or get off the pulpit."

Bindel stood immobilized, as if turned to stone.

Seymour Kraft muttered into Bindel's ear. The cantor sagged against the lectern. Kraft and Cline propped up the Torah-scrolls in their arms. Bindel signaled the choir. He intoned the introduction to Kol Nidre:

> *B'yeshiva shel malah, u-v'yeshiva shel matah...*—By the authority of the court on high and by the authority of the court below. With Divine consent and with the consent of this congregation, we hereby declare that it is permissible to pray with those who have transgressed.

Tali backed away from the lectern. He removed his prayer shawl, folded it in half and draped it around one arm. He surveyed the disbelieving faces staring up at him, as if he had brought on the Apocalypse. His eyes lingered on the two vacant seats in the first row. He pivoted, swept past the pulpit and walked into his dressing room. The turmoil building in him since Hadassah had left gradually ebbed, disintegrating like wavelets lapping at the shore. He packed his pulpit vestments into the closet and put on his jacket.

He stepped into the September night. A refreshing breeze caressed his face. The moon seemed to be smiling down at him.

Strains from Kol Nidre pursued him, then faded into the crisp night air.

Morning stole under the window shades. The bureau clock displayed seven-thirty. Tali climbed out of bed and snapped the shades. Sunlight streamed into the room. He padded into the bathroom and sprinkled water on his hands and face. He selected a lightweight blue suit, white-on-white shirt and muted blue tie, then dressed quickly. He stepped outside, taking care to close the door softly. Happily, the street was empty.

He set out at a brisk pace.

Bet Emet's makeshift bulletin board was mounted on twin brass

Israel Jacobs 345

poles temporarily driven into the quarter acre lawn. It stood six feet high, at right angles to the street. The bulletin board listed the schedule of services.

Kol Nidre	7:15 p.m.
Yom Kippur	9:00 a.m.
Shofar and conclusion of Yom Kippur.	7:30 p.m.

Tali threw his cuff. Nine fifteen. The walk had taken under an hour. He entered the white clapboard building. A wooden staircase curved up to the first floor. To the right a narrow stained glass window brooded above the landing. The building's function prior to being converted into a synagogue was etched into the grillwork under the sill, NORTHVILLE FUNERAL HOME.

Tali followed the narrow hallway to the end. It opened into a long room with old-fashioned crenelated walls. A tall wooden cabinet, screened by a white linen curtain, stood on a raised platform flush against the Eastern wall. About seventy worshipers sat on metal folding chairs facing the home-made Ark. A bridge table served as Jeremiah's lectern. He announced,

"Please rise for *Borhu*—the call to worship. Page two hundred—."

Yarden glanced his way. Surprise plastered the physician's face. He signaled Hadassah with his eyes. She turned, blinked several times, as if in disbelief. She erupted into quiet sobs, crying softly and smiling through her tears. Silvano followed Yarden's signal, caught sight of Tali and hastened to the door. He pumped Tali's hand and escorted him down the aisle. A woman next to Marduk shifted one seat to the left. Marduk, displaying a wide grin, moved into the vacated chair. Tali squeezed between Marduk and Hadassah. Silvano motioned with his fingers. Tom Carter came forward, greeted Tali warmly and passed him a prayer book and prayer shawl. Yarden about-faced to the Ark. He bowed. The congregation followed his lead, "*Borhu et Adonoy ha-m'vorah*—Bless the Lord who is to be praised."

The congregation responded, "*Boruh Adonoy ha-m'vorah l'olam va-ed* —Blessed be the Lord who is to be praised to all eternity."

Tali draped the *tallit* around his shoulders.

Hadassah searched for his hand. Their fingers intertwined.

Epilogue

June 11, 1984

Dr. Jeremiah Yarden
33 Tel Hai
Jerusalem, Israel

Dear Uncle Jeremiah,

Hopefully, you and the family are in good health and that your decision to settle in Israel continues to fulfill the promise that initially moved you to make *aliyah*. If memory serves me right it is twelve years since you made that decision. Much has happened during these years. What has not changed is the courage and commitment it required for you, Rebecca and Jonathan to quit the security and comfort you enjoyed in the States and start over in a new land. Those qualities of character encouraged me to pursue my current career. It was your patience and willing ear when I visited with you in Jerusalem that firmed my decision to enter the Seminary.

Time plays tricks with our perspective. On the one hand, it seems like a century since that fateful Kol Nidre night Tali walked out of the Pineville Jewish Center. On the other hand, when I look back, it sometimes seems as if all happened yesterday.

By the time this letter reaches you, I will have been ordained by the Seminary as Rabbi, Teacher and Preacher in Israel. It is of interest

348 The Convert

to speculate how the Sumtara Rebbe would have reacted to my ordination as a liberal rabbi. His ideas regarding God, Torah, Jewish Law are in many ways radically different from mine, and have been ever since I could think about such subjects maturely. Nevertheless, not once during my student years at the Sumtara Yeshiva did he intimate that I was less of a Jew for not subscribing to his theology. I think he expected me, perhaps even wanted me, to follow in Tali's footsteps. He would never have admitted this publicly, but he hinted more than once that he believed Judaism needed troops in the "progressive" trenches so we do not entirely lose our "marginal" Jews, who are rapidly assimilating into what he termed pagan America. Paganism, he said, is the arch enemy of the Jew. Not Christianity, not Islam, not even agnosticism. Certainly not liberal Judaism.

Thousands clogged the street in front of Ohev Tsedek for the Rebbe's funeral. The police cordoned off the street. Traffic was rerouted all that day. In my judgment, no hasidic Rebbe in our time, possibly in the last century, was as venerated as the Sumtara Rebbe, and as deserving of veneration. Heschel has inherited his father's crown. He is a changed man. I suppose responsibility will do that to a man. He's matured. He's softened. He's no more the rabid dogmatist, ready to excommunicate anyone who differs with his version of Judaism. He and Tali are now reconciled. Tali initiated the rapprochement shortly after the Rebbe died. To everyone's surprise Heschel embraced his cousin. Will marvels never cease?

I am happy to report another reconciliation, the Zeigs and the Russels. That reconciliation was also precipitated by a death. Zalman Lutvak passed away a month after his 92nd birthday. He went to sleep one evening and did not wake up. Tali said he died like a *tsaddik*—like a saint. We attended the funeral. The Russels attended the service. Tali approached Everett. That sparked the reconciliation. Hadassah was open to renewing the friendship. Now that she's the mother of two children, she better understands how far parents will go to protect their children, even to the extent of compromising cherished principles.

Tali has done exceptionally well in the academic world. The thesis he wrote for his Ph.D., *Chinese Humanism and Ethical Monotheism*, is

Israel Jacobs   349

currently being used as a textbook in universities across the country. He's been made professor at Triton University, and is visiting professor of philosophy at the Seminary.

Now the big news. If you are standing, I suggest you sit down.

The Pineville Jewish Center has plowed through four rabbis since Tali left. It seems they can't a find rabbi who is able to strike a balance between the die-hard traditionalists and the progressives. The Seminary graduates nowadays, with rare exceptions, don't have the yeshiva training Tali had. He was able, because he combined both tradition and modernity, to span the opposing factions. The Sumtara Rebbe was very much aware of how crucial it was to the survival of Judaism for the varying Jewish denominations, Orthodox, Conservative, Reform at the least to communicate with one another, else the Jewish people would splinter into irreconcilable obscure sects. He called Tali a bridge between two worlds.

And according to Professor Arthur Teitlebaum, who still reigns supreme at the Seminary, none other than yours truly also possesses the necessary background to be a bridge. He is urging me to submit an application to the Pineville Jewish Center, which at present has no rabbi. He assures me that if I do, I will be elected. It may smack of nepotism, but Arthur Teitlebaum was never one to worry about what others think.

What is my connection to Arthur Teitlebaum?

I'm his son-in-law.

The first time I saw Rachel, his daughter, I went into a tailspin. Like Jacob did, as described in Genesis, when he met her namesake at the well. It must have been the same for Tali when he met my sister at your home. My first encounter with Rachel occurred at Professor Teitlebaum's home. He was giving a seminar for senior students. Rachel walked into the den to help her mother serve coffee and cake. I tell you, Uncle Jeremiah, from that evening on I could concentrate on little else but Rachel.

Professor Arthur Teitlebaum's students think he is a tyrant. They've dubbed him the Seminary's anti-Semite. He fails more Jews than professors in universities throughout the country. But Arthur

Teitlebaum's primary interest is truth and scholarship, in that order. He is blind to skin pigment. And that's how he raised his children.

Ecclesiastes wrote, *Only that shall happen which has happened, only that occur which has occurred. There is nothing new under the sun.* Ecclesiastes was a keen observer of life, I grant him that. In my judgment, however, the Sumtara Rebbe was equally perceptive. He came to a different conclusion. The Rebbe took his cue from the verse in our prayer book, with which you are, no doubt, familiar, *Awesome in praises, Sovereign of wonders, day after day He renews Creation.*

It does appear that the more things seem to change, the more they're the same. Maybe, I haven't lived long enough, but I believe things can and do change. Blacks are still far from achieving the hoped-for millennium. But things have improved considerably. During Tali's tenure, no black family could break into Pineville. Today, a dozen black families reside in Pineville, with no problems. Ironically, none of them are black Jews. But that, too, can change. If I do apply, and am elected, it will be a different ball game. Rachel will not be riding into Pineville on my coattails, as Hadassah did on Tali's. In fact, she'll be in the majority, while the rabbi of the Pineville Jewish Center will be a minority in that still predominantly white community.

I'm strongly inclined to apply.

God, in his good time, will determine which construction of life is correct: that of Ecclesiastes, or the Sumtara Rebbe, may the righteous be remembered for blessing. Despair or hope, that is the difference.

With much affection,

Mordecai
Rabbi Mordecai Adams

Printed in the United States
2918